SILENT NIGHT

WILL IT BE OVER BY MORNING?

Also by this author:

THE DEVIL'S TEARS

SILENT NIGHT

WILL IT BE OVER BY MORNING?

M.C. DUTTON

Matador
5 Weir Road
Kibworth Beauchamp
Leicester LE8 0LQ, UK
Tel: (+44) 116 279 2299
Fax: (+44) 116 279 2277
Email: books@troubador.co.uk
Web: www.troubador.co.uk/matador

ISBN 9781848762404

British Library Cataloguing in Publication Data.
A catalogue record for this book is available from the British Library.

Typeset in 11pt Stempel Garamond by Troubador Publishing Ltd, Leicester, UK
Printed by TJ International Ltd, Padstow, Cornwall

Matador is an imprint of Troubador Publishing Ltd

To my children
Helen and Ben,
Richard and Amanda,
Andrew and Nansel

To my grandchildren,
Isabella and Kiera, Rebecca, Josh and Thomas,
Bradley and Maxwell

To my sister,
Pamela Cumberworth

Thank you for your support

CHAPTER ONE

He was resigned to the fact he would be dead by the morning. Did he deserve to die? What sort of fucking stupid question was that? He would have given himself a slap for being so ridiculous if he could. He might as well ask himself if he was a good father, which was as useful a question as the last one. He needed to think clearly and sensibly. He was scared, he conceded, but that was shitty as well, he was terrified and it was about time he owned up to that. He had to confront the thing that terrorised him, and continually tortured him. It was not death itself, but that promised state of creative, exquisite, deep, relentless, unforgiving pain that would make him beg to be killed and released from his agony.

They had promised him, in barbed, urgent whispers, that he would be begging and screaming for death, that he would give them every penny he had, and he would willingly beg, borrow or steal, more money for the right to die quickly. He wished he had what they wanted, it would have been so much easier to give it to them, but that was not possible now. He mentally beat himself with the thought of how did he get to be so stupid; he was an intelligent man, or so he thought, but right now he really did not know what sort of man he was.

He had been born into an old farming family, not quite landed gentry but good enough to have a name in the county. They were rich enough for it to be the norm to send the two sons to good private boarding schools and employ 10 full-time staff to help run the farm and maintain the house. Christopher Cross was the youngest of the two brothers. He was by far the better looking, tall and erect, he was often thought to be ex-military in later life, but of course, he was not – discipline was not his best subject. So how did a well spoken, good looking, reasonably intelligent, and by most standards, a rich man, get himself into this deadly mess?

He had plenty of time to think about it, to unravel the tenuous threads that started in his childhood. He knew it was too late now to change anything, but he could try and make some sense out of it. He supposed this was part of his own torture to see how through his life he had been a complete, blinkered, and perhaps, a little selfish, arrogant bastard. How could he, and the thought brought tears of frustration to his eyes, have believed so implicitly that money could change his life, that money earned as easily as possible would make him a better person? Once again, if he could have, he would have kicked himself but he was tightly bound. He had always wanted adventure, but this was too big for him, too dangerous, and he had been caught. "*If only*" had become his saying and it was driving him mad.

He was alone in this hellhole by choice. He walked round him rubbing his chin and looking into his face, he was still breathing hard from the beating he had just given Christopher. Swooning from the stinging pain to his face and the deep, hard pain he felt in his stomach and chest, Christopher was being forced to listen. He had never heard such kind words said with threatening menace. He said they wanted him to ring a friend to help him, that they only wanted what was best for him. He knew he could not have done this alone, so why should he have all the aggravation. A slap across the face punctuated each sentence, making each word stingingly clear, and hard enough to keep him alert. He said he just wanted to help him resolve this difficult situation. Christopher listened but was certain that there was no way he would drag her into this, it was his problem, she might have gone along with it but she didn't make him do it. One of them had roughed him up a bit to get him to talk. It was pretty frightening and it hurt like hell, but he wasn't going to involve anyone else in this.

They didn't believe him at first, but Alice had nothing to do with this. It may be a loveless marriage but he would make sure she was not harmed, it was the least he could do; she didn't deserve that. He realised his children needed their mother, they did not need him. It was too late to feel sorry about that, he told himself, but it didn't stop the ache in his chest at this realisation.

He would never involve Neil, who was probably one of the only people who was in a position to help him. Neil was his best friend and was too good a person to be hauled innocently into this mess. Neil's family was worth at least a billion pounds but Christopher could not, and certainly would not, ask them for money; he could not put them in such a position. Passionately, he thought he would rather die than involve his friend in this mess. The humour of this struck him and he smiled to himself at the stupidity of such a thought. Christopher's only consolation in this terrifying and deadly game was he still had a semblance of honour left.

He thought there were four of them in this room. Only one had seemed to be asking the questions and administering the beating. Christopher wondered now who the hell the others were. Bastard number 1, as Christopher called his tormentor, had tightly covered his mouth with masking tape, leaving just enough room for him to breathe through his nose. In a tone more reminiscent of a soothing lover, he had caressed Christopher's cheek and bent forward and intimately whispered his fervent wish that Christopher would not tell him what he wanted to hear. He explained he loved playing games and looked forward to hearing Christopher scream for mercy. He asked that Christopher would not disappoint him. They were going to give him a few hours to think things over and suggested he think long and hard and come up with the right answer. With that chilling whisper, and a gentle slap to his face, Bastard number 1 and the silent watchers left him to the dark and his own thoughts.

Left in this dark and dank place he could hear distant noises, which he tried to identify. He thought he was underground and near a tube line because he could hear trains rumbling and as the sound got louder he could feel his chair shake gently. He hadn't heard any trains for some time and supposed it was after midnight when the trains stopped for the night. The odd squeak and rustle of rats didn't bother him too much. What bothered him more was his mind, which seemed to be vomiting up every horrific and frightening scenario he must have stored there. He felt like he was on a collision course that would turn him into a gibbering wreck. They were going to kill him he did not doubt, but the twisted torture of what they might do to him before they killed him was more than he could cope with. It had been implied they were going to enjoy watching him suffer more pain than he could cope with. He was left with the implied knowledge that they were good at torture and were happy in their work. They were South American types, either Columbian or Mexican, or such like, he had heard how these types had ways of administering torture. He had read books or seen something on the television about drug cartels and how they work. The beating had been administered without emotion and he was assured of more interestingly painful ways to get him to talk. He shuddered in despair at the thought. They wanted the money and that was all that had spared his life so far.

He needed to gain some control over his thoughts. He wasn't a wimp, he wouldn't give them the satisfaction of seeing him out of control. He didn't have the money anymore. He couldn't pay them, even if he wanted to, but they didn't know that yet. He had taken what was not his and someone had taken it from him. Once again, he could feel himself smiling at the irony of such a thing. The smile turned to frustrated anger quickly and shocked him. He needed to keep his mind off such treachery. Now was not the time to consider who was the more treacherous; himself or her. The frustrated anger surfaced again at the thought that he was utterly, totally stupid and it would cost him his life. Tears began to sting his eyes and he decided enough was enough of this pathetic display of feeling sorry for himself.

Christopher booted all self-pity out of his mind and returned to the area that was his to control. His memories would keep him sane and he would use this to keep himself together. He realised that somehow he had lived a life without reflecting on who he was and what he had to offer anyone. He had the time, so he would journey back to his earliest memories to find out how he had got to be him. Ironically, he thought, with nothing better to do, thinking about himself seemed a good way to spend an hour or so. Christopher realised that many of his thoughts had made him smile and he wondered if, at this belated hour, he was developing a sense of humour. To leave this "mortal coil" laughing seemed a good way to go. The tears welled up at this thought and he gave in to a few minutes of snotty, salty discomfort. That was enough of that he told himself and settled down to thinking back on his life.

CHAPTER TWO

He dredged his memory for his earliest thoughts and he came upon the knowledge that he had known, since a very small child, that his elder brother would inherit the family farm. He chose at this time to try and ignore the frustration that he had felt when he realised that his family would leave nothing for him to inherit. The family fortune and land would go, regardless of talent and fairness, to his boring, humourless older brother. Perhaps, in retrospect, he thought, this was the reason he had spent such a carelessly selfish and wasteful youth. He preferred this line of thought, it made his misuse of such precious time seem justified and therefore more palatable. He took that thought further and wondered if his father's actions might well have altered his perspective on life and led to this present predicament. He knew he was making excuses for himself and with a careless cavalier attitude thought to himself, "So sue me for it!" The humour was definitely developing.

Life was easy and simple until he was 16 years old and in his last year of boarding school. James, his elder brother, was already two years into farming college and a credit to his family. Christopher had been spoilt and indulged by his mother. His allowance was generous and additional presents of clothes and money came his way with loving regularity. His mother could deny him nothing. Although there were constant hints from his father that he might like to have an involvement in the farm and help his brother, there was no pressure or insistence. Now Christopher was being asked to go into a local accounts office to learn the ropes. It was a respectable job and his family would expect and insist on that. They had a name in the county and their younger son must work hard to maintain their standing. He had no plans to go in that direction. The thought of working in accounts left him feeling sick and petulant. He would make his own arrangements. What was the point of going to private school if you did not make good contacts and connections for life.

He had a good friend in Neil, whom he had known for some three years. He remembered when he joined the senior school at 12 years of age. He spent at least three months orientating himself to the other pupils and assessing which ones would be of benefit to him then, and in the future. Thinking back on that now, he chose to believe he had not consciously chosen his friends based on their usefulness, more likely to him, they were chosen because they were on the same wavelength. It was well known in such circles that good friendships forged at boarding school were often maintained throughout life. He did not want to believe that even at such a young age he had put usefulness and ultimately money before comradeship and honourable friendships. He would ask himself many times was he really that conniving, and where had that attitude come from?

Sitting tied up in this dark, dank, room on a rickety wooden chair, he tried to take his mind off his aching shoulders and the pain in his back. Alone in the dark, his mind kept darting from one area of his life to another, trying to find where he had started to go wrong, but he just kept feeling confused. Feeling sorry for himself and hating the *"if only"* thing. He wasn't a wimp, or a coward. If he deserved this, then so be it. Such a heroic statement did not make him feel any better. Where were the women in his life? Where was Amanda the temptress or Jenny the rich and grateful one. He could have laughed. Both had been such fun, but worth it, never!

He could feel himself getting melancholy and panicky, a most distasteful and base emotion. He knew he had to calm himself down. The tape across his mouth only allowed him to breathe through his nose and this was not enough. His nose felt blocked and he suddenly realised it was hard to breathe. He could feel himself panicking and this was making him inhale heavily through his nose. His lungs were craving more air, which in turn, caused more panic as his brain was telling him he was suffocating, that breathing through his nose was too small a channel, that his lungs would stop working through lack of air and he would die. He mentally slapped his face, told himself to shut up and sit quietly. He tried to regulate his breathing, the more he thought about it, the more panic stricken he got. He had to think of something else, he felt unbearably hot, the sweat was dripping down his face making him itchy and desperate to get free to tear off everything that held him.

He was going to die, one way or another, he could not see that he would survive the night. He wondered where the sprouting sense of humour had gone, he could do with the light relief it had initially given him.

CHAPTER THREE

His mind settled quite quickly on Neil. He had a few good memories, his school days and his best friend being an easy one to remember. This was a good time for Christopher, a slight smile played across his face in memory. His school years were happy. He had learned early on to survive and enjoy this part of his life. He frowned and remembered how he had been taken to his first boarding school at the age of 7 years. It seemed to him that he was abandoned. He was left with strangers in a building that was huge and cold. The people he trusted the most in his short life had left him and although the feeling lasted only a short while, the damage was done. There was something deep down inside him that had curled up and died. The feeling was so deep he would not recognise where it had come from in adult life. Trust he determined was not something a clever, sane and sensible person gave another. The air of mystery he would carry throughout his life was based on his childhood, no one ever knew everything about Christopher, he preferred it that way. Most privately educated boarding school children were affected in some way. Christopher thought being dumped in a boarding school at a young age was akin to castration.

After the initial settling in, his school life got better and better. Christopher took on the boarding school culture and succeeded. He found he had a natural talent for making friends easily, and his height enhanced his commanding manner. He was not only head and shoulders taller than most of the boys but he had a way about him that ensured he was treated as their acknowledged superior. He found himself top of the pecking order and his confidence grew during those school years. It became normal for him to be treated with respect, and any mickey-taking he encountered was always greeted with genuine amusement and laughter, it was now not in his nature to believe it could be anything but a joke. He was, after all, the most popular person at school. Even his many escapades, like going out for an evening and then having to climb back unseen into his dormitory, remained unnoticed by school staff. He knew he was invincible and had a charmed life. This caused him to be big-headed in his later school years, but by then, there was no one to tell him so. He sailed through school. He was academically middle of the road but his personality positioned him top of the tree and he ruthlessly maintained his hold over his peers throughout his school years with the help of his Crossword gang. Strong leadership attracts weaker souls who will do anything to be part of the group. Christopher was not a thug and did not aspire to bullying. But he did use this leverage to get what he wanted without resorting to anything physical. Everyone wanted to please Christopher and conform. Those who did not were ostracised. As he examined his past he saw more things than he cared to remember.

He could see his school life as it really was without

the romantic storybook version of "Christopher the Hero" he had imagined he was. It was as if he were looking at a stranger all those years ago. He wanted to make excuses now for the young person but could not. School had been his success and he wanted to remember it as such now. With a sigh, he closed his eyes and realised what a pompous little shit he had been.

CHAPTER FOUR

It had not been part of Christopher's game plan to have a genuine best friend. Almost as soon as he met Neil, he liked him. There was a certain amount of curiosity at the start of his friendship. Could someone be so naïve, so considerate and kind be for real? It took a few weeks before Christopher believed it. He had never met anyone like Neil. What clinched the friendship was a small incident that Neil would not have remembered but Christopher would not forget. Boarding school pupils were always looking for forbidden food like cakes, burgers, hot dogs and sweets. Boarding school meals were nutritionally good but they lacked any imagination in the taste bud department. Many smoked and were looking for spare cigarettes. Pocket money was never enough for these young men. They spent robustly what they were given and no one had enough to last the month until next pocket money day. The school was strict on how much any one boy could have in pocket money and it was decided no boy should have more than £4 per month. The school saw this as a learning experience in character building. Consequently, money was always short for those things that boys want and need. Christopher had more than £4 per month. He arranged for his mother to give him at least £10 extra every month when he visited home. Neil, as with other boys, was having a very lean last week of the month. When Christopher dropped a £5 note in Neil's room without realising, Neil had found it quite quickly and picked it up. He ran down the hall after Christopher to hand it back to him. Christopher had been surprised and suspicious. Why would Neil return it to him? He waited for the punch line. What did he want? Neil's reluctance to hang around after handing the note back, his pleasure in having found it and his refusal in taking any reward mystified Christopher. Christopher would not have been distracted from taking the route that "finders is keepers", however much money he had. It was after all quite normal he considered, feeling quite incredulous that Neil was not so like minded. It proved to be quite a momentous discovery for Christopher. Neil was, after all, exactly what he seemed, a great and good chap.

Neil became the only truly close friend Christopher would ever have. In the early days Christopher was surprised to enjoy feelings of comradeship and support with someone else. Neil had always been there for him and it never occurred to him not to gladly be there for Neil when he needed support. He felt good. Hey! he was a nice guy. Neil would vouch for that, perhaps the only person who would. It was a relief to know that his friendship proved to be more important than the fact that Neil came from an incredibly rich family. Neil's father was a multi-millionaire who owned, amongst other things, the finest chain of quality car show rooms throughout the most exclusive areas of Britain, he dealt with Rolls-Royce, Mercedes, Lotus and Lexus vehicles and any other four wheel vehicle manufactured for the rich and discerning required by his clients.

Neil's friendship was one of the few instinctively unselfish decisions he had made. He wanted to stay in this area of memories for a while, it made him feel good. His initial plan had been to keep all friends at arm length. He knew he needed friends to help with his success but they were not going to be close enough to hold him back. He consciously made Neil an exception to this rule and decided he could afford to keep Neil and his long term plans in the same frame and intact. His rationale had been that Neil was too good and naïve a person to interfere with his long term plans. Now he understood he needed a close friend, someone who he could care about. He had never cared about anyone until that time. As a 12 year old boy, he viewed everyone he knew as either useful to him or as nobodies that he would discard or put on the back burner for recall at a later date. The long term success plan had been his only companion and at that stage in his life he finally understood being popular and respected did not warm the chill of loneliness. Still so young, he decided he could have it all. Neil would be his luxury.

Christopher was quite fascinated to experience a new way of living by watching and listening to Neil. Although he never seemed to learn from Neil's goodness, he liked to bask, and relax in it. Neil had an infectious laugh and he seemed to be in awe of the power Christopher commanded with all the boys. No-one challenged him, or made his life difficult, he saw

Christopher could stand up for himself. Neil did not see the ruthless streak Christopher was developing. Boarding schools were tough places, even for the seriously rich. Christopher found himself protecting Neil, who was the butt of other lads' jokes and mickey-taking. It seemed to Christopher, all those years ago, that youngsters living in a closed environment seemed to have a sixth sense of who is a susceptible and weak and who are strong and should not be approached. Neil had a weakness that was not on the surface but understood by others and used against him. Neil was a gentle child who seemed to have a foot in bygone days and a much slower and kinder way of acting that was not the norm for boisterous and often cruel boys of his own age. He was sensitive to comments about his height, his inability to play roughhouse games, and his fear of fighting.

Christopher watched Neil make mistakes at school knowing he had to learn. He was not popular with the boys so he did everything possible to make and keep friends with the other boys in his dormitory. He arranged for trips in one of his father's sports cars, driven by a chauffeur of course, picnics with all the favourite foods imaginable, and any pop concerts in London worth going to he had tickets. This worked for a while, but of course, they too came from wealthy families, and after a short time, everyone became bored with him trying to organise events and as they saw it *"buying their friendship"*. The mickey-taking that was always around suddenly got more ferocious and intense, Neil instinctively knew he could not cope with it and the other lads knew this too.

Christopher stepped in at that point and took him under his wing and protected Neil. Neil's school life was much better than it could have been due to Christopher, he knew that, and would always be indebted to him in lots of unspoken ways. The initial reason became buried under years of growing up, the strong commitment and friendship he felt for Christopher was imbedded in his soul and they became more like brothers.

Christopher had many friends, but there was only one close friend, Neil, and even Neil only knew what Christopher wanted him to know. Christopher's friendship with Neil, was based on an implied familiarity that made Christopher feel he and Neil were kindred spirits. There was a natural honesty and correctness about Neil that Christopher admired. He would protect this wonderfully good person even though his own jaundiced view of life would not entertain such naïve integrity.

Christopher was to spend many holidays and weekends in the company of Neil and his family. He preferred to spend his time off with them. There was a buzz in Neil's home that he had never experienced in his own family, which he found exciting and fun. He considered Neil's friendship and his family the best thing that had happened to him. He had lived on the periphery of family life, now he felt accepted and belonged to his surrogate family. It lasted many years and they were some of his most happiest of times.

His capacity for not learning from this experience was awesome. He was in his fifties now and wished he was 12 years old again. Would he do things differently given the chance? He fervently hoped so. If only this was all just a dream and he was lying in his dormitory bed all those years ago waiting for the 6 a.m. wake up call. That much hated bell, would be a very welcome sound now; so pure and wonderful. If only he had a second chance.

CHAPTER FIVE

Neil was not particularly small, but at 5'6" he was smaller than most boys in his year. The inferiority complex that had attached itself to his height should have been placed at the feet of the towering inadequacy he felt in his father's company. Since he was a small child, all he could remember was his father trying to instil in him the work ethic steps that must be adhered to:

- Money is power,
- Trust no one in business,
- Work is the only reason for getting up in the morning,
- Success is an aphrodisiac,
- Make useful friends,
- Do it to them before they do it to you.

These golden rules had made his father, James a rich, ruthless, star in the business world. They did not understand each other, that was the problem. Neil saw his father as a very successful, aggressive fighter who always got his way. It was the 1960s and everything was up for grabs, Neil's father grabbed everything and was doing very well thank you. He had fingers in many pies and it was working. You cannot turn off that sort of energy when you go home, patience was not something James had a lot of, and sometimes, Neil pushed his patience too far. The boy had no get up and go, he found it difficult to believe that the boy was his son at all. But he loved him and of course he knew exactly who he was like. He could see he was a throw back to his father, who had in the past done well in setting up his own businesses but now seemed to be stuck in a time warp. All Neil had ever seen of his grandfather was this parody of a Norfolk man.

James Davies-Clarke was a self-made man, or so he told his acquaintances, but the inference of no help from any quarter was not quite true. He rose quickly and magnificently using his own initiative and skills to be the leading star in his field. His family background was fairly wealthy and he had been well educated at a good private school. He must have inherited his business acumen from his father, but it was a brave man to suggest this to either James or his father. Neither thought the other had any of their skills; *"chalk and cheese"* was a favourite saying of each to describe their relationship.

James knew his father would look on Neil as his heir. He had watched him grooming Neil since he was a small boy to take over his shops. James had never wanted anything to do with the old fashioned, cheap shops that catered for the working class masses. James had decided many years ago that his father's area of work was too small and limiting for his liking. James was big in the corporate world and he reckoned he could retire, if he wanted, in a few years time.

His father, Bertram, owned shops in Wroxham, this

was a modest statement, he actually owned all the shops worth having in Wroxham. This lovely little village nestling by the side of the river, grew into a busy, bustling, tourist village due to the success of boating holidays on the Norfolk Broads. Whilst other local business men were fighting over what was considered to be the prime businesses, the boat yards and building boats for hire for holidays, Bertram Clarke was quietly buying up the department store and shops surrounding it and the supermarket. He extended bit by bit each shop and added a dress shop and sailors wear shop until those alighting from boats to view the joys of Wroxham, spent most of their money in his shops which were filled with souvenirs, and all supplies needed for boating on the Broads. There were also the wonderful bargains to be purchased that could be taken home, such as china, cheap towels, table lamps, books etc. If you knew of anyone who had taken a boating holiday near Wroxham, you could be assured they possessed several items purchased happily at one of the Bertram shops as they were called. When the dust had settled and the locals looked around to see where other business could be made, the prime shops had been taken by Bertram Clarke. He was an astute business man and James had inherited his business sense but would build his businesses in a different direction.

Where Bertram was a gruff, no-nonsense man, James understood, due to his schooling no doubt, that bluntness got you nowhere, but a little charm and flattery worked wonders. Bertram did not approve of his son's work ethics or his careless disregard of honour, integrity or values held dear to Bertram's heart. He had always noted that James looked nothing like him either, very much a throw back to his wife's side of the family. The blonde hair and chiselled looks belonged to her father and the lean taller build to her mother, although James was only 5'10" he looked taller because he was so slim.

Bertram resented his son for not wanting to join the family business, for affecting airs and graces and for talking in a posh voice; he could not understand why he was so ashamed of his Norfolk accent. Bertram had taken to telling those around him how his family had been in Norfolk man and boy for at least six generations and all had been proud of their humble beginnings. He would regale his family with stories about herring fishing, and how he remembered as a boy all fishermen smoked their catch of herrings in a special smoke house attached to their homes and sold them either from their front door or took them to market. James found these stories boring, exaggerated, old fashioned and not helpful to him in his future career. Bertram and James were well aware of each others views and had over the years exchanged heated words on the subject.

Neil, on the other hand, loved to listen to his grandfather's stories and views on life. His grandfather showed a very gentle side of his gruff nature when Neil was around, and gave him time, something James never had. The warmth and love that was generated between Neil and his grandfather was comforting for James. Neil was safe and happy with his grandfather, this left James with the much needed time for his businesses.

Christopher remembered, in looking back, how

fortunate Neil was to be so loved by his grandfather and father. It was the little things that came to Christopher's attention. He supposed Neil did not notice the looks of pride Bertram would give him. The pats on the back that were soft and caressing without being soppy. James was very busy indeed but he always tried to ring Neil once a day to see how he was. Perhaps if his parents had shown that type of care and attention he might have turned out to be a good person like Neil. Christopher still felt a little pang of jealousy.

Holiday times in the Davies-Clarke household were especially busy, with lots of house guests, normally two or three businessmen would stay for a few days at a time combining business with pleasure and Bertram always had one or two cronies around. The house as Christopher remembered was a thriving, bustling, argumentative place full of characters and tensions, but with an underlying sense of love and family. It was an enormous house and certainly needed to be, to give space to such large egos.

Bertram, James and Neil all lived together in a country home that had 12 bedrooms, 6 sitting rooms, a Pool House with games room close by and accommodation for live-in staff. A house this size should allow for individual space and alleviate the necessity for communal living. Bertram would have none of that. Where ever James went, so did Bertram. They would argue from morning till night, if James and his father were ever around for that length of time. James' wife had vanished from the scene many years ago when Neil was a small boy. They saw her very occasionally when she was in the country, but she had remarried and lived abroad in various hot and interesting countries. Bertram had always said Clare, that was Neil's mothers name, was not good enough for James and good riddance to her. He and his wife had been very supportive of James and it was then they decided to move in with him and Neil to look after them when she left. Since Mrs Bertram died some 3 years ago, Bertram had taken to going fishing, he said he liked the peace and quiet. He had never said much, but her passing away had been a bitter blow. He had never got used to her not being there, always expecting her to bustle into the house, organising him, and everyone around. He spent many an hour on his fishing trips sitting quietly thinking of her, talking to her, crying for her.

Bertram made sure that no one knew of his suffering and quiet despair in the loss of his beloved Ivy. It was a shame James would only find out how he felt through reading diaries of his father after he had died. If Bertram had only known how bitter James would feel in later years when he had passed on, perhaps he would have allowed his son to realise how much he missed his wife and they could have mourned her passing together. Bertram had made noises about moving out of James' home after Ivy died but to his private relief, James made it very clear that he would not consider his father living anywhere else. They all lived together in a comfortable tension.

The staff who ran the house and grounds were, it seemed to Christopher, rather unusual and certainly fun. Bertram and the butler had built a friendship that had been cultivated over the past 10 years. The butler was a drunken old soul, very close to Bertram's age. He could be found many a day in the kitchen annexe of the Swimming Pool with Bertram drinking rum. They told stories of adventure, cunning, and daring that were blatantly untrue, but in their drunken state, neither cared. They roared with laughter that got louder and more uncontrolled as the day wore on. The swimming pool was housed in a building quite close to the house but far enough away for the two old codgers to get some peace and quiet, and they thought secretive enough for no-one to be aware of their little drinking games. Of course everyone knew, it was a source of concern and to a few members of staff, a source of money in bets as to whether either Bertram or the butler would make it to the house without falling in the swimming pool. There had only been one or two occasions when a dripping wet Phillips had entered the big house. Bertram has always been that bit more agile where the swimming pool was concerned, but he had in his time decimated a few rose bushes that had leapt out in front of him. By the looks of him, he had come off worse with scratches all over his face. Thankfully, it was not painful, the alcohol had acted as an anaesthetic and Bertram felt nothing. So on days when it was known they were together in the kitchen annexe, the staff were on red alert for any injuries. No one dared to suggest that perhaps Bertram and Phillips should stay in the big house where it was safe. It may have been the worst kept secret in Norfolk, but Bertram and Phillips gained much enjoyment out of the clandestine meetings and drank in the clear knowledge that no one knew about it. Phillips the Butler did a little work, but his main job seemed to be to keep the Captain amused and happy.

Then there was Mrs Matthews who cooked the best spotted dick and custard in the world. She was a chirpy, happy woman, it was her way to burst into song at any given opportunity in the kitchen, if she only had a voice, it would have been a joyous place to work in. As it was, she caused pain to anyone within earshot who was not stone deaf. All had to agree though that singing with such volume and passion gave her star quality. When sober, Phillips appreciated Mrs Matthews in a professional manner and gave her due respect for her culinary skills. When drunk, Phillips' view of a plump rosy cheeked Mrs Matthews turned to seeing her as a voluptuous temptress who was "begging for it". Although Mrs Matthews complained long and loudly at Phillips' advances, all could see she enjoyed the attention. Christopher had been around when Phillips, obviously the worst for drink, had proceeded to chase Mrs Matthews round the kitchen table. Her shrieks had made him rush to her aid, but he was held back by a bored Jacob and Peter, who were having a tea break and had obviously seen this scenario many times and found it all rather noisy and intrusive in their 15 minute break. Christopher, against his better judgement, sat down and watched. He marvelled at this drunken, old man chasing this large woman round a kitchen table. Phillips was more agile drunk than sober. Eventually, Phillips was allowed to kiss Mrs Matthews on the cheek, much against her better nature, she would loudly tell everyone, and then all would be calm, until the next time. It was whispered by those who should know better that Mrs Matthews husband had forgotten what a woman was for except cooking and cleaning for him. Christopher surmised that the rosy cheeks Mrs Matthews had was more to do with the pleasure of Phillips attentions than the exertions of running round the kitchen table.

Rosy and Maisy were the cleaners who doubled as waitresses when necessary, they were two young girls who always seemed to Christopher to be giggling, when he turned 15 years old, he realised he was the object of their giggling and rather enjoyed the attention. It would be at least a couple of years, at a time when he was feeling a little bored, that he would test out how much they liked him. He found they liked him a lot and were most willing to please him.

The grounds were cared for by three gardeners, two were old and called Jacob and Peter and the third was their apprentice and shifter and mover called David. The two old gardeners had a status in the scheme of things, so David was never allowed to have his tea break with them or eat with them. They were Lords of the garden and David their servant. Christopher found it strange, but David accepted his lot and understood his lowliness, besides, he enjoyed his breaks with either Rosy or Maisy.

When guests were expected, three local women were hired to help prepare the bedrooms, assist Mrs Matthews, the cook, and the two girls. Phillips the Butler, more on auto-pilot, co-ordinated all the necessary work and organised supplies of food and drink, the house ran surprisingly efficiently. To Christopher, there never seemed to be a dull moment in this household. He felt sure now, that if he had been born into that household instead of his own, he would be a different person today. He realised he could be kidding himself, how could he blame his family for his problems today?

Christopher was an ear for Neil during their school years so he knew how Neil felt about the in-fighting that was happening in his family. Neil was his grandfathers natural heir. Bertram had got nowhere with his son, but his grandson was another kettle of fish. The old man would sit with Neil as a child telling him about how he started his business, and as Neil grew older, he would take him to his shops in Wroxham to meet the staff and he would be introduced as young master Neil. This was very comforting to Neil, he seemed to have found his place in the scheme of things, he felt tall in the company of his grandfather and the Bertram shop staff. Bertram always kept the personal touch with his staff, and they stayed with him, Neil understood that.

He had an empathy for his grandfather and enjoyed all his stories. He thought his grandfather was an honourable man who conducted honest business. Neil seemed to inherit a country gentleman's attitude of *"what you give to the land and people who service you, you reap in kind"*. So he was not one for the subtleties of business and rather thought his father was a little underhand and his business practice often tacky.

Bertram was proud of his grandson and somewhat relieved that the "la-de-dah" schooling had not driven out all the inbred decency and pride in the county that was their birthright. Bertram often wished he had not listened to his wife's family all those years ago and sent James to a day-school where, at least he would have had some influence on how his son was being brainwashed. What really upset him was James adding Davies to his name and making it double-barrelled. It just was not true, he had made the name up and did not seem to care that he upset the old man who was proud of his family name of Clarke, one he traced back many generations, and all were Norfolk people. He was disgusted with James for thinking he needed to lie and have so many airs and graces. He found it hard to look locals in the eye with a son betraying his roots in such a manner.

Bertram, as he got older and more eccentric, seemed to become far more Norfolk born and bred. As a young man he was in fact very much like a young Neil, not very tall, mousy coloured hair and stockily built with a barrel chest. He conducted himself in a business-like manner, his Norfolk accent hidden beneath a middle-class veneer. Now, with time on his hands, he had grown into a strong Norfolk accent that he took much pleasure in exaggerating, and had for many years sported a bushy beard and moustache which had gone Father Christmas white. He had taken to wearing a double breasted blazer with gold buttons and a peaked cap. Behind his back he was affectionately known as Captain Birdseye. He had over the years heard this nickname and, although he never acknowledged it, rather enjoyed the picture he created.

For some years Christopher had seen a quiet in-fight underway in Neil's family. The chemistry of high finance, versus good old fashioned business with Neil in the middle. James had, of course, noted the bond between his son and his father. The two strong characters of James, Neil's father and Bertram, Neil's grandfather played the push and pulls game with Neil for many years unaware of the damage they were inflicting on the lad. When Neil reached 16 years old and was on the verge of a minor brainstorm with all the pressure that had been exerted none too subtly over the years, his father gave up the tug of war for his son to join him in his business. He realised Neil would be an embarrassment, with no get up and go. He had noted that he did not have the required flair, a will to win, or a strong business sense. He had for many years tried to instil in Neil a sense of adventure in business, to try and induce the buzz it gave you when the hunt was on for a new piece of action, and the high of winning. Neil never understood. It took many, many, years for James to understand that Neil was not made of the right stuff.

So all in all, James had to make a decision about his son. He conceded his father had won the battle, and although he never liked to lose, he realised Neil would be heir to a nice little business. He was giving his father his only son, he laughed to himself, it was absurd, his last thought sounded almost biblical. Perhaps now his father, might, at last, forgive him for leaving the family business and going it alone. Perhaps now he would give him some recognition on how well he had done.

James' motivation for business had always been that he could do it. He pushed for success for no one but himself. He was feted by the corporate world and the

Newspapers as the "Business Man of the Year". His shares continued to rise and he was treated with due deference by his fellow Board of Directors, but at home, his father would never acknowledge his success. He was always saying to him that he was lucky and a fly-by-night, using business methods that were not ethical. James did not bother talking about business to his father, but Bertram knew everything that was happening by avidly following his sons businesses in the newspapers and from talks to other business men on his monthly visits to his Club in London. He would not concede even to himself that he was proud of James. As he saw it, he would not be seen to condone his business methods as he, Bertram, had respect in his community as an honest Norfolk business man.

When James purchased a helicopter, telling all how time was money and it would save him hours of travelling, Bertram nearly died of shame. He told his son in no uncertain terms that "This is England not America". Almost clucking with indignation, he told James his lawn, which swept down to the river, was not Heathrow and not for James' noisy, smelly, expensive, toy. When he thought James was not around, Bertram had gone outside and given the helicopter a good inspection inside and out. James watched him from the house, the usual resentments were trying to surface, his father would make sure he took no pleasure in showing or telling him anything, that the cleaner in his buildings got more attention from his father when he visited than he ever did.

This is when James started to laugh. Good humouredly, he at last saw the game, the one his father had been playing for many years. In a blinding flash he remembered all his father's comments and whilst he was continually putting him down, he seemed to always know what the business was doing, he knew where his son was going in any given week. He laughed again and thought the old bastard was just playing his Captain Birdseye game. To have achieved what he had entailed a certain amount of, and he paused for the right thought, "sharp practice". If now he wanted to play Mr Kind and Respectable, why not, he would not spoil his game.

He could see in Neil a similar streak, honest but naïve, James thought that was no bad thing. Yes, he admitted to himself, he had played some rather ruthless games to get where he was today. Yes, he was far more ruthless than his father had ever been, but the world today was pretty vicious and would chew up and spit out anyone who did not have the balls to get stuck in. Neil would not last a minute out there. All these revelations had taken about 15 years to understand. James now felt more relaxed and contented. The resentment he had felt towards his father for not being visibly proud of him, and his impatience and disappointment at Neil's attitude towards work was now laid to rest.

James lightened up, looked 5 years younger and gained a sense of humour. Those working around him noticed a vast difference in him. At first they were mystified by the change, then they found his new laid back attitude made working life better, and in turn, more prosperous. The spin off for this understanding seemed to have improved his relationship with his father and

Neil which was fine and dandy. He continued to build and consolidate his empire, unhindered now by negative thoughts. Christopher was to join the Davies-Clarke business at this very relaxed point in their history.

Looking back, he recognised how important Neil and his family had been to him. In some ways, he thought of them as his family. He stayed with them often enough for him to have his own bedroom, blend in and be accepted as part of the house. They liked him. Until now, he had never realised how much they meant to him, and with nothing but time, he was on to his "*if onlys*" again. He could have been more loyal to them. He wished he had told them how much they meant to him. Sitting here now he could only hope that they knew how much he thought of them.

The Captain and he had a great rapport. Christopher recognised the game he was playing and in good humour, often pulled his leg with jokes about Norfolk and Turkeys, and Christopher was always saying Bernard Matthews, the biggest Turkey farmer in Norfolk, and famous for his personal wooden acting advertisements on television, should be Prime Minister of England. The Captain would always take the jokes in good part, but always added that Bernard Matthews' acting may have been a little under-rehearsed, but his heart was good which was more than he could say for the la-de-dah public school boy Prime Ministers that had been around. Over the years he had noticed the Captain giving him some very knowing looks, he had been following Christopher's career and always made a point of talking to him about what he was doing and showing an interest. Christopher realised he was acting like his father should have, God! he thought, he missed the old man.

What a wonderful man the Captain had been and Neil was so like him. He had plenty of chances over the years to tell Neil what a great guy he was but he had blown that now. Neil had shared everything with him, his family, his friendship, his caring, his support, even when he did not fully approve of what Christopher was doing. He could feel the tears starting and that would not do. He thought back to where he was in his life story. He had to find the point his life went wrong. He remembered when he had to leave his boarding school and look for work.

CHAPTER SIX

As his school life came to an end and the big wide world beckoned, Christopher called in a few favours. Neil had arranged for Christopher to meet his father for a business chat. James Davies-Clarke already knew Christopher well, he had spent many a holiday and weekends with him and Neil. He liked Christopher and thought he was a resourceful young man with possibilities. So when Neil asked him about a job for Christopher, he was happy to arrange an appointment over lunch in the RAF Club in Piccadilly.

The RAF club was a regular haunt for James, many a business deal was discussed and settled within the portals of this elite and plush gentleman's club. Christopher enjoyed the atmosphere and vowed one day to be a member. Over a lunch of saddle of lamb with lyonaise potatoes with green beans and carrots cooked in orange juice, washed down with a good red wine they chatted about this and that. Watching James look through the wine list and pick a suitable bottle with skill and confidence made Christopher put learning about wine top of his list of important things to do. He noted it would be useful later in his career. It didn't take him long to acquire this skill.

Whilst eating, James, under hooded eyes, watched Christopher conduct himself with a confidence and assuredness that belied his youth. He liked what he saw and their discussions confirmed his thoughts that Christopher would make a very good salesman for his exclusive car showrooms. He was obviously too young to sell at present but he would groom him in that direction. The only reserve James had, and he was an astute judge of character, much used and needed in his meteoric rise in business, and he could see problems with Christopher in the future. Christopher was a gentleman, he had been brought up a gentleman and had the manners, air and considerations of a gentleman, but there was something else there, just under the surface that told James to watch out for sharp practices. He should easily have recognised the signs, after all, James and Christopher were more alike than each would care to admit. Each were under the illusion that, that part of their character which did not play the game, that knew it was not cricket to act in a certain way, was not on display but well hidden from view.

Christopher joined the team as James put it, his job would be background work, admin work, telephone work, studying the specifications on the exclusive vehicles they sold, but not client-face-to-face work, not for a few years anyway, he had much to learn. He received a wage that was higher than most would receive for his age and experience and a title that would please his family and friends as a trainee Sales Executive for such a prestigious Company. Davies-Clarke was known as a high powered corporate business with many business arms to its name. Christopher was known as a family friend that James had taken under his wing for the car side of the business. This ensured Christopher had an easy ride with other members of staff.

Peter and Helen Cross were proud of their son. At first they were concerned that joining Davies-Clarke was not the type of work they wanted for Christopher, but when they looked into it, and noted how Davies-Clarke was doing on the stock exchange, they changed their minds. Christopher was his mother's favourite. When he reached about 14 years old she discovered Christopher had grown into an amusing and very handsome young man, with a somewhat similar nature to herself she thought. She did not have many maternal instincts when her boys were small, but she began to take an interest in them as manhood beckoned. John, she had noted, when he reached 13 years old, took after her husband, solid, sensible, hardworking, and honest. She was bored with her husband; those traits that had looked admirable when they married now looked old and boring. She surrounded herself with good works and was on enough committees to keep her busy and interested. She had a lively mind and looked forward to dinner parties where she could talk to others of the same ilk. In the county they were known as an interesting couple and were invited to many occasions in the area. He was a successful farmer and had much in common with other land owners and she could talk interestingly on almost any subject, it was never a dull time when they were there. Christopher had lived a privileged life style and it felt to him that he could have anything he wanted out of life.

He lived at home whilst learning his trade. Norwich was not too far to travel each day and the trips to London to work were bonuses and kept him overnight in a hotel for something like one week out of every month. He was enjoying what seemed to him to be an easy job. He saw clients with his manager, he would act as his gofer but it enabled him to see close up real money people. He could almost smell them, they looked, acted, and were different to anyone else. The assurance that you could buy anything in the world must alter the way you handle yourself Christopher would often muse. He found it fascinating to watch. He wanted to know for himself how that felt, to be so rich, you could have anything you wanted.

When he turned 18 years old he started taking an active interest in girls. He liked them before, and was not unknown in the area by all eligible and non-eligible girls. He soon realised the pleasures of young women, and how, especially the local girls who one would not normally associate with, were quite happy to share their charms with this handsome young man. He had a pleasant few years learning the ropes from some very experienced accommodating girls. About the time he turned 27 years old, many things were starting to happen.

The first, his mother, who up to now indulged her son, had learned through gossip at the many functions she attended, that her son, not to put too fine a point on it, was whoring with some very dubious young ladies and causing the family much embarrassment. It was time he thought about settling down, his job was assured and he seemed to be doing very well. He could afford a wife, and a suitable one she would find for him.

Secondly, James Davies-Clarke was very happy with Christopher and his development. Although he was very involved with other aspects of his businesses, he kept a close eye on Christopher and tried to work with him as often as possible, this realistically meant that once per month he would spend a day with Christopher. He was quite fond of him, and felt like he had known him all his life and began to look on him almost like the son he would have wanted Neil to be. He liked the way the boy thought and conducted himself. He saw the time was right for Christopher to try some face-to-face selling. He had been talking to clients on the phone for some time and had impressed James with his knowledge and salesmanship, he was a respectable age and had honed his skills, now he could meet with clients.

Neil and Christopher were able to meet regularly, their continued friendship was a source of pleasure to them both. Neil was always the one to confide everything to Christopher, never the other way round, Christopher always erred on the side of caution when disclosing information. As time went on, Christopher realised through his conversations that Neil was never going to join his father's corporate businesses, that he loved and would always stay with his grandfather's business. Up till then, Christopher assumed that as Neil matured, he would tire of his grandfather's old fashioned business and be ready to join his father. It occurred to him that with some certainty he could assume that Davies-Clarke would not have a working heir apparent. He knew he had what it took to succeed, but he was not blood related, he figured it was worth going along with how his career was shaping for the time being and see where it took him. He was earning good money, but he wanted more, much more.

He was learning a lot about selling, he was meeting important people who, if he decided he wanted a change, were good contacts. His money was getting better now he was selling cars, with commission he should have been able to save many thousands of pounds per year, but he enjoyed the good things in life, holidays, cars, quality clothes and clubs, he wanted for nothing else at the moment, but soon it would not be enough.

CHAPTER SEVEN

His mother had other ideas about how he should spend his money. Before long, Christopher seemed to be on a whirlwind of dinner parties and suppers with good families in the county who, by chance, had eligible daughters, most of them of a type that did not appeal to him. He did not want to marry a well spoken, highly educated *dumbo*. Actually, he didn't want to marry anyone, he was having fun and didn't want to be responsible or accountable to anyone. Whilst his mother was busy trying to sort his life out, his brother John, had been quietly and steadily going out with some young women who were farmers daughters. He was rightly considered quite a catch with a farm to inherit. One young girl in particular, Alice, was a pretty young thing and she caught Christopher's eye. She seemed far too lively for jaundiced John, as he was referred to by his brother.

A chance meeting in town, and a cheeky remark by Alice ended with Christopher and Alice becoming closer than they should, in an indiscreet amount of time. The two months of laughter ended when she announced she was pregnant and Christopher was the father. He argued that it could just as much be his brother who made her pregnant, why him, he asked and she replied she had never slept with anyone else before. He actually realised that this was true.

She was from a good farming family, a marriage between the families would be a good move. Peter and Helen Cross had, in fact, planned to add her to the family, only they hoped that John would marry her. A lively person is what John needed, it would have been like Helen and Peter, and everyone knew what a good team they made. Her family owned the farm quite close by and it was hoped that in years to come, the two farms would go to the grandchildren as Alice had a younger sister and no brother.

Helen Cross was angry. She understood why Christopher liked the girl, but it was unforgivable that he would steal from his brother. He had messed with her plans, she had done everything for Christopher over the years, and this was how he repaid her. John, meanwhile, was beside himself with grief and speechless with anger over the treachery of his brother. He worked long hours and it was many weeks before he realised something was not right with Alice and him. He could not understand how his brother could do such a terrible, dishonourable, detestable thing. He had grown to love Alice, she was all he wanted, so lively and bright. She would make a good farmer's wife with all her family experience. He knew they would have been happy. It was true, he admitted to himself, that they had not as yet made a commitment to each other, but he loved her and he felt sure she would have grown to love him in time.

He had always viewed his brother as a waste of

space, a little of that was jealousy, he saw how popular Christopher was with the girls and he seemed to get on well with everybody, something John did not find easy. Favouritism is always a gnawing, festering ulcer in any sibling rivalry. John knew his mother adored Christopher and gave him the time she never seemed to have for him. Some would say that he was the favourite of his father but he knew that to be not true. He knew he had worked hard and studied hard to be a credit to the family and to be ready to take over the farm at the right time. Of course his father liked him, they were the only two in the family who understood how important the land was, they had something in common, that was not favouritism.

There had been many brooding thoughts about Christopher over the years, but this was the most treacherous, and this had given him the right to make a stand and assert his position as eldest son. He did not want Alice now, she was tainted, it was for his brother, Christopher, to sort this mess out. It was not normally in his nature to be vengeful he told himself, but he decided, quietly and without fuss, that he no longer had a brother and he would never be welcomed in his home again. He made his mother and father promise to abide by this. As he said, one day he would inherit the home and the farm, he demanded they listen to him and stand by him for once in their lives. His father agreed readily and his mother was forced to agree.

Christopher and Alice were married quite quickly within 3 months in the local parish church. It was a beautiful but simple ceremony attended by Helen and

Peter but not John. Good and faithful Neil acted as best man and tried to jolly Christopher along. Christopher remembered how Neil kept telling him that it was the honourable thing to do to marry her, that he would enjoy his life. Neil said he wished he had a beautiful child to look forward to and that Christopher must consider himself lucky. Christopher admired Neil's optimism but was not sure if it was going to be that good. That occasion would be the last time he would see his parents together. His mother sneaked visits to Christopher's new home but she was never accompanied by his father who stood by a wronged John.

Christopher had never been that close to his brother and father. To him, they were from a different planet, the bonding that usually happens between fathers and sons missed those two. Having spent his early years at boarding school, and spending holidays anywhere away from the farm had not helped. Although he had been brought up in a farming family and had associated with other farming families, he had never, and would never, get to grips with the boring rotation of crops, even with modern machinery, it was still labouring work, something Christopher found distasteful. However much money anyone earned in farming, and despite all farmers constantly saying to the contrary, there were many rich farming families in Norfolk, he could not see anything that was sophisticated or classy about working on the land. He found it hard to put into words how he felt about being banished from the family home, inconvenient and regrettable was the nearest to how he felt. He still had his mother, and she would always be there for him, he knew that it was enough, resentment was an emotion that would come with the fullness of time.

Since she found out she was pregnant, everything had moved so fast for Christopher and Alice. Christopher was a gentleman and took the honourable path and asked for Alice's hand in marriage, he simply had no choice, it was the only course of action available to him, anything else would have been unthinkable. She accepted, partly because she wanted to marry Christopher, not quite in love with him yet, but certainly in lust for him, and partly because her parents insisted that no daughter of theirs would have a child out of wedlock. It was the 1970's but in Norfolk, life was still buried in the 1940's.

Christopher did not love Alice, he liked her, thought she was funny and sweet, but he did not love her. Marriage was not in his plans and he was distressed and uncomfortable at the way his life was going. He did not want a kid, house, or wife, he wanted freedom to do things, to go places, to experience life. All those thoughts caused him sleepless nights, he had to marry her, it was the right thing to do and there was no way he would shirk his duty. He had to stop the torture he was feeling at seeing his life run away from him. Rather than go forward reluctantly, he would embrace the situation and make the best of it.

A house was found and bought for them in a small village called Winterton. It was close to Norwich, just 20 minutes by car so it would be good for Christopher's work, and Yarmouth station was 10 minutes away by car, if he needed to travel to London. Winterton was a small, picturesque village on the East Coast of Norfolk. It was by the sea, the air was good, and offered very pleasant walks in the sand dunes by the sea. It was considered an ideal spot for the newly weds, close to the towns but so close to the sea as to be an ideal place to bring up children. The house was bought for them as a wedding present by Alice's parents. It was a 1940's built house with 5 bedrooms, 3 bathrooms, one en-suite, and 4 reception rooms downstairs. The house was set in an acre of grounds and was thought to be the most appropriate for raising a family. Both Christopher and Alice loved the house, and they spent many months arranging for interior decorators to come in and make the house theirs for them. Christopher's parents paid for all internal decorations and furnishings.

Christopher's father told a resentful John that he had been seen by those that matter to discharge his duties correctly for his youngest son. He explained he had seen him married, set up with a home, and now his duty was finished. He had now washed his hands of Christopher and was no longer responsible for his welfare and thus could not be criticised by their friends and respected colleagues for his treatment of his son. He made it clear that it was at an end, he could, with a clear conscience, and with God as his witness, now have nothing else to do with Christopher. John still felt too much had been done for Christopher but he understood why his father had to been seen to help Christopher. Privately, John hoped Christopher caught a long and painful terminal disease. Only Helen found her husband's attitude distasteful and wrong, but she could say nothing to John or Peter, they were too petty and small minded. She vowed to keep faith with her son and help him if needed.

Christopher found he was enjoying the adventure of marriage, much to his surprise. The birth of a daughter, Emily, completed their happiness. Christopher was at this time happier than he thought possible. His job was doing well, he had a beautiful home and now a daughter. Life would run in domestic bliss for many years. Winterton had a typical village atmosphere with the hierarchy that goes with it. Top of the pile would be the Vicar, followed by who ever owned the largest house in the village, the Chairman and committee members were next, down to those who cleaned and cooked, and worked for the higher members of the village. The farm labourers and household staff lived just outside the best parts of the village, passing visitors would note the quaint little houses with gardens just outside the picturesque village. These little terraced houses were built at the end of the last century and although land workers houses, were built with a style and grace not undertaken for the working classes today.

Both Alice and Christopher's parents knew the hierarchy in Norfolk village life so to ensure they both continued in the style they had been accustomed to, they were bought the largest property in Winterton. As was normal, Alice had been asked to join all the committees available which she readily accepted. They were invited to many dinner parties in the area which Christopher found fun for a while. Christopher employed two gardeners to look after their acre of grounds. He arranged for flowers to be grown in a plot of land furthest from the house and these were picked and sent to the local hospital and church. This was a permanent gift that would be continued throughout the years. Being a benefactor to the local community had a charm that Christopher enjoyed. It all still felt like an amusing novelty, he seemed to have attained a good position in his community without really having to work at it, he had the best house in the area, a beautiful child, with another on the way, and Alice was easy to live with and caused no disharmony in the house with arguments. None of this had caused him to break sweat. Life was easy, too easy.

One of the first visitors they received after settling into the house was Neil and the Captain. With time on his hands, the Captain liked to keep in touch with his friends, and he considered Christopher a friend. Both he and Neil were house guests for the weekend about 3 months after their marriage and with the work on the house more or less complete, Alice and Christopher took much pleasure in entertaining the Captain and Neil. Alice liked Neil very much indeed and thought him such a gentleman. The Captain she found odd, she did not fully understand his eccentricity, which the Captain found most amusing and made him much, much worse. By the end of the weekend visit, Alice was avoiding the Captain and looked like a frightened rabbit caught in the headlights of a car whenever they had to meet at meal times or in the evening. Christopher could see the Captain was having a wonderful time teasing

Alice. Good manners prevailed, and all meal times were conducted in a tense but polite manner. Christopher had such fun, he would remember fondly that weekend for many years.

He and the Captain took to walking each morning in the sand dunes at Winterton. Christopher had rarely seen the Captain so animated. He loved Winterton. He pointed out the small worker houses near the beach and showed Christopher where the herrings were smoked those many years ago. Now he sadly told Christopher, herrings were outfished in the area due to foreign boats overfishing the area. Before the old man's rage got too much, with his swearing and promises of killing anyone in Norfolk who was foreign and responsible for the overfishing that happened years ago, Christopher showed him the nature reserve just south of Winterton. He took pleasure in pointing out the nesting areas for skylarks, all the types of wild life that lived in the area which included rabbits, foxes, adders and funnel webbed spiders. He showed the Captain the man-made waterholes for the natterjack toads, and pointed out how important Winterton was to conservation in the area. The Captain was thrilled and examined every rabbit hole, heather clumps and waterholes giving his view on conservation as he went along. Christopher had caught some of the Captain's pride in Norfolk and laughed at the thought that he was becoming an expert on wild life. The Captain felt proud that Norfolk took such conservation responsibilities serious. Christopher felt relaxed and at ease with the world in the company of the Captain. He made most things seem simple and easy.

That was a particularly happy and relaxed time in his life. It may not have lasted very long but he was content to bask in that trouble free time when just married and enjoying the pleasures of a new wife, a beautiful house, a good job, a child on the way. With lots of new experiences and a certain amount of respectful attention from the village people, he had accepted his lot and was surprisingly enjoying the life of a country gent.

On one of their walks, the Captain seemed uncharacteristically at a loss for words. After what seemed a long time, Christopher offered his assistance, and tried to prompt him into getting started. What came forth was what Christopher had christened *"fish finger talk"*. This was the Captain talking, using words and sentences that were normal but when they hit your ear, the words had become mashed into a new unrecognisable form Christopher called "Captain Birdseye *"fish finger talk"*. So for half an hour, it seemed to Christopher, he was listening to some profound words spoken obviously for his benefit that made no sense whatsoever. The Captain strode along the beach, in full volume, expounding the virtues of nature and how Christopher should mind the way nature worked, how if he emulated natures gift of life he would be a happy man. During this sermon, he brought in the sea, the birds in sky and the trees. At the time Christopher had no idea what the hell he was talking about but nodded at appropriate stages. It was some time later, on reflection, he understood the Captain was wishing him a happy life, and he thought trying to say be happy with what you have.

He felt that prickle of a tear again. He thought that perhaps he had always known it, but only now fully acknowledged how much he loved that eccentric, loveable old man. He realised the Captain had hidden so much love for his family behind a crotchety facade. If only he could go back in time, he would have dropped the English stiff upper lip stance and given the old boy a hug.

CHAPTER EIGHT

A second daughter, Jane, was born. He felt very proud of his children, his mother told him how beautiful they were and they looked, both of them, just like he did as a baby. At the time, on reflection, he tried to remember if he was upset that his father had not shown any interest in his grandchildren, but although in later years he felt much resentment at his lack of care, at the time, he could not remember being at all concerned. Christopher noted that Alice had, after the birth of their second child, settled rather comfortably into domesticity, not employing a nanny saying she would look after her children and not a stranger. He saw that the comely figure she displayed as a young bride had expanded into a rather portly look.

Alice did employ two cleaners full-time to keep the house and to do the washing and ironing. There was also the two gardeners and the young girl who baby-sat for her whilst attending committee meetings etc. Alice thought they may require another gardener to help tend the allotment they had created along with the flower bed at the bottom of the garden. Alice had insisted they grow their own vegetables, the farmers daughter was coming out in her. Christopher thought she would add keeping chickens in the not too distant future, he found the thought depressing. He did not want to turn his lovely garden into a smallholding. Alice also thought they may need an additional house help to cope with the dinner parties they were having. It seemed to Christopher that his wife was accumulating more and more staff. Alice insisted though on doing the cooking herself saying good homely cooking was best. Her domesticity did not run to cleaning up after cooking and she wanted to hire a woman to help her prepare vegetables and clean up at the end of the evening meals.

Most men, on the face of it, would have paid good money to swap places with Christopher, such a dutiful wife and mother. Alice had fulfilled her destiny and was happy with her life, domesticity and a place in her community, she wanted for nothing. Christopher slept alone at night with Alice in with one or the other of the children. She insisted they did not want to be alone at night. Since the birth of her second child, Alice found sex distasteful, and painful, so she made sure the opportunity did not arise. He conceded she was a good mother, the home was run well, but he wanted more from life. After 6 years of marriage, he was restless, bored, frustrated in all sorts of ways and worried about money. Something had to happen soon.

CHAPTER NINE

He had in the last 3 years taken to commuting to the London Showroom each day. As he told Alice, if he wanted to expand his area of work, he needed to be in the heart of London, where the real money was. Not quite true, but believed by Alice, he enjoyed getting out of Norfolk, away from the same provincial people, and having some fun. He found a wine bar not far from his workplace and would spend many an hour relaxing and socialising. London buzzed, there was not even a flat fizz in Norfolk. On one of his quiet afternoons in the bar sipping lager, he hatched his first plan of action.

Alice did understand, she said so. Of course the journey to London was long and tedious and very tiring. She knew that many men who lived in rural England but worked in London did the same. If he could find somewhere to stay for the week in London and travel home on Friday afternoon and spend the weekend with her and the girls, that would be fine. Although that was what he wanted to hear, and it was so easy, a bit of him realised she could not give a toss really. It mattered not to her whether he was there or not, she had the children, the house, the position in the community, she had everything, what did she want him for? Nothing would come to her mind. It might have made a small difference to him if she had said she would miss him, that she could not cope on her own. Of course, he thought later, she would not be on her own, she was in the process of employing half of Norfolk to work for her. This made him laugh.

Their marriage was a sham, one that would work nicely if only he would settle for that, but of course, he would not. So without any arguments, or questions about why, where, or when from Alice, he would organise the next day somewhere to live for the week and then organise his freedom, he laughed again, still so easy, everything came easy to him.

Looking back now, his laughter seemed a little hollow, he was a shallow, self-centred person who did not realise that no one cared what he did, as long as he paid the bills and kept up a respectable front for the community. Everything does come easy to someone who no one else cares about, of course he could do what he wanted, it mattered nothing to his family, and until now he never understood that. Tears of pity hanging about in the wings were pushed roughly away by the thought that he deserved it, he had done nothing in that marriage to make Alice feel special so why should she care. He wondered what his girls thought of him. It never occurred to him that they might think anything other than he was their father and he loved them. That was a tough one to think about, he decided now was not the time to consider that one, it was too much.

He thought back to that important but unemotional thing that had driven him most of his life, money, and the lack of it. Although he earned a very good wage, his house, his wife, his children were swallowing up a fortune. They had a standard to maintain, and he for one would not like to see it drop. Renting a place in London was also costly. He found a small one-bedroomed flat, fully furnished in Tooting. It was not the best of areas, he would have preferred Fulham, but this was close by and all he could afford. The need to make more money that had always been an underlying want of his now came to the fore with vengeance. He knew he could not live a life without more money. He could barely afford the flat in Tooting, if it had not been for his mother who agreed to pay for half of his rent, he would never have managed. He hated to penny pinch, he was not born to do that and his life style could not include being broke. He was used to an easy life, he could not bear to live hand to mouth. Apart from always doing the pools, and betting on what he thought were certs in horse racing, he did not have a plan to get more money for the future, but he would work something out.

Thinking back now, he thought himself a pompous, stuck up, snobbish, money orientated bastard. Why did he have to learn so much about himself now? He reasoned with himself that if only, yes, he thought, into the "*if onlys*" again, he had thought clearly years ago, none of this would have happened.

CHAPTER TEN

Sally thought his flat in Tooting rather sweet. Her own flat was much nicer, but as she conceded, this was only his weekday home. She had heard about his estate in Norfolk, and understood that he did not mind roughing it for the week. He had told her he was considering buying a penthouse in central London, but did not know how long he would necessarily be in the London area, so a small rent was sufficient for him. She thought him a typical man, never bothering himself where he lived as long as it had a bed and a fridge. Her aim for the two years they were together was to give his flat the woman's touch and to that end, she bought him many little bits and pieces that made his life easier. She had offered, when he first said he was looking for a place, that he could move in with her, but he declined which she thought so gentlemanly. In fact, he was not sure how long they would last together and did not want to be living in her home. He was looking for space and freedom and keeping his options open for alternative company.

Sally was a successful director of her own small but lucrative employment agency. She earned enough to buy her a 2 bedroomed apartment in Fulham furnished by

Maples of London and decorated throughout by a Kings Road interior designer who charged extravagant prices and sprinkled all his conversations and designs with famous named clients he had worked for. Sally was an intelligent, hardworking, career woman. Something Christopher found most appealing, that she had a nice figure and a pretty face was also an advantage. Sally had spent her early career working to achieve her present status. Now at aged 36 years old, she had fulfilled her ambitions and owned a lovely apartment, but it felt empty. She was a today woman, but her urges were still buried in the past. She wanted a husband, a family, and a big home for them all. It was hard for her to realise that most acceptable men were married or living with a partner, her biological clock was ticking to the beat of *"Hurry, hurry, last day of closing down sale"*. Part of her was hoping Christopher would be her partner. She knew he was married, but not happily, she would make him happy.

For two years they were happy, although he never promised her anything, she felt he implied their togetherness. They had fun, they had great sex, they could talk about business and understand each other. They spent many weekdays together and he would go home at weekends as arranged. He enjoyed his two years. They would eat out, or as was quite regular, Sally would cook something special at her home and Christopher would stay over. He kept a few items of clothes at her place because this had become quite a regular way for them. He spent at least two nights a week at Sally's home. Alice had commented on how he was putting on weight. He could not tell her it was all the rich meals Sally was cooking for him. There was no pressure from Sally, she understood he must go home at weekends as she said, she had him all week.

After two years, Sally's biological clock started ringing and panic set in. Christopher did not know what had hit him. Suddenly Sally was putting pressure on him, subtly at first, but after an indecently short time, she bluntly told him what she wanted. He had no idea. He thought she was the modern business woman she said she was. She was saying she wanted a child now, that she wanted him to leave his wife and marry her. That they loved each other, understood each other and should be together. He was shocked, and in a jokey manner he asked where the independent woman he loved had gone to. Her response in rage, took him aback and frightened him, he certainly did not understand her. What had he let himself in for? He did not love her and had no intention of settling down with her, let alone marry her. He just wanted the nagging to stop and for things to go back to how they were. Pushed into a corner he did what any red-blooded man would do under similar circumstances; he stalled for time. Sally interpreted this ploy as action, and let him run rings round her with excuses for six months.

She ran out of patience; disappointed and let down, Sally left him loudly, on an ocean of tears and recriminations. Christopher felt nothing but relief as she went, he did not need all the nagging and tears. He had really thought at her age that there would never be any expectation of marriage or children. What did a modern woman in her late 30's want with kids? He honestly thought she was just like him and wanted some fun without responsibility. On further reflection, feeling let down and prickly, he concluded that perhaps she had tried to trap him because she had obviously lied to him about being a modern woman. He had learned something from this and that was he would never trust a woman again. It had been great fun while it lasted, but not worth all the hassle. He decided he would be more selective and careful in the future. He threw himself into his work. Something he had been working on for some time now got his full attention.

CHAPTER ELEVEN

Neil had been very busy indeed. He took to his grandfathers business like a duck to water. He had many ideas, plans, expansion, modernisation, advertising, staffing. He breathlessly and with great excitement gushed all his ideas in one fell swoop. The Captain, overwhelmed by such a jigsaw of information could not get a hold on what Neil was trying to say. He stopped the lad in mid sentence after a string of ideas that had taken 10 minutes without a pause for breath. The Captain laughed and patted Neil affectionately on the back. He was impressed by his enthusiasm, it took him back years to when he had been like that.

The Captain felt good, with a new spring in his step, he took Neil to the waterside pub for a business chat. Neil agreed with his grandfather that he had ideas but they were not structured as yet. He decided he would go away and put each idea down on paper with the necessary costings and time scales and advantages and disadvantages. He knew this would take him many months but went away happy to have a project to work on. The Captain's smile got broader and more self-satisfying. The lad was going to be good, he would make sure the business stayed safe and progressed as it should.

Bertram shops and staff were safe in Neil's hands.

Neil had looked closely at the department store and realised the stock was getting very staid and boring. What might have interested holiday makers years before was not interesting now. Yes, everyone wanted a bargain, but they also had more money to spend now so items that were different and exciting were needed. They had a very old fashioned line in crockery that needed to be got rid of. Tastes had changed and the old fashioned dishes were not always dishwasher proof or microwave or oven proof. The patterns and styles had a charm that was from years ago, not eye catching but very practical. The whole store had a look of 1940's which was quite austere and did not promote the feeling of wanting to buy. He checked the takings and the stock and realised business was not as good as it used to be.

When he came to London, Neil looked in all the department stores to see how they looked. Bright colours, fun things as well as practical items could be mixed and work together. He needed something to bring the people in, then once there, they should find everything they needed at reasonable prices. He wanted Bertrams name to be on everyone's lips like it used to. He had an idea, and he was to spend the next month researching a manufacturer in Portugal. He did not want to pay the middle man again, his idea meant he would deal direct. It would take him a further two months to build a plan and costings for expansion work. It would take a further month to convince his grandfather that this could be the way forward for Bertrams, and the costs upfront would pay for itself in the following summer holiday busy time. The Captain thought the idea was worth exploring, and decided he must put his faith in Neil to the test. He realised it could be a costly test, but told himself, what was money anyway, Neil was his heir and must be given his chance.

Neil asked Christopher if he would come to Portugal with him for moral support. Christopher did not think Neil needed support, he had never seen Neil so strong and determined to undertake this. But yes, he would go, it would be fun, Neil did not ask him to do much for him. Christopher told Neil's father he was taking a weeks break to go to Portugal with Neil to look at a supplier. James was curious, no one had mentioned anything to him about Neil looking at a supplier, perhaps someone would tell him about it in the near future. Until then, he would wait and see what was what.

Before leaving for their appointment in Portugal, Neil was very busy indeed. He had a procession of builders looking at the area out the back of the Department Store. There was a large carpark at the rear, some of which Neil wanted converted to enlarging the store and incorporating a warehouse for storage. He wanted the job done quickly, professionally, and priced reasonably. He had a friend on the local council and arranged for planning permission to be given. He settled on a builder who would get the work done in a promised 4 months. Neil took a deep breath and told his grandfather his plans and the order things would happen. His visit to Portugal that week would trigger the work starting. If all went well, the work would get underway on his return, it would be finished by February, and then they had over a month to get the shelving up and get stock in, bar code everything and put out on shelves for April, the start of the boating season. The Captain patted him on the back, he was tempted to hug Neil but they did not do that sort of thing, instead he took his hand and shook it warmly. He wished him good luck and said he would be waiting to hear what had happened on his return.

Neil and Christopher travelled club class, Christopher hoped they might have a few days in Portugal to look around Lisbon before travelling back. Christopher could see Neil was uptight, in control, and the glint in his eyes did not hide the tension that was mixed in the excitement. Christopher knew this was Neil's first test, he was running this show and he wanted to succeed to please his grandfather and repay his trust in him as his heir. Also to prove something to his father, that he was not a waste of space as far as business was concerned. Christopher thought it was most probably a shock to Neil to realise he was quite disturbed by his father's view of him. Neil had always said it mattered nothing to him, that his father's style of business was not something he wanted to be associated with.

They had booked into a very pleasant hotel and that evening availed themselves of the excellent room service. The following morning they kept the appointment made by Neil with Mr Rodrigo, the owner, managing director, and sales manager of the ceramic manufacturers. After a polite introduction, a brief chat about both their needs, and a cup of coffee, Mr Rodrigo took them to the factory and display room. What they saw was colourful, and some pieces quite extraordinary in shape, use, and gaudiness. It was just what Neil was looking for, now to bargaining.

A table had been booked for lunch at their hotel. They wined and dined Mr Rodrigo, and enjoyed small talk about this and that. It was over brandy and cigars that they got down to business. Christopher sat back and watched and listened to a very impressive Neil. He was surprised as the conversation turned in a direction Christopher did not anticipate. Neil was not interested in the standard pottery, he wanted to buy the seconds, the items Mr Rodrigo could not sell, the practice pieces, but he wanted to buy them at next to nothing. They argued for quite some time, but Neil had researched Mr Rodrigo's buyers and what they wanted. Mr Rodrigo sold to top London stores, his designs cost a fortune in those shops. Neil wanted to buy the ceramics that were not good enough for these stores, to keep ahead of the market, Mr Rodrigo had a healthy design department that produced many items that were not wanted by the top stores, Neil would buy everything they could not sell. Neil got his knock down price, practically for nothing and he was promised at least 20 containers to be delivered when Neil was ready for them.

Christopher had to ask why. He could not understand what Neil was doing. Surely no one would buy discarded rubbish? What was his reasoning and was he going mad? Over a drink in the hotel bar Neil explained he was not going mad. It was really very simple. It was to do with Bertrams style. Everyone knew

Bertrams was a cheap shop selling items that every home needed. Neil looked at Christopher and asked him to be honest.

"If we stocked Royal Dalton would you buy from us or would you go to London or a stockist in Norwich?"

He did not wait for a reply but went on, "Of course you would not buy from Bertrams because it is not the type of store you would associate with quality goods. Expensive goods are from big shops, cheap goods, value for money, interesting bits and pieces would be bought from Bertrams. So my friend, Bertrams will be cheap as ever, but far more interesting. People will buy because they can afford these items. They will never necessarily consider these items bought at full price. We can, however, let everyone know that the perfect items are sold in London stores at vastly inflated prices and purchased by the rich. That will please some purchasers." Neil was determined this would work. Christopher raised his glass in a toast to his friend wishing him good luck.

The same routine was gone through over the next 4 days. Different ceramic companies were looked at, their Managing Director wined and dined, a knock down price was agreed and contracts were signed. As Neil said, he needed about 3 different suppliers to ensure a variety of stock.

The last two days they spent in Lisbon, sightseeing. Christopher particularly liked Lisbon and the way the modern city and the old city could be so close together. One minute they were getting lost going up and down steep cobbled narrow roads in old Lisbon that drew them further and further away from new Lisbon only to find that on a turn of a corner they would find themselves back in the new cosmopolitan town. New Lisbon where shopping was as good as Rome or Madrid and the clubs, bars and restaurants offered all the entertainment they could want. Neil was exhausted but elated. Christopher never stopped saying how impressive Neil was, how he did not know he had it in him, how he would make an excellent salesman. Neil laughed and said he was a salesman.

Over a glass of champagne to celebrate, Christopher asked how much Neil was going to put on the price to Bertrams. Neil had got such a ridiculous price, he could afford to take a cut himself by charging Bertrams half again for the goods. Neil, patted Christopher on the back and laughed, of course he would not do anything like that. Bertrams would make a fortune from selling the items on to customers at over treble the price they paid and the customers will still be getting the bargain of a life time. Neil would never do anything that underhanded, Christopher knew that, but it gave him ideas for his own business.

CHAPTER TWELVE

His return to Wroxham was heralded as the victor returning. The Captain wanted to hear all the details, and where modesty prevailed, Christopher filled in the blank areas. Neil was a hero. James heard what he had done and congratulated his son. He felt a bit disquieted by the idea but would not say anything to upset his son's elation. He wasn't sure people would be interested in such junk. The building work started with vengeance, there were many tears where work was held up by some problem or the other, the deadline was getting closer and closer and nerves were on edge. The work was finished in mid March and with Easter two weeks away, the panic that had threatened for months exploded and Neil dug deep and found a ruthless streak. His usual laid-back style of working at Bertrams was forgotten for the moment. Pressure and blackmail seemed the order of the day. Overtime was required and expected, with the promise that those who had been most helpful would be remembered, which translated meant if the shopworkers wished to continue working at Bertrams they must stay late every evening until the china area was ready.

With one day to spare the China Department was completed and ready for opening. Christopher had been invited to look around the 5 aisle area with shelves covered from floor to ceiling with an assortment of colourful and extensive array of china. There were many items on display that required explanation. Neil explained that many people were not aware that when eating, say, corn on the cob, the small corn shaped dishes that looked intriguingly like real corn on the cob, were an essential item for the table. That would also apply to individual servings of broccoli, served, as Christopher was to guess, on those long dishes shaped and decorated like broccoli. On being asked his opinion, and wanting to sound as positive as possible, Christopher remembered how pleased everyone was when he said that Bertrams was going to teach the ordinary man in the street that there was a crockery item available for all types of vegetables and fruits. In case that was not enough, he added quickly at prices the ordinary man could afford. Everyone was most happy with his comments, and the nervous hand wringing and fidgeting that had accompanied his tour of the crockery department was now overtaken by clapping of hands and an invitation to the drinks table by the cash out tills where all the Bertram staff were happily supping the wine and beer made available.

That evening was very tense. Neil, was very proud of his stock, and very frightened it would not be a success. Bertram blustered and strolled around the store, he exuded confidence in everything, and pride in Neil, but Christopher saw the tension in his eyes. James was unable to attend the exclusive get together due to business commitments, but he sent his good wishes and promised to be home over the weekend. The first day of the Easter holidays, the next day being Good Friday, was the start of the tourist season. Christopher did his best to put everyone at ease, but quite honestly he realised nothing would help, the following weeks would tell. In speaking to various members of staff, some of whom had taken full advantage of the drinks available and were feeling friendlier and happy to give their honest opinions. The general view was it was all rubbish and monstrous and they would not be seen dead with any items in their home. They added quickly, and slightly slurred that they hoped it went well because they liked Bertram and young master Neil. As the talking got louder, Christopher thought it best not to keep asking that question, Neil did not need to hear such pessimistic talk. Christopher stayed that weekend with Neil and Bertram. Although Wroxham was only a short way from Winterton, Alice had agreed he could stay and support Neil and Bertram through this time. She certainly did not like the alternative which was to ask Neil and Bertram to stay with them, she never got used to Bertram and his funny ways.

On the morning of Good Friday, the Captain was up early as was normal. Christopher could see him from the house down by the river edge feeding the ducks and swans. For a few minutes Christopher watched and wondered whether to join him or not. He walked slowly down to the river edge. The weather was cold, and clear, the wind had not risen yet so it felt very spring-like, and if you used your imagination, almost warmish. The watery sun shone casting a zigzagged pattern on the rippled river and the blackbirds singing loud and furiously to protect their nesting areas, made Christopher feel that Norfolk must be the best place to be in the world. As he walked closer to the Captain he realised Bertram's brainwashing talks about Norfolk had got to him as well. Today felt good though, the tourists would be here soon, and the empty river in front of him would soon be full of boats driven by office and factory workers who had never had a days boating lessons in their lives. Bertram would have his photo taken hundreds of times by those travelling by boat who were photographing anything that looked remotely interesting.

Christopher had reached the Captain and just stood quietly by him and just stared out to the river. The swans, he noted, were getting very greedy and taking all the bread being thrown. The smaller mallards and moorhens were swimming as if their lives depended on it to reach the thrown bread only to be pecked and shooed away by the swans. The Captain, always one for the underdog, was busy trying to ensure the mallards and moorhens got some of the bread. Without acknowledging Christopher's presence, he nodded to the moorhens and mallards and said for Christopher's benefit, "They will have youngsters too soon, they need food." Still without looking at Christopher, he asked "Do you think he will be O.k?" Christopher knew exactly what he meant. "He's got enough of you in him to make a success of this, I'm sure of that." The Captain smiled at that and turned and nodded to Christopher. They stayed at the water's edge for a further thirty minutes, neither felt the need to say anything. The busy life of the river with all the wild fowl, and fish seen surfacing almost ready to jump and just before they came out of the water they flicked their tails and dived down. The odd local boat went by, they would wave and the Captain would wave back, no shouting, just lazy, quiet, acknowledgements. After half an hour the Captain sighed, turned to Christopher and with some gusto said it was time for breakfast. They walked back to the house with a resolve.

Neil was already eating breakfast. He raised his head from the newspaper and grinned his good morning to them. They had a comfortable and amusing breakfast. Christopher decided to take the mickey again out of the Captain. He regaled to Neil an absurdly exaggerated tale of the Captain that morning feeding the ducks. In an incredulous voice, he painted a picture of the Captain making the ducks and swans line up for their bread, of making them swim past in formation and he added, he felt sure one of the birds raised its wing in salute. Christopher professed his admiration for such uniformity and neatness. As he said, most people just throw bread to ducks willy nilly, but the Captain had to do it in an orderly fashion. It made Neil laugh and the Captain joined in pretending to be offended but ended up laughing as well. He was pleased to see Neil so relaxed. Neil said he would go to the Store for a couple of hours before lunch just to ensure the bar codes were working alright and the staff were up to date with prices. As he said, "This was going to be a lot of new items in one sitting for the staff to cope with, if by chance any bar code was not available, I want to be there to give them support and help." With a playful smile, he added, "Anyway, I reckon I know all the bar codes off by heart having worked for so long on setting up the systems."

Christopher thought that was probably nearer the truth than Neil would like to admit.

Neil in a flourish of determination to get on with the day, threw down his napkin and pushed his chair back and wished all present a good day and he would see them later for lunch. Christopher and Bertram offered to join him but he said he preferred to go alone, they nodded quietly understanding what he meant but each silently willing the day to go well for Neil. James would arrive by helicopter either later that day or Sunday and Neil wanted to be prepared to face his father with the success or failure of his opening weekend, that, they knew, he had to do alone but by God they both vowed silently to stand side by side with Neil and support him.

Lunch was organised for 2 p.m. Neil arrived back at the house exactly on time. Over a hot lunch of Mrs Matthews Steak and Kidney pie, Neil always said it was a masterpiece and certainly one of his favourites, he told Bertram and Christopher that all was going well. It was early days yet, but he told them not to worry, there was already interest being shown by the locals who visit the town. The tourists would not arrive properly until tomorrow. Everyone who lived near the river knew how it worked. Tourists would pick up their boat sometime during the day. By the time they had got on board their holiday boat, there would be an excited look around their new home for the week or so, and after some brief instructions on how to drive the boat, would immediately cast off and take to the river. Locals knew every man who hired a boat did so with the explicit belief that they were born to take the wheel of a boat and had a natural gift for sailing. As most boats had engines and not sails, it should have been easy but it would take most new boat users a few hours to get to grips with driving, gears, and mooring was fraught with accidents, happily nothing too serious. Stops for food and shopping would happen after the captain for a week or two had got to grips with the boat and the river. After two or three days each temporary boat captain was feeling quite laid back and ready to wear a captain's hat, and a seaman's jumper. Where else would they buy these items but at Bertrams in Wroxham?

On Saturday morning whilst the Captain, Neil and Christopher were having a leisurely breakfast, the comfortable, relaxed quiet was disturbed abruptly and violently by the roar of blades, the barking of dogs, the shrieking of disturbed swans, ducks and geese scurrying away from their resting place on the lawn outside. They all looked up from their respective morning papers, realised James had arrived, and continued to read, making the most of the last few minutes of peace. Five minutes later the front door slammed and heavy footfalls could be heard echoing around the hall. In case no one had heard his arrival, James shouted a friendly hello and waited for a reply. By the time he had reached the breakfast room, papers had been folded and all three were waiting in anticipation of James' entrance. It was only after James had deposited all his paperwork, briefcases, he always carried two, and carelessly threw himself into one of the empty chairs at the breakfast table, that the questions started about what was happening, how was it going, and who had the coffee pot, and was there any fresh toast. It was at least 5 minutes before James realised that no one had answered him and that he was still asking different questions. He sat back, took a deep breath, and smiled. He apologised for his heavy entrance, as he said, he had forgotten he was not at a business meeting where everyone was waiting to answer any question he threw at them. He asked to start again, and wished them all a good morning. The Captain, his chest and face puffing up ready for any argument, was hovering between keeping quiet and blowing his top. Christopher could see that. Feeling indignant at his lack of manners, and angry at the way he just walked in and took over, the Captain opened his mouth to start. Neil seeing this, butted in quickly and tried to diffuse an argument, he did not need that this morning. Neil updated his father on what was happening with the store, and added before anything could be said, that it was early days yet, and time would tell. James, never one to sit still and let things happen was ready to go to the store with Neil there and then, to see what people thought, to encourage them to buy, and to ensure the staff knew what they were doing. That was more than enough for the Captain to hear. Without waiting, he barged into the conversation and told James to leave well alone, that Neil was doing an excellent job and knew exactly what he was doing. He added unnecessarily that, people in Norfolk handled business differently to the fly-by-nights of London, that subtlety was not something James had any of, but Neil, and he paused and pointed at Neil and continued this son of Norfolk was on top of everything and had worked long and hard and did not need any interference from James. If the Captain had feathers, they would have been well and truly ruffled. James had to smile at his father. He knew Neil was being well protected and would be alright. Having been put in his place, he turned to Christopher and they had a brief discussion about the car business.

Once again, Neil said he would prefer to go to the store by himself. Christopher, bored with staying at the house and not wanting to be around James all day, knowing that it would be business first, second, third, and last in the conversation stakes, asked if he might go with him, he promised not to get in the way. Much to the annoyance of James, and to a certain extent, the Captain, Christopher got to go with Neil to the store that morning. Christopher remembered how glad he was to get out of the house. When the Captain and James were together there was always a tension, it was usually quite fun and it looked to Christopher as if it was always the Captain who pushed for an argument. He noted though, if you watched closely, none of the barbed comments were really meant. But today, he was not in the mood for the tension that he saw had started to build.

They arrived in Wroxham high street about 12 noon. It was a busy, bustling village high street. There were far too many cars for the narrow roads that were built originally for horse and carts, and not many of those. The pavements allowed for the odd person to walk along not the hundred that now casually strolled around the village, spilling onto the road where possible. The noise of people, cars and angry horns being sounded as cars and people continually nearly collided, changed this sleepy village of winter months into something resembling a mini London street. Much to the annoyance of older residents, the Local Council had found it necessary to install a traffic light system for the benefit of cars as well as pedestrians. Many would have preferred these 20th Century tools had been left in Norwich where they belonged along with the cars, and some would mutter darkly, the tourists should stay there as well.

Today was a good day, the sun was trying to shine, boats were chugging along the water way, the streets were crowded with tourists who all seemed in good form. Neil parked in his special space behind the store and together Christopher and Neil entered Bertrams by the back staff door. When they walked through to the shop the buzzing of voices was deafening. Neil rushed ahead of Christopher to see what was happening.

The shop was crowded, even for a Bank Holiday, the sound of china crashing to the floor sent Neil in the direction of the newly opened china department. He found his way blocked by people and trolleys trying to enter or exit the china area. Red faced, breathless, and very excited, Neil pushed his way back to Christopher. All he could say was it was working. Neil's eyes sparkled and in his excitement he grabbed Christopher's hand and shook it hard and long, and then he started laughing. Neil continued shaking Christopher's hands and before his arm dropped off, Christopher disengaged himself and patting Neil on the back edged him to the side of the aisle so customers could get by. Many viewed curiously the two suited men standing in an aisle laughing and patting each other on the back. Seeing the looks they were getting, Neil pulled himself together and still hyped up, went to the checkouts to see if the girls were coping. He noted straight away that they had not considered how people were going to wrap the china and he saw his large plastic bags being wastefully used for wrapping sometimes very small items. He looked around and spied two warehouse lads and despatched them to the warehouse with instructions to bring to the checkouts any paper packaging they could find in the bins. Usually they accumulated a lot of paper which had to be collected and placed in huge bins for disposal, now Neil had found a use for it. He also noted it took ages for each customer to wrap and pack their china so the queues were getting longer. Neil took off his jacket, hung it in the staff room and rushed to the busiest checkout and acted as packer for Linda. She had recently left school and was a new employee. She was obviously finding some of the questions being asked about certain items of china difficult to answer. The older women had an answer for every question, not always correct, but said with such certainty that they usually satisfied any customer. Linda blushed at the sight of her boss helping her and made her very aware that she must make sure she was doing her job properly. Her embarrassment turned to relief when as well as packing, Neil also answered all questions on the china pieces. Linda was a nice girl but none too bright and totally uninterested in anything that did not have anything to do with boys, pop music or make-up. All she could see was the rotten china was dead boring and making her have to work harder.

Christopher, seeing what Neil was doing, took off his jacket and started to help pack at the end of the check-out next to Neil. Mary, the young girl working the till, blushed and started giggling. Neil told them to get on with their work because Mary's giggles had started Linda giggling and the customers queuing were not amused with the wait. Christopher was fumbling a little with the crockery, certainly not used to handling and wrapping these items, and he was concentrating hard to try and do it quickly. The female customers in the queues, bored with the wait, watched this handsome man and many gave little giggles. Christopher looked up to see all the women looking at him and smiling, it was a very distracting sight for him and he continued wrapping but keeping his head down hoping they would not see him blush. An hour passed and the queues were moving quicker. Neil grabbed the two warehouse lads and got them to take over packing from himself and Christopher. It was 2 pm and Neil thought they could both do with a spot of lunch.

A table was found in the Red Lion and with a glass of lager in front of them and a ploughmans lunch on order, Christopher raised his glass in salute. Neil acknowledged his praise and raised his own glass to Christopher as a thank you for your help. They tried to guess how many pieces of china had been sold during their hour on the check out but it was impossible to say. As an attempt at humour, Neil wryly wondered how many pieces of china had been broken. He thought he would look at how the china area was set out next week, although he thought it unlikely he could do anything to stop clumsy people dropping pieces. Neil fidgeted throughout lunch, his excitement almost contained but little bubbles broke out every now and again and he was becoming quite irritating to Christopher. Neil obviously wanted to get back to the shop as soon as possible. He was saying that he was worried about the stock, was anyone replenishing it if necessary. He certainly did not want the interest to die down because there was no variety of stock on the shelves. Christopher could see that the china was very popular, but he thought it highly unlikely that all the variety of stock on the shelves would have gone already. He thought Neil was getting a tad carried away. A success it surely looked, but Neil was forgetting that not everyone in his store was buying china that day.

Christopher had had enough, it was only Neil's good manners that had held him on his seat and stopped him rushing out of the place and back to the store. Christopher sighed, downed his second lager and beckoned Neil to get up and leave. Neil did not have to be asked twice, he was out of the door before Christopher had put his jacket on. Christopher could feel indigestion starting, they had eaten, drunk and talked for only half an hour and now Neil was already out of the door and striding towards Bertrams store.

By the time Christopher had caught up with him, Neil was already in the warehouse looking for Ian, the stock Manager. An open crate of assorted plant pot holders, some with very unusual designs, was obviously waiting to be emptied.

Ian was a 45 year old manager who had been employed about the same time as Neil joined Bertrams. He used to work in the warehouse of Sainsburys in Norwich. He liked it better at Bertrams, it was near home and he had been promoted to assistant stock manager when he arrived. The work had been easy in comparison to Sainsburys, the money was not marvellous but he did not have the fares so all in all, he was happy with his lot. He remembered when Neil started work at the store, the Captain made him work on the tills, unpack stock, stack shelves and even sweep the floor. The staff had a good laugh about that and took the mickey out of Neil, behind his back, of course. Generally though, they thought he was a good soul and as he progressed in the business, the Bertram staff showed him a lot of loyalty and goodwill. He had always been fair, he understood their jobs because he had done it, but today he was not himself.

Ian was not happy, he had been at work since 8 a.m. he had not had any lunch, his two lads had been taken from him by Master Neil to help pack on the check-outs leaving him to cope with filling shelves, clearing up the broken china and generally being accosted by customers who wanted to know about the various bits of china. He had just taken a 2 minute ciggie break out of the back when Master Neil bounced in and caught him. Unable to push himself forward and tell Master Neil his predicament, he got carried along with the mild ticking off for smoking at a time when Bertrams needed him to be working hard. Neil helped him unpack the large case, all the time, in a good humoured but pointed way, chiding him for not getting staff to help him today. Neil was surprised and disappointed that he had not realised he would need help in the warehouse and that although Ian was, he admitted, an experienced Manager, how did he think he would manage alone today? Only Christopher saw the resentment in Ian's eyes.

Having been an outsider watching what had been going on all morning, Christopher thought it might be a good idea to get Neil to go home and leave the staff to get on with their work. He could see that Neil had upset nearly every member of staff he had come into contact with. The tourist season was always busy in Bertrams and the staff had enough to cope with without Neil acting out of character and upsetting everything.

Over the evening meal, it was decided that tomorrow, being Sunday, they would have lunch at the usual restaurant in Wroxham, and as such, it would do not harm to just look in on Bertrams to see how Sunday opening was going. Christopher had decided that after lunch he would go home to Alice and the girls and spend the remainder of the Easter break with them. Everyone, especially Neil, was grateful for Christopher's support and, Neil made a point of saying later, that he would not forget what he had done for him. Christopher made the usual noises of don't be silly, and it was a pleasure, but Neil would have none of it.

A few days later he realised just how serious Neil was. This was no ordinary business deal, it was much, much bigger than that. Thinking back on his words Christopher realised the China store was Neil's nemesis, his Armageddon, the point of him being where he was. The covert words he used did not hide the fact that if the China store had failed, Neil being the gentleman that he was, would do the equivalent of Captain Oates in that tent and leave by the back door uttering the immortal words *"I'm going out now, I may be some time"*. It made Christopher stop and look hard at Neil. Up until then, he had not realised how determined and brave he was. Nothing in his own life would make him take chances like Neil if it would in some way destroy his life style.

He laughed at the thought, what was he doing now he asked himself if not taking chances and getting caught. He thought it ironic that his life style was about to change drastically. Of course, Neil was honourable and everything he had done was legal. There was nothing honourable or legal about this predicament. He wondered if he was developing what he used to consider a useless emotion, shame. He was certainly not familiar with that feeling.

CHAPTER THIRTEEN

Sunday came, and the Captain, Neil, James and Christopher arrived at Bertrams about 11.30 a.m. The shop had opened at 10 a.m. on a Sunday, but only during the tourist season. During the rest of the year it closed all day Sunday. This being the first Sunday opening, the staff were not at their happiest. The morning was bright but sharp with an implied frost that could be felt but not seen. Bertrams was buzzing with customers, not as many as Saturday, after lunch was usually the best time. It allowed the small entourage to tour the China shop, inspect the set up, and talk to staff. Feeling much less pressurised, Neil unwittingly put right all the wrongs of yesterday. He was full of praise for all the staff and the way they had worked so hard with the new stock and Easter excess of customers. He made a point, in front of Ian of saying how proud he was of the way Ian had coped alone in that department, how he worked from morning till evening ensuring the shelves were always stocked. Ian received congratulations and pats on the back from the Captain and James. Ian, basked in the glory of it, and would later relate to his wife how he had been specially selected by Master Neil and thanked for his work. He told her that Master Neil was just like the

Captain and his job at Bertrams looked on the up and up because of the new china department he was in charge of.

Christopher was amazed at the mans innate goodness, he was so generous with his praise. Neil's man-management was instinctive, nothing learned.

Christopher, on the other hand, was very good at getting people to do what he wanted, but he knew what he was doing, nothing said that was not thought out, but Neil, did not even know he was doing it. If it had been anyone else, it would have made him sick.

They spoke to the check-out supervisor to see if she had a feel for how the china went yesterday. Molly, a 35 year old woman who had always lived in Wroxham, had risen from check-out girl on leaving school to supervisor at Bertrams. In between, she had married and had three children. She blushed at the four important men standing before her. It was not very often she had Master Neil, the Captain, Mr James and that handsome man, Christopher, all together just hanging on her every word. She went into efficiency and posh-speaking mode.

"Hi don't quite know yet, seeing as Hi 'aven't done the books, but it ain't 'arf looking good. Hi'll know tomorrow, if that's alright."

They all suppressed a smile that could easily have turned into a giggle. Neil thanked her solemnly, told her she was doing an excellent job and said he would see her tomorrow.

The party left Bertrams after a short while and made their way to the Riverside Restaurant where a table had been reserved for them. The talk throughout lunch was all about Neil. Although it was early days and no figures had been supplied yet, it was obvious to all that the risk had paid off. James looked at his son with an admiration not felt before. Both James and the Captain were far too modest to take credit in public, but in private they would each say that Neil's business skills were most certainly *"a chip off the old block"*.

Christopher watched the pair fuss and praise Neil, who was enjoying the attention in an embarrassed haze. Christopher was pleased and relieved for Neil, he really was, he deserved all the praise, especially from his father. He knew he deserved it, but he could not understand why he felt this pain in his gut. While relaxed and watching the three of them at the dinner table, it overpowered him from behind, he did not see it coming and was not prepared. The feeling of jealousy was deep and took him over for a short while. The emotion was so strong it made his body heat up and his face turned red. Shocked at such an unusual and treacherous emotion, he struggled to control it and push it away. Christopher summoned up as much goodwill as he could and made noises to leave. Lunch was over and he wanted to get home to spend time with his girls. They all understood, thanked him again and with many handshakes Christopher left. The Captain walked him to his car. The old boy was very astute. For ten minutes Christopher listened to Captain Birds Eye *"fish finger talk"*. It took him many days of dissecting to realise he was being told he was loved. He remembered now and tears fell at the bitter sweet memory.

In the car, driving back to his home in Winterton, he tried to find out where the jealousy had come from. It didn't take any deep soul searching find the reason. Whatever he did, whatever ideas he had, there was no one who was proud of him. He was going home knowing Alice would not be interested in anything he was doing. The girls, obviously were far too young to be interested in anything that their parents did.

At that moment, on the road to Winterton, he would have given anything to change places with Neil; to have what he had.

CHAPTER FOURTEEN

He arrived home to find Alice was out. She was doing something or other at the church for Easter and the message on the kitchen table said she would be out for most of the afternoon and early evening. Donna was baby-sitting the girls. A lumpy, short girl, who when not looking sullen, blushed brightly when talking to Christopher. He never could, or for that matter, wanted to get on her wavelength, and found even the smallest conversation with her tedious. She was always chewing gum, not too quietly and often with her mouth open producing smacking noises that set his teeth on edge and made him want to grab her by the throat and pluck the nasty, noisy, piece of shit from her mouth. He thought his girls were baby-sat far too often by illiterate morons and he despaired at their development.

As he walked into the house he could hear the usual video on the television. The girls were mad about the Smurfs and had watched the same video so many times, it would not be long before it was stretched and worn and would need replacing. He kissed the girls and asked if they would like to go for a walk along the beach. Without taking their eyes off the television screen the cries of "Oh no daddy, we're watching our video" put an end to that. He would make eye contact with them later when the video was finished. He could have sat with them he supposed, but to watch the Smurfs the first time was bad enough, a second time would be hell. Donna, through hooded eyes, and chewing gum, open mouth style, watched him head for the garden.

He thrust his hands in his pockets and hunched his shoulders slightly against the chill that was developing as the sun began fading in the spring mid afternoon. It all felt rather flat. He wished he was somewhere else. He walked towards the rear garden where the vegetables were grown and he noted that, yet again, the area had increased by many square feet. Every spring for the past few years, Alice added more and more vegetables and fruit. At the last count he noted they possessed 4 large chest freezers full of the usual meat, bread, etc and the rest contained home grown vegetables. He tried to appreciate her efforts and the saving of money but for Christ's sake, if they bought their vegetables instead they would save more money, because they would need only one full-time gardener and they could afford to drop a house help who did most of the preparing and freezing of the fruits and vegetables. He reckoned if they acquired any more chest freezers they could compete with the Bejam shops for frozen foods. He dropped that thought quickly, although he would put nothing past her, even she would not open a shop, he shrugged the awful idea away and continued to the back of the garden.

He noted the grass was looking good and the ornamental trees and his pride and joy, the weeping willow were all budding. Spring in England was a good time. He noticed a piece of ground at the rear and to the left of the vegetable garden had been cleared and levelled. On closer inspection he saw concrete had been laid as a base. With a sinking feeling he knew the chickens would not be far away. His lovely big garden was slowly turning into a small holding. Standing there in the cold, sharp, dying spring sunshine, that was the moment, in despair, when he decided things must change.

He was sure now, that this was the turning point in his life. He knew he had always looked for more, but that was the moment, innocent to any onlooker, not understood by his family. To anyone looking, he was just a man looking around his beautiful garden, but he had made the decision to seek and make his own, a different lifestyle, as far away from Norfolk, and England as possible.

His hideaway in London, fine for a time was now not enough. His long term plan was to work abroad, to see what was out there. England was too small and restricting. Norman Harvey-Colland was an upper class, middle aged gentleman who was ex-Army and genuinely had the bearing of an army officer that Christopher only implied by his stature. Norman was the overseas International Salesperson for Davies-Clarke Plc – Luxury and Customised Vehicles for the Discerning. Christopher had noted that Norman was very successful with clients in the Middle East, where money was nearly as plentiful to the chosen few as the sand that invaded everywhere. The files that he spent days poring over showed that attempts to infiltrate America, Australia, parts of Europe and Asia had proved time consuming, costly and an embarrassing disaster. The Great Britain, parts of Europe and Middle Eastern clients had kept the company in good condition, but Christopher wanted to get work out of England, and he would work on that, not for the company, but for himself. Over the years he had proved himself an excellent organiser and had developed a natural, believable honesty as a salesman.

CHAPTER FIFTEEN

For about two years he worked closely with Norman. He had gained approval from James to travel to the Emirates States with Norman on his regular visits. Christopher found it a God forsaken place. All the women were covered from head to toe, no booze and the heat was unbearable. No way did he want to muscle in on Norman's area. He soon realised he would be kidding himself because Norman was nobody's fool and although he enjoyed Christopher's company, he could, at that moment, outsmart him and out-think him. Christopher knew Norman was the master of all salesmen and he would sit at his feet and watch and learn.

It would take many visits with Norman to fully understand these foreign clients. The wealth in the Emirates was awesome. These people wanted the best of everything. It was the younger males of the powerful families that wanted everything now. These rich communities were rivals and wanted to be different and better than their neighbours. It caused Norman many a headache and many a whopping bonus. Christopher watched intently and learned. Rich he understood, so rich that nothing was important and costly possessions were discarded like worthless trinkets. He could not understand this mentality, and if they wanted to throw away such costly items, why not in his direction? No one ever benefited from such wastefulness, except Norman.

A particular event was burned into Christopher's brain, something he would never forget. It still shocked him and he found it incredible that any living person could be so shockingly wasteful and disrespectful of property Christopher would have worshipped and loved. He remembered a top of the range Mercedes-Benz Sports that was ordered by a Sheikh's son. The SLR McLaren was worth about £300,000. It was the most beautiful of sports cars and had a supercharged 5.5 litre dry sumped 90 degree V8. Christopher loved the sleek look and the power of this fantastic racehorse of a car. It had been customised with real gold fittings, the softest kid leather in the rarest pastel blue, it reminded him, in colour, of the eyes of a new born sheepdog, one of the few things in his childhood that had struck him as beautiful and wonderous. The stereo and TV that was so state-of-the-art that it was still in the experimental stage of development and cost this Sheikh the same as a small army.

He actually witnessed the following event, he remembered he would not have believed it otherwise. Norman and he drove along with the Sheikh's other two cars to the beach where upon Norman told Christopher to follow him to a higher point on the beach. He told Christopher to watch, behave himself and say nothing.

The new car was driven onto the sandy beach. This beautiful, stately, deep blue car with customised features at a total cost that would have cleared a third world country's debt was used as a racing car on a none too even beach outside Dubai. Christopher watched the especially sensitive and shock absorbing suspension rise up and down as the SLR McLaren was driven at over 100 mph across the unwelcoming surface. Christopher winced at the memory; to the beat of a deep bass rock song, indefinable to them standing at some distance except for the unrelenting beat, the car drove up and down the mile length beach and regularly skidded into a 90° turn. It was after nearly 45 minutes of trying to roll the car, that finally Christopher watched it being driven at high speed into the sea. As the waves licked at the door handle, the Sheikh struggled out and swum to shore. His servants rushed clapping and cheering towards him and he was covered in towels and made comfortable. Christopher watched speechless. When dried and pampered, the Sheikh strode over to Christopher and Norman. In quite a matter of fact tone he told Christopher that last time he managed to get his sports car further into the waves and with some pride, said it took days to get it out due to the strong currents. As he walked away, he shouted over his shoulder in the direction of Norman that he wanted the same again within a month. They watched him stride to the backup car, a rather beautiful gold coloured Bentley, driven by his chauffeur and throw himself into the back and before anyone could say anything the car was a distant speck on the horizon.

Christopher turned to Norman opened mouthed at what he had just witnessed, mute with an inability to comprehend such disrespect for a wonderful piece of machinery. Now they were expected to replace the car within a month, there was nothing that could be done at such short notice. Christopher knew it was impossible. Disgusted at such waste and incredulous that someone like the Sheikh really existed he shouted in frustration at Norman.

"A month, is he serious, the fucking kid leather takes a month to hand stitch into place, let alone everything else. What the hell are you going to do?"

Norman smiled and said: "Never you mind laddie, he will have a new, identical, Mercades-Benz SLR in 3 weeks." Norman, apparently had been dealing with this client for 10 years. Most of his Emirates clients were older business men who ordered good quality, customised vehicles and he had enjoyed many a social evening with these men. The youngsters were a different kettle of fish. He said they were spoilt and had never done a days work in their lives. Not all of them were like this Sheikh, but he was not alone in his temperamental wasteful habits and Norman had got the measure of them. In answer to Christopher's quizzical look, Norman told him, quite smugly, "Every year this particular Sheikh buys at least 3 cars for his own use, and everytime without fail, the first one has ended in the sea and he orders an identical duplicate. The duplicate," Norman told him, "was already waiting for delivery but I make the bastard wait 3 weeks. One day he is going to want it quicker and then I will charge him double for the special round the clock work necessary to get him his car earlier than usual. As it is, I make a fortune out of the little bastard. One of his cars is the Bugatti Veyron, at a cost of £800,000 he never rides that one into the sea, I think I would shoot him myself if he tried. Christopher, I will be retired and living a very comfortable life in not too many years thanks to that little wanker."

Christopher looked at Norman giving him full admiration and respect. No wonder he was so successful.

The Bugatti Veyron always made them pause and reflect, any red blooded man would fall in love with the power under such a sleek and full bodied car. The engine 7993cc, 16 cylinders in a W its power 1001bhp @ 6000rpm and with torque 922 lb ft @ 2200rpm transmission 7-speed DSG, manual and auto fuel 11.7mpg (combined). It was like a mantra to these men. To be in control of this stallion was a lifetime dream and Christopher had test driven it. Nothing in the world could compare with the exhilaration of the sound and speed and class of this temple. 0-62 in 2.5 seconds. Speeds of up to 253 mph. After driving a Bugatti, nothing in the world would ever compare with it. Christopher wanted to sell a Bugatti Veyron in his working lifetime and preached its biblical roar and its angelic curves to the very rich masses. It was the most powerful and expensive car in the world.

Christopher had been working on his plans for some time now. Whilst looking after his European customers he had worked long evenings in London on his ultimate goal. He had made many contacts over the years and initiated friendships for one purpose only; to get out of England and make his fortune. He was nearly ready to present his Business Plan to James. Before he did that, he had to sort out a minor distraction on the home front.

CHAPTER SIXTEEN

His eldest, Emily, was due to start Junior school within a couple of months. Alice, unbeknown to Christopher, had put both the girls down for a particularly good boarding school not far from Sandringham, just months after they were born. It was by pure chance Christopher found out.

Last weekend, he went for his usual Sunday morning walk in the dunes at Winterton with the girls, this time only Emily came with him, and as usual she was prattling on about this and that. He always said to anyone who would listen, "That girl could not keep quiet if her life depended on it."

She spoke to him in a squeaky, high toned manner that he once found charming and funny, now he thought she was sounding like a pretentious, middle class snob in the making. She was tugging on his sleeve to keep his attention. Emily was 8 years old going on 20 years by the way she talked, she had listened to her mother and mimicked her tones. At 5' she was tall for her age, and slim like him, with the most beautiful long golden blonde curly hair, that had been gradually changing to a mousy brown like her mother over the last few years. When she was 4 years old, everyone said she looked like

Shirley Temple, now she was a mixture of her father and mother.

Whilst she loved her father, she understood that he did very little for her, she assumed because he was tired and busy doing other work. Her mother was always there for her and she would go to her for anything she needed. Today she had wanted her father to do something for her. Emily was determined that daddy would listen to her and do what he should for her. It was the words *"Boarding School"* that caught his attention. Up to that point he had made a habit letting most of what she said go over his head when she started her prissy little conversations. He asked her to repeat the bit about the Boarding School. Irritated by his lack of attention, she sighed deeply, stopped walking only long enough to scold him for not listening properly. She started walking again, as she took step after step she repeated slowly in a condescending manner, something she had learned from her mother, that she would need her own suitcase with her name on it for Boarding School. He felt irritated and blustered, trying to shut her up as she went on to say what colour her suitcase should be, and how the school colour was green and so perhaps her suitcase should be green, her friend was having green so perhaps that was good. She only stopped walking and talking when she heard her father shout louder than she had ever heard before for her to shut up. While she contemplated this order, her lower lip started to tremble and she could feel tears building ready to overflow. Christopher saw the effect of his words and immediately felt sorry for Emily. She sounded so like Alice at times he forgot she was just 8 years old and mimicking her mother. He crouched in front of her and dabbed her eyes with a tissue he found in his pocket. She was such a little soul he felt quite horrid to have nearly made her cry. On promises of a piggy back ride to the house and an ice-cream on the way from Mr Hooper of the General Store, they returned to Winterton singing her favourite song "One Man went to Mow". They only sang up to 10 men and then started from one man again. By the time they reached Winterton village they were onto their third time of 10 men, 9 men, 8 men, 7 men, 6 men, 5 men, 4 men, 3 men, 2 men, 1 man and his dog, went to mow a meadow. They both needed an ice-cream after that. They arrived home laughing.

Alice and Jane had stayed in the house. Jane was 6 years old and wanted to stay that day with her mother. Jane was plump and small with straight mousy hair and looked the image of her mother. She had wanted to stay with the chicks that had been purchased. Three dozen hens would be squawking, pecking and digging in the back of the garden soon. The girls had been so excited when they had arrived. The gardener had prepared room in the shed for them with a small heater and lighting. Jane had been guarding them. She had told her daddy that they would get lonely by themselves so she was going to stay with them and bring her dolls into the shed for them to play with. The arrival of the chicks had done nothing for Christopher's mood which was getting blacker by the minute. Once back at the house, Emily went to join Jane in the shed with the chicks. Her little sister had laid out her tea set and offered Emily an imaginary cup of tea and a biscuit when she arrived. Both girls would happily spend the rest of the day in the shed with the chicks. They told the chicks all about their new school and the big adventure that mummy had told them about. They would live during term time in a big school and have their own bed in something called a dormitory. They would make lots of friends and have swimming lessons. Jane would be alone with mummy for another year before she would join Emily at the Boarding School. Emily would be alone for the first time ever. They told the chicks that mummy said they must be brave little girls and not cry. They made the chicks promise not to tell mummy or daddy that they were frightened and didn't want to go away from each other or from mummy and daddy. They tried not to cry but Jane cried, then Emily did too.

When the girls had closed the shed door, Christopher went looking for Alice. He found her in the kitchen cooking something or other. He asked where all the help was and she said they were around somewhere. He needed to find a time when they could talk in private. The house was always full of other people, this was usually a distraction that did not cause any problems as they spent little time talking to each other, only to talk diaries and dinner parties to be arranged. It had up to now been comfortable, but Christopher realised that they were strangers to each other. He could feel his temper building and he needed to talk now. On seeing there was no staff around, he closed the kitchen door and told her tensely to sit down, now! He had something to discuss that would not wait. She felt quite prickly at being disturbed whilst preparing dinner and did not like to be told to shut up and sit down when she remonstrated about leaving the cooking. As she dried her hands on the tea towel draped permanently over her shoulder she told him through pursed lips and a stiff back that if it was about the chicks she had bought, it was too late now to send them back. She went on about how it made sense to have fresh eggs, how much cheaper it would be, and how anyone would think he had been raised in a town and not on a farm for his silly objections to chickens. She was just adding the point that he wasn't being asked to do anything like clean them out or collect eggs when he shouted for her to shut up and listen for a change. She turned, shocked at his raised voice and squared her shoulders ready to answer him back when she saw the look of a barely contained temper and decided this did not happen often and kept quiet. He had objected to very little over the years. What had made him so cross now she waited to hear.

Holding himself in restraint, he asked her what was all this he had heard about his girls going to Boarding School. He asked in a calm, quiet voice that frightened her. She did not know what to say. He had, over the years let Alice do what she liked. He never complained when she took on more staff, upgraded the family car, decorated the house. She thought he was not interested. She knew the vegetable plot was disliked and the chickens would cause a stir because he had always said he didn't want them in his garden. To a certain extent, he took pride in the garden and would talk to the gardeners about what he wanted and where. But the girls schooling, he had never mentioned anything about that. Yes, she had put the girls names down for St. Hillary's a few months after they were born. She had meant to talk to Christopher about it but what with a new baby she forgot. As the years rolled by, they had become more and more distant with each other, it had felt unnecessary to discuss the girls schooling, she dealt with everything else without talking to him about it. What was the big deal now she wanted to know.

He had great difficulty in controlling his temper but felt he deserved a medal for the way he controlled himself. He told her calmly and coolly that his daughters would not ever be going to a boarding school, that they would go to a good school locally on a daily basis, and she had enough staff to help her look after them so why in Gods name did she want to send them away? Alice was lost for words, not knowing what was going on. All children from good families go to boarding school. You make friends for life, it was well known. She had gone to boarding school, he had gone to boarding school, she really did not understand. He was so angry he did not have the words to explain properly why, he did not even know if he wanted to tell her this intimate and personal worry. At that moment Susan came in to help with the dinner. In a quiet, intimidating way, Christopher bent towards Alice and told her this was not finished and he would talk to her again, if not tonight, certainly on his return next weekend.

He seemed a little distracted to all at work in the London Office. That week he drank alone poring over papers sent to him, and seemed to spend hours on the phone. By Friday he seemed his old self and went for a quick half with Norman, Phil and Ted before starting his journey home to Winterton. He had sorted the problem of the girls schooling and had the answer. He hoped Alice would not argue, he had made his mind up. He realised he had not done much for his girls. If nothing else, he would know he had protected them from boarding school life. It had cost him dearly, schools like that do not come cheap. Jumping the queue meant he owed someone a favour big time, and he had promised to repay them whatever the price, and he didn't mean money. He knew his life was about to change and hoped, in later life, the girls would recognise that he had done something for them, that he did love them. He would never be able to tell them that.

Now, as the middle-aged man he was, sitting in this room, he realised he had never told his girls he loved them. He had smugly told himself it did not matter. He would give anything to hold them and tell them how much they mean to him. He might be tied to this chair now, but he had made his own chains that had bound him for years restraining any decent emotions, and holding back real love. It was unbearable for him to realise, he wished they would hurry and kill him now.

CHAPTER SEVENTEEN

He arrived home at 4 p.m. on Friday. All was very quiet in the house. He looked in the kitchen and found Lindsay peeling potatoes for the evening meal. She told him Mrs Cross was at a meeting and should be home soon and the girls were at a tea party at a neighbours house. Christopher paced. He felt everytime something important needed to be done, Alice was not there.

Her car pulled into the drive at 4.30 p.m. and Alice eased her way out of the car and into the house. In her arms were files of papers, a bunch of flowers and two bags of produce. Christopher wondered what on earth she did with herself all the day, and if they had an allotment at the bottom of the garden full of vegetables why the hell had she bought more. He could feel irritation taking him over and he had to push it away. This weekend was to be devoted to sorting his girls schooling out.

Alice gave him the obligatory peck on the cheek as she entered the kitchen. He told Lindsay to go and sort out a drink for him. Alice looked at him quizzically. He never asked her to do this, he always said a whisky should be poured by someone with love and intelligence for the smooth liquid, and she never thought Lindsay knew anything about whisky. He seized the opportunity and quickly told Alice they must talk in private, and asked her to walk in the garden with him. She pursed her lips, knowing there was going to be trouble. As her back stiffened ready for a fight, Christopher told her that he did not want to fight and he had an answer to the girls schooling that she will be very happy with. He was positive that she would jump at this offer, but because the cost to him was so high, he had to make sure, there was not room for doubt. He brought his salesman techniques into play and promised her it would be everything she wanted for them. He would play on her snobbery, for she had become a prize snob and since becoming chairperson for the W.I. in Winterton and surrounding areas, had decided that everyone in Norfolk was watching her and she needed to be a shining example of middle, nay, upper-class folk for all the poor, lower-class people in Norfolk. So everything she did or her children did was important to those she knew were watching her as a role model.

They strolled to the bench by the Rhododendrons that were in full bloom. For ten minutes it was very comfortable just talking about the plants and what beautiful colours they were. Alice said she had never seen such a Rhododendron plant full of so many flowers. Christopher told her he had spoken to the gardeners about special fertiliser for acid loving plants and it had worked. This cosy chat had the effect of bring them, for a few moments only, closer than they had been for years. Christopher broke the easy silence.

"I want the best for the girls too you know."

Alice, without looking at him sighed and said, "You have been in such a funny mood about this. I want the best for the girls, you should too. I won't let you ruin their chances in life because of some silly reason about boarding schools. Look at us, we're fine, we are both examples of former boarding school pupils."

He thought she had no depth, how could she have gone through the boarding school experience and want that for her children, if she had any real feelings? He would not verbally attack her, that was not the plan. He must present her with an alternative that was so good, she would grab it with both hands. God knows, it had cost him to secure this. He wanted to build on this peaceful, comfortable moment, he put her hand in his and pointed to the willow tree.

"If we hadn't tended that tree so well, would we have such a beautiful specimen of a willow to admire today, I think not. We have two beautiful girls, what we give them today will sculpt them for tomorrow." He wondered if perhaps he was sounding a little like the Captain and his *fish finger talk*. He definitely was not going to mention acorns and oak trees. Alice seemed to understand what he was saying and waited for what else he had to say, so far they seemed to be on the same wavelength. He had to get down to the point of all of this.

"I made enquiries about St. Hillarys and yes, it's a good school. You picked well there Alice."

She smiled a satisfied smile, she knew it was the best in the county. It was going her way.

"I have spent the week looking into all schools in Norfolk and you picked the best alright. But, and listen to this, I made enquiries and there is an exclusive school on the borders of Suffolk and Norfolk in a village called Blythe St. George. The school is a boarding school but will take day pupils. Wait for this Alice, it's called Blythes, heard of it eh?"

Of course she had, it was so exclusive that you put your child's name down before it is conceived, that is, unless you are so rich you have seriously rich on your cheque book, and only if it was a Coutts & Co, cheque book. She would never have tried to get her girls in there, it was far too expensive, far too exclusive, and well, out of her scope of possibility. She shook with surprising emotion.

"For god sake Christopher, tell me more, what are you saying?"

He could see he had won and continued in an easy manner to fill her in on the details.

"I have a place for Emily this year and Jane next year. They will be day pupils only though. I pulled every string I could find to get them in. A couple of my clients have children at the school, and through them I found out who the Governors were, and surprise, surprise, one was a good friend of one of my clients. It took lots Alice, I promise you, but I did it. It's going to cost every bit of spare money to have the girls there, but I promise to work harder to pay for it."

She looked at him with pride. So she had thought him a mistake, a disappointment, but today in one fell swoop, he had redeemed himself. She realised that not only were her girls going to the very best school there was, perhaps in the whole country, but her standing in the community would rise immediately. Already she was planning how to get on the parents school committee. Then a thought struck her.

"But Blythes is too far away for the girls to go each day Christopher. How will that work?"

"I have thought of everything Alice, we will get a new gardener, instead of old George who should retire, he will be a chauffeur as well and take the girls to school and collect them. The journey is no more than 45 minutes, so I think I've thought of everything. You can interview for a gardener/chauffeur, you're good at that."

She looked at him like she hadn't looked at him for many years. She saw again the remnants of the man she married. She squeezed his hand in excitement and gave him a hug. He broke the quiet moment by giving her hand back and jumping up, he wanted none of that. His plan was to save the girls, he had no plans to save his marriage. With a deep inhale of the afternoon air, and a broadening of his shoulders he told Alice to buck up, tomorrow they were all going to Blythes to have a look. Excitedly, Alice jumped up and started to twitter about clothes, and what the girls would wear. She left Christopher to his garden while she went indoors to prepare a list of what was needed for tomorrow, and she must ring Belinda and Lucy to thank them for a wonderful meeting today, perhaps she might let slip where they were going tomorrow. She hadn't felt so happy for a long time.

He looked around his garden. He knew he had done good. He could, with a clear conscience start his plans.

His girls were safe, Alice had what she wanted, he would always look after their interests. Now was his time, he hoped within a month he would start his tour abroad, this would be settled tomorrow and next week he would have his meeting with James to settle his long term plans.

CHAPTER EIGHTEEN

He had a meeting on Thursday with James to go through his initial plans. Today was Tuesday and he was unaccustomedly twitchy. He went over and over the papers to ensure it was all there and made sense. This was the biggest deal for him so far. With this idea, which he had to sell to James, he would be on his way. Thursday was a long time coming and Christopher was getting more and more anxious. It had to work, there was no point to what he did if he could not get out of the country; England was choking him. He needed relaxation and there was only one answer to that, he deserved a treat.

Amanda was his bit of home comfort, just the thought of her relaxed him.

He had known her for some 3 years now. Since Sally he had trusted no woman. He would not get his fingers burnt again. He wanted to shake the depressing idea that women were not to be trusted. All he wanted was some fun and sex without commitment. He realised if he continued to feel like that he would never have a relationship with all the trappings he wanted. The six months without a woman had been uncomfortable and miserable. He had even contemplated Alice, his wife, a not unreasonable notion in times of hardship, but thought better of it. She would expect many favours for sharing his bed and yes, he could close his eyes and think of England, but the lead up to sex always put him off, he found her repulsive and a complete turn off. He had decided he was not that desperate.

By chance, a Saudi client of Norman's arrived in town. Norman was out of the country and it fell to Christopher to entertain this very rich and feted client. No hardship at all for Christopher, he found the older ones very amenable and good company. A good meal and one too many drinks later saw Christopher and Sheikh el a benia knocking on Amanda's door in the fashionable and expensive part of Kensington.

The white house with the steps up to the front door took a few minutes to negotiate but Christopher, triumphant and busy focussing on where the door bell was jumped with surprise when the door was opened by a tall, dark haired, long-legged woman with an amused look on her face. Her slight puzzlement changed when she spotted the Sheikh propping up the pillar by the door. With a shriek of delight she grabbed him and pulled him to her. She called out to a space behind her for Lisa and Emma to come and help. She hugged and kissed the Sheikh, Christopher, in his drunken state, deduced that she knew him and was not just being friendly. Linking arms with both of them, and with Lisa and Emma now helping, Christopher felt himself wafted into the house on a cloud of perfume and softness. He found himself in a sumptuous home, although he was made to sit down, everything around him was still swaying and his brain was unable to connect with his mouth. He wanted to say something but he could not remember what. Coffee was served hot, black and strong. As Amanda explained later, if you had a bad head cold you would not enjoy a gourmet meal, so how could you enjoy a good fuck if you were drunk? All this came out of the mouth of a woman who had so many plums in her mouth she could have made jam. Amanda went to Blythes, the top class school. Her daddy, she would tell clients, could buy and sell England, he was so rich.

Christopher had a night to remember, paid for by the Sheikh, God Bless him Christopher would utter many times. He had to do nothing he didn't want to. There was no having to work for sex, he laid back and everything was done for him and to him and it was pleasure, pleasure, and don't you worry, you rest honey, greatness takes time to recover. Every time he thought of her he would exhale loudly and feel a disturbing ache in his groin. The thought of the women and especially Amanda, made the many weeks until the next visit seem a life time away but the memories of the last visit would keep him drooling and yearning.

Now he had found the answer to his prayers, the frustration of not being able to afford to visit as often as he needed caused Christopher a lot of heartache. She became that treat at the end of each month when he was newly paid. He worked towards the visits, counted the days, planned what he would do, remembered what she did so well. For a few months everyone noticed he seemed to be going off the rails, he had gone from red hot tempers over stupid little hindrances in his job for the past five or six months to being buried in thought for a lot of time, the men reckoned it was a woman, they assumed his wife. Christopher did not share his private life with anyone and no one knew what he did when he left work. He felt contentment in having found his second home. Amanda and the girls, all ten of them, were ex-public school girls with class and style. He had never considered a prostitute before, thinking them common and disease-ridden.

Amanda was a dream come true, he cursed himself in not thinking people like her existed and waiting so long. He dreamed of her often, her long legs, so smooth, so accommodating, so athletic. Her long dark hair with a hint of a wave that became quite curly round her face when she got hot and sweaty. Her features were chiselled and her nose quite pointed, it was the typical features of a beautiful, middle-class, English woman without the hang-ups he had found in women of this class. She enjoyed sex and always insisted on making sure he enjoyed himself and she expected nothing from him except money. A perfect relationship, made not quite in heaven, but in paradise for him.

Amanda liked him very much. She looked forward to his visits. He was good looking with an almost shy and school boyish naïve attitude to women which she found rare and very sexy. He was obviously from a good background and in a regular job. It made a nice change for her to enjoy a client's company, it did not happen very often. She found something appealing in all her clients, usually they were very rich, very powerful, and very married. This was her aphrodisiac and she enjoyed her work. It was just nice every now and again to have a client that was particularly delicious. She kept Christopher to herself, no one else serviced him and he was happy with that too. This was no love match. Business and pleasure rarely meet, but it did for them. She indulged him, he paid, of course, but enthusiasm like hers could not be bought.

Some time later it would be Amanda who helped him get a place at Blythes for his girls. He almost giggled now at the thought, what would Alice have done if she had known that, torn as she would have been between the best school for her girls and gaining their entry because of a prostitute. It would have been fun to watch her struggle to reconcile that one. He reckoned she would do what any self righteous hypocrite would do, she would take the places for her girls and make him pay penance for his infidelity and indiscretion for the rest of his life.

Amanda was a naughty girl with naughty habits as she coyly told him one hot night. He found out this included an expensive coke habit which she shared with some of the other girls and many of the clients. Christopher had never indulged and had no intention of indulging in that sort of habit. He was not adverse to others using it, and in fact, he quite liked on many occasions the results of the girl's coke habit, which made them very amenable and creative.

That Christopher was not a cokehead was of great interest to Amanda. She knew he travelled to Europe regularly for Davies-Clarke Plc – Luxury and

Customised Vehicles for the Discerning. One evening after a pretty hectic time, as they lay resting, Amanda, as was her habit, would stroke his leg enticingly looking for a reaction that would take at least another half an hour to happen. She told him she had a plan that would allow him to visit more often, this got a small reaction she noticed. She hesitated long enough for him to settle, she had his interest. Whilst making circles lightly on his stomach with her index finger, which he found quite disturbing, she whispered her idea. It was so simple, she would tell him, it would not involve him in any time or trouble, but would make him lots of money. She wanted him to collect and deliver some recreational drugs for her and the girls use. She told him how easy it was nowadays, that the police and customs were looking for those who sold to the street market, hers would be for her use only, besides, some of her best clients were judges and top policemen, so he would be safe. She knew he travelled regularly to Europe and it would be so easy to collect a little package on every trip. She kissed him lightly on the neck, using this as a full stop to every sentence whispered. She giggled as he grabbed her, fifteen minutes this time for recovery, she knew the idea excited him. Afterwards, worn out and sweating heavily, Christopher agreed to her plan, after an obligatory statement of not wanting to get caught and it would have to be worth his while. The finer points would be sorted out at a time when neither were so distracted.

Over the next two years Christopher's short hops to Europe increased, obstensively to build relations in Brussels at the UN, his pick ups were now for clients of

Amanda's as well, and he was making a lot of money. He felt safe carrying the packages and the money. Amanda had given him a special plastic bag that he put the packages in and the money in. She told him it was a protection against the sniffer dogs in any airport. The plastic bags were impregnated with a proven something that masked the smell of drugs or money. Christopher at first felt spooked by this high tech stuff. What had started as just a little bit of recreational drug smuggling for the use of a few people now took on a dark and sinister tone. He looked to Amanda to make this whole business feel safe and give him an explanation he could deal with. Alarmed at his back tracking, but sensing he wanted to hear anything that would make him feel better she had sat beside him and calmly explained everything. With a little laugh and a gentle scolding of what a silly sweetie he really was, she explained a client of hers had been boasting about these bags and how you could smuggle anything into the country using them. Apparently, he had told her, the contents of the bags could not be seen on any X Ray machine, and sniffer dogs could not smell their contents.

"Just because he worked for the Ministry of Defence," she told Christopher through pouted lips in that coy and sweet way that women do, "does not mean it is anything for you to worry about. In fact my darling, I only want to protect you, to make sure you are safe. Just think, sweetie, no worries going through customs. You will have no problems getting the packages home. You are far too precious to me to allow anything to happen to you."

She told Christopher her Ministry of Defence client had given her a huge package of these top secret stash bags. She didn't tell Christopher how she had threatened him, that he did not give them to her willingly but because he had no choice. Blackmail was such an ugly word and she preferred not to use it.

Christopher soaked up this explanation because it suited him to accept her every word. Of course she cared for him, he knew that, and it made such good sense to use whatever means were available to keep him safe. He was happy with his lot. Going through customs gave him a buzz and he was loving the thrill of these illegal operations. He felt invincible and untouchable and with the added tingling bonus of Amanda's ample thanks Christopher was feeling quite arrogant and smug.

A few times James had given him a lift back from Europe in his private helicopter when their meetings had coincided. Christopher had found it hard to suppress a giggle at the time. When he knew he was getting a lift back with James he ensured his pick up was big. He would bring back a street value of nearly one million pounds in coke. The VIP trip, he knew, meant no searches at Heathrow and he would walk away with a cool stash of money. He made an absolute fortune which he kept safely in an off-shore account. By the time the girls entered Blythes, he was worth, with interest, 200 thousand pounds sterling. Naturally, no one knew of this wealth, Amanda could guess at how much he had, but he was telling no one. Far from being satisfied, as far as Christopher was concerned, it was obviously not enough. He wanted freedom and that would take much more money to keep him in a style he wanted to become accustomed to. He now knew how he would make his money and he would use Davies-Clarke Plc – Luxury and Customised Vehicles for the Discerning as the best vehicle to achieve this.

Thursday was approaching and he needed some relaxation, Amanda was always willing to help his stress levels. He spent Tuesday night talking and lying with Amanda. He told her his plans for Thursday and she thought they were brilliant and he was so clever. She rewarded him with a night of excessive passion that left him happy, breathless, weak and tired. He slept the best he had slept for months.

Thursday at 9 a.m. he arrived for his meeting, rested, confident, and with a spring in his step. James, as always, had been at work for an hour and half. He always said he got more done before 9 a.m. than after. Christopher collected two cappuccinos en route and made straight for the conference room.

"So you're going to share with me at last the plans you've been working on for the past months." James knew everything, this still surprised Christopher. He should have known by now, James had a finger, thumb and eyeball in all parts of his businesses. It crossed Christopher's mind that James might have a spy on the payroll who kept him informed of all that was going on. Christopher snorted at such a stupid idea, James was not James Bond 007, he was just a successful, rich, bit of a bastard, workaholic.

He presented his plans simply and clearly, as a good salesman he knew how to pitch an idea. He wanted to take Davies-Clarke Plc – Luxury and customised Vehicles for the Discerning successfully across the world. He knew this had been tried before, unsuccessfully and at great expense, but Christopher had a new slant that would cost an insignificant amount of money to test the waters of customised cars. He had researched thoroughly and spoken to many key people and Christopher cited many examples of how where and when. To James it had the unmistakable whiff of success. He could put the cars on show for maximum effect at minimum cost. He promised the cars would be seen by the right type of clientele. He could see James was interested and wanted to know more. He explained it had taken many months to put together because of attention to detail and costings. Now James was getting impatient, so before he could bellow for him to get on with it, he stopped side tracking, got straight to the point, and laid his plan out.

"Across the world at different times of year, countries and continents have global events planned that attracted the upper income and discerning clientele. In Asia there were the Asian Games to be held in Thailand, the Air Show in Singapore, a yearly cultural Exhibition in Kuala Lumpur that attracted money from all over the world. In Melbourne, Australia, there would be the Olympic Games in the next eighteen months. In America the PGA Open attracts mega rich clients from all over America and the world, that goes on for months in different locations. California has a smaller but very select gathering regularly of tennis matches, garden parties and galas for charity. All those attending have more money than we've ever seen." Christopher leaned forward towards James in a conspiratorial way, knowing he had him. "They would love it if we offered a vehicle for them to raffle at one of their exclusive gatherings, please note all are attended by not only the richest in California but by the press as well. The cost of a car, although high, would allow us to advertise to a group we have not been able to pitch to before, even the cost of a car is less than an ad on American television and we might not pitch to the right client, this way is a winner everytime. Then, of course, there is Salt Lake City, they have more money than sense and events happening that will attract our type of clients. Then, of course, there is England. Why haven't we been involved in events like Farnborough Air show and such like?"

James shifted position and wanted to know how specifically Christopher saw the route to achieving this success. "Well," Christopher tried to wipe the smug look off his face. "It is going to be so easy. At all the events we have a pitch to show our products. The cost would be minimal, we only pay for the area we use, we don't have to bother with advertising, setting up of the event, etc, this would be taken care of by the events organiser. We just sit back and take orders." Christopher could see James trying to find fault and moved on quickly before he got distracted with negative comments. "With target clientele coming to us we should know our market in a short while. I reckon 5 – 6 cars to start with should be sufficient to cover our first venture say, into America. I have spoken to organisers of the PGA tournament, the Singapore Air Show and

California charities. There seems to be no problem with us having a part in their shows at a cost we can afford. From these starting points I would look for other markets available for us to show our cars. California and the PGA would be our springboard, our showcase. We have nothing to lose."

Christopher took a deep breath and sat back and waited. James was excited, he could tell by the way he was tapping Morse code on his teeth with his pen, the far away look meant there would be a hard and fast grilling coming. The questions came, and Christopher spent the next few hours answering questions on every aspect as James tried to find holes in all his ideas. He couldn't find anything, Christopher knew that, he had spent many a long night working on this and had it sewn up. There was nothing James could ask him that he didn't have an answer for. At the end of a gruelling two hour meeting James stopped, looked at Christopher for what seemed ages, then with a smile, a deep breath, he offered him his hand and congratulated him on his idea and gave him carte blanche to go ahead and make it work.

It would take another six months to organise the cars and set everything in motion. In the meantime, Christopher would go to America to cement relationships and pave the way. James had, in effect, given Christopher an open cheque book to spend 6 months out of the year in America alone, Asia and Australia would follow. They had decided that America should be given priority to see if this new venture stood a chance of working. The time scales of Asia and Australia could wait a while.

He figured later that he was a better salesman than he thought. He had got exactly what he wanted without any hassle, James was not an easy punter to sell to but he was eating out of his hand. Christopher celebrated that night in the only worthwhile way he could, Amanda was his for the night. He told her how well things had gone and their plan could be put into effect. If the car deal took off, then Christopher was in the money. The spin off would be he would spend 6 months in top hotels at the expense of James, so he could get rid of his London flat.

The reason for expanding James' car business was, of course, cover. He needed it to succeed because he needed a legitimate base in other countries. He was earning good commission on the sale of customised cars and America would give him more scope and therefore more money. It would never be enough money. The only way he knew to make more was to expand on bringing in drugs from America. The recreational drugs he had brought in for Amanda from Europe had been so successful that there was now a market for larger supplies. Christopher had forgotten his original concerns, Europe had never been a problem for him, and the special bags had always kept his cases safe from examination. He had found it all so easy. Cockily, he realised everything came easy and USA for starters, was his passport to a fortune. He wanted to know nothing about the people he bought from or who the people were it was going to, it allowed him to keep his mind off the dirtier details. Amanda would sort out all of this for him, so he could just pick up the packages and bring them to England. This made the whole procedure very simple and extremely worthwhile.

He celebrated with champagne and full of admiration for her, toasted Amanda and her business acumen. It was her planning and her idea of expanding to America that was going to make both their fortunes. This was a big deal for her too, she saw many possibilities for the future through Christopher. She didn't want to run a brothel all her life, she wanted money, fun, and oddly enough, respectability. She had always told anyone who would listen that upper class values were outdated and a girl could do whatever she wanted nowadays. She had taken to prostitution as a liberating and exciting lifestyle. Of course, she had never slept with anyone who was not of her class and all had breeding so it never seemed sordid to her. Her favourite saying was that she had been doing it for nothing for years, the difference now was she earned very good money.

Where the feelings of guilt had come from so suddenly she did not know, she was getting older and wanted a more acceptable and respectable lifestyle, she supposed it came from an inbred attitude to earning money in this manner. She knew marriages, deals, and society functions often had a lot to do with behind closed doors sex, which had always been acceptable. However much you think you can, you can't turn a silk purse into a sows ear. This twisted phrase had made her laugh inwardly. No one would ever know how her life had fallen into the abyss. It was a well kept and guarded family secret. She came from a diplomatic family, daddy knew many heads of state and anyone who was anyone knew her daddy. Oh yes indeed, she came from a wealthy background with the best boarding school, finishing school in Switzerland and in her budding years had been introduced to young men one of whom would eventually be considered for a suitable partner. She had been a wild child at 14 years and continued with drink and drugs and the uproar and mayhem it caused at parties and clubs. She had been mentioned in all the papers and celebrity magazines and at 18 years after many exclusive rehabs that did not work, her father decided she would go away to a retreat to contemplate her future.

Amanda wanted none of that. She raided her bank account which contained £4,000 and promptly opened a new account in another bank under a different name. She was now Amanda Blackstock. Her old Etonian boyfriend at the time enjoyed snorting cocaine regularly but it was at variance with his job in the city and his family. She blackmailed him into giving her enough money to buy a house in Kensington. He could afford it, his family were loaded and his "job" was on the Board of a very lucrative Bank. He was more frightened of his father who, as a Methodist, disapproved of drink and drugs and his inheritance was something that he would never compromise. Amanda left everything behind and moved just around the corner and using the skills she had learned and given for free, opened a high class brothel. It had been fun and such good business. Her father was now in Dubai but a few years ago he was just around the corner from her and it gave her pleasure to think she was snorting and screwing right under his nose. Through a friend she learned her father had let it be known that she had moved to a retreat and was doing good works in some part of Somalia. That made her mad. How dare he dismiss her so easily. It made her laugh to realise what it would do to his career if it were known what his daughter was doing. It occurred to her she must have had customers who knew her father and it gave her exquisite pleasure to carry the secret. She was now making more money than he ever did and the increase in drug trafficking was incredibly profitable. At 35 years old she wanted to settle down. She was getting older, maybe it was time to find a husband and have a child and move to the country. She just needed to complete her plans for a little longer to finally make the move into respectability.

She had seen in Christopher a way of fulfilling her plans to move on to a more respectable lifestyle. She recognised his naïvety, his greed, his middle-class arrogance and his sharp sense of survival. She knew the heady promise of more money than he could earn honestly and unlimited access to her was the carrot that would keep him close to her and at her bidding. He had done well so far, and to that end, she had prepared a special surprise for him as a reward. She told him if he had never experienced three skilled women in a bed with him before, he should cancel all appointments for the following day, the pleasure will render him useless for work for at least 24 hours.

He was on a promise for a good evening, and as he remembered now, it was all he could have hoped for. It was the start of a wonderful, rewarding, and scintillatingly exciting partnership. At that point he was grateful and pleased with everything if not a tad too complacent. It would be later that it would not be enough and greed would set in.

CHAPTER NINETEEN

It was easy for him to tell Alice that he would be out of the country regularly from now on. She knew he was only doing it so that their girls could have the very best education possible. She could only guess at the sacrifices he had made for her and the girls, but she was well aware that it was costing him more of his leisure time and he would be working much harder and longer for them. Her gratitude and abundant respect for him grew to the point of sainthood.

He would arrive home Friday afternoon to find Alice waiting for him, something he was not used to or particularly liked. He had found Friday afternoon his time, one where he could wander his garden, chat with the gardeners, make himself comfortable in the study with a large neat whisky and feel master of all he surveyed, that was until the girls came home. They would burst into the house, giggling bustling, and were always full of questions and chit chat. Invariably they would scold him for something or other to do with not asking how the chickens were, not noticing their new hairdos, or other such silly things. He had found it all quite endearing, especially after one or two large whiskies. By the time Alice arrived home he would feel mellow, amiable and able to cope with her sourness. She would goad him, always nagging about anything she could think of, making disapproving noises about his drinking, his lack of conversation, even the way he ate seemed to invoke pointed comments. This seemed to go on all evening until he left the room and went to bed. His whisky was like a painkiller, he knew she was there but he had covered himself in an alcoholic protective shell.

Now, he had her waiting for him as soon as he arrived home on a Friday afternoon. He was to find a very different Alice. Her gratitude for getting the girls into such a top-notch school had provoked a humbling attitude of servitude and deference to him. After the visit to Blythes, Alice was stirred and overcome with pleasure, pride, and superiority. She had sat Christopher down and earnestly promised him that from then onwards when he came home from his trips she would wait on him hand and foot. She added quickly that he would never have to worry about anything to do with the house or the girls as she would sort everything for him. She promised never to nag him about anything again. He was happy with that, although he hoped the bit about always being there, waiting for his return, would wear off, he would have preferred she stayed away. All the same, the package of an easy life, a grateful, dutiful wife, a beautiful home was very appealing. What more could he want, his life was getting better and better by the day.

Her standing in the county of Norfolk had risen considerably. Alice had climbed further up the social scale and was perceived jealously as a very lucky woman who now belonged to the Parent teacher committee of Blythes. This was a huge step up because the rich and famous sent their children to Blythes and Alice was on first name terms with many names she was unable to say above a whisper. Of course her close friends heard every bit of gossip and name dropping that Alice had to impart. She always put in the proviso that they tell no one, this proviso was always quoted when friends passed on this information to their friends. In the end, as Alice always knew, everyone was aware of her famous associations and it pleased her greatly.

In truth, Alice had found the man she had always wanted, kind, giving and undemanding. This allowed her the lifestyle of the upper middle class. With that, inevitably came respect and envy, both qualities she liked to see reflected in those around her. Her girls, her standing in the community, her charitable works were her reason for being, her pleasure, her much preferred sexual substitute. Christopher and Alice had reached a good compromise.

CHAPTER TWENTY

Neil; good, kind, honourable Neil, was happy and confidently running Bertrams. Christopher would have a meal and a few drinks with Neil once every month to talk about this and that. Christopher always looked forward to it. The Captain had *sailed off into the sunset* a year ago. Christopher and Neil had found solace in each others company, sharing anecdotes and laughing and sometimes almost crying at their memories of him. When the Captain died, Christopher felt he had lost his grandfather too. Christopher was glad he died peacefully in his sleep, he deserved that. He was there to comfort and help Neil through his grief. Neil, he remembered, was inconsolable, James and Neil could not mourn together and a deeper rift in their relationship was forged.

Christopher fervently wished he had spent more time with the Captain, he always knew he was lonely and missed his wife. God! He felt so useless a person. He should have done something to make the Captain feel loved. He promised himself, if he ever got out of this mess, he would be a better friend than ever to Neil, but he thought it very unlikely he would survive. He wondered where all this sentimentality was coming from. He couldn't make up his mind at that moment if it was a bad thing or not. He knew that every time he thought about the Captain he realised more and more what that gruff, eccentric old codger meant to him and it hurt.

The Captain's death had brought Christopher and Neil even closer. Those who did not know them would think they were brothers, such was their bonding. Neil and his father did not share this bond, James had never learned to share grief, and would bury his feelings deeply into work and even more work. If Neil had realised, he may have been able to share his grief with his father, but he just saw him as an unemotional, hardfaced workaholic. The British stiff upper lip was working overtime in that family.

Christopher and Neil's meetings happened on a Saturday night at the beginning of the month, and this get together was set in stone, nothing broke this important date. Alice had never known Christopher so keen to keep appointments that were not work orientated. He would drop everything so as not to let Neil down. There had been many dinner invitations received from friends and acquaintances over the years that had to be turned down because Christopher would not cancel any of his dinner dates with Neil. She had always liked Neil and thought him a gentleman. He had always seemed friendly and appreciative of her and was always interested to talk with her. As time went on, Alice found her feelings of admiration had changed to jealousy; she thought Neil had an immense power over Christopher. Christopher had never given up anything for her, his loyalty to Neil was something he had never given her. Of course, that was to change with the girls new school, now she had Christopher working so hard to pay for the girls to go to Blythes. His devotion to his family was fully recognised and appreciated by Alice.

People watching the two successful business men chatting and laughing over dinner surmised they were family. There was something in their attitude, an indefinable knowledge that family members have. Perhaps it was the way they did not have to try hard, that each appeared to know and accept what the other said, the comfortable air that surrounded them. Those people watchers that made up a part of every crowd, bored with waiting for whatever, and happy to watch those around them, had thought one was very superior in looks and charm to the other. One was obviously the older, classier brother.

Neil, as usual, was talking ten to the dozen. Christopher was the only person he felt comfortable enough to do that with. He had never noticed that Christopher always encouraged him to talk about what was happening in his life, how when Neil asked what Christopher was up to, he got a short answer and the conversation would go back in an indecent amount of time to Neil. Neil was very animated tonight. He blushed, did an embarrassed jerking movement of his shoulders that told Christopher he had something to say but modesty was making it hard. At 35 years old Neil was to be made a Justice of the Peace for Wroxham and surrounding areas. Christopher knew this was a very big deal. No one had ever been made Justice of the Peace before they were 40 years old. That Neil had been nominated and appointed showed what high esteem he was held in Norfolk. His congratulations were genuinely over the top. The other diners looked over at the noise of scraping chairs as Christopher got up in one stride went round to Neil's side of the table, where he grabbed him in a bear hug and with much patting of the back and cries of "Well done" ringing through the air, ordered champagne from a passing waiter. The other diners were now embarrassed and put out by such un-British behaviour. To make such a fuss in a crowded place and disturb their quiet gatherings was just not cricket. All those people watchers averted their eyes from such an embarrassing sight.

Neil was still unmarried and the source of good humoured ribbing from Christopher. In truth, Neil had never been in love, never met a girl he felt strongly about. He had many women as friends but no one special. Years before he would have been called a confirmed bachelor, today quiet rumours were made about his sexual orientation. Christopher had heard this and strongly defended and where possible, protected his naïve friend from those who took pleasure in such accusations. Neil, he thanked god, went through life oblivious to the mutterings of others. As he saw it, Neil would never live down the shame if he knew people were calling him a Poof. Political Correctness had not arrived in Wroxham.

Christopher's thoughts would often turn to the Captain and remembered his sayings that Neil was the son of Norfolk. With a tear glistening in his eye, he knew how proud the Captain would have been of Neil had he been alive that day. He smiled at the thought of how the Captain would have strutted around telling everyone how wonderful Neil was, and how embarrassed Neil would have been by the attention. He hoped Neil would survive as a Justice of the Peace, but then, perhaps naïvety with a blend of goodness was a perfect requirement for the job, Christopher hoped so.

Neil put aside his own news, and wanted to hear more about Christopher's plans abroad. He was given the abbreviated version and how his first trip was to America. Neil thought him brilliant and clever and how James must be proud of what he was trying to accomplish. Christopher did not want to hear this praise from Neil. It seemed inappropriate, not called for, and he wanted to change the subject. It was decided that Neil would keep in touch with Alice to ensure she was O.K. while Christopher was away. No amount of arguing from Christopher could dissuade Neil from this course of action. In fact, the more he argued the stronger Neil's resolve got. In the end Christopher gave up the fight, he did not want Neil involved in anything to do with his trips, but could find no valid reason for keeping him away.

Christopher left for Atlanta, America, on a tide of goodwill from Alice, promises of care for his family from Neil and instructions from Amanda on where to collect the items and from whom. To start with he had to collect a rather large package of coke from Atlanta and on his travels take it to California. Not unsurprisingly he had arranged for his first business meeting to be in Atlanta. He did not know why he felt uncomfortable and not at ease with himself, and why he could not get rid of the jittery feeling that seemed to have invaded his body. He had a good seat on the plane, the food looked good for plane food but he was not hungry and kept wanting to get up and walk around. Club class was very comfortable and he was glad of it. At least he was not squashed into seats like the sardines in economy and he could at least walk around without being told to sit down. He had many things to worry about not least was the fact he had never been to America before. Europe had, so far, been his work and playground and he knew what to expect there. He wondered if he would like America and if America would like him.

The airhostesses were busy offering pillows and those small thin blankets to everyone in Club class. It was 1 a.m. English time and the cabin lights had been turned down to slumber level. Christopher thought it highly unlikely he would sleep at all but after half an hour of tossing and turning, he fell into a fitful sleep that covered three quarters of his journey time.

CHAPTER TWENTY ONE

He woke with a start to the rattling of the food trolley. Breakfast was being served. He felt better after his sleep and pushed away his feeling of unease. He told himself it was just him being wary of a new way of working. This was further from home than normal and the stakes were much, much higher. He knew he was a good salesman and realised if he could sell to the suspicious and difficult French, then he could as sure as hell sell to the Americans. His telephone conversations with them had been successful, and although he didn't want to make any assumptions, they seemed pretty easy to do business with. The drugs were just a small part of his trip and no big deal. He was, of course, kidding himself.

After a boring breakfast of scrambled eggs and a tiny roll with something that was supposed to resemble bacon, although it was the smallest, most uninteresting piece of leather he had ever tasted. The raspberry jam and the roll were pleasant. He never expected much from flight food. He looked out of the window and as night changed to day, he saw land. Over the intercom the pilot told them that it would be another hour before they commenced their descent into Atlanta.

When breakfast had been cleared he watched as his

fellow travellers reached into cases around them and took out their laptops. Christopher looked on, glad he had never indulged in such a mindless task. No computers or laptops for him. As he was fond of saying, "If God meant for man to work computers he would have made man 3 armed to cope with that stupid mouse thing as well." He would hand write most of his letters and at some point, would fax them to Pamela in the office in London to type up. James was always having a jibe at his hand written letters. No way would he go down that high tech route, it looked pathetic to see grown men spending what should be relaxation time peering into the screen of a tiny laptop.

Christopher knew he was a strange contradiction of a man in this day and age. Everyone was using computers, surfing the internet Superhighway and sending interminable e-mails to each other. He did not know why he hadn't cottoned on to this most fashionable and masculine way of working. He always got all the information he needed through Pamela, his secretary. She was an expert in such matters and would surf for hours to find any bits of information he required on the internet. He concluded that since his schooldays, he had always had someone to do his research for him. He saw himself as someone who planned and thought. He had secretaries who did the actual physical work of typing up his programmes of work, leaving him to use his skills in other directions. He would conclude that those men typing away on their laptops had not, and did not spend time evaluating situations and planning ahead. Why bother spending tedious time on an overpriced typewriter when you could pay someone to do it for you? He also did not play golf. He understood from his peers that he should, to help him network and meet clients, but he arrogantly came to the conclusion it was not necessary. He could network without it.

As the plane circled Atlanta, Christopher glanced out of the window to see this new sight. They circled for 15 minutes at what looked an extremely low height. The landscape below, to his surprise, captivated him. The plane, it seemed, circled just above the tree tops and he could see houses nestled amongst these tall testaments to nature. It seemed to Christopher that the forest ruled and the suburbs were allowed to nestle around their space as a favour. He found the sight of nature and sprawling houses so close to the obvious concrete and glass of the city a wonderful inviting compromise. He wondered if the people of Atlanta would reflect this convivial style. The heat hit him as he left the plane and he looked forward to arriving at his air-conditioned hotel. He had booked into the Hilton in Atlanta. First, he went to Alamo car rental and picked up a Buick he had hired for the week. With directions ringing in his ears he found his car in the lot just 5 minutes walk from the airport reception and drove to the Hilton. It was not far and he knew he could ask directions. He found everyone in the airport falling over themselves to be helpful.

He thought Americans strangely naïve and open. It would actually take him a little while to trust this naïvety. On hearing the vastly repeated phrase of "Have a nice day" Christopher mistook this for sarcasm and had to bite his tongue on many occasions. After a short while he realised Americans did not understand sarcasm or irony. He found them an up front, eager to please culture with simple, honest humour. He liked them very much. The hotel was, naturally, very comfortable. On his travels in Europe he had looked for and got used to the good service of top hotels and relished the luxury of it all. He unpacked, and poured himself a miniature whisky from the fridge. He took a good sip, swallowed and inhaled deeply of his Silk cut duty frees and relaxed. He felt at home in Atlanta, stupid as that sounded. He knew no one, he had only just arrived but he felt comfortable.

He phoned the number Amanda had given him. A cold disembodied voice asked him what he wanted. He repeated the sentence Amanda had told him and the voice, devoid of character or charm, barked directions and a meeting time. As Christopher, with inbred politeness, tried to thank him, the phone was slammed down at the other end. He realised this would be business without any pleasure. He poured another miniature to steady an uneasy feeling, which smacked of fear and trepidation. Part of him wished he was here only on business and not for the drug thing. Another part of him laughed at his stupidity. The drugs were going to give him the life style he wanted. The cars were just cover and would never make him rich enough. Besides, he had been doing this in Europe so why did he feel so weird about doing this in America? He finished his drink and smoked another cigarette and got a grip on the situation. He told himself business was business and to get on with it. All the plans had been made and even if he had a choice, there was no way he could not go through with it. He felt better for this chat with himself.

He had decided he would never give in to jetlag so his first meeting had been arranged for the same afternoon. The disembodied voice that called himself Chuck would be met the next day. An invigorating shower, some real food sent to his room and a change of clothes saw Christopher primed and ready to do business. Not familiar with American driving and wanting to make a good impression, he chickened out of his first drive up town and took a cab. He was deposited outside a towering building made of mirrored glass. He had seen Dallas on the television but he found the inscrutable buildings awesome in real life.

He made his way through a cavernous entrance hall to a very eager looking security guard and asked for directions to Mr Carlotti's office. Curt, polite instructions would have been helpful, but Christopher's irritation mounted at the same pace as the security guard's laboured, childlike instructions. On mistakenly calling the elevator a lift, the guard all but took Christopher by the arm and was about to personally show him to Mr Carlotti's office. Christopher extricated himself from this stifling over enthusiasm and with a polite smile, told the guard he could find the 23rd floor by himself. With "Have a nice day sir" ringing in his ears, Christopher found the lift. He breathed a sigh of relief as he journied up to the 23rd floor to the gentle music of madness. The tunes were obviously composed in mental institutions for the musically challenged.

He was feeling a little unsettled and the far too personal behaviour of the guard had made him feel jumpy and prickly. He was used to an indifferent but courteous politeness in England but this felt too close, too cloy and made him feel claustrophobic. He was determined to get the hang of this culture, the French are rude, the Spanish O.K. and the Belgium ignorant in his view. The Americans he would reserve judgement on until he had been there a bit longer. As the door of the lift opened, he put on his nice, professional attentive face and strode towards the door marked USA Special Events. Mr Carlotti's office was about 5 minutes down the corridor. According to the young girl on reception he must be escorted to Mr Carlotti's office. She walked ahead of him, but turned every few steps to check he was managing to follow her and giving him an obligatory well-done smile. He was getting used to this nursery type of treatment.

After many meetings with his subordinates, the eventual meeting with Carlotti was easy, friendly and to the point at last, but he still left without any firm decisions. He found the office did not contain Mr Carlotti but one of his associates. Christopher found the tedious meetings were what appeared to be standard preliminary discussions, with various people who purported to have the permission of Carlotti to make decisions. Much time was spent outlining each laboured point on when, where, what and money. The real meeting with Mr Carlotti would be another two meetings down the line. Americans, Christopher was to find out, were enthusiastic, agreeing, and helpful. That was until you got to the part that said, "shall we make this a firm deal?" Then no one would take the responsibility of saying yes to anything. Christopher, fed up with such a waste of time sarcastically thought these little yes men could not say yes if offered a free shag.

Mr Carlotti was to be the first of many such meetings throughout America. The game would be played again and again of saying yes, until crunch time of make a decision and then no, not me, until someone was found brave or stupid enough to say yes, or they dragged in the big boss to say yes or no. It took one week to get a yes and a further week to organise the finer points and future meetings. Nothing got signed and settled, it seemed as if he would have to return many times to America before that happened. They called him a real English gent and he quickly realised he had to get used to their ways of working. He quite quickly lost a lot of his priggish attitude and accepted the American way of doing business. He would not recognise that his frosty and stiff attitude was softening as the days went by and he was falling under the spell of America but that was what was surely happening.

Jennifer Logan was an interesting addition to the retinue of Mr Carlotti. This smartly, and if he was not mistaken, very expensively classically dressed woman was introduced to Christopher as his right hand woman. Quietly, when Jennifer was not in earshot, Carlotti added she was a widow. Christopher thought her quite fascinating, with a gentle sense of humour that he found very pleasant. She had a very pleasing figure and a smile that beamed up at him. At what must have been about 5'0", she was a lot smaller than he was and he reckoned she would eventually get a crick in her neck if he stayed talking to her much longer. She made intelligent small talk and he could see she had a brain. He liked her; she was funny and so good at making him feel like the only person in the room. He felt comfortable in her company. He wanted to know what type of relationship Jennifer and Carlotti had, and he made subtle enquiries to that effect. It was important to know whose toes he was treading on. Mr Carlotti apparently thought she was a brilliant business asset, an interesting addition to any dinner party but definitely not the one to share his love life. She was in the same category as his wife, at 50 years of age she was too old for fun, but handy for those occasions where an intelligent and mature woman was needed as a host. He had a mistress who his wife knew about and he divided his time between the two homes with the approval, so he was told, of both women. Christopher found it hard to believe, but once again, he had to admit this was America and anything could happen there.

Mr Carlotti, was interested in Christopher's proposition and keen to keep him around to see if there was more to be made out of the customised cars. Carlotti had seen the interest between the two of them and suggested to Jennifer that she invite Christopher to the charity ball being held in her home the next evening. Jennifer readily agreed and gave Christopher her address. He asked what the charity was and she said it was an Aids awareness. He wondered why it was being held in someone's house and why Aids when there were many other worthwhile charities about. Aids was still quite new to Britain and had not been taken seriously. Articles in English newspapers had explained it as a homosexual thing. The general view in the English media was that America was just being hysterical as usual. He was told it was an eveningwear occasion and he would be expected at 7 p.m.

He spent the next day driving around Atlanta. The centre of town was very business-like and not somewhere a tourist would want to visit. He travelled out a little to be near the trees he had seen from the plane. The air was fresh, the countryside enormous and different. He could not get over the size of everywhere.

He stopped at a little diner for coffee and cake and enjoyed a conversation with the waitress in the diner. She told him his accent was lovely and asked about England. She thought London was small, quaint and covered in fog. Christopher didn't have the heart to tell her different so remembering all the Sherlock Holmes films he had seen he painted a picture of old England. She even believed the bit about horsedrawn carriages still being used in London. She was enthralled by his stories of old London and the queen who always wore a crown when she went out anywhere. He inwardly laughed at her naïvety but after a while he looked at this eager young woman who was so grateful and earnest and realised he was just being a cad. He found out she was 22 years old, married with 4 small children. Her husband worked nights and she worked in the diner during the day. The children were aged 6 years to 3 months. This hardworking young girl had never had much of a life by the sounds of it and he was taking the mickey out of her. He felt ashamed of himself. He left a 20-dollar tip, which was so excessively over the top he made his excuses and left in a hurry. She did not know what to say and thought English men must be just the best in the world, apart from her Eddie of course.

He got back to his hotel at 2 p.m. and got out his evening suit. He wondered what to expect. He presumed he would have to pay as it was a charity function so he made sure he changed travellers cheques to the value of two hundred dollars. He figured this would see him through the next few days or so.

He took a cab to Jennifer Logan's address. It took 30 minutes to get there. It was in the suburbs and he was travelling towards those wonderful trees again. The cab driver chatted on and on during the drive. He talked about some type of football game that Christopher was not familiar with and made rude remarks about the English which Christopher could not be bothered to reply to. He looked at the homes they passed and was suitably impressed. The long drives hid some houses from view but Christopher was sure they were huge. The ones he had seen ranged in size from big to enormous, from chateau to ranch, or colonial style. All looked amazing and had really spacious grounds. He would not get over the amount of land available in America. His own one acre garden, pretty big by England standards now seemed like a postage stamp. He expected Jennifer to have such a lovely home but he was totally unprepared for what he saw.

The cab pulled up outside a set of gates that were locked and large. They looked to him like the gates outside Buckingham Palace and nearly as big. He was unsure what to do. The cab driver, impatient by now, told him to go and talk into the intercom by the side of the gates and get the god dammed people to open it and let them in. Tentatively Christopher pressed the button on the intercom and stretching his neck towards what he thought was the microphone piece he spoke into. "Hello, anyone there please?"

A crackling sound and a disembodied voice asked who he was. He told the voice his name and he was told to get back into the cab and the gates would open. He wondered how they knew he was in a cab. He spotted the camera as the gates opened. It was on a 10' pole to the left of the intercom. It gave a good view of everything going on in front of the gates.

The cab made its way up the long curved driveway. The house was hidden and it was not until the driveway curved for the last time that Christopher saw the house in front of him. It looked like a palace. The gravel driveway in front of the house was large enough to park 60 cars comfortably. The house didn't look that old but it was built in a style preferred by English nobility. It looked familiar and he thought Blenheim Palace was probably the role model for this fabulous place. He could only guess at the rooms it must have. Judging by the vast amount of windows he could see, Blenheim Palace would have difficulty rivalling the size. It took his breath away and he wondered absurdly if Jennifer wore a tiara to these occasions, the house could stand that sort of over the top fancy dress. It had majestic steps up to the front entrance with a long and wide stone terrace that would have allowed for at least 100 guests to look out onto the lawns that fronted the house. Christopher paid the cab driver and started his climb up the vast steps to the terrace. He presumed only fit people were invited here because by the time he reached the front door he was quite out of breath. The stone was all in grey brick that was very familiar to English old houses and the stone wall that surrounded the terrace was relieved at each corner by a rampant lion. Christopher thought that was maybe a little over the top but the house was big enough to take it.

He walked up to the oak front door and rang the bell. The door was opened by a very distinguished, middle-aged man with a regal bearing who politely invited him inside. Christopher had seen enough butlers in his time to recognise who this person was. "What shall I call you?" asked Christopher.

"Cameron Sir."

"English eh. Where do you come from?"

"Lewisham, London Sir."

Christopher was surprisingly glad to hear an English accent. It made him feel at home.

Everything about this house seemed very English. He stood in a large hall which could have accommodated a symphony orchestra. He looked around this oak covered everything, it was on the walls panels, on the doors, the staircase, the floor. It reminded him of his old school assembly hall; all polished wood and dignity. The staircase at the end of the hall merited a long look. It was one of those staircases that seemed to be made for beautiful women to descend in long, and flowing evening gowns. The central staircase rose and split left and right towards the first floor. The highly polished thick oak handrail swept downward towards him and finished in a beautiful curl at the bottom. He could have studied it further but a slight rustling made him look up to the right of the staircase as Jennifer descended towards the central staircase. She stopped at the top of the central staircase to allow Christopher to appreciate her light blue sequinned dress. It shimmered and sparkled in the light of the huge crystal chandelier suspended from a ceiling that craftsmen must have slaved over for many a year. Her blonde hair was swept up into a chignon, he thought she looked the epitome of sophistication. She had walked down these stairs many times and knew the reaction her entrance would make. Christopher was dazzled in more ways than one; the light certainly reflected off her dress highlighting her beautiful figure. It was a figure that had never borne children, known anything other than to be pampered and spoilt with the best of everything. Jennifer, toned and tanned, knew the sequinned dress was doing everything it should. Christopher found himself staring at her, he pulled himself together and pushed away the thought that she looked so sexy. He struggled to keep his good manners in the forefront and smiled at Jennifer as she put out an elegant hand as she gracefully wafted down the last of the stairs. Christopher was there to take her hand and place it on his arm as she reached the bottom stair.

"Thank you for coming Christopher. May I call you Chris? Christopher is such a long name."

Of course he didn't mind; he quite liked it.

She explained that her guests were arriving at 8 p.m. and she had invited him earlier so she could show him the gardens. She called Cameron to fetch them both a drink as she gently pulled him towards the garden. The terrace at the back was just as big as the one at the front. There were steps down into the garden. He looked out from the terrace and in a sweeping glance drunk in this beautiful garden. This looked like a reproduction of a Capability Brown garden with undulating lawns sculpted with trees and shrubbery. It was a huge garden, he could not see any boundaries and in the distance ahead of him he could see what looked like an English forest with what appeared to be oak, ash and sycamore trees. The main focus of the garden was what could only be described as something he had only ever seen in Chatsworth House gardens in Derbyshire. It was an oval shaped lake as large as his garden back home with the highest and most dramatic of fountains in the middle. It shot all of 60 feet into the air and cascaded impressively into the lake. He took a deep breath and tried to inhale the evening musk. He could have been in England, it was confusing and he thought the climate would not be appropriate for English trees but it was so amazingly beautiful. He would have lingered on the terrace all evening, just looking out across the lawns but a gentle nudge from Jennifer encouraged him to follow her towards some tables set out on the lush grass.

The weather was kind. It was a warm evening and

there was no breeze to distract the cascade of water from its majestic thrust into the sky. She put her drink on one of the tables with chairs set out ready for her guests. She smiled at his amazement.

"Chris, I know this seems very strange to you. It is strange to Americans as well. My late husband loved everything English as you might be able to tell."

She had a beautiful voice and her accent was immaculate, almost English but with a slight American twang. "The joke has always been that he should have married an English woman to complement the house. But he chose me," she smiled and added, "I became more English as the years went on, or so my husband used to say."

There was one of those silences that one never interrupts. She took a deep breath and smiled at him. He realised her husband had been very special to her.

She asked if he would like to walk in the shrubbery. He readily agreed and they strolled leisurely through a magnificently green cascade of shrubs and woodland flowers. He would have liked to take a closer look at the variety of plants, but they were chatting about this and that and it would have seemed bad manners to stop and inspect the plants. He thought that perhaps later he might find some time to come back and have a closer look at the amazing area, he did note the rhododendrons, one of his favourite plants. They both found themselves laughing at silly little jokes and comments which made for a pleasant stroll as they followed the path that took them through many twists and turns. To his surprise, they came upon a pool house and swimming pool. He laughed and said this was the last thing he expected to see. He said her path gently illuminated by many tree lights casting magical, fairy shadows amongst the branches had reminded him of a childhood story where a young man followed a similar path to find his princess. She thought his interest and delight at her garden very attractive indeed.

He liked her, she had a fine sense of humour that was understated and gentle. She thought him a gentleman and wondered if he was married. The hour passed very quickly and Cameron came to find her to say the first of her guests had arrived. A stringed quartet started playing something gentle by Beethoven and the lights around the garden sparkled playfully. Jennifer made her excuses and went to welcome her guests. Christopher took himself to the terrace and placed his arms on the wall overlooking the garden. He thought there was nowhere more beautiful. The music seemed to be in tune with the gentle movement of the water on the lake. The reflection of the moon in the lake shimmering in the ripples was gracious to watch. He could have stayed there all night caught up in his own thoughts and the beauty of the gardens. He looked around him, at the house, and the garden, and decided if all of America was like this, he could live here in America.

A tap on his shoulder brought him far too quickly back to reality. With a smile he turned to acknowledge Jennifer. She had come looking for him as more guests arrived. She introduced him to many people, some of them he promptly forgot others he stayed with. She watched him in the company of some of her dearest friends. He had a lovely sense of humour and didn't mind making jokes against himself. He seemed very popular with her friends. He was intelligent, had beautiful manners and was rather nice to look at too. She wanted to get to know him better.

He circulated, got another drink and nibbled the food, which covered 5 long tables. With the many waiters and waitresses on hand to help him with his selection of food, his plate was never empty. He joined in many conversations and was pleased to realise that those present were in the main intelligent, business people with manners. It was all very gentile with an English style which was very pleasant. He felt mellow and at ease. Again, the thought struck him that he wanted this type of life, he liked it here, it was what he was born to have.

Jennifer whispered to Christopher that Brett Kincade was making the opening speech. He had never heard of this Brett Kincade. Jennifer explained he was a famous young actor and all red blooded women wanted his body. Christopher could tell that Jennifer was one of those women by the sigh in her voice. He thought she should have been old enough to know better. He would see later what all the fuss was about.

The evening went well. Brett Kincade made his appearance. To Christopher he was a 25 year old with a sullen attitude and bleached blonde hair. The ladies present obviously found him most appealing. There was an impolite rush of women to stand close to Brett as he spoke quite movingly about Aids. Christopher did not join the throng and stood back and listened. Christopher did not like this Brett and thought him a short, smarmy bastard who would never make it in England. English women would see right through him. Jennifer had mentioned that Brett had kindly agreed to step in when the main speaker fell ill. He thought she said that was going to be Liz Taylor. Now there was a real star! He wished she had been there instead. Brett finished his speech, made his excuses and left. The women stopped twittering on about Brett this and Brett that and settled down for the next speaker.

A gaunt young man who professed to all present that he had full-blown Aids and was not expected to see another Christmas, made another speech. Christopher thought him brave to spend what little time he had left attending fund raising parties to help others, because by the sounds of it, it was too late for him.

Jennifer made the final speech. Christopher listened with admiration as she skilfully manipulated those present to part with lots of money. She had whipped up all the sympathy so far with Brett Kincade and the Aids person and she finished the evening with a heart rending speech, which left everyone present incapable of leaving without having given a massive donation to the Aids foundation. Christopher was so moved he gave all the 200 dollars he had with him.

When the evening ended and he was leaving, Jennifer thanked him for coming and asked that when he was next in town to contact her. He was very happy to do that. She was excellent company and her home was very beautiful. He was pleased she wanted to see him again. He was due back in Atlanta after his visit to California and he arranged to ring her then. He gave her a peck on the cheek and left in a cab ordered for him.

Back at his hotel he happily sat in his room thinking about the evening. It was the best evening since coming to America. He would tell Neil about the people he met, and the beautiful house and gardens. He had one more day in Atlanta before flying to California. The thought stifled his contented feelings and he was worried and a little scared about meeting the Chuck person. It left him restless and sent him to the mini bar for a whisky before bedtime.

The next evening he went to the pick-up address by cab. It was in a part of town that didn't feel safe. Christopher asked the cab driver to wait for him. The cab driver was not keen. Feeling jittery, Christopher was very nervous about being left in this area of town and didn't want to wander the streets with bags of stuff on him. He offered the cab driver a hefty tip if he waited, he said he would be no more than 10 minutes before he returned. He didn't think the man he had spoken to would want to be sociable. Reluctantly the cab driver agreed to wait. Christopher checked the piece of paper on which he had scribbled the motel room number 16 and knocked on the door. It opened abruptly and the man gave a quick look around outside before he pulled Christopher into the seedy motel room. A very quick look at the standard cheap fixtures made Christopher feel it could be the 70's again when orange was the in colour. It took Christopher a few seconds to collect himself. He was shocked, scared and wanted to be elsewhere.

He gave Chuck, a skinny, middle-aged man with an unhealthy pallor the money as arranged. Christopher fought for control of this situation and in doing so, misread the signs. He thought the villain in front of him was just a joke and a little worm, this thought projected to his face and Christopher, without realising it, gave this Chuck one of his contemptible, snobbish, snotty looks. To this day he didn't know why he did that. The reaction was swift and very frightening. Before he had time to take the situation in, he found himself pushed against the wall and held there by one hand round his neck. The eyes were dead, the words deadly. Christopher was told to give more respect and Christopher nodded as much as he could and promised faithfully that he would. The package was pushed in to his chest and he grabbed hold of it before leaving. He was very scared and left the motel room panting for breath. It was a most disagreeable and worrying meeting, that had left his body soaked in stinking sweat. He would go back to his hotel room and have a long bath. The reality of playing at drug dealing left him scared. It was a dangerous and murky game and he wanted to go home.

Looking back now he bitterly wished he had remembered those feelings, instead, he knew he had just got bolder, more conceited and plain greedy. He wondered, as he had all night, where the brains he was supposed to possess were. The thought popped into his head that his brains were buried deep in greed. Even now, he couldn't accept that. There had to be more to it. He needed to justify his own stupidity, but of course, he couldn't. He thought he heard footsteps again. His heart would not take much more pounding. He had never experienced such fear. It would be a relief if they got it over and done with. He wanted some peace. He hoped it would be quick and painless. The footsteps faded and he realised he could just have imagined them.

He searched his memory to get back to where he was in America. He remembered. He was still the arrogant, stuck-up prick who still thought the Americans were stupid and he, the English man was sophisticated and clever. He didn't want to go there but he knew he must remember how his arrogance got him to where he was now.

He left Atlanta the next morning with the stand partially organised and agreed. The package was stashed inside his case. Onwards to California to pass on the package to some rich fellow Amanda knew. He was to meet an Associate in his hotel later that evening. He would nearly double the outlay for the drugs which was over £100,000 and the last meeting would be with Chuck again in Atlanta before flying home and taking with him a large amount of drugs to give to Amanda to sell on.

If it all sounded so easy, he had wondered why he was becoming a gibbering wreck. He could get caught was all he could think about. Bravery was not the concept he was trying to find. With a case full of dope he did not feel this was the appropriate emotion. Hell, he was not James Bond defeating Smersh. He was a villain dealing in something sordid and nasty. Realisation was nearly dawning, but before something akin to shame entered the equation he quantified what he was doing. He was not encouraging kids to buy this stuff, it was for existing coke heads who could afford it. If he didn't deliver it someone else would and he needed the money so why not? Strangely, it took only a couple of sentences to confirm that what he was doing was not that wrong. That was the first and last time Christopher's conscience made any stand on the subject of drugs and it had lost big time.

He flew into Los Angeles airport early afternoon and took the free Alamo bus to the Alamo Office and car park facility just outside the airport. He liked L.A. airport. It was one of the easiest airports he had passed through. He had his luggage in a short time, got through customs and was told how to get to the Alamo offices and on his way to pick up his car within 30 minutes. He picked up his rented car, a Buick Park Lane, the business was done and he was on the road within 20 minutes of arrival at their office. Everything so far in L.A. was friendly, efficient and relaxed. Armed with a map he travelled towards Palm Springs. It was a 200 mile drive but, as he had found, American roads were so good it never took that long. The Buick was a comfortable car, similar to the Jaguar in comfort and size, which he found a pleasure to drive. He would enjoy the views on the interstate. He arrived at his hotel feeling relaxed and confident. He was staying at the sumptuous Wyndham Hotel in Palm Springs. The company he was visiting was having their Annual seminar there. They had gathered senior personnel from 20 car showrooms in California for the 2-day event and Christopher was lucky enough to have the ear of many managers. The owner, Harvey Little, was the main man Christopher had to impress and hopefully, no middle men to see first.

He observed that in America, all adverts seemed to personalise products with names of owners of the business. For such a big country, it seemed strange to him that anyone would be bothered who owned a particular company. In England you knew the company name but who ever had heard of the owner, except, of course, for Richard Branson, everyone knew him. Christopher still had lots to learn about America.

It was Christopher's first visit to Palm Springs and he found, just like its name, full of palm trees. The Wyndham was classy and big. Christopher was getting used to this concept. Palm Springs was dry, hot and almost desert like but that did not stop every hotel he passed, including the Wyndham using water like they had reservoirs of the stuff. Each hotel he passed was gushing gallons of water in fountains, mini waterfalls and ornamental pools as part of their entrance grounds. He ruefully thought that one week of hot weather in England caused a hosepipe ban across the country. He wondered how in America, they could use so much water in an obviously dry area. It was another thing that amazed him about the country.

He was told the Wyndham had the biggest swimming pool in Palm Springs, and judging by the pools he had experienced so far, this was the biggest. He had a dip before his evening meal and felt better for it. He would be refreshed and ready for his meetings the next morning.

Thinking back now to his first visit to America he remembered how much of a tourist he was. America was like no other country he had visited so far. He wanted to live there. He was in no doubt that his destiny was firmly set in America.

The business in California went well. It took, as he now understood, a few meetings to get to the point of serious discussions. The Wyndham had a suite of conference rooms in a building just outside the hotel itself. Christopher did not have to go far to attend the meetings, which started at 8 a.m. in the morning. With a booked meeting in one month's time with Harvey Little at his Hollywood office, he could assure James he was well on the road to securing a sponsorship deal for his cars be shown in this rich and glorious state. He was initially promised that there would be places available at six functions throughout California and especially Hollywood. He was very excited about the Hollywood aspect and hoped he would get to look around some studios or something. However much he was trying to be the business man, he was still acting like a tourist in many areas of America. It had felt a successful day and he remembered feeling good when he got back to his room that late afternoon.

Handing over the drugs and collecting the money proved to be so easy. He had not long arrived back at his hotel room when a knock on the door disturbed his early evening whisky. He remembered feeling at that moment a little apprehensive of whom he might have to deal with. He had opened the door to an immaculately suited young man who gave him a respectful smile and handed him an envelope. Christopher ushered him into the room and closed the door. It felt odd entertaining a stranger in his room, he never saw clients in his hotel room, he did not consider it appropriate behaviour and he liked to keep somewhere that was his. Christopher was not sure what the etiquette was for a situation like this. The stranger shook his head when offered a seat, and a drink. Christopher had thought he could have been a film star with his chiselled looks, blonde college cut hair and his obviously very fit body. Christopher stood and opened the envelope presented to him. The note said the young man was representing the client and to give him the packages in exchange for the agreed amount.

Christopher looked at the young man and realised he had not said a word and he wondered if he had a problem or something. On seeing Christopher had read the note, the young man opened the briefcase he was carrying and took out the agreed amount of money. Christopher took the white packages from his suitcase and awkwardly tried to give the packages to the young man and at the same time grab hold of the money proffered to him. Christopher nearly dropped the packages in his effort to grab the money. They each gave an embarrassed laugh. It wasn't just they were not trustful, it was more to do with neither knew the right way to conduct this exchange. The hand over happened successfully on the second attempt. The young man said thank you, put the packages in his briefcase and went to leave. Christopher dropped the money on the bed and rushed ahead to the door to open it for him and mumbled something about pleasure to do business and see you again no doubt, or some such words. When he had closed the door his shoulders relaxed and he exhaled heavily. It had felt very strange and tense and now he just wanted to scoop up the money and count it. It was a lot of money £110,000. He enjoyed the counting so much that he poured another whisky and counted again. He slept well that night.

The next morning he travelled back to Atlanta. He phoned Jennifer and arranged to meet her for lunch. He told her he had a meeting that evening and the following morning would be travelling to Salt Lake City. He enjoyed lunch at Marcello, a restaurant chosen by Jennifer. They talked about where he was going and whom he was going to meet. Jennifer said he must let her know when he was next back in Atlanta. He thought he would be back in one month's time. They said goodbye and with a peck on the cheek, Jennifer rushed to a meeting of her own.

Christopher had booked into the Hilton and rested for an hour or two before it was time to meet Chuck. The venue was different but the same cheap, uncared for motel in an area you wouldn't want to go to at night. Mindful of their last meeting, Christopher gave him a respectful nod and handed him the small fortune in exchange for one of the largest stashes that he had taken. When he got back to his hotel, he opened his case and just stared at the bags of white powder inside. He was frightened, excited, and he would be glad when he reached England and passed the packages on to Amanda. With the small bags of stuff dotted between his underwear and shirts in his case, he took the plane to Salt Lake City. He put the thoughts of what would happen if his case was opened to one side and assumed his very English stiff upper lip attitude. Three more days and he would be going home. He knew they were going to be a long three days.

Salt Lake City was the important meeting. If this were not a success he worried the other companies would not be so keen to let him use their venues. He was going to discuss shows for the following year. For once he hoped that he was going to be able to talk to the right person straight away. The scenario so far had been going through the tedious and repetitive procedure of talking to minions before the important meeting. He was getting bored and frustrated with the "Yes, yes", to everything he suggested then when the crunch question was asked about being part of the show, a resounding "No, I can't make that decision". He would have to go through this at least twice before he reached the man with the power to say yes.

The travelling was weird. He was catching planes like he would catch trains in England. He seemed to journey a distance that was longer than a trip to Cyprus or Greece going through different time zones and yet he was still in the same country when he arrived. It gave him a buzz realising how vast America was. He was losing and gaining 5 hours per day with all the travelling from one time zone to another. He had vowed that the next time he was in America he would travel less and maybe stay in one place for at least a week at a time. He thought the size of America was something he would never get used to. Sitting in this dark room now, he reckoned his trips to America would not be a problem in the future.

The trip to Salt Lake City was to meet a chap called Henry Fitzjohn III who was staying in the Hilton for a 2 week convention of car dealers. Henry was the big fish and the one that counted. The PGA tournaments were his baby, and he had fingers in all pies in America. Christopher had done his homework and he knew Henry Fitzjohn III was the key to America. His name and company were highly respected throughout America and Davies-Clarke Plc needed to be associated with such a prestigious company to have credibility in the American market. There were others to see as well and a meeting with Bill Hartman was scheduled to be the first. He hoped to use the flight to read up on this car convention, a weird concept by British standards, but as he kept saying to himself, "This is America where anything can happen".

A Marty Klein took the seat next to Christopher on the flight to Salt Lake City. Marty made an in your face introduction that Christopher found hard to ignore and after Christopher politely reciprocated by introducing himself. He tried to retrieve his hand but Marty was having none of that and continued to shake the now numbing digits.

"Hi Chrissy baby. Are we going to have a good flight together? You bet we are. Auto Convention isn't it?" Before Christopher could agree Marty answered. "Of course it is. Got a nose for these things. Can always tell."

Christopher smiled politely and extricated his hand from Marty's podgy, hot vice. Christopher was not at all sure of this Marty fellow and didn't particularly want to share a 3 hour flight with him. With an inward sigh he realised that business could be business and he should stomach this crass fellow. It had, in fact, proved to be a very useful flight. Apart from realising "Marty baby", as he wryly thought of him, was a facile, loud, uncouth American that Christopher would never befriend if there was a choice, he got to know everything about his upcoming appointment.

"So you're seeing Henry Fitzjohn III. He's an evil bastard who would sell his mother, brother and children to a brothel if it helped him." After a nano second of thought, he added, "Great guy though." He added, as if it was a validation, "Has four wives and he keeps them all happy. Takes some doing Chrissy. I've got two and they drive me up the wall. The only thing keeps me sane is the mistress but she knows she's out if she doesn't behave." Marty baby laughed and nudged Christopher "Know what I mean Chrissy baby?"

Christopher hadn't a clue as to what he meant. After the shock of hearing they had two, three or four wives, he concluded they were all very odd. One wife was bad enough in Christopher's eyes. Marty continued gabbling on asking questions and answering them himself, a habit Christopher got used to, so he sat back and just listened. It seemed Salt Lake City was his home. Christopher wondered what on earth he would find there having been told about harems of wives, and religion. He got the impression that Salt Lake City had a view of women that would not go down well with the likes of Germaine Greer, or any self respecting feminist. It was *a man's world* and he for one was glad and grateful that he was one! The journey passed quickly.

It was 1 a.m. when he said goodbye at last to Marty who stuck to him like glue and they shared a cab, much to Christopher's dismay. As Marty said, it was on the way so they could continue to chat. The cab stopped at Marty's gate and Christopher was interested to note the house was big. The drive up to the house was fairly short but the house was enormous. It had a white colonial feel that Christopher liked very much. As Marty got out of the cab he turned and promised to call in to the Hilton for a drink in the next few days. Christopher hoped he would forget. The cab took him to the hotel where he looked forward to a little peace and quiet.

He arrived at a Hilton in disarray, an unusual sight for a Hilton hotel. It was nearly two in the morning and there were men in groups milling around everywhere. There was a lot of backslapping and good natured talking going on. The shouting was bad enough, but the dress sense was too hideous to be true. It looked to him like a golfers convention gone wrong, with each man obviously trying to outdo the others with tasteless check suits and loud shirts.

He registered his arrival and got his keys before heading straight for his room. All the rooms were now looking the same. A king sized bed, with matching cover and curtains, a dressing table, television and en-suite. The service, as always, was immaculate, he had his dirty clothes ready when the knock at the door brought a far too chirpy porter to collect his washing, saying all would be ready by breakfast the next day. Tomorrow was another day and for now he wanted a quiet drink from the mini bar, a bath and a good nights sleep.

He had breakfast in the dining room. It was 7 a.m. and not many were there enjoying a good breakfast of ham, eggs, pancakes, syrup and soda bread. The service was fast, with waiters in professional happy mode, he still found that annoying, especially in the mornings. He went back to his room and found his shirts, t-shirts, trousers all washed, pressed, and sanitised in cellophane. Christopher put the clothing away in the wardrobe. He had two more days to kill in Salt Lake City, most of which would be spent in the Hilton and then he could go home.

He lit a Silk Cut and phoned Amanda. It had been 5 weeks since he left Britain and he was missing Amanda badly. She sounded husky and glad to hear from him. He could almost smell her. She said all the right things to make him feel good and he hoped the next few days would go quickly so they could be together. He had suggested often that she join him in America but every time she had declined. He didn't bother asking again. She told him to be careful coming through customs on the way back. Her promise that she would be waiting for him made Christopher's stomach knot in anticipation.

At around 10 a.m. Christopher joined the mishmash of dealers in the foyer to assess the competition. The back slapping and hearty laughs were a bit beyond him but they seemed to like him. He was certainly polite, and the pole stuck up his backside was their answer to his stand offish manner. They would comment that he was English after all. Funny lot the English, they all agreed, lots of class but no money to back it up. There were various seminars to attend on taxation, selling techniques, etc all of which the experienced good old boys present had no need of. They were a good natured lot, especially after the many drinks that oiled the day. He was seen as no competition, a mistake on their part. He made some good contacts. Perceived by those present as no threat, they treated him with kindly goodwill, he made a nice change to all the other hard ass salesmen there.

His meeting with Bill Hartman was set for 2 p.m. that afternoon. Bill Hartman he was to discover was not like the good old boys he had met in the foyer. The meeting started with a couple of Bill's "yes" men. He knew they were "yes" men because they had developed an ingratiating way that obviously worked for Bill but had become the norm in their dealings with potentially important businessmen and they could not stop it. Christopher wished the top boss was as easy as these pair were. They fussed and got him coffee, asked about him and said how lovely his accent was. He thought they were fags. They did not quite understand his humour, it was rather subtle and dry for them but they laughed nonetheless. They loved him, and thought he must be related to a king or prince or something. He spoke so nicely and carried himself so regally. Christopher found this a useful tool and although he never said he was related to nobility, he never denied it either. They thought him so English and reserved and embarrassed to admit he was royalty. In fact, Bill Hartman was to be told later that Christopher was asked outright if he had ever met the Queen of England. They had studied his face when Christopher had said no. They noted he had averted his eyes and a slight smile had played across his lips which confirmed he was lying. Bill was to relay this information to his cronies at a later date. He proudly told those present that no one pulled the wool over Bill's eyes. Of course Christopher knew the Queen of England and Christopher was stupid to deny it. He smugly told all at his table it would have done Christopher a mighty power of good business-wise to use his royal connection, but he would remark with a sigh, what do Brits know about business. When Bill stated his often repeated saying of "Bill Hartman never had the wool pulled over his eyes" every one with him nodded their agreement.

His meeting with Bill was not bad. He saw the "yes" men and then Bill followed not only in the same day which made a change, but later that afternoon. Christopher was on a roll. Bill was direct, and friendly and didn't waste time going through every item again, his "yes" men had obviously briefed him. Christopher knew the only reason he had got this far was because of curiosity. Some of the special features in Davies-Clarke Plc – Luxury and Customised Vehicles for the Discerning were very tempting and would be an added interest to any car show. The Texas customised car, whilst vulgar, was of great interest to Bill. In fact, all clients Christopher had seen were sold on the fact that the cars would not only be an additional attraction to their events but a sale would make them money as percentages of sales had already been agreed and they all knew sales of these cars would be mega bucks. After one or two logistic and operational questions that needed answering, this achieved, Bill agreed to the date and space allocation. Christopher could see that although agreements had been reached Bill needed to say something else. His final word as he left the room was that Christopher should consider himself lucky that he had given him a chance, as Brits don't usually get a shot at his shows. Christopher took that comment with a pinch of salt. He had got the show and that was all that mattered. He was glad the power-hungry prick had left the room and he could go and get a drink.

He had time for a whisky, or Bourbon as the Americans called it. Tasted good to him anyway with ice and soda. He met some of the good old boys in the bar. They were on form and insisted he sat with them. He was regaled with stories of cars, hunting trips, women and guns and murders. Each story, however gory, ended with raucous laughter and back slapping. Christopher quite enjoyed their company. After one too many drinks they made their way to the restaurant. What he was going to eat was taken out of Christopher's hands. Good natured shouting gained the attention of the waiters. The largest steak with fries and salad was presented to Christopher. He looked at it, all 30 ozs of it, the plate was the largest he had ever seen and then there was the fries along side what looked like half a cow on his plate. He realised from the intent stare from his drinking pals that they wanted him to eat it, and eat all of it. He laughed and gave it his best shot. It was the best steak he had ever tasted. After he had got half way he realised there were bets taken on if he could finish it all.

Well, he was British, and he would not let the country down. The whisky he had consumed and was still consuming was giving the whole meal thing a surreal feeling. As he got to the last quarter of the steak and the fries were nearly gone, a whoop went up on the table and they chanted "get it down, get it down" as he struggled to chew and swallow. He begged his stomach and mouth to co-operate, it had become an important victory for Christopher.

He woke the next morning in the right room, in the right bed, with his clothes over the chair. As he lay there moving nothing but his eyes he could feel the pain queuing behind his eyes waiting for the doors to the rest of his body and head to open. He remembered he had been pretty drunk that evening, but it had been a long time since he had felt this bad. As he tried to sit up a pain shot across his forehead. His head ached and he felt sick. He tried to put a hand to his head but the muscles in his arm had melted. Between the pain and the waves of nausea he remembered why he was there. Henry Fitzjohn III would be waiting to see him that afternoon. Walking and talking was causing him a problem at the moment. He looked at his watch, it was 10 a.m. He cursed himself, his meeting with Henry Fitz etc, was the one he did not want to screw up. There were mega bucks to be made with Henry F. If he got the business he could line up a series of shows for next year. If his information was correct, HF had a reputation of excellence and to be on his ticket was vital for Davies-Clarke's PLC to have credibility in the American Events market. Christopher was betting on the HF ticket to bring home the other companies he had been seeing. It would make his next upcoming visit in a months time more interesting.

He had 4 hours until his 2 p.m. meeting. He would have panicked if he had the strength and energy. A shower, some fresh air, and time to go over his strategy was something he would do after he ordered some strong hot coffee from room service.

He stayed under the hot shower for half an hour, letting the water wash away the throbbing ache that started in his head and had spread to all parts of his body. He had managed to keep down the coffee and paracetamol and hoped they would work soon. The water running over his body relaxed him and he made himself calm down and stop panicking. He chanted continually under his breath, "I'll be fine, I'll be fine," until he believed it.

He dressed casually and sat at the table on his balcony. The air was warm and clear. He was feeling better. His head was beginning to feel like his own and he could think a bit more clearly. He had two and a half hours until his meeting and knew he would be ok. He ordered a club sandwich and hoped he could eat just a little of it to settle his stomach.

He made bullet points of all the important areas he needed to bring into the meeting. If he screwed this up he was sure the other companies he had courted this trip would follow Henry Fitzjohn III's lead and back out of their verbal agreement. He was very well aware of the importance of this meeting and he felt ill again. All the promises made so far were verbal, nothing had been signed and he knew he was still on trial. He took a deep breath, cleared his mind and was determined not to scare the hell out of himself by worrying, it was a waste of his time. His club sandwich had arrived and more coffee. He sat back on the balcony and enjoyed the air. The sandwich was staying down and the coffee was making him feel better. He was going to be a winner he told himself.

As he sat on his balcony enjoying the midday air he decided he was going to like being in America. Next time, he was determined not to travel so far in so short a time. He felt exhausted but success would make him feel much better. He had psyched himself up for the meeting so much that he was on a high. He could do it, he knew that. He knew the opposition and they were not his equal. Feeling better he closed his eyes for a short nap in readiness for his meeting.

At 1.45 p.m. Christopher was suited, prepared, and ready to go. The meeting was in the hotel on the top floor. With a look in the mirror, a minuscule movement of the tie and a final tug on his suit jacket, he picked up his briefcase and made his way to the meeting room with his confidence flying high ahead of him.

The meeting with HF was strange. On entering the meeting room, Christopher saw Henry Fitzjohn III was already seated at the head of the table with his entourage of four men around him. He nodded at Christopher who made his way to a seat a few feet from HF. HF resumed immediately his discussions with his group and did not give Christopher a second glance. Christopher tried not to look as if he was listening as he put his papers neatly on the table. HF was talking in a low murmur and could not be heard outside of his group. It took Christopher only a brief glance to get a picture of HF and what he was. This was the first time he had seen him and it matched what he had heard. HF was a distinguished looking man with black hair greying at the temples giving him that intelligent look that women seemed to like and men trust. He had the body of a man much younger than his 50 years and his slim, toned physique showed off the very expensive suit he was wearing. He had a presence that took full command of the room. Christopher could see he was handsome and understood how he got his legendary reputation with women. Personally, Christopher could see what he was. The thin cruel mouth and piercingly cold eyes gave away the fact he was a bastard of the first order.

HF had invited other car dealers to be present. They entered the room and got the nodded acknowledgement and were then ignored. Christopher surveyed the competition, he knew them all from previous meetings. Marcel Gambeau was the intense French candidate who spoke quite good English but was out of his depth with an American accent. Martin Shultz was an American car dealer who should have known better. He was brash and very Texan, arrogant, loud and big. A stupid Italian car dealer sent the most gorgeous woman called Begonia to represent them. By Italian standards this was a good move. Christopher watched as she moved into poll position by placing herself next to HF.

When everyone was seated and papers shuffled into neat piles, Henry Fitzjohn III raised his head to survey the table in front of him. Everyone present took their cue from HF's group who were now sitting back and waiting for HF to state what he wanted. Begonia got a very interested "hello there" look which she took to be a result and gave him a very intimate look. He welcomed everyone to the meeting and nodded at Martin and Marcel. For Christopher he reserved a special word of thanks for coming all the way from London, England. Christopher immediately discounted Martin and Marcel as competition. Begonia was the only one at the moment who was to be watched. That was until Henry turned to Begonia, gave her a smile and asked, "Hey honey, can you organise some coffee for us all?" Mustering all the good grace she could, Begonia left the room in search of someone to bring in coffee.

Christopher gleefully saw all the competition demolished. He wondered why he was getting his chance so easily, but the floor was his and he was going to take it, why he had got it he would worry about later. As a consummate salesman, Christopher took the meeting his way. Martin, the loud Texan was not going to let Christopher get away with hogging the show and loudly muscled his way into the conversation. Christopher was more than a match for him and with a smile told him very grandly that his attitude was rather boring, and turning to Henry F, he apologised for the vulgar way the meeting was going. Henry F seemed to enjoy that. Martin watched Christopher intently. He was seething and hoping Christopher would hang himself. Christopher took over the meeting. He had sorted out one of the opposition, now for the next. He talked fast and used analogies that the

French man would not understand ensuring no sensible interruption from him. As for Begonia, she returned flushed with frustration and indignation after 5 minutes. It took her what seemed ages to get someone to organise some coffee and she was spitting nails at the thought she could be so easily dismissed by Henry F. But for the moment she was all smiles and girlie looks at him. Christopher saw no challenge from her.

Christopher could not believe his luck. He knew Davies-Clarke had far more gimmicky cars to put into a show as well as the standard bullet proof, latest electronic gadgetry types. The Texas car had not been done by anyone else so far and it had proved to be the clincher in all his dealings. He knew it was not going to be long before it was either copied or someone would go one step further in producing something more ridiculous. This, he reasoned, must be why Henry F was giving him such an easy time. Henry F had said nothing for the past 30 minutes, he had just watched. Christopher had used the time to put Davies-Clarke up as the only company worth dealing with. He was running this show and paused to allow Begonia, Martin and Marcel to interrupt on cue. It was fun to watch as they fought amongst themselves to be heard. Christopher was enjoying himself.

After 5 minutes of shouting and arguing Henry F raised his hand and the table went quiet. "Thank you Gentlemen and lady, I will let you know." He rose out of his chair and strode out of the meeting room with his retinue of 4 men, leaving the bewildered four standing around the table. They were not, and never would be allies, so they picked up their various papers and left silently and individually. They all had the same thoughts of what had they done, and what do they do now. Christopher was really worried and panicking. He was catching the next evening flight home and he couldn't go without something from Henry F. He was totally unprepared for this reaction and wondered what the hell to do now.

He went back to his room and raided the mini bar for a whisky. It was a little early, but what the hell, he needed it to help him think. He lit a cigarette and took his whisky onto the balcony. It was mid afternoon and very pleasant. The sun was shining but the slight breeze made it feel warm enough to sit and cool enough to feel comfortable. He mulled over the events and wondered what the hell was happening. It hit him quite suddenly and he was angry. This had to be a game and Henry F was playing with them. Why he would waste his time he could not fathom out. He surmised he wanted something from one of them, he didn't know what. He came to the conclusion if he didn't know what was wanted, he would just have to ask. When he had finished his whisky and cigarette he picked up the telephone and asked to be put through to Henry F's room. A woman's voice told him he could have a meeting with HF at 8 p.m. that evening in the meeting room. Christopher asked if it would be just him and HF and was told yes. It was 3.30 p.m. and he decided another drink and cigarette on the balcony would go down a treat.

He had a meal sent up to his room at 6.30 p.m. He didn't want the distraction of meeting the others downstairs. He had a shower and ate his dinner in his dressing gown. He was scared and worried. Everything he was doing would be for nothing without HF. He wondered if HF knew this. Of course he did. He was kidding himself if he thought otherwise. This mental torture went on all afternoon and would not stop intruding into his every thought. He got dressed and went up to HF's meeting room in time to arrive outside the door at precisely 8 p.m. He was ready by then to agree to almost anything suggested to get HF's backing and business. Christopher took a deep breath, gave his tie another tweak and knocked on the door. He entered the room after hearing HF's shout of "enter". HF nodded towards a chair and with a thank you smile and nod Christopher sat down.

HF had finished playing games and got straight to the point, there was no need for niceties. His voice was smooth and quiet as a shroud, "The deal is non-negotiable. I want a customised car of my choice for my personal use. A higher percentage than the crap offered on sales so far. I want a percentage of all deals throughout America as Broker/Agent for all Davies-Clarke vehicles. Give me your answer no later than 9 a.m. tomorrow morning. Goodnight." With a wave of his hand in the direction of the door, he was dismissed. Christopher picked up his brief case and left. It was the strangest meeting he had ever attended and he had no words other than a mumbled quiet "Thank you". Which HF acknowledged with a nod of his head.

Christopher was taken aback by the meeting he had just left. He felt out of sync, not in control and having lost face somehow. Back in his room he poured himself a whisky and lit a cigarette. He went over every aspect of his brief meeting with HF. He paced the room and with every drag of his cigarette he whispered, venomous "Bastard". He realised he had been played better than any virtuoso could. HF had known what he wanted from the start and so Christopher could only assume the purpose of the earlier meeting was just a power thing. He needed another whisky. He wasn't as clever as he thought and HF had *stitched him up like a kipper*. After a few more "Bastards" filled his hotel room, Christopher looked at the time which was now nearly 9 p.m. and decided 2 a.m. in the morning English time should find James still awake. He had kept in regular contact with James on all developments throughout his trip.

James had the names of all Christopher's contacts, especially Henry Fitzjohn III. It was part of his usual business practice that when a new player was entering the arena, as James liked to put it, he would get his contact in a commercial private detective agency to prepare a dossier on HF. James knew all about HF and his business practices. He was one of the most powerful people in America on the corporate hospitality and event scene. The dossier contained information on his businesses, his wives, his corporate style, and even included his preferred confectionery. Belgium chocolates were especially flown in for this guy every month. He was a tough cookie and would not be toyed with. James looked forward to meeting him. James had been informed there would be a meeting at 2 p.m. that day with HF. With the knowledge of the man set in the

30 page document in front of him, he knew Christopher would be calling soon for help.

James was still working when the phone rang at 2 a.m. After the polite greetings, he listened in silence as Christopher told him about the earlier meeting and HF's demands at the final meeting. James' reply was short, sharp and to the point. "Christopher, find out what car he wants and get it, offer him 5% more as our sole agent and anything else he wants just do it, get it all in writing and thank him. Well done Christopher to get this far. I want to be in on the next meeting with him so get me dates as soon as possible, speak to you when you get back. Goodnight."

After he had put the phone down, Christopher lit another cigarette. He knew just how he felt; he felt like a piece of ham. HF and James should get on fine, they were very similar and Christopher felt like the filling in a sandwich between these two. He admired James more than ever at that moment, the man knew all the games and was a top player himself. America was going to be a great big success.

First things first, he sat down and wrote out an agreement for HF to sign in the morning. It took him 30 minutes to compose, a legal document for signing would be sent by Davies-Clarke Solicitors at a later date. For the moment, Christopher wanted something signed in principle. When he had finished it he went to reception and asked them to fax it to the number written down. He had sent it to Pam, his private secretary at Davies-Clarke. When he returned to his room he searched the mini bar for another whisky. O.k. he had drunk a few whiskies that day but, what the hell, he needed another one. He drank to his success.

Tomorrow he was going home. He would see Amanda first and get rid of his packages and have a little fun. He had earned some pleasure, it had been a long and tiring trip. Amanda would credit his account with his share of the profits on the drugs as usual. For now, a good nights sleep, a restful breakfast and the exquisite anticipation of a grateful Amanda made him very happy. Although James did not come in the same category as Amanda, his congratulations would be most welcome. Christopher settled down for the night and with a giggle, he had the relaxing thought that he was going home as a huge success with everyone who counted in his life.

With the 5 hour difference Pam would arrive for work and find the fax on her desk. She fully understood the importance of the note that said it must be done immediately. She got a thrill from the confidential note addressed to her only, saying she should tell no one about the fax enclosed. He made most pieces of work seem clandestine and for her eyes only. It was exciting and thrilling and felt part of a James Bond intrigue. He trusted her with this and he trusted implicitly her alterations to his letters. She felt special. This fax was no different from others sent to her in the past and she would type it up putting in full stops and commas as appropriate and any other neat touches to make the letter look professional as was entrusted to her by Mr. Christopher as she called him. The document was typed and faxed back within the hour. By 6.30 a.m. America time he would find the fax pushed under the door when he awoke. He had time to check it was correct, and time to send it back if not correct for alteration and still be ready for his 9 a.m. meeting with HF. Pam was not quite his confidential secretary but she knew more about most things he was doing. When she added two and two it always made four. She was sensible and could keep her mouth shut. She never revealed anything about Christopher's business ways to anyone. She took far too much interest in his business because she had developed a deep affection for him over the years, which gave him the sort of loyalty only seen in sheep dogs.

Her loyalty was never in dispute with Christopher. He accepted this rare and precious gift as a right. He never gave her a second thought, bought her a Christmas card or birthday card let alone a thank you present for all her hard work. Other staff at Davies-Clarke could not figure it out. Pam was tall, blonde, middle aged and very attractive. She was still in love with her husband of 10 years and would talk about him all the time. Everyone had met Pam's husband Peter and the affection between the two was noticeable. Pam would talk to everyone about anything other than Christopher and what he was doing. Even James when asking where Christopher was got a standard "I will look into this and come straight back to you" reply. Pam would then ring Christopher and ask where he was as far as James was concerned. Her protection of Christopher was intense but all were convinced it was not a sexual thing between them.

The faxed letter was just as he wanted. After a good breakfast Christopher went back to his room, collected his jacket and briefcase and made his way to HF's meeting room. He stood outside the room at 8.57 a.m. adjusted his tie again and knocked on the door.

HF was already in the room and told him to come in. Christopher showed him the document he had prepared and told HF that James agreed with his demands. With a short nod and a hint of a smile he told Christopher to see his secretary about future appointments and he would talk directly to James in England. With a strong shake of his hand Christopher was dismissed. It still felt most odd and he felt a spare part to this discussion. Still, he assured himself, all was going well and he was on his way home today. A comparing of diaries with HF's secretary, a Miss Welling, who suggested a date in September when HF would be in Atlanta. This suited Christopher, Jennifer crossed his mind and he only had to convince James that the September date was necessary and he should clear his diary for this.

His only problem now was to get through customs with all the little packages he was carrying. He felt rather nervous but he had done this before so he told himself to stop being stupid and just get on with it. He adopted his haughty attitude at the airport which he felt helped him get through customs. He hoped they thought he was far too high class to be interested in anything to do with drugs. He considered this attitude a proven winner because he had never been stopped before.

He was right, he got through customs without any problems. The little packages snug in his case amongst his clothes. He had to summon up all his self control to go through customs in Atlanta and Heathrow. He was feeling a bit spooked and felt everyone looking at him. He knew he had to act normally or they would pick him out. He didn't relax until he left the Heathrow terminal at 9 a.m. in the morning and caught a taxi to take him to Amanda. The journey was long and the anticipation of seeing her unbearable, he deserved this treat. It had been weeks and weeks since he saw her last. She was waiting at the door as he paid the taxi. They went straight to her private room where he unloaded the little packages and gave them to Amanda. Apart from the odd delivery when James' helicopter was used, this was the largest delivery Christopher had made and Amanda whooped with excitement. It had been a practice really to see if this would work and it had. She grabbed Christopher and hugged him in excitement. He wanted that hug to last longer and move on but she had other plans for the moment.

She sat him down and asked him for all the details on how the plans had gone for getting the drugs, who he had visited and what they said and the delivery he made and what he did with the money until he handed it over to Chuck for more little packages. She was full of praise for the way he handled himself. He told her about Chuck and how he grabbed him. She thought him brave and told him as soon as she had put the packages somewhere safe, she would not be able to contain herself any longer. He liked that thought very much but made do with a cup of coffee in the meantime while Amanda disappeared for about 20 minutes.

He never knew how or why it happened but as he sat there waiting for Amanda, the tremors started gently in his hands as he lifted the cup of coffee and got stronger and stronger. He put the cup down with half of the coffee in his saucer. His legs started to shake and finally his whole body shook. So shocked at this it was almost as if he stood away from himself and looked at this gibbering wreck sitting in an elegant Louis XVI chair. He had to get himself under control before Amanda came back. He realised quickly what a shock it had all been to his system. He had worked hard for James in America and gone backwards and forwards buying drugs and selling drugs and bringing a big stash into the country. Of course he was shell shocked by it all. It had become his favourite saying that, of course, he was not James Bond and the past weeks had been packed with more tension, suspense and long days than most people experienced in a life time. He allowed himself a few minutes of uncontrolled emotion and then reigned himself in.

It was over, he returned with the packages and he had earned himself a nice little fortune. Amanda was pleased and he looked forward to her gratitude. He was a success and now he was going to enjoy the rewards. When he looked back over the past weeks in America he took great pleasure and satisfaction in realising it was really very easy. Life was good and he for one was going to enjoy it to the full.

Sitting here now he remembered his words clearly. The feeling of satisfaction that the first big success gives you is very warming. It was a pity he did not stop there. He had made a nice bit of money so he could have stopped. Davies-Clarke was going to be successful in America and that should have been enough. But of course there was Amanda. Even now, knowing the truth, he still knew he would not have been able to give her up. She was the main reason he stayed with the drugs, he could not imagine a life without her. She was worth all the danger and anxiety. She spent that day proving it as he recalled.

CHAPTER TWENTY TWO

The following day Christopher went to the London offices. The meeting with James went well. He was happy with the way business was progressing and congratulated Christopher on his success again. A date in September was confirmed in James' diary and together they would return and speak with HF. James would, as always, make sure everything was set in concrete and nothing could go wrong. Christopher did not think he would be needed particularly for that meeting but James wanted him to go. It suited Christopher fine, he would tell Amanda about his visit and, on reflection, he would contact Jennifer and they could maybe meet for a meal or something.

After that de-briefing in London with James, Christopher drove home to Winterton and his family. He arrived home at 4 p.m. on a gloriously hot summer day. He had phoned home to say he would be arriving at 6 p.m. The house was empty except for Lindsay who was preparing vegetables in the kitchen. She was surprised to see him, as she said, Mrs Cross was expecting him to come home at 6 p.m. Christopher mumbled something about being able to get away earlier than he thought, surprise for everyone. He smiled at Lindsay and went to his study. He knew Alice would be at home just before 6 p.m. to greet him. He wanted a couple of hours alone to look at his garden and wind down.

Off came his tie, and he unbuttoned his shirt a little. He poured himself a large whisky and took it with him to the garden. He sat on the bench near the rhododendrons and looked at the willow tree. It was a beautiful spot to sit and contemplate with the birds singing in the trees and bees buzzing with contentment at the explosion of flowers that summer always brings. He stared at the movement of the willow branches. A gentle breeze had disturbed the long flowing branches that swept near to the ground. He thought the branches moved like long delicate piano playing fingers across a key board. He could almost hear the tune the willow tree was playing, *"Moonlight Becomes You"*. Relaxed and at peace, he sat there long enough to finish two cigarettes. He was disturbed from his deep contentment by the sound of chickens squawking. It was a rude awakening and he cursed them soundly for invading his thoughts, his garden, his life.

He looked at the rhododendrons, they had finished flowering long ago. The leaves should be dark green and glossy. He thought the leaves were lighter than they should be. He would have a talk to the gardeners about making sure they were being acid fed. He got up and walked the garden avoiding the corner where the chickens were housed. It was a most beautiful walled garden. Even the bricks in the wall had plants growing out of the cracks. There was alyssum, forget-me-nots, nasturtiums and lovely lavender which made the wall a jigsaw of colour.

He watched the bees going in and out of the flowers as if they could not believe their luck. The gardeners were doing an excellent job and worth every penny of their wages. He made a note that tomorrow he would tell the gardeners what a sterling job they were doing

His peace was broken by Alice shouting his name. He looked at his watch, it was 5.30 p.m. Depressed, he thought she was keeping her promise of always being there for him when he came home. Surprisingly, as she appeared, she was a very welcoming sight; she had brought the whisky decanter with her. A little out of breath, but smiling and welcoming, Alice greeted Christopher with: "Goodness! You are early. You silly thing, you should have rung and let me know. I should have been here for you, I'm sorry. Here, let me top up your glass."

She gave him a peck on the cheek, then made sure he had his drink. She asked as always how his business had gone. He would reply, as always, that he was doing very well and preferred not to talk about it on his days off. She really wanted to please him but had rather ran out of things to say that would interest him. He had made it clear in the past that he was not interested in gossip, name dropping, or anything to do with her committees. Thinking hard, and wanting to please him, she continued, "The garden is beautiful isn't it?"

She had said the right thing because he smiled and looked at her.

"It is a joy to come home and see it Alice. You are doing a good job with the gardeners, they make it more beautiful every time I get home."

She smiled her thanks, knowing she had nothing to do with the garden arrangements. The gardeners had decided between them what they wanted to do in the garden and just got on with it.

"I hope I won't see any more surprises in the garden."

She knew he was referring to the chickens again. He never stopped going on about them. They'd had chickens now for some time and she was really quite fed up with his little snipes. Not wanting to upset the atmosphere, she tried to be conciliatory.

"Don't spoil it Christopher, I haven't expanded this area and I won't. I keep telling you that. Now, can we go back to looking at the wonderful flowers? Have you seen the delphiniums in the corner, the mauve, blue and white is stunning."

He hadn't, and they walked arm in arm to explore the right corner of the garden. To anyone watching they looked the most perfect and contented, married couple. It was the preferred view both Alice and Christopher wanted others to have of them.

Alice said she had lots to do for dinner. She told Christopher that Neil would be bringing the girls home and staying for dinner. The school holidays had started and the girls had spent the day boating on the broads with him. Christopher thought "Good old Neil, he did what he said he would and kept an eye on my family while I was away."

Alice added, "By the way, your mother is also joining us for dinner. I told her to arrive at 8 p.m." Alice was none too keen on her mother-in-law, far too snooty and always all over Christopher and ignoring her. It had been many years, but she would never forgive Alice for deserting John and getting pregnant and marrying Christopher. Alice had built herself a high profile in the county of Norfolk and was not used to being so dismissed. It was going to be a busy dinner so he told Alice he would stay a little longer in the garden and enjoy the early evening peace.

At 7 p.m. precisely the girls bounced into the house and garden. He had only been away for 6 weeks but they had grown. They rushed to Christopher and he crouched down to cuddle them. Emily had got taller and he could see the young woman beginning to blossom. She was still enough of a tomboy to try and swing herself around his back and grab him round the neck. She wanted a piggy back she kept telling him. Jane skipped up to him and planted a big soppy kiss on his cheek. Her smile showed him she had lost her two top front teeth and on closer inspection the new teeth were just beginning to show through the gum. He had forgotten what it was like to listen while two little girls both talked excitedly at the same time, each tugging at him, vying for his attention and expecting him to answer their various questions. In the end, from a squatting position, he just toppled over on to the floor with Emily still clinging to his neck and Jane hanging on to his arm. He lay on the floor laughing and the girls started to giggle. Neil, who had stopped to say hello to Alice, arrived in the garden to see an undignified mass of arms and legs intertwined. When the giggling calmed down, Neil shouted his hello. Grinning at such a happy family sight, Neil offered his hand to any one of them who wanted a hand up.

The girls were called into the house by Alice to have their supper. She wanted them clean, tidy and fed before mother-in-law arrived. Christopher and Neil strolled into the house and headed for the drinks cupboard. Alice had put back the decanter half full of good malt whisky. Christopher got clean glasses for them both, poured a generous tot in each glass and sat down to hear all the news on the Bertrams front. They had nearly an hour of peace and quiet to catch up on news. Alice interrupted their chat with a syrupy smile and using a particularly gentle tone of voice asked if they would both like to come to the dining room. Christopher knew his mother must have arrived. Alice was very different when mother was in the vicinity. He ignored the tension these two women created when together. Each vied with the other to be very nice and attentive to him and he always found their actions very acceptable. Neil had been an onlooker often enough to know what dinner would be like with these two women. They joined the ladies in the dining room as Emily and Jane were about to say good night and go to bed. They asked if grandmother would read them a story and of course, with a smile, she agreed. Alice thought that her own mother not only read to her girls, but played with them and cooked with them. Alice thought how her mother was a proper grandmother and was not just the token grandmother Christopher's mother was. But with a smile, Alice wondered if she might like to go up with the girls now because dinner would be ready in just over half an hour, she added she would call her when dinner was ready. A reluctant grandmother walked up the stairs with the girls. She hadn't wanted to stay with them that long. Alice smiled more brightly as they left the room. She knew the old crow wouldn't have given them more than 5 minutes, but half an hour was the least she could give her girls. It had been months since she last saw them.

The meal was pleasant and by the end of the evening Christopher was pleasantly drunk. His mother noticed but forgave his indiscretion. She came to the conclusion living with that woman was enough to drive her poor son to drink. Alice was mortified by his behaviour which was only a little slurred and certainly not unacceptable. Neil thought it funny and found himself left to keep the women entertained while Christopher seemed unable at that moment to continue with any small talk.

Christopher was to spend the next 4 days at home. It was pleasant and restful. Alice was out for some of the days leaving him to enjoy his time in the garden in peace. He had many chats with the gardeners. He enjoyed their company. As Norfolk men used to the land and the seasons everything in life had a simple answer which Christopher found refreshing.

He and the girls went for a walk along the dunes. They took with them bottles of water and kitkats. The walk took 2 hours there and back. In that time Christopher listened to their chattering about school and friends and their ponies. Thank goodness he did not have to buy the ponies for them. They visited nearby stables regularly for horse riding lessons. At present they rode the ponies, Emily said Glenda, her riding instructor, said she would soon be ready to ride Black Beauty the 6 year old horse at the stables. She told her daddy that she was excited because Black Beauty was her favourite and she always gave him an apple when she was at the stables. He interrupted and asked about her school. Christopher could see the chat would have gone on for ever about what horses were at the stables, what they ate, ad nausium, and he didn't need to hear about all that.

He had found over the years that once a question had been asked of Emily, that was it, she talked about everything possible and at great length, given the chance and his job was to just listen and make appropriate agreeing noises. He heard all about Emily's new school, how she had told everybody there that Jane would be starting next term. Her friends have the most strange names like Moonbeam, Boston, and Zoltan for Christs sake! Who, he wondered, was twisted enough to call their child that? He thought it was supposed to accommodate lords and ladies but as he was to find out, it also accommodated rock star's children. Emily also had friends Alice would approve of, she mentioned names like Tristran, Isobel, and their mummies who were Lady this and Baroness that. He remembered Alice all a twitter one weekend going on about how Lady Diane had visited the school for tea. The parent/teacher committee she was on had wondered if, perhaps, when *the you know who* boys get old enough if they might be going to Blythes. He remembered Alice phoning all her so called friends to tell them and asking them if perhaps the girls should learn how to curtsey correctly. She gave him a headache that weekend but the girls took it in their stride.

He quickly got back to listening to Emily who was looking at him. She could tell he was not concentrating on what she was saying. "Silly daddy," she said and tapped him on the arm and plunged straight back with a deep breath and gulp into her story about her teachers. He had acquired the knack of half listening but something caught his attention and he stopped her and asked her to repeat what she had just said. A little peeved that he had not been listening properly but with a sigh she slowly repeated what she had said: "Mr Evans is my favourite teacher I said daddy. He is our Games master if you remember. He says I am getting really good at netball. He says I hold the ball correctly, like this daddy." She demonstrated how she upturned her hand and clasped her fingers around an imaginary ball. Christopher could see she was going off at a tangent again and had forgotten what she had said before.

"Emily, you said something about "F" and Mr Evans."

"Oh yes daddy. Mr Evans always says the "F" word. He says we should all use the "F" word in everything we do." She looked triumphant and smiled up at Christopher. She liked Mr Evans, he made her laugh. Christopher thought she had said that. He licked his lips not quite sure what to ask in response to this. He tried to sound light-hearted in his response but was struggling. "So, Emily, Mr Evans likes the "F" word? What does that mean exactly?" Emily put on her reciting tone. It was obviously something Mr Evans said often to the class. Christopher waited with baited breath.

"Now girls and boys. The "F" word is just a small word but it should be an important part of your life. Everything you do should contain the "F" word. **Fun** boys and girls is something you should find in every part of your life. If you can see the fun in life then life will be fun."

A relieved Christopher let Emily carry on talking about her other teachers. He pondered that Mr Evans must have lead a sheltered life if he was not aware of what the "F" word meant in the real world.

Jane had patiently listened to Emily talking ten to the dozen and now she wanted to join in. She told Christopher all about her junior school and how she was going to have a uniform just like Emily's and she wanted to learn about the "F" word. Christopher let them argue about who was going to be in what class and all those silly little bits of information. While they chatted and argued between themselves Christopher could look at the sea, the sky and the dunes. The fresh air, space and familiarity was so relaxing. They arrived home with the girls still arguing about Mr Evans and who he would like best, and how Emily had lots of friends and Jane would have none. They were obviously getting tired and Jane was quite weepy. Christopher told Emily off for being such a little teaser. He picked up Jane and gave her a cuddle. He told her in whispers that she would be much more popular than Emily because she was so beautiful. Jane liked that.

Christopher had arranged to meet Neil in Wroxham

the following evening for a meal and a chat. Christopher drove to Bertrams in Wroxham to see how Neil was getting on. The shop had been rearranged yet again. It was looking better and better. The china area had been enlarged even more. On inspection, Christopher discovered an outside additional area full of plants and pots and other sorts of gardening bits and pieces. It was difficult to see much because of the throng of people and shopping trolleys. He could not remember seeing the shop so full. One of the staff had told him Neil was across the road in the dress shop but was due back by closing time. It was now 6 p.m. so Christopher waited. He didn't have to wait long. He saw Neil at a distance entering the shop. He was looking so like the Captain. He was wearing a blazer. He had never seen Neil wearing one of those before. Neil spotted Christopher lurking outside of the check outs trying to keep out of the way of customers and rushed to greet him. After back slapping and shaking of hands they both headed out of the building towards the Red Lion for a drink.

Christopher heard about Neil's plans for Bertrams. He was going to add a small café with home made scones, cakes and pasties. There were many boating tourists who spent many hours in Bertrams stores, so a tea place seemed a good idea. He thought there was a market for it because all the Wroxham cafés were burger and chips type places, his would be for a cup of tea and a cake type of café. Christopher could see that everything Neil had done was a success and he did not doubt this would also be a success. It was as always a most pleasant evening. Christopher made Neil laugh reciting what the girls had told him, especially the bit about Mr Evans. He thanked Neil for keeping an eye on the girls for him while he was away. Neil looked a little embarrassed and said it was a real pleasure. He thought Christopher very lucky indeed to have such a wonderful family. They talked as ever about the Captain, James and his work load. Neil said his father was bringing home a woman he had met somewhere in London. She was half his age and he did not think it was her brain he was interested in. This seemed strange for them both as James never seemed to have time for women friends. Neil thought his father found the house empty since the Captain went. Neil said his magistrate work was taking a lot of his time. He didn't like to talk about it except to say that Teddy Waring, the local drunk, had come up before him so many times that Teddy thought he could call him Neil. Neil laughed and said this had to be discouraged. Christopher found it difficult to see Neil as he was now, to him he was still the young boy of their youth. People everywhere in Wroxham saw Neil as a distinguished, authoritative man, a pillar of the community. When Christopher tried to pull Neil's leg by reminding him of his insecure youth, Neil went to throw a bread roll at him then remembered that yes, he was a pillar of the community and must behave like one. They both laughed at what they had become and how they must behave. Christopher thought there was no one else in the world that could bring out the carefree person that lurked inside Christopher like Neil could. He would remember always how good it was to be in this great and good persons company.

They ate a good meal, drank more than they should

and put the world to rights. Christopher told Neil bits about America and the people he had met. He told him about Jennifer and how charity work was so different in America. Everything was big there. No jumble sales to raise money, more likely huge, expensive parties with wealthy people invited who gave generously but easily to whatever charity was being hosted that day.

Neil started that embarrassed jerking movement that told Christopher he was going to be told something that modest Neil did not want to brag about.

"Well, funny you should mention that. I am involved in a charity that gives inner city children the chance of holidays in the country."

Christopher wanted to ask – why? But knowing Neil, he asked instead what did that involve. Neil was excited, and the words just blurted out.

"Well. I bought this piece of land on Martham Broads. It slopes down to the broads and had not been used for farming land as most is around here. It is dry ground but scrub land. I bought 30 acres of land but it wanted work done on it to make it good and safe enough for farm animals. I am building a house with dormitories for up to 20 children at a time. There will be rooms for mothers if they wish to come with their children. Do you know Christopher, some children from inner city homes have never seen farm animals in real life? Some have never seen the countryside in the way we have. We are so lucky and we don't know it. I am going to have cows, goats, chickens, ducks, lambs for these children to pet, touch, and we will teach them how to milk the animals."

"How can you milk a chicken Neil?"

"Stop it Christopher, you know what I mean. This will not be a profit-making farm, it will give the children a view on life they have never seen. It might help towards keeping these children away from drugs and a life of crime. I can only try."

Christopher felt a mild pang of guilt at the mention of drugs but shooed it away quickly. Neil was on a roll and had more to tell.

"I have bought a motor boat for the broads that will take up to 10 children and 3-4 adults to look after them. I plan to make the holiday an intense, one adult to two-three children. While 10 children are on the boat for the day learning about what birds and fish and animals live around the broads, the other 10 children will be spending the day on the farm learning and helping with the farm animals. They will be given more time and attention than these youngsters are used to and if they need to talk about anything time will be set aside for private chats. But above all, it will be fun with music, games and laughter. We are on course for the opening to be next summer, fingers crossed. I am so excited Christopher. I feel I am giving something back because life has been so good to me."

Christopher was quite taken aback at such an unselfish view of life. Neil was rich, he could afford to do this, but surely this would drain his money reserve. He tried to say this to Neil without sounding a complete bastard, long term this sounded a plug hole project. He had to ask the question of was he rich enough to guarantee money for years to come. Neil smiled and thanked Christopher for his concern. He knew he was only looking out for his well-being. Neil did not know how he deserved such a good and caring friend. He explained he would fund the setting up of it. The long term plan was that the charity he had set up would fund the running costs. He said he would be employing up to 6 full time workers on the farm plus the many volunteers who would still need feeding and bedding for their stay, then there would be the office staff who would organise and arrange for the visits. It was going to be a daunting task but worth it. Christopher asked what the farm would be called. Neil smiled with emotion. "It's going to be called *Captains Farm* after Bertram. He would have loved this if he had been around today."

They both nodded and a moment of sadness crossed the table. Christopher broke the silence in an effort to lighten the conversation, robustly offered his thoughts.

"He would have strutted around that farm of yours telling stories to the youngsters about Norfolk history. I can see him now, he would have been in his element." Neil sighed. "He would have loved it, bless him." After a short pause, Neil looked almost apologetically at Christopher. "My father is not so keen you know. He thinks I should use the money to diversify into other fields as he has. You know how he thinks. He says what if Bertrams was to collapse and no one wanted to buy from the shops any more. He thinks I should have other business interests to ensure I don't go broke."

Neil leaned forward towards Christopher and earnestly told him.

"You know me Christopher. I am too long in the

tooth now to get married and have a family. It's not going to happen. I want to do something to carry on the Bertram name. I won't have children so I feel bound to help other children. This is my way of saying my life has been worth living."

Christopher was a little taken aback. This was a very important project to Neil. He obviously felt very strongly about it and he for one was going to support him.

"You are one of the best people I have ever known Neil. What can I do to help?"

Neil was so pleased with this reaction. He told Christopher he just needed to have him on his side. He viewed Christopher as a successful businessman whose opinion he sought and considered very important.

"Just listen and watch what I am doing and give me your honest opinion if you think I am not being professional in my approach. As my friend I value your input."

He didn't deserve for Neil to think so highly of him. If only he knew what type of businessman he really was. Still, there was nothing to stop him supporting Neil. He had smiled at the thought, that it just might make him a better person.

His four days at home went very quickly. His final evening was organised by Alice. They were holding a dinner party for 10 friends. With Christopher away for so many weeks and in the knowledge that he would be away regularly for about one month at a time, she had to get the dinner parties in when he was at home. Alice wanted to climb the social ladder as quickly as possible.

She was already half way up the ladder but the top was still so far away and such a wonderful place to be. She told Christopher many times that when they reached the top of the ladder they would have exceeded both their families expectations. She knew Christopher's family had a higher standing in the county than her family but her and Christopher were closer to the top than they had ever been.

It would give her a lot of satisfaction to have a better name in the county than Christopher's family. To be invited to the homes of the rich and famous would be something Christopher's parents had never experienced. She did not say much, certainly not to Christopher, but she smarted at the way Christopher's father and John totally ignored her, the children, and their marriage. How dare they take this attitude? Alice and her mother had often talked about the Cross family and their uncaring and embarrassing attitude. Alice's mother was the only person she would confidently talk to, knowing it would go no further. Alice would have preferred it remain a family secret that Christopher and Alice were not included in the Cross family anymore, but of course, everyone who was anyone knew. It was a source of constant concern and something she refused to talk about, even with her friends. She felt contempt for the Cross family. Who did they think they were? They were a joke in her eyes and she would have the last laugh.

Christopher enjoyed the dinner party. Alice invited her ladder climbing friends, the women had eyes everywhere, and seemed uptight, but he found the men usually good company. Why, he would ask himself, is it always the women that make life difficult, who want to play the one-upmanship game. The men he had met were mainly quite relaxed and amusing company. It was his way to invite the men to either join him in the study or the garden, depending on the weather, for cigars and a liqueur. It left the women to hatch schemes, gossip or do whatever they do, as long as he didn't have to be a part of it.

It was his pride and joy. He found most men appreciated his garden. Gardens, Christopher felt, were the domain of men. He knew women were supposed to be the gardeners, and flowers might seem girlie, but his garden was different. He had a manly garden with trees, grass and big chunky flowers and bushes. He had never met a man who did not appreciate its look and felt comfortable. It allowed for loud talking, plenty of space to move around and lounge around. When talking, men did not have to worry about knocking cigar ash on the floor. Men could be men in the garden.

Four days at home was enough for Christopher. He returned to London with relish. He spent the month checking details and realised he must find somewhere for the cars to be garaged on their arrival in America. He suggested to James that Atlanta would be a good middle distance for some of the cars. When venue dates had been agreed, perhaps a further garage and cars in a different area would be necessary. He was working on the basis that he needed one of their top mechanics and engineers to regularly check the cars with an assistant. Christopher was going to have to work out what was the best cost effective way of doing this. He rang regularly and kept in contact with all the people he had spoken to in America. He let them know he was back in America the following month for a meeting with HF. They all knew who he was and he made sure they understood that he was going to be their agent in America. Christopher thought that all the contacts he had made were not necessary now. HF would be his main contact and HF would deal with all those smaller companies Christopher had tried to get on board. He hoped his life would now be easier in America.

He arranged to see Amanda two days after his arrival in London. Amanda was busy until then but promised the wait would be worth it. He knew that would be true. She had a disturbing way of making him feel aroused from a distance. He had known her for many years now but she still had this extraordinary effect on him. He did not believe he would ever tire of Amanda. She made everything worthwhile and life bearable.

Before pleasure, Amanda told him his share of the America stash had been put into his off shore account. He had earned £90,000 for that one return from America. He was very pleased indeed and wanted to celebrate with her straight away. She had laughed and told him to wait a little longer. She asked if he realised what a lucrative little deal America was. She told him they could make mega bucks in the future. Christopher thought they were still only getting supplies for her and the girls plus a few clients as a favour. Amanda kissed him and called him silly. She said they could make so much more money if they supplied others as well. If he could make £100,000 every few months, he would be so rich so quickly. She wondered if he was bored with money. She tempted him with the knowledge that if they became regular business partners, how could she expect him to pay for his visits. Of course, they would be free, she considered him more than a client, she pouted and hoped he knew that anyway.

His arguments were weak but she knew that. He said he did not want to go to America and have to travel all around to buy and sell drugs. He told her that in future he might only visit one city on business. She reassured him that it would be fine, that she would arrange for a meeting in whatever city he was visiting at the time. Amanda was hoping he could carry more drugs in future. Yes, she recognised he had brought a large stash back into the country this time. He argued that the delivery must have had a street value of at least a million pounds if he earned £90,000, so why did he need to bring back more? Her rich velvet voice dampened his arguments and made him feel very receptive to her attentions.

"The more you bring back darling, the quicker we can make our fortune and settle down to do whatever we want. Money is freedom. If you had so much money it allowed you to do anything, wouldn't that be wonderful?"

He had to agree, yes, it would be wonderful. He understood he did not have to bring that much more back. Just a little more would make a big difference to their pay out. As she told him: "if we sell to others we make more money. It is really very simple."
With that comment she grabbed him by the hand and led him to her room.

CHAPTER TWENTY THREE

The month passed quickly and before Christopher knew it, he was boarding the plane to Atlanta with James. The flight was pretty boring with James again going over the business plan and arrangements. Christopher tried to sleep for a few hours but James worked on his lap top.

Atlanta in September was beautiful; still very warm but with a hint of autumn on the way with subtle colour changes in the trees and foliage. James had brought a carry on bag because he was staying two nights only in Atlanta, so the wait for James luggage to arrive on the luggage carousel was tedious for them both. Christopher noted that as James got older his patience got shorter. A cab was hailed to take them to the Hilton in downtown Atlanta. They had until tomorrow before their meeting with Henry Fitzjohn III.

Today was the day that Christopher took James to see the buildings he wanted as garages and repair rooms for the cars. They were outside Atlanta and the cost was within the budget. After James approval of the site and the security arrangements, the leasing documents would be left to Christopher to finalise. James asked for a report to be faxed to him on how the negotiations proceeded and what the final conclusion was. The cars were ready to be shipped to Atlanta when this little detail was finalised.

That evening a meal had been arranged with John Carlotti and Jennifer Logan. The business part of the evening was dealt with quickly. James understood that HF would orchestrate most of the business dealings and therefore negotiations with John Carlotti were not necessary. At present, John Carlotti was not aware of the extent of the liaison between Davies-Clarke and HF. It was a pleasant social evening. James was very good company and was a hit with their two guests. Christopher thought dryly that the fact he was a billionaire might have helped. Was he feeling a bit prickly, you bet he was. He noted the way Jennifer flirted with James and he didn't like it. James was polite back but he never mixed business with pleasure. Christopher thought that maybe that was why he hardly ever had a woman friend. It was well known his only hobby was work. Still, Christopher found the whole dinner experience unsettling, but at that point he was not sure why.

The following day was the meeting with Henry Fitzjohn III. It was in his office in the plush downtown Kennedy building. HF had the top floor suite. Christopher had read James' report on HF so he knew all about his many business interests throughout America and the various offices he had in strategic places around the country. HF lived in Salt Lake City with his many wives, but this week he was residing in Atlanta.

The meeting set for 10 a.m. was going to be easy for Christopher. The contract between Davies-Clarke and

HF had been signed by both after many alterations and copies going back and forth across the ocean. This meeting was designed to start operations and discuss how this would happen. It was also an opportunity for these two men to meet. As James had ordered a full report on HF, HF had also spoken to his contacts and read a full report on James. They each knew this and their meeting would be a relaxed affair with these two powerful men. Christopher watched them talk and negotiate. He was envious of the fact that James had it so easy. Christopher had to sweat blood and did not always know where he stood. Obviously, he thought with a hint of bitterness, if he was a *zillionaire* then perhaps he would be treated with the same respect and deference.

It was arranged to meet HF for a meal that evening and Christopher had organised a table in Atlanta's finest restaurant, Luigis. James and HF were getting on very well indeed. They liked each other and had a great respect for each others business acumen. They roared with laughter at misfortunes of rivals they knew and gave opinions on how they would have handled the same business. The meal ended with an open invitation for HF to visit James at his home in Norfolk. Christopher felt a little out of control and was glad James was leaving the next morning. He could get his business sorted. James left the next morning with a list of things for Christopher to attend to. James was practically pushed into the cab to take him to the airport.

Christopher had a week in Atlanta to finalise the storage garages. He had to arrange to bring over his senior engineer and mechanic. It would be his job to stock the garages with whatever was required to keep the cars in tip top condition. There was also a need to put in place trained local people for cleaning the cars and small repair jobs, and organising transportation to the various events. The garage renting was already in the bag with James signing the agreement before he left for England. He spent some time phoning England to organise his next visit to America. He had organised for Syd to come over with him on his next visit, which he arranged for one month's time. Syd would inspect the garages and bring some specialist equipment to install in the garages. Christopher arranged it so Syd knew his role would keep him in Atlanta to finalise training of new staff. Christopher was working on the basis that his presence in America would only be needed at the shows to sell the cars and acting as good will representative of Davies-Clarke. He did not want to have to deal with the various companies like before. It was not his style to have to deal with the egos of so many different men.

He had meetings with HF's organisers to arrange the first showing of Davies-Clarke cars. He understood a Karl Klingerman was his contact. He met Karl for a drink to cement their relationship. The two men got on well and decided they would be able to work through any problems that might be encountered in this new venture.

He had a very busy week. By the end of it, Christopher had a list of the first dates that Davies-Clarke vehicles would be shown in Atlanta and Salt Lake City starting in two months time. The first, Atlanta, had some upcoming mega huge charity events that would work well with Davies-Clarke vehicles. He had organised the cars being shipped over by cargo ship with two engineers accompanying them. Syd was organised, the garages organised, and surprisingly so, Jennifer was becoming an important item in Christopher's itinerary.

Jennifer rang Christopher's mobile to invite him for a meal at her house. Christopher, still prickly from the James meal, pompously told her that he was the only one who could attend because James had gone back to England. Jennifer, puzzled, laughed, and said, "Well good, because I was only asking you, not the whole company." Embarrassed, he realised how stupid he had sounded. With all the good grace he could assemble, he thanked her and said he would love to have dinner with her. She confirmed he should arrive at 8 p.m. the next day. When he put the phone down he had cringed at the thought of his childish comments. His conversation with Jennifer came back to haunt him all that day and he would almost curl up at the thought. She was a sophisticated, worldly woman and he reckoned she would be regretting asking such an ass to dinner.

He had a wonderful evening, he found her funny and fun. They talked incessantly about what was happening in the world. It had been a long time since he had talked to anyone in that sort of depth. It was at that meal that Jennifer asked him to be her escort to the many dinner parties she was asked to attend. She knew he was not always in the country, but she asked if she had invitation that coincided with his visits to Atlanta would he mind being her escort. He was taken aback at such an invitation after what was such a new friendship. It seemed really strange to him but he quickly qualified this with the knowledge that this was America and Americans were very upfront people. He was flattered and rather pleased to be asked. Of course he would be delighted to escort her, he told her. She was very pleased with his acceptance and they finished the evening sitting on her terrace watching the fountain in the lake.

It was his best week so far in America and it had left him with a warm feeling of contentment. He still had the one area to deal with, it was, after all, the main point and the answer to his long term plans, but it was certainly not the most pleasant. He was having such a good time that he refused to allow the finale of his visit to upset the feel good factor of his American visit.

He had been given a number to ring to arrange to meet this Chuck. He was to arrange this for the end of the week. He did not want to have all the packages in his possession for too long. On the evening before he returned home he took a taxi to the address Chuck had given him. He had the money in his briefcase. He was carrying a lot of money, one million dollars, it felt hot and heavy in his case. He had carried the money from England and was getting used to taking it through customs. He knew the most difficult part was getting the packages back into England. He refused to worry any more about that. He had never been looked at whilst going through customs, let alone had anyone stop him. He treated Chuck with the respect he was due and the transaction went without hitch and was over in minutes.

They were getting used to each other. He had many packages to fit into his case and he just about managed to close the brief case. With a nod to each other, no words exchanged other than a grunt, Christopher left the motel room and returned by taxi to his hotel.

He spent the remaining evening in his hotel room, drinking whisky to celebrate a good weeks work and re-arranging the packages to fit between his clothes and papers in his various cases.

It was still so easy. A bit of him remembered Amanda saying she had judges and top policemen as her clients and he would be safe. He literally laughed all the way to the bank.

CHAPTER TWENTY FOUR

Over the next year, Christopher travelled back and forth to America. He was feeling more and more confident. The shows in Atlanta and Salt Lake City were fun. He had the technical crew to deal with siting the vehicles at each event, Karl Klingerman, working for HF was very good at his job and dealt with all the arrangements. Christopher had the arduous task of getting himself booked into a hotel nearby and attending the shows. Christopher's job was to talk to interested visitors about his beautiful cars and their customised features. He sold quite a few, and he hardly broke sweat. Karl and he were becoming good working colleagues. Christopher sold cars and young Karl ran around like a blue-assed fly getting everything organised. It was a good arrangement as far as Christopher was concerned.

Of course, the lovely Chuck was contacted on some of the visits. He bought and carried the packages on almost every alternate visit. Christopher always referred to the drugs as packages. He knew he was deluding himself, but he felt more comfortable not thinking about the lethal parcels. As he told himself whenever he had to think about those business transactions, he reconciled it by saying "Well, it's only a recreational drug, no worse than drinking whisky. It's not as if it was stuff that could kill you." If he said this to Amanda, she would always readily agree and tell him how sensible he was to realise the difference. She blamed the Government for making it necessary to buy the stuff in this clandestine way. Each preferred to forget how much money they were making out of this illegal racket. Amanda said it was best not to buy the stuff on every visit. She reassured him it was safe, but it would be silly for him to carry stuff so often. He was visiting America regularly and even alternative visits made him a cool £100,000. It helped to make him feel better about the drug thing. It had become normal to exchange one million dollars on each visit for the requisite packages.

Christopher had noticed that the packages had started to look different and there were fewer given for the money. Amanda told him not to worry it was just a design thing and prices had gone up so not so many packages for the money. Christopher was happy with that explanation and it would be much, much, later before he would question this again.

Each visit to America would last about 3 weeks to 5 weeks, depending on the show in question. He had noticed that all the shows were in the same area, something for which he was thankful. Atlanta was becoming the much-preferred place to be. There had been the odd shows in Las Vegas and Phoenix when the cars had been put on a truck and driven to the venues. This had been a 3-month showing that Christopher enjoyed very much. In the first year these visits were just practice runs for the eventual setting up of garages and cars in California. Davies-Clarke customised vehicles appeared to be a huge success in America.

Christopher loved the American trucks, they were the kings of the road. He was pleased to see the truck selected to take his cars to Las Vegas and Phoenix was a shiny red and chrome model. He arranged to be a passenger in the truck for a short ride on the highway so he could experience travelling in one of those magnificent beasts. He was a big fan and showed respect to the driver, whose agility in getting into the cab was astounding, considering he was carrying a stomach that defied gravity. Christopher noted Art, for that was the drivers name, was wearing outrageously tight trousers for his size. Trousers reigned his solid, prominent, stomach in with only one small button holding the ensemble together. Each exhale of breath pushed the waistband and this little button to the extremes of resistance. In conversation with Art outside his truck, Christopher was obsessed with watching the button fighting to hold together Arts options of decency or prison (the American laws on exposing oneself was very strict in most States). Christopher had to stop looking because Art was getting suspicious and had begun thinking Christopher was a fag or something. Christopher came to the conclusion that America had everything that was bigger and better and that included stronger cotton and buttons. He would have laid odds that one more breath and the button would have hurled itself away from the trousers leaving Art to hang on to his modesty.

Phoenix had been good and he stayed in Scotsdale, a

very upmarket town and one he had been to before. Scotsdale is just outside Phoenix and is home to some very wealthy corporations. It has its own airfield for private planes to come in and out for business meetings, golf, and corporate affairs. He sold 10 cars in Scotsdale. The Synphax Corporation took 6 for their Chief Executive and five top Directors. They were like children in a sweet shop. He watched them fiddle with all the accessories, argue about colour schemes, and fight over stereo systems and plead for that marvellous electronic hood system that was so smooth and quiet. They were not allowed convertibles because of security, all had to be bullet proof with tyres that could not be shot out. Christopher had dinner with them and they were very excited about when they would receive their cars. Christopher understood their pleasure in choosing a car. These were top business men who were used to the best, flew in private jets and stayed in the best hotels. *Boys and toys* was something he called it. Christopher had come to understand that the richest people in the world still got childish pleasure out of choosing their car and all the accessories to go inside it. He understood that being at the top of high finance was a sobering, responsible position. His cars, although sold as necessary protection with a corporate image, were also fun and could be adapted to make travelling everything a *boy could want*. Video games were an essential part of a Davies-Clarke interior and they had made it their business to get access to games before they hit the market place. It was also a Davies-Clarke guarantee that *"If you had a Davies-Clarke car with a video game system, all updated games would be sold to you before they reached the general marketplace.*" He was actually quite amazed at how many CEOs and millionaire bosses, often quite young, in their early 40's, found this exclusive access one of the most popular features. In the Corporate World of one-upmanship, Davies-Clarke cars with exclusive video games access was envied by those who did not have it.

It was the first time Christopher had been to Las Vegas. There was a 3 week show booked in the CarDrome Casino. The CarDrome was a new hotel on the strip that wanted unusual cars on display in their foyer. They said they would buy the Texas car from Davies-Clarke. They had seen it in Atlanta and, along with most prospective buyers, they showed a big interest. It was the most bizarre and fun car that Davies-Clarke had produced. It was so not English and stood out from the sophisticated vehicles on display. Christopher let it be known that he had designed this spectacular vehicle. He knew that he needed a fun car to catch the eye of the American market. It was never expected to be a vehicle commissioned for a customer but to everyone's surprise in Davies-Clarke, it was regularly ordered around the country.

This absurd vehicle was designed over a few glasses of wine with the help of a very merry and intoxicated Syd. What they came up with to start with was a Cadillac, for it had to be an American car. They painted the car in the dapple colours of cattle in America and put the biggest pair of steer horns on the front fender. The car horn played a choice of two sounds; the tune called

Land of the Free or alternatively, it sounded the call of a steer, at a volume that could be heard 2 blocks away. Christopher and Syd giggled at the thought that the warning horn could kill more people through heart failure at the shock than would be saved by the warning sound. The increasing number of drinks helped fuel their imagination and they let themselves get carried away with the interior of this machine. The seats were covered in the Stars and Stripes of the US flag. When the electronic hood was lowered the car played the last post and when the hood was raised it played reveille, all automatically and very loudly. When the prototype car was finished, Christopher and Syd spent far too long testing opening and closing of the hood with the appropriate loud bugle music. Christopher, who was enjoying himself immensely, was fortunate not to hear the mutterings from the factory floor. They had heard the bugle music one too many times that day and were more than willing to grab Christopher and stick the bugle music in a place the sun would not shine. Fortunately, as much fun as Christopher and Syd were having, they had to leave after a few hours, to everyone's relief.

Christopher and Syd had not stopped at the music, there was much more they wanted to do to the Cadillac. There were small Stars and Stripes flags attached to the wing mirrors and rear bumpers; something they thought the most patriotic of Americans would approve of. The state of art stereo system played all the latest country and western music, very loudly, of course. They added suede tassels, these were to hang as a fringe on the top of the windscreen, very tasteful they giggled. The boot of the Cadillac had a built in casing in the same spot you may usually find a spare wheel to house a pair of 4 bore shotguns and a bull whip. Christopher had wondered if it might look a bit more like an Indiana Jones type set up, but Syd, who was well into the design thought it was coming along just fine. When this design was put forward for James' approval, they were surprised to hear that after he stopped laughing, he gave Christopher the go ahead.

What had brought Christopher and Syd for the wonderful 3 week stay in Las Vegas was the loan of all the Davies-Clarke vehicles to show for the opening of the new Casino. The Texas car was on order but would take at least another 3 weeks before it would arrive at the CarDrome casino. Christophers 10 vehicles would be put on show with 50 cars of all kinds in the foyer and outside. The Casino organisers said Christopher could stay in the hotel, and although he must not actively sell cars, he could be there to hand out cards and answer any questions on the cars. Christopher brought Syd with him, partly as a treat, the chap had been invaluable at all venues, but also because he could answer any technical questions. Christopher found this site a challenge. When the hotel opened with the Casino fully operational, it was a 24 hour venue. After discussions with Syd, it was arranged that they would take turns on rota to keep the cars monitored from 8 a.m. – midnight. It was a long day but they both agreed it would be an experience to remember.

Christopher and Syd had two days in Las Vegas

before the hotel was officially opened. They had a wonderful time together. As drinking pals, they had lots in common and laughed at the same things. CarDrome was situated at the Luxor, Mandalay Hotel end of the strip. They were amazed at the size of the place. The food and drink was not expensive. They visited as many hotels as they could in two days but succeeded in only managing to visit about 5 hotels. There was too much to see and do in each. The Luxor with those anamotronic camels, and this hotel was in the shape of a pyramid, something they thought amazing. It had sphinx as high as the ceiling that made your neck ache to stare up at them. The casinos had banks upon banks of machines, more roulette tables, craps tables than Christopher had ever seen. They would spend hours looking and watching lounge shows of singers, all very professional, magicians on a small stage on the first floor of the casino. Christopher and Syd walked around this small part of Las Vegas with their mouths open. They had never experienced anywhere that had such ideas, such as a Pyramid shaped hotel, and a Hotel in the shape of the New York skyline, the ideas, the size, the razzmatazz, the hospitality, it was nearly too much to take in. They played the machines, and had fun losing, which was a first for both of them. They both agreed you could tell someone about Las Vegas but you had to be there to understand what it was really like. In his conversations with Neil later he would recall all the details of Las Vegas in an incredulous voice, "The MGM hotel and casino had fucking lions in it, can you believe that! Neil, get this, there was a river running through it and a restaurant that looked and sounded like the forest. It, it, was so huge. You've got to come over and see it, if you never see anything else Neil. It's amazing."

Neil would listen and see the excitement building as Christopher told him more and more. His mouth would get wetter and wetter until spittle was unsophisticatedly being projected in Neil's direction. Many times, whilst talking about this casino or that casino, Christopher would have to stop and get his handkerchief out and wipe his mouth. Neil was surprised to find Christopher so excited about a place as brash and tawdry as Las Vegas, but he laughed at the genuine excitement portrayed by Christopher. Christopher had never been this loud about anything before.

To this day, Christopher did not know what happened to him in Las Vegas. He was acting so out of character and was enjoying something, that previously, he would have emphatically said to anybody listening, that Las Vegas was the most tacky place on earth. He suspected he had been sucked in, chewed up and now reformed as a new person who embraced America. He loved the country, the wonderful breakfasts, the steaks, the vast country that changed from tropical to ice-cold weather, from southern hospitality to New York bad manners. He loved the size, the general friendliness of the people, the openness of the country and people, and the opportunities to earn a good living. The good humour of most people he met who seemed to prefer to think the best instead of the worst of situations. Over the year he had decided he wanted to live in America.

His choice would be Atlanta, he had fallen in love with the State of Georgia.

Over the year, he saw Jennifer frequently. In fact, she travelled to Las Vegas to be with him. For the first six months of his visits, he accompanied Jennifer to the many dinner invitations she received. He had enjoyed this, he was always sought out by other guests. He thought it was his height in the first place, then his Englishness. They all loved to hear him talk. He was very flattered by the attention and was by no means beguiled into thinking that he was, perhaps, an interesting person, he was a novelty, but that was o.k. by him.

One of his most memorable functions he escorted Jennifer to was at an Aids Charity dinner held in a magnificent white house very much in the colonial style with balconies and pillars. He saw the house and expected all the ladies to be dressed in those long voluminous dresses he associated with the film 'Gone with the Wind'. Of course, it was not like that. He met many famous people at these occasions, but found himself quite overawed when he was introduced to Elizabeth Taylor. He was not told she would be there, and was totally unprepared for a face-to-face meeting. He had been tapped gently on the shoulder and when he had turned round, Jennifer was introducing him to this icon, this vision, this Elizabeth Taylor. He had always liked Liz Taylor and seeing her close up, he thought her still the most beautiful woman in the world. To meet her in person was something that took his breath away and caused his tongue to stick rigidly to the roof of his mouth. She was very gracious and shook his hand and smiled at him. He thought she said something to him but his ears could hear noise but not the words. He was speechless, and for many weeks after would kick himself in mortification at the way he just stood in front of her ramrod still with only his head moving; he was just nodding at this beautiful woman like a man possessed. He closed his eyes at the excruciating thought that she must have thought him a totally stupid idiot. Jennifer had laughed at his embarrassment. She told him he would get used to meeting such people after a while. She added that Liz had thought him rather sweet. He had found this comment rather hard to bear as well. He did not think of himself as a *sweet* person, rather, he would have preferred a sophisticated, intelligent, amusing Englishman, but he glumly realised Liz, would never see him that way.

CHAPTER TWENTY FIVE

Jennifer was increasingly becoming the person he looked forward to seeing. She had taken him to so many parties and dinners during his many visits to America. After six months, the invitations were addressed to both of them. He had become part of her social life and he was happy with this situation. She was still his client and their relationship had stayed on the basis of a kiss on the cheek at the end of an evening. Christopher loved her lifestyle, her friends, her house and servants, and especially her garden. He hoped he did not seem too obvious, but on every visit to Jennifer's house, Christopher would make excuses to walk around the garden. It took nearly an hour to walk across the lawns, around the lake, into the shrubbery. The rose garden actually deserved much more time, and left to his own devices, Christopher could have spent an hour in this area alone with so many rose bushes, climbers, and miniature roses, the standard bushes were amazing and he had lots of questions he knew Jennifer would not have the answers for. He did have good manners and tried not to take advantage of Jennifer's goodwill. He was her guest after all, and was not there to spend his time wandering her wonderful garden alone. She would just laugh, and say how like her husband he was with regard to the garden. She did not talk much about him, but Christopher found out the garden was his domain and he could see the similarity. Jennifer would walk with him sometimes but did not want to talk about the advantages and disadvantages of horse manure over chemical fertilizers. Christopher realised women did not think about these things in the same way as men.

Jennifer and her home and social life was becoming his preferred life. He had the best of everything and he knew it. He had Amanda for the intense, tingling pleasure of sex, Jennifer for a social life that was far more exciting than anything in Norfolk. Jennifer was so much more though. He enjoyed the life of being waited on by servants in her household. He found her an amazing host and he enjoyed her intelligent, worldly conversations and her sense of humour. He realised a lot of his time was spent with the name of Jennifer never far from his mind. She was a client, as he kept telling himself, so he kept his fascination with her on a strictly friends only level. He was kidding himself, this relationship had been steadily growing, whether he wanted it to or not, and it could not stay on a friends only level for much longer.

For the past six months he had regularly diarised all parties and dinners he was attending with Jennifer. He had arrived in Atlanta early that morning, and after attending a short meeting early afternoon was preparing for a dinner party to be held at Jennifer's mansion. He always made an effort to look his best for Jenny. The valet returned his newly pressed evening suit together with his shoes, which had been cleaned to an impossible shine. After a shower and a good splash of Armani after shave, and cufflinks suitably straight, he was ready to leave for Jenny's place. He had found the dinner party details a little sketchy, something about six other guests, so just a small, intimate dinner party. He thought the others would be the Mitchells, Bernsteins, and the Harveys. All were good friends of Jennifer's and he liked them. He knew he was in for a good evening.

As was usual when a dinner party was held at Jennifer's, Christopher would arrive at 7 p.m, always an hour before the guests arrived to give Jennifer and Christopher a chance to talk and relax. He was not a guest in her eyes and she did not want him arriving as a guest. By the time 8 p.m. arrived both were relaxed and at ease, ready to greet their invited dinner companions. It was a mutually agreeable arrangement.

It had been quite a few years since Jennifer had a male companion to rely on, but she wondered if Christopher felt more than friendship for her, he was always attentive and kind and caring but just stopped short of real affection. She had always found him to be such a gentleman and being English to boot, she had assumed he would find it difficult to bridge the gap between friendship and lover. She had heard all about Alice, and although Christopher would never say anything deliciously nasty about her, she knew they did not have a marriage worth talking about. He was all the things a woman would want with the added spice of never quite knowing what was going on in his head. She presumed this was an English thing, but it gave her something to unfurl, to open up, to delve and to discover. This sort of closed book intrigue was something she had never found in an American man. Her quiet times alone had been spent thinking about him, about how handsome and tall he was, how he carried himself like a movie star, back straight and head held high. She had watched him in company and loved his manner. He was always a real gentleman and he could be so, funny, kind and discreet. What was really endearing to her was that although he appeared worldly, he seemed not to have a clue about real women, she found this very sexy and so sweet. She found most things about him charming and agreeable and liked the way it made her feel like a school girl again and she wanted more. She had wanted him for a long time and now she had decided she was going to have him.

Christopher arrived promptly at 7 p.m. without a clue of what was about to unfold. Jennifer opened the door to him. This was unusual, he expected Cameron, the butler to do this, but he gave it a momentary thought and followed Jennifer to the lounge where he accepted the prepared whisky from her. Jennifer would invite him to follow her as she led him to the terrace. Each time he arrived for a dinner party, she would lead him out onto the terrace, weather permitting, and they would look across the lawns to the lake. It was a beautiful night with only a breath of a breeze to disturb the trees. He sighed in a relaxed, *this is as good as it gets,* way. He so loved Jennifer's gardens; he had to put them in the plural because no one garden could be so big, so varied, so utterly beautiful. Jennifer watched him. She knew that his first love was her gardens, she had seen the way he always made every excuse to be in the garden and relaxed as soon as he got there. She hoped if she could not be his first love, she could become his second, after all, as she would say, she and the garden came as a package. His love of nature was something she found rather beautiful.

They stood looking across the lawns and talked about this and that, light and simple conversations. She broke a comfortable silence and told him she had spoken that day to the gardeners and asked for Bird of Paradise shrubs to be planted near the house and a bed was being prepared to the right of the house, in front of the small shrubbery area. She pointed out the bed for him to see, it was at present quite empty. He did not remember a bed there and Jennifer said it had been prepared especially for him and his plants. She knew Bird of Paradise flowers were one of his favourites. He was enthralled by the shape and colours of this flower that did, indeed, look like a bird with blue body and red head. It was something he had never seen grown in England, and he had presumed this most delicate flower would not grow in such a wet and cold climate. He was truly touched that she would do such a lovely thing for him. Overcome with warm feelings, he looked at her, and in an uncontrolled moment, he hesitantly moved a millimetre towards her. Somehow he stopped himself before he got too embarrassingly close to her lips and instead, breathed in deeply, pulled himself up to his true height and thanked her with a smile. She had turned her face up to him as she sensed he was tempted to kiss her, she managed to smile as he changed his mind and turned away. She was always one for a challenge and grinned to herself at his coyness. She thought with an impish glee, he was in for a surprise tonight.

As ever, the hour in the garden passed far too quickly. Jennifer quickly checked her watch and saw it was just past 8 p.m. She suggested to Christopher that they might make their way to the dining room. Christopher found this strange. Cameron would always be the person to trigger their entry back into the house when the first guests arrived. He wondered if, perhaps, Cameron was on holiday, then promptly forgot his puzzlement and followed Jennifer through the French doors and into the dining room.

The lights were low and the candles on the table unlit. He stood and watched as Jennifer picked up the matches on the side table and lit the two candelabras on the table. With all six candles lit, the table was beautifully illuminated and he realised the table settings were for two people only. He was actually quite bemused and a little scared, and quite honestly did not know how to react. She took command of the situation and told him the dinner was a surprise for him as her way of saying thank you for all his help in being her escort to so many occasions. She told him quite candidly, she would not have wanted to go with anyone else. She would always be grateful for the way fate brought them together. She hoped he felt it was enjoyable for him. He nodded in agreement. He felt quite relieved to know what all this was about. They had a comfortable dinner of Steak, salad and new potatoes and some hash browns. She knew what he liked and made sure all his favourites were on the menu. They finished with a sumptuous cheese cake, the likes of which Christopher often said could only be found in America. They drank white wine, which although not correct to have with steak, was once again, something Christopher preferred. The meal was very pleasant indeed. They joked about silly things, chatted about this and that, all very simple, and all very pleasant.

Still laughing, Jennifer led Christopher to the lounge where the coffee was waiting for them. She liked to see a man smoke and she encouraged Christopher to light up while she poured them both a coffee. She explained that the staff had all been given the night off so she and Christopher could, for once, have a little time to themselves. She sat down very close to him and handed him his coffee. He certainly wasn't that stupid, he did realise this was a strange turn of events. As yet, he still wasn't sure how this would proceed. All he was sure of was he felt uncomfortable, out of sorts and not in control of this situation; something he told himself a good salesman never was.

When the coffee was finished Jennifer took both cups and put them on the table by the door. She turned and looked at Christopher sitting with his bow tie undone as she suggested and looking very relaxed. How stunningly handsome he looked. His long arms outstretched across the back of the settee. She wanted to see his chest, to kiss his chest, to run her fingers through his hair. The build up to this evening had taken its toll and she could barely control her lustful feelings. When she sat down beside him he was surprised and quite stunned when she took his head in both her hands and kissed him full on the lips. Before he could say anything she became quite frenzied and breathless and in words punctuated by kisses planted all over his face and neck, she told him of her love for him, of her lust for him and she would have him now. As she continued, she started to undo his shirt buttons, take off his jacket and anything else within reach, she promised him it would be the best night he would ever have.

Shocked and totally unprepared, Christopher's mind exploded into overtime and he tried to consider his options, as if he could think clearly under these circumstances. His mind shouted "Oh my God! She's a client. This is not right. What do I do?" If he did go along with this, what would be the outcome? How would it affect business? What if he stopped her now? Oh my God! He knew she would never forgive him and there would be no business, and no her. He loved being her escort but whatever happened now, it would never be the same again.

He was scared witless and felt totally out of control. She had by now started to undo his belt and he knew his trousers would go next. He couldn't believe this pocket sized woman was doing this to him. As she caressed all the areas she accessed, he found his body was responding and decided that perhaps it would be best to go forward in this direction.

The sex was frenzied, uncoordinated, and dreadful. It was over quite quickly. He had known much, much better. It actually left him feeling a little dirty and he thought he knew maybe a little of what it was like for a woman to be raped. Jennifer seemed happy with the outcome, she lay in his arms panting with pleasure and exertion. She suggested they make their way to her bed, but he just wanted to get away from this situation and to go back to his hotel where he would feel safe. He told her, in quite a formal manner that he thought it was not right to stay the night under these circumstances and perhaps they should talk in the morning. She could not read him, and didn't know how he felt about her, she didn't want to ask now. They both felt a little embarrassed, and after a short recovery time, Christopher dressed, thanked Jennifer for a lovely evening, and returned to his hotel. He left her feeling quite confused by his *oh so* correct attitude. She presumed it was English etiquette to thank a person for sex. She thought that rather curious.

He tossed and turned all night trying to decide what he thought about all this, and what the hell he was going to do about it. He knew that as sure as eggs is eggs, something would have to be done but he didn't know what. He wished with all his heart this had never happened, that she had never thought of him in that way. He couldn't sleep and smoked more cigarettes than ever. He ran out of whisky quite quickly. He thought distractedly that he would ring the hotel reception to ensure more whisky was put in the fridge the next morning.

She slept very little. Toe curling embarrassment played a huge part in her lack of sleep. She hit her pillow, cursing herself for putting herself in such an awkward position. It was obvious to her he did not have the same feelings for her. She loved to have him as her escort and she had blown that right out of the window. She thought it highly unlikely he would go within a mile of her. She had felt frustrated before, why now did she take this huge and none retractable step and thrown herself at Christopher. As an intelligent, controlled and contained woman, how had this happened? She cried herself to sleep in the early light of morning.

Next morning both felt more in control of their feelings. Jennifer rose, red eyed at 8 a.m. with only 2 hours sleep. Christopher rose at 7 a.m. with 3 hours sleep. By the time breakfast was over both had made decisions that put them firmly back in control of their lives. Jennifer was the first to make the telephone call to Christopher asking him to meet her for lunch. She suggested a lunch in the garden would give them the privacy they both would need. Christopher happily agreed and asked her if she was o.k. She thanked him for asking and said she was. He confirmed he would be with her at the time suggested of 1.30 p.m that day.

He arrived with confidence at Jennifer's home. Cameron answered the door and led Christopher into the garden and pointed to where Jennifer was sitting. Christopher thanked him and watched Cameron return to the house. Christopher walked down towards the lake, which took a few minutes to reach, giving him time to collect his nerve, for he had come to the conclusion that he had acted dishonourably and cowardly last night. He had run away and left Jennifer thinking goodness knows what. He discovered in the early hours of the morning that he cared about her and was very worried that his cowardly reaction would have given a strong message that he did not want her.

A table had been laid by the edge of the lake. As he got a little closer, Christopher could see the table was covered with salads, bread, and place settings for two. A wine bucket with a bottle of white chilling in it was beside the table ready for pouring. Although the day was warm, it was overcast giving the setting a bleak and cold look. Jennifer was seated and waiting for him, she was looking across the lake to the trees in the distance with a far away air about her. He thought she looked rather forlorn and he couldn't have that.

He strode down to the water edge and grabbed Jennifer in his arms and kissed her. He knew it must have looked very much like a Mills & Boon scenario but he had decided that after last night, he had to make a statement. He had left her with nothing but embarrassment and humiliation last night, today, he had decided, he would make it up to her as best he could.

She had waited for him with some trepidation. She was going to make light of what had happened, she thought about telling him she had a brain storm, that she had drunk too much, that the moon was full and it always had that sort of effect on her. Of course she could not be that flippant and so she was going to just play it straight and apologise for misreading his signals, she really thought he felt the same. It would hurt her greatly to have to say that, such a loss of face would be quite unbearable, but she decided to be honest and hopefully, that would help clear the air between them. She didn't feel very confident and knew it was all going to be embarrassingly awful. To that end, she had steeled herself accordingly. He had gently but firmly pulled her out of her seat and kissed her in a lingering passionate embrace, and when he released her, she just looked at him, breathless and speechless. She had thought of all the possible ways he might react today, but this was one scenario she hadn't rehearsed and she was left not knowing what to say or do.

As she struggled to find the words to break this vacuum of incredibility, he took her hand and made her sit again. Grateful to sit down as she was decidedly confused, she did as he required and waited. After all her agonising, she now had the relief of just waiting for him to say something. She watched intently as his face contorted with many thoughts and she watched his struggle to say something meaningful.

Christopher had decided on the tone and content of what he was going to say. It wasn't as if he hadn't bothered. He had spent the morning preparing how to say it succinctly. He intended to put this situation right and leave Jennifer in no doubt as to his intentions. The problem was, he had not planned his opening gambit. It was important he got it right and started correctly to gain her confidence. She was looking up at him expectantly and it was putting him off.

This had to work. His stupidity, his cowardice in leaving last night had jeopardised something that was becoming a very important part of his life. In fact, his relationship with Jennifer was the one honest partnership he had. Amanda was Amanda, no more than a wonderfully pleasant distraction in his life. What else could you say about her, she was a prostitute, a drug dealer and an altogether very naughty girl. His relationship with Alice was far from honest. He had never said an honest word to Alice but their relationship worked in a mechanical fashion. Jennifer was as near as he would get to a proper relationship. They talked, laughed, and liked each other. If he were worried about any aspects of business he found himself able to discuss it with her, something he rarely did with anyone. She would listen intelligently to him, something he very much appreciated. He admired her for many reasons, she was honest, always up front, diplomatic and intelligent, as well as being a rich, worldly beautiful woman.

Honesty was needed now but it would be tempered with a realistic amount of necessary white lies. He cleared his throat and told Jennifer he loved her. He added that he had always loved her from the first moment when she walked down the staircase in that sequinned dress. She raised an eyebrow at that comment but was pleased he remembered the dress. He told her how sorry he was for his behaviour last night. Jennifer looked away at that comment, and he sensed her deep embarrassment. He took her hand and made her look at him. He looked into her eyes and wrinkled his forehead as he again apologised and then proceeded to take the blame for everything that happened last night. He was so convincing that even she nearly believed he had made the first move. He gave a wonderful display of sorrow and asked again for her forgiveness. He explained he had wanted her since their first meeting. He thought last nights charming surprise of an intimate dinner was too much for him to bear and it caused him to lose his self-control. He confessed how he was mesmerised by her looks, her body, and her mind.

She understood quickly what he was doing and how he wanted to save her from any embarrassment. He was being her knight in shining armour, saving a damsel in distress, she being the damsel and he saving her from distress. Jennifer loved him from that moment.

Christopher could see this had worked. In truth, he really could not bear to lose her and hoped this ploy, would help her save face and allow them to start again on a more understanding footing. He kissed her and whispered a promise that next time would be so much better than last night. He had finished and with bated breath looked at her, waiting for her to say something.

She was much calmer than he was. Jennifer could see what he was doing and gratefully played along with his explanation of last night. It was readily agreed with nervous laughter that they would start again and next time there would be no misunderstandings. Christopher suggested that tonight she would be his guest. He invited her for an intimate late night supper to be held at his hotel. He added that they would require privacy so he hoped she would agree to meeting him in his room. She agreed and was quite breathless at the thought. He decided to order champagne and smoked salmon nibbles, both favourites of Jennifer's.

They enjoyed a pleasant lunch, each rather too excited to eat much. The tingling expectation of later made each blush and struggle to talk about mundane things. Christopher left to attend a meeting arranged that morning with one of his engineers. The Texas car had blown a gasket or some such thing and the part they needed to replace would not be delivered for two days. He would meet the engineer, Patrick, in the suite of garages he had rented on the outskirts of Atlanta City. There was a show tomorrow and The Texas Car was a firm favourite. They would decide between them if it could be towed to the show and displayed without having to mention it was faulty. It was by far the most popular car they exhibited. The Texas car was the one that stopped all visitors to events from passing the Davies-Clarke stand. Invariably, after playing with the Texas car, prospective buyers left the ridiculous and examined the sublime and more practical vehicles. Christopher was not asked to do very much now in America, so sorting out the Texas Car was the least he could do. His job now consisted of selling cars, and quite honestly, they sold themselves. Life was getting easier and easier.

He was expecting Jennifer at 8.30 p.m. It was 8.15 p.m. and he checked the trolley to ensure all was as it should be. The champagne was in the ice bucket and the two glasses had been wiped clean for the third time. A silver platter covered in stripped lettuce contained the little rolls of smoked salmon nestling on small but beautifully formed pieces of brown bread. There were two small plates and napkins ready. He made sure the trolley was positioned near the balcony so they could sit and enjoy the night air if they wished. He was nervous, but for the life of him he did not know why. Perhaps he liked her more than even he realised.

She arrived at exactly 8.30 p.m. With all the emotional turmoil of yesterday and today, she was quite tired but the excitement of what was to come kept her wide-awake and interested. She had never met anyone like him before. He had talked that afternoon in such a polite and correct manner and his invitation to join him in his room that night had been couched in such a gentlemanly way it had taken her breath away. She found it a huge turn on.

The evening was fun. They sat and chatted and laughed on the balcony drinking two bottles of champagne and finishing the smoked salmon. At 10 p.m. Christopher took Jennifer by the hand and kissed it gently, then he led her towards the bed. He whispered in her ear, "Yesterday was a fiasco, but tonight darling, is going to be a triumph." He hadn't drunk any scotch that day but he felt a little heady. He picked up the remaining half bottle of champagne and she took the two glasses to the bedside with them so they could enjoy a glass afterwards.

Sitting here now, he remembered how wonderful that night was. He loved her more and more as time went on but the first night in his hotel was something else. His plans to stay in America started and finished with Jennifer. He wanted to be with her for the rest of his life.

She suggested not long after they became lovers that it was silly for him to stay in a hotel when he was in Atlanta. She asked him to share her home when he was in Atlanta. She had called him her lover, her escort, and her friend, so what could be more right than to be with her whenever he could? He did not need persuading. To have the love of an intelligent, beautiful woman, to share her fabulous house and those amazing gardens, then there was the servants, and that pampered lifestyle; it was something he had only dreamt of. Of course he said yes. For the next two years he stayed with Jennifer on his many trips to America. She became his sounding board and helped and advised him if asked. She introduced him to people that might be useful and generally helped him absorb into the American way of life.

He owed her much. She was his friend and he truly loved and admired her. She was well respected in Atlanta and knew all the top judges and law enforcement agents, which added to Christopher's feeling of being invincible. He was carrying larger amounts of drugs and money in and out of America. He felt so safe. What with the impregnated bags, Amanda's contacts in the police and now Jennifer's contacts, no one could touch him.

Here and now was reality. He ached badly and could not alleviate his intense back ache. His hands were tightly tied behind his back making every muscle in his shoulders and the tops of his arms hurt. He felt so uncomfortable it was getting harder to think. He knew he would go mad if he didn't take his mind away from this place.

Looking back now he could not believe how his life had been so easy. Everything he ever wanted fell into his lap. Of course he had great times, he remembered Amanda and how she made him feel, that was real enough. Jennifer was so good to be around. Her home felt like his home. He was comfortable, at ease, and had a life with her that was opulent. Davies-Clarke was successful and he was doing very nicely. He was making money hand over fist one way or another and his girls were doing well.

On paper he reckoned he looked good but in reality it felt as if he had lived his life in a bubble. He saw everything, and thought he felt everything but his life was a cruise where he visited but never stayed. Nothing had got through to him, he wondered if he really understood what he had done. Once again, looking back he could not understand how he had allowed himself to get sucked into the drugs thing. He was an intelligent man, or so he thought. A woman suggests he carries drugs for her, and like a tart, without hesitation, he says yes and makes a deal on how much he would make out of it. It was so easy now to say that was wrong, he shouldn't have gone down that road. He earned good money with Davies-Clarke, he was a good salesman, that should have been enough. He wondered if he had his time again if he would do things differently. He rued the day he met Amanda, none of this would have happened except for her. The involvement in drugs had led him into more trouble. All this, he raged, was Amanda's fault. His temper had made him feel hot again and the itchy, sticky feeling of sweat dripping down his back and chest was fighting with his aching back and shoulders, making him wish it was over now. He was so tired and feeling weepy again.

"What a way to go" he thought. "As a snivelling,

cringing, wimp". He reckoned he would rather have *smug bastard* as his epitaph than *wet wimp*. He had to go back to his memories and try and find something else to think about. He knew he had more integrity than his memories were telling him.

He got back to remembering Jennifer. He had lived with her for 6 months out of each of the two years they had been together. He realised that perhaps he had not appreciated just how easy his life was. He never had to think about his clothes, they were laid out for him and kept clean and ironed without him having to think about them. Jennifer had bought him items of clothing every now and then. He could not remember having thought about anything domestic for years. Alice did the same for him in England. The difference was he slept in the same bed as Jennifer and he certainly hadn't shared a bed with his wife for more years than he cared to remember.

He had become very comfortable with America over the years. America loved him. His deprecating sense of humour was considered very amusing and his company was sought at all the parties he and Jennifer were invited to. He had made many wealthy contacts through the dinner parties and events he was invited to, and this had helped his customised car sales go through the roof. He walked on cloud nine in America. Everything he touched earned him money. Even Chuck and he had an arrangement that was mutually rewarding. He gave Chuck money and Chuck gave him the little packets of powder. Over the years they had exchanged few words but Chuck had said if he needed more packets and had more money, he could supply him. This snippet of information was stored in Christopher's brain under *so what*. He had no intention of doing anything other than what Amanda had told him to do.

Thinking back now, he could not remember much about anything because it all ran as slick as butter. He would arrive at Jennifer's, a meal would be served, his cases unpacked and anything creased ironed. Cameron kept a check on his diary and informed him of where he was going the next day. Pamela in England rang him regularly with reminders of phone calls to make and people to see.

Jennifer was available to him as and when he wanted her. She didn't make many demands of him but was always delighted with his advances. He had talked to her about Alice and their relationship. He explained to Jennifer that he would never desert Alice and his girls. He would remain married to her and maintain the façade of a married life. He told Jennifer he owed her that much. Jennifer was not jealous of Alice at all. In fact, she had the best of him, she knew Christopher loved her and wanted to be with her so it was no big deal that he remained married to Alice. Once again, it was all so easy, he was being spoon fed cake and eating it. Jennifer demanded so little of him yet shared everything with him. Of course, he was grateful, he told himself, but in reality, he just took it all for granted.

The only area he remembered in great detail was the garden. He remembered when the summers had been so long and hot that the lawns were losing their greenness. He had conversations with the gardeners and arranged for sprinkler systems to be installed to water the lawns during the evening and early morning. He also arranged for lawn fertiliser to be bought. He even brought a sample of the one he used on his lawns in England for the gardeners to look at. He took a great interest in their compost heaps and what they mixed in it and when they spread it on the gardens. He arranged with the gardeners to get a tree surgeon to inspect the American Oak trees, conifers and redwoods, he thought they needed some attention. He noted some of the branches were dead and some trees needed culling and saplings needed to replace the old trees.

The lake needed dredging, he thought there was too much weed in it and it was choking other oxygen making water plants. There was not enough fish and he organised the restocking of the lake with trout. He watched with delight the growth of the Bird of Paradise shrubs and how the flower, very small at first, bloomed into the beautiful and big flower imitation of a bird. He introduced rhododendrons into the area near the forest. He found approximately 6 different colours and varieties. They were growing but it would take many years for them to establish. He had spent many days over the years with rolled up sleeves digging holes for plants or helping to prune some of the shrubbery. He remembered how he loved Atlanta after it had been raining. Everything was very aromatic and smelt of leaf mould. He would stand and look at the gardens, so lush and green after a rain fall. Then there was autumn, when the leaves turned golden and fell, creating a carpet of gold. The gardeners were kept very busy throughout the year, planting, pruning, and then cleaning up in the fall.

Looking out across the gardens from the terrace, he often thought that although it was not quite Constable country, it did resembled very clearly those paintings of great English country houses with magnificent gardens. Jennifer's home felt more like England than England. He remembered now how Jennifer teased him about his love of the gardens and how he loved them more than he loved her. He wondered if there was not just a little truth in that. But of course, he loved her. "You couldn't make love to a garden for Christ's sake!" He would tell himself.

Looking back now, it seemed to him that the only area he remembered in fine detail was the gardens. He had visited many places, clinched many lucrative deals, had many, many great times with Jennifer but he could not remember minute details like he could about the gardens. He wondered why that was.

He was spending on average two months in America and then returning home for a couple of months. When he returned to England Alice, Amanda, and James treated him like the hero returning from the wars. Although the novelty of his return to England had never worn off, his visits were as short as possible. The only place he wanted to be was with Jennifer in America.

On his return visits to the office, Christopher was to find that he was now the blue-eyed boy of Davies-Clarke. James wanted to hear more and more about what was happening in America. They had sold so many cars that the American factory, opened hastily to cope with the surge of new orders, was hard pressed to keep up with the demand. The English factory tried to help out, but at such a distance, James was looking to expand further. Christopher was earning bonuses he had previously only dreamed of. James gave him a £25,000 *well done and thank you* bonus at the end of the second year to mark his appreciation for a successful opportunity being realised. He had, by the end of the second year, several million pounds in his off shore account. He spent very little these days. Now he was staying with Jennifer he put everything he spent in America down to expenses and James sanctioned this without a murmur. Of course, James knew all about Jennifer and how Christopher stayed with her and not in a hotel when in Atlanta City. He kept this information to himself and would not tell even his son Neil for fear of Alice finding out. He did, however, rib Christopher intensely over his ménage à trois.

Alice was blissfully unaware of Christopher's arrangements in America. Alice was very happy indeed with her life. She thought everything was as near perfect as any person could hope for. She would count her blessings often, verbally and especially in company. When at any one of her considerable amount of charitable duties, she would tell other members how lucky life had been to her. She would say that not only had she two beautiful, gifted, and charming children, but a loving husband who worked hard in a very prestigious field of work.

Irritated, Christopher never understood why his visits home always seemed to coincide with Alice's rich, bitch, cronies from one of her committee things or such like, arriving at the front door. Audrey

Milton-Green was the most monstrous of women, according to Christopher. It was always her that interrupted his quiet drink with an apologetic and embarrassed, "Hi, I'm sorry Christopher, took a wrong turning to the bathroom/kitchen/garden". She would stay far too close to him and ask him things like how was he, and what he was doing in America. It always felt to him she was asking a totally different intimate question. His manners kept him civil, but his blood pressure would rise by the nano second. He practically had to push her in the direction of the bathroom. He always promised himself a lock for the study door but that little chore would be forgotten on his return to America. He complained to Alice and she soothingly promised to keep them out of his way. Alice took much pleasure in the jealous gossip of how handsome her husband was. Yes, her life was near perfect. There was just one little area that would make her life so very, very, perfect and she was working on that. But for now, she happily spent money like it was going out of fashion. She was the only person using Christopher's cheque book, and there was room for only one user. Christopher was amazed at the amount of money she could get through. Fortunately, he could afford it and the only brake he put on her spending was to forget to tell her about half of his bonuses and commissions he received which he had transferred to a separate account in his name only.

Pamela started her working life at Davies-Clarke Plc as a junior copy typist and rose through the ranks to become secretary to the top sales people. She had started about the same time as Christopher, in fact they had made tea together on more than one occasion. As the years passed and Christopher started to grow in his job, Pamela became his unofficial helper and typist at a time when he was not allowed the use of either. It was at her suggestion that he asked for his own secretary but the best he could achieve was the use of Pamela in conjunction with other sales staff. It was not many more years before he had Pamela to himself, only James had a secretary of his own. There was nothing she did not know about Davies-Clarke and was a most skilled, intelligent secretary who knew everything about all the staff and clients. Their alliance was built over many years. She loved him and he found her the best confidential secretary anyone could have.

Pamela was middle-aged in experience, dress and life-style with a teenage crush on Christopher. Pamela was working class with higher aspirations. She was known as a "right cow" to those who crossed her at work, and a "joke" by most who saw her fawning over Christopher. Pamela was married to Darren, a Carpenter who left College with high ideals and a City and Guilds Certificate. Over the years he earned fair money, enough for holidays in Spain and a mortgage to buy their Council House in Ilford, the first in both their families to own their own home. Pamela's standing in her family was high, she was well off, had a husband who worked for himself and a new car every 3 years. The fact they had no children was put down to Pamela's high flying career. Pamela knew different but would never tell anyone. She had everything except passion and excitement.

Christopher was her James Bond, her illicit, unattainable, love god. She wanted to stay married to Darren, he might be boring but was always dependable. She wanted her lifestyle, perceived by the neighbours and family as rather grand, but her imaginary love-affair would stay as a fantasy – she had thought about it and decided it would be far less messy and disagreeable than a real love affair. Her imagination made her fantasy more satisfying and fulfilling than any real thing she might have experienced in the past.

Her imagination was fired by everything that Christopher did, a look, a whispered confidential tit bit of information, an intense thank you was all that was needed. Pamela could fill in the gaps, a thank you was *"I want you now but can't have you"*, a look could mean volumes of suppressed longing. She drank in his little schemes, thinking him clever, and so scheming in a gorgeous, wonderful way. Christopher fed her need to feel sexy and desirable. As long as she could feed her safe, private fantasy, she had everything she could want in life.

Her loyalty to Mr Cross was non-negotiable, and she knew he really appreciated it. They were Anthony and Cleopatra and she was certain he felt the same. Their unspoken love was perfect and pure. Unbeknown to Christopher, he had made Pamela the happiest woman in the world.

Christopher never fully appreciated her, but he did understand he could not survive without her. He knew she was his for the taking which he felt amusing but not something he would ever consider, she was not his type at all. Pamela, Confidential Personal Assistant, was his eyes and ears whilst he was out of the country, and she would tell him anything she picked up in gossip at Davies-Clarke. He liked to hear how all the other salesmen were of envious of him. She made him laugh with her impersonations of the bitchy secretaries who said he had just got lucky in America. Pamela kept an eye on everything in the office for Christopher. If she thought anything was happening that Mr Cross should know about, she would let him know immediately. She had his mobile number and the telephone and fax number at Jennifer's house. She did not know exactly who Jennifer was but she put two and two together and bingo! It made four.

The one she could not place was Amanda. On occasions, Amanda had phoned Pamela asking for a number to contact Christopher. Sometimes his mobile did not respond and she needed another number urgently to contact him. Of course, Pamela would never give out a number. What she would do, was telephone Mr Cross and pass on the message for him to ring Amanda. She wondered many times who that sexy sounding woman with the upper class accent was. She suspected that Amanda might be a girlfriend of Mr Cross. Pamela had always thought him so gorgeous and sexy, it seemed quite likely to her that he would have a girl in every port, so to speak. She was actually confusing Christopher Cross with James Bond but it made her days more interesting.

Of course Pamela knew who Alice was. Mr Cross had given her strict instructions to tell him immediately if there were any messages from Alice. Christopher always ensured Alice, his wife, was treated with respect and he ensured everyone else did too. Pamela knew that they did not have a happy marriage. She had watched the same scenario many times: he would return from America and the last person he rushed to phone was his wife. Pamela knew this was not normal for a married couple. The first call he would make would be to someone who he was obviously doing some sort of business with. She knew it must be confidential because he would stop talking whenever she went into his office. She knew at some point he would tell her about it, because she was the only person he trusted. That always gave her a lot of satisfaction. The next call would be a long, confidential and loving conversation with someone who she absolutely knew was not his wife. Obviously she knew all about these calls because she had to go in and out of his office bringing him papers and such. She admitted to herself that she was a little curious, but listening to his calls was o.k. because she would never, ever repeat anything to anyone. It was just that everything he did was so interesting and sexy, it gave her a buzz she could get nowhere else.

Pamela had spoken quite a few times to Alice, although she had never had a proper conversation with her, always answering Alice's questions politely, like a good secretary should. She did get a good idea of what this woman was like. There was never any more than a "How are you Pamela?" and "Hope you are keeping well Pamela". Pamela knew she didn't want real answers to these questions and she had no liking or feeling for this woman. Pamela found her very hoity toity and much too grand to talk to the likes of her. Pamela wondered why on earth someone like Mr Cross had married her. She had seen her photo on Mr Cross's desk with the two girls and she certainly was not beautiful, in fact she looked rather fat, not Mr Cross's type at all.

Alice was always busy with the many committees she chaired and the organisations she worked for, but, as always, she was there waiting for him when he arrived home. As she would tell all her workers and committee members, "My husband and children must always come first in my life". She had acquired a reputation as a snob who tended to patronise the workers, but no one could fault her on her devotion to her hard working and by all accounts, incredibly handsome and successful husband.

She was in contact with Pamela from the office and ensured Pamela kept her up to date with the day and time he was returning home. He wished she wouldn't, but she had promised to always be there for him and whether he liked it or not, she kept her word. He would arrive home and find her waiting. The first thing she would do was to pour him a glass of whisky. He actually found that rather nice of her. He knew she used to disapprove of his drinking.

He would always take his drink and wander through his garden. Whatever the time of year there was always something new to inspect and enjoy. Alice allowed him his time in the garden. In the summer he would be out there for at least an hour before coming in to replenish his drink. Even in the winter, he would stay out there for at least half an hour. She thought him a silly billy for making such a fuss about the chickens and the vegetable plot because she could see he was at heart a farmer's son. She would never dare air her thoughts to him but anyone with half an eye could see he had replaced the farm with a garden. However much he said he hated farming, his heart would always be in the country.

The girls were often out when he arrived home. They were teenagers now and as such often stayed with friends. Alice encouraged the girls to stay weekends with their friends. As she would explain to Christopher on many occasions.

"The girls need to keep a broad base of friends and get to know their families because we have got to ensure their future. All those well-connected families will love our girls and the introductions will be so exciting. We have got to ensure they meet the right type of suitor in the years to come. Our little darlings must marry well, we owe it to them to help as much as possible, don't you agree Christopher?" He would nod his head, which pleased Alice, but it felt miserable to Christopher to think the girls were going to be married off to some rich, gormless, twits. He hoped the girls were developing a mind of their own and would rebel at their mother's attempt at arranged marriages.

What he had found over the years was the girls no longer wanted to walk with him over the dunes. They were young ladies now and spent their weekends playing tennis or going horse riding. They were becoming little Alices and so had more in common with their mother. When they were home he found them in the kitchen with Alice discussing parties and clothes and gossiping about this one and that one. They would giggle and tease their mother but she would smile and enjoy their teasing. She understood them, shared their little secrets and thoughts, and knew all about their friends and their family. They were growing into beautiful young women and wanted to do things that young women do. He understood very well why things were changing. They still loved him, and were always pleased to see him but he didn't understand their conversations anymore and was not on their wavelength. They would laugh indulgently at him and call him an old fashioned, silly daddy when he tried to understand about the latest fashion, or music, or boy they had met. It felt like they were dismissing him with a pat on the head and he understood that this was the way of things from now on. He was a little sad to see the young girls who liked to jump on his back, giggle at his jokes, and give him big, sloppy kisses disappear.

He could see times were changing and he had no right to be sorry about the way the girls were now closer to their mother than to him. For gods sake! He would tell himself, he was hardly ever at home so it was obvious they would be closer to their mother. She did everything for them, and was there to wipe their tears, advise them on what to do in girly situations, and those many areas of womanhood he knew nothing about. He might not approve of all the social climbing she did but he could see the girls were benefiting from it and enjoying it. As usual, he regretted not spending more time with the girls. It was too late now and not the time to get maudlin. He should have thought more about the girls before now. He realised you only get back what you put into a relationship. It was beginning to feel as if there was not much to keep him in England anymore.

Although she knew Christopher had never shown much interest in what she was doing, always calling it *"Just gossip,"* Alice ventured to talk about something that was becoming very dear to her heart. She had become a career volunteer. She could, she would tell her family with a little laugh, rival royalty with the amount of good works she had become involved with. With much huffing and puffing, she would say that it was nigh impossible to keep track of where she should be on any given day. What with a home to run, and her commitment to all her organisations she had no time to spare. She had confided that nothing happened as it should, with all her organisations unless she attended them in person. She didn't want to say she was indispensable, because, of course, she knew in all modesty that was not right, but, why oh why she would lament, could no one understand simple instructions and leave her to have some time to herself. She would joke that she needed a social secretary to organise her and her diary. Christopher, glumly, could see another member of staff being employed in the not too distant future.

Over a dinner for two, Alice told Christopher about her involvement in Neil's project. Christopher was surprised to hear about Alice's involvement. Apparently, Neil wanted to use Alice's expertise in setting up a committee to deal with the running of the project with Alice of course as Chairperson. Everyone who was anyone in Norfolk was aware of Alice's abilities in organising and motivating volunteers. She was also well known as Chairperson for most local and county wide charitable committees. There were mutterings about how pushy and bossy she was, and so regal, some wondered darkly, if they should curtsey or bow when they met her. She always said her skills were in planning and delegation. Those around her saw it more as her giving orders and sitting back whilst others did the work. Begrudgingly, those same people admitted that whatever she was involved in worked well, kept within the approved budget, and was successful.

According to Alice, Neil had thought her the only woman to consider for chair of his committee and had asked her to help with his project. Alice told Christopher that the only reason she agreed to take on this additional responsibility was because Neil was such a good friend of Christopher. She added, everyone knew how little spare time she had. She patted Christopher's hand and earnestly explained that she would do anything for him and if it helped his friend, she would willingly give up her precious spare time. He knew she was going over the top but still, he was impressed.

Christopher had never taken much notice of what Alice got up to until now. If Neil wanted to use her, then he figured she must be good at something. He congratulated her, which pleased her no end. At this point she started whispering, why, he had no idea, as no one else was present. He could see this was going to be a very big deal and so with elbows on the table, he made himself comfortable and listened. She told him, very modestly, about the noises various committees were making about her to the sort of people who put names forward for MBEs and such like. She could not help herself and started giggling like a schoolgirl and fidgeting in her chair. Once again, she whispered that her name was being put forward for an, and here she just mouthed the letters, MBE, in recognition of all her good works for charity. He let her ramble on and listened. It became clear to him that the idea for an MBE was undoubtedly hers, and she had coerced, bribed, blackmailed, or whatever women in these circumstances do, to get their names put forward for such honours.

He had begun to mellow towards her a little, and had been lulled into a false sense of her kindness to him. He realised, as she wittered on in a quite guileless way, that she was just the same, snobbish, social climber she had always been. She had never joined any committee for the good works part but more for the social standing and power it brought her. O.k., he knew he was no saint, but he never pretended to be something he was not. He felt no pride in her trying to get an MBE or such like. He hoped he had more integrity than she had.

Alice and the girls had built a very different life from his. He knew it would not be many more years before the girls left home, either married or perhaps to University. He could see that Alice would then go into overdrive on the Committee circuit. He wondered how much longer it would be before Alice decided their home in Winterton was not big enough for her social climbing. He could see her aiming for Charities in London and if this were the case, then a more magnificent home would be required. He wondered if the Queen was considering selling Buck House he reckoned Alice would be first in line to buy it. He was feeling more and more depressed.

Over the years, his mother had visited less and less. He knew that he wasn't in the country as often as she would have liked. She had, sarcastically, asked him why he hadn't considered an American passport because he spent more time there than in England. He had laughed at the time but noticed she stopped visiting him when he was in the country. He asked Alice if she heard from his mother. Alice cautiously said she hadn't. What Alice did not want to say was how the two women had spoken on the telephone some time back when Christopher was in America and how an argument of biblical proportions had developed.

Afterwards, Alice had got straight on the telephone to her mother, and in tears proceeded to tell her all about her conversation with Mrs Cross.

"That woman is the most selfish woman on God's earth! Never a word about her beautiful granddaughters, never any questions or interest in what I'm doing. You know mother, I work so hard to keep the good name of Cross in the forefront of Norfolk society, and is she at all grateful for all my work. Never! I know you are proud of me, so why isn't she. Whenever she phoned all she ever wanted to know was" (she mimicked Mrs Cross's voice) "where is Christopher and when was he coming home. I have been patient mother, you know I have, but I have been forced into telling her what a disgrace she is to the Cross family".

Alice's mother agreed with her daughter and made soothing noises. Alice, feeling a little calmer and less tearful continued in her injured tone.

"I know I shouldn't have said it mother, but you know it had to be said, and Christopher would never do it. I told her Christopher was ashamed at her lack of family commitment to us whilst he was away. That she was just as bad as Mr Cross and that awful other son of hers. She was very upset mother, but I was upset too, not that she cared. She said if that was how Christopher felt, she would never call again. What shall I say to Christopher?"

Alice began to cry at this point but her mother, who had grasped all the relevant points told her to stop crying immediately. She told her that Mrs Cross was not worth crying over and that part of the family was a disgrace. She thought her daughter so brave and forthright, not like the scheming, devious way the Cross family operates. She told Alice to say nothing to Christopher. She said if the mother doesn't telephone then he would never know. She also added that she could never, ever, not ring Alice to see how she was and how her beautiful granddaughters were. Alice's mother concluded that they were all just jealous because she was so successful and she would have to get used to this type of reaction. She had instilled in Alice the realisation that all successful people have this type of cross to bear. After reassuring Alice that her family loved and admired her, she realised that was all that mattered to her.

Alice's mother felt quite justified in advising her daughter, she had never liked the awful Cross woman and was secretly very pleased her nose had been put out of joint by her daughter. She was quite frightened of Christopher, he always seemed polite but distant in her presence, but she knew her daughter could handle him. Alice, comforted by her mother's true words, would continue as if nothing had happened and put Mrs Cross firmly to the back of her mind, in the full knowledge that she was a woman scorned by the treacherous Cross family.

Christopher was to remain blissfully ignorant of the family problems. He wouldn't think to ring his mother, there was so much else to organise. His life in England was also as slick as butter. He never really knew what was going on or recognised the undercurrents of family strife.

He kept in contact with Neil as best he could. Neil was very busy indeed these days and what with the shops, his Justice of the Peace work and now his Captain's Farm project, it was becoming increasingly difficult to make a time to meet. There had been many occasions when Christopher was in Norfolk that a distracted and pressurised Neil had apologised for cancelling dinner dates.

Sitting in this dark, damp place, Christopher finally realised the real reason he lost his head and allowed the madness that had led to this unexpected and filthy situation. It was a revelation to him and he wondered why he had never recognised it before. He ached badly and his hands felt numb. The rope tying his hands together seemed to have got tighter. The gnawing feeling that he had kept at bay all night came up and flooded his brain. He was desperate for a cigarette and a drink. He shook with the worst desperate feeling he had ever experienced. He hadn't had a cigarette or drink for what must be 24 hours. He wished they would come back now. Even a condemned man was allowed a cigarette, if they shot him then so be it, just so long as he had a cigarette first. God he needed one now, he couldn't think about anything else. The panic was rising but it had no where to go. His heart pounded and he wished it would just stop still and let him slip away from this misery. He was acting like a yellow bellied coward and that would not do. He fought to control himself, it had worked so far, going over his life had passed quite a bit of time and now he forced himself to think back to his meeting with Neil, to carry on with this unrealised story of his life. A life he had most certainly lived but never fully participated in.

Finally, after 4 months of last minute cancellations by Neil due to pressure of work, they met for dinner. Christopher, waited with a fresh whisky and cigarette, sitting back at a quiet table, relaxed and enjoying surveying the ambience of nondescript people enjoying conversations and meals in this comfortable, familiar restaurant. This was the Little Fish restaurant which was always the preferred choice of Christopher and Neil. The joke between the men had always been just how inopportune a name this was, no one remembered why it was called this, although it must have meant something once. The Little Fish restaurant was, in fact, primarily a steak bar with a token few fish dishes.

Christopher saw the door of the restaurant open violently with a bang as Neil arrived. He stood puffing and panting as he surveyed the restaurant for Christopher. Christopher studied Neil and watched his movements. He was amazed that Neil hadn't changed at all, maybe a little slimmer but no noticeable change. The only difference that Christopher noticed was the worry lines on his forehead that had arrived over the last 5 years were now deeper. Neil was 10 minutes late, Christopher had never known a time when Neil was late for anything. It had been a source of mild irritation over the years to go anywhere with Neil; he would worry and cajole Christopher to ensure that their arrival was early and they would have to wait often in an unimpressive waiting room for sometimes as much as 30 minutes. Christopher in a state of mind numbing boredom would try to hide his frustration as Neil would remind him that it was worth the wait to be considered a gentleman and always on time. Christopher wryly thought "Times were a changing".

Flustered, and apologising far too much, Neil greeted Christopher. Christopher watched as Neil disturbed the relaxed air of the restaurant by making more fuss than necessary in taking his coat off and settling himself into the seat opposite Christopher at their regular table. After blowing his nose, and taking a deep breath, the questions started and came thick and fast.

"How are you Christopher? Been here long? How are the girls? Saw Alice the other day, she is still working hard on that committee that does things for unmarried mothers or something."

Christopher noticed how as the questions were being shot at him, Neil kept looking at his watch as if Christopher's reply would be timed. It had a surreal quality that almost made Christopher smile. "This is your starter for 10 – How are the girls? I'm sorry, that was not the correct answer and we have run out of time- Give that man a cabbage". It was funny how childhood programmes suddenly pop into your head he had mused. 'Crackerjack' had been the favourite of all children all those years ago, but it had no place here.

Realising there was no reply, Neil stopped searching his pockets for his wallet and looked up at Christopher who sat looking at him with an amused look. Irritated, Neil wondered what on earth was the matter with him.

Christopher thought he was getting more like his father than the Captain. He had sat through many meals with James and was familiar with late arrivals, inappropriate fuss and disturbed meals. He smoked his cigarette with more determination.

Time was precious to Neil, goodness knows he filled his day from start to finish and this meal with Christopher cost him valuable time away from his projects. He had been looking forward to this meeting for days and he didn't want it wasted with silences when there was so much to catch up on, he could feel himself getting more annoyed with Christopher's belligerent demeanour. He had many invitations to dinner at various homes, he had found himself in demand over the last 5 years, certainly since his business, and his charity work had all become very successful. Christopher was never around long enough to know, but his time was very valuable and much sought after, he wanted to tell Christopher this but good manners just about won the day and he kept quiet.

Christopher could see Neil's irritation and was shocked. Both used their impeccable manners to hide any uncomfortable thoughts and feelings and they passed the evening away with pleasantries, thoughts from the past and once again, Christopher steered the conversation in Neil's direction. Neil spent many hours explaining his works as Justice of the Peace, how Bertrams was expanding and succeeding and finally, his pride and joy, the Captain's Farm.

Christopher had never found farm animals particularly charming or interesting, they were stupid, smelly, and messed everywhere. Neil's long explanation on the wonders of artificial insemination and its relevance to the Captain's Farm left him feeling rather sick and he picked at his food anxious to conclude a rather vulgar evening.

As Christopher drove home that night he felt unsettled, restless. On arriving home he headed for his study, poured a large whisky and sat in the Reddish brown leather Chesterfield Alice had purchased for him many years ago. She had told him it was a chunky, manly chair just right for a husband's study. He had argued at the time that it was not worth buying as he was away so often, he had muttered hadn't she got better things to waste his money on. As usual, Alice just laughed and called him "a silly billy" which annoyed the hell out of him. She had learned to laugh at his moaning and he had learned to keep quiet and let her do whatever she wanted. He had actually got very fond of his chair and had placed it in front of the french doors to the garden so he could look out and enjoy the view. Apart from a couple of cigarette burns on the arm, the chair still looked as good as new.

The house was calm, Alice was in her bedroom and the girls were away for the weekend with friends. He put on the outside lights and sat in the darkened study looking out to the artificially lit garden with shadows held back by the bright garden light mounted on the wall above the study window. Christopher took a long sip of Glennfidik, swallowing the smooth nectar slowly hanging on to the taste for as long as possible. It was the most wonderful drink and usually relaxed him making him feel all was right with the world. Tonight was different, he recalled the events of the evening and how he had so looked forward to meeting Neil, but even with his second glass of Scottish comfort, he could not stop the deep depression that was taking him over.

It was the next afternoon when he was sitting in his garden, alone with his cigarettes and a large whisky, that his confusion cleared and he wondered if he had ever been part of a life in Norfolk. His mother hadn't rung him for months, his wife had a climbing career in charities and her life revolved around the girls and their social lives, and none of them needed him for anything.

Neil was the real shock, he was so busy and successful and without Christopher's help which rather dented his ego. He had always known that Neil could never instigate anything without his knowledgeable input, but Neil had proved that was no longer true, he could manage very nicely thank you without him. Christopher felt very unsettled, a feeling he did not fully recognise. To be quite honest, he didn't like it at all. It was a disconcerting feeling, almost as if he was in an air bubble that didn't touch anyone else's life. He yearned for Jennifer and Atlanta, he was comfortable there, to be wanted, needed and valued suddenly seemed very important.

As was usual, when he was about to return to America, he would visit the London office and of course, visit Amanda. He still looked forward to visiting her, although the novelty of their sexual encounters had waned a little over the years, it was still relaxing and enjoyable and naughty Amanda still dared to do things that no self respecting woman would consider, he liked that. It had been a while since he last saw Amanda and that old feeling of anticipation that left him breathless and with a throbbing, heavy, tight pressure in his groin made his needs unbearable as he paced the room waiting for her. God he wanted her now, he was quite exhilarated by the pain and anticipated pleasure of the moment. He mopped his brow, he was sweating profusely.

He knew he had arrived unexpectedly but he was not prepared for rejection. Lucy quietly came into the room and whispered that unfortunately, Amanda was busy with a client at present. He was offered a drink if he cared to wait or if he preferred, he could return in maybe 3 hours when she would be free. It took all his willpower to keep his temper in check, which was boiling fast and furious, with restraint he didn't know he had, he thanked her as best he could and said he would return later. She eyed him warily, she could see that one wrong word or gesture from her would be enough to trigger something unpleasant. He left in a fit of ungraciousness but told the astonished girl that he would return later that night and warned her to be sure Amanda was available or else. Lucy smiled, promised to tell Amanda of his visit, and closed the door.

As the door closed behind him, his temper came back with a force that startled him. "After all these years, how dare she not be available to me". Incandescent with rage at this snub, his first reaction was to leave and never go back, but there was business, of course, he had to collect the money for the next batch of drugs to be brought back to England. He had come to rely on the money that this regular and easy courier service afforded him. He would not cut his nose off to spite his face, although he was close, very close to telling her to fucking stuff it all and then enjoy watching her squirm because she needed him as much as he needed her – the fucking bitch.

He was steadily getting drunk, having spent more hours than he should have in a bar around the corner from Amanda calming himself down with whisky shots and assessing why the hell he was being treated so badly by everyone. Ungrateful, fucking ungrateful is what he thought of Alice, she was nothing without his money. Neil was a fucking wimp, he was only who he was today because of Christopher. Amanda, the fucking whore, without him she would be just another cheap, street corner whore, not quite true, but he didn't care, that's how he felt so fuck her! England was becoming a dull, grey place to visit. America was bright, warm, fun, and people fucking respected him, it was the only place to live and Jennifer was the only person worth being with. He was angry alright, fucking angry. Even his girls didn't appreciate him, they had become just like their mother!

America and Jennifer was where he wanted to be but he had to be rich to live the good life there. Jennifer would not stay with "a has been" of that he was sure, and he did not want a life without her and he could not bear the thought she might see him as he really was. To her he was a successful, rich sophisticated English man and she loved him, but he was sure she loved the package and not just the man. But hey, he thought drunkenly, he was that man and the package was him also. He had decided many years before that money and lifestyle was what made him who he was, he could not bear to live without the trappings that money had given him. There had to be a way to live the good life in America, to stay for ever in America and leave England behind. When the anger left him, he realised he had, in fact, emotionally left England many years ago and his visits had been him just going through the motions. With a deep sadness he realised it was not his home anymore.

Amanda was there waiting for him when he arrived 3 hours later, swaying with nearly a bottle of whisky in him. In an alcoholic haze, Christopher enjoyed a subdued evening with Amanda, unable to focus or think straight, his performance was rehearsal standard and neither wanted to remember it as anything memorable. She made him stay the night in a spare room so he could sleep off the booze, she didn't want to give him the £100,000 he needed for the next collection while he was so drunk. This was a small collection, but £100,000 was still £100,000. The amounts of money varied, it was thought safer and easier. It was thought prudent that £1,000,000 was not couriered regularly in case he was followed by a lowlife who had got wind of the sums exchanged. Christopher thought this strange because surely he would say, £100,000 was worth mugging him for. Amanda had laughed at him and said her contacts had told her no one would think it worth getting on the wrong side of them for a measly £100,000. He tried to follow that by asking who they were. Amanda never would tell him, saying it was best he did not get involved in that side of things. She inferred that they were dangerous men to know and frightened Christopher enough to stop him asking any questions. Of course over the years he had thought about what type of people were behind the drug collections but came to the conclusion it was maybe safer for him not to know. He reckoned that as long as he got his money, it was far preferable just to deal with Amanda. He could convince himself that really he was not doing anything that wrong, that with just Amanda as his contact it was a personal thing really and that Chuck, his contact in America, was just a person he did not have to meet or talk to socially. Over the years Christopher had built up a nice, cosy excuse for his drug collection, something he found easy to live with and something he did not lose sleep over, he took his money and invested it with quite a clear conscience.

It would take another year before any real plans were put in place. His visits to England were shorter and his visits to Atlanta were longer. He became preoccupied with money. He constantly checked his accounts, worked out what he was spending per year, what he would need to last him for the rest of his life, and if he could invest it elsewhere to maximise return. He became obsessed to the point where Jennifer sat him down and asked if he had money problems. Until then he had not realised how his obsession had started to interfere with his day to day life.

On the scale of a Doctor's life style, Jennifer would be considered a rich woman in her own right. Her home and the land surrounding her home made it worth $4,000,000 alone. Her husband had bought it when land prices around Atlanta were still reasonable for a millionaire, since then, Atlanta had become so much more prestigious and house and land prices had risen dramatically. It would be fair to say that Jennifer would never have to compromise her standard of living. She could afford the gardeners, cleaners and maids together with the obligatory English Butler and chauffeur. She did budget for her cars and since her husband's death, sold most of the vehicles that took up room in the bank of garages to the side of the house. She had surmised that cars were a man's thing and therefore she only needed four cars instead of the 50 assorted vehicles her husband had spent so many hours admiring and driving. She found it quite amusing that the only man she had seriously considered as a partner dealt in cars.

Poor she would never be, but her extravagant lifestyle which included the latest in fashionable clothes, perfumes, her hair, jewellery, make-up, holidays with friends in exotic places, travel, parties, all cost. A woman in her late 40's was high maintenance work if she wanted to delay ageing and improve her looks, maintain the ideal size 8 figure, and consolidate a position in the right circles. All in all, and known only to herself and her accountant, was the fact that Jennifer was just about maintaining her standard of living and subject to a recession, war or stockmarket crash, she should survive and carry on with the lifestyle she demanded. She did not earn the sort of money to keep her in the style she was accustomed to. She was well aware that her money would not carry two people.

When she met Christopher she was delighted and charmed by him and quickly fell head over heels in love with him. One of the first things about him she was pleased to note was he had money in his own right, maybe not quite old money but he was not a brassy get rich quick type. For her this was essential on all levels. In the circles she mixed with any companion must be able to meet the criteria of being financially sound. It would have been so embarrassing and such a social black mark to be seen around town with a partner who was not of the same financial status as yourself, it was akin to a consort who was ridiculously younger than yourself, that only worked for men, never women. Her husband had come from old English money and that was considered very classy indeed. There were no class wars in America but sure as hell money class was important.

Christopher picked this one up quite quickly and made it known to anyone who seemed remotely interested that he was not only an English gentleman, which was impressive in its own right, but a rich one to boot! She also hoped that not only was Christopher rich enough to be considered favourably by everyone as a suitable partner for her, but that he would help with maintaining the house and gardens. With more money she would love to buy breeding horses and convert some of the garages into a stable area. Then of course, there was the yacht. She wanted a yacht to entertain her friends on. She had been the guest of many yacht owners over the years and had developed quite a taste for the high life only a yacht can bring. All in all, Jennifer counted her lucky stars to be loved by and have fallen in love with someone who was perfect on all counts. She could see that they would make a wonderful partnership and raise the profile of their social standing higher than it had been when her husband was alive. With his money and her style, they would be the envy of their entire social circle.

Jennifer found it odd that the happier she had become with Christopher the more she thought about her dead husband. He had died far too young of a heart attack. Their social standing had been rising quickly since they had bought the house and settled in Atlanta. She remembered the parties they held with congressmen, actors and actresses and church leaders. Those were the happiest days of her life. They had everything, youth, looks, money and they knew and were known by everyone who was worth knowing in the whole of Atlanta and Washington state counties. Then suddenly it all stopped with his body found at the bottom of the pool. He went for his usual morning swim and did not return and suddenly her life had changed forever.

She felt they were about to launch themselves further and higher in society. His motto had been move up, consolidate, move up again until you reach the top. The top of course being top of the "A" list on everyone's schedule but she knew the top meant being made Ambassador of England. It has been her fervent wish too. She thought they were half way there and all the plans, hopes, dreams, and the child they were talking about having faded into nothing.

For the first two years Jennifer did not venture out and refused all invitations to functions, did not receive visitors, and became a recluse. She loved her husband, he was strong and it was his hopes and dreams that carried them along, he was the driving force in their life together, and with life as she had known it gone, he had left her alone without any idea on how to carry on.

She pulled herself together and discovered that she had more strength than she had given herself credit for. Over the following years she started to pick up the tenuous threads of a social life, found herself a little job and a routine that got her through the day. Her charity work gave her a reason to keep going, it became her baby. She had taken up the fight for Aids sufferers long before it had become fashionable and to that extent, made her one of the leading charitable authorities and her contacts made for exciting reading. All the top

Hollywood stars supporting Aids started through Jennifer and her contacts and knowledge. She was on the President's list of dinner guests, making her now a confident, knowledgeable, and well known public figure. This is the person Christopher knew. He would never know that until she met him her personal life had been kept in the freezer, she had thought she would never get over losing her husband and her inward life felt like a long and deep winter.

Now she had Christopher and it felt like spring again. All her hopes and dreams and plans were again sprouting and there was renewed vigour in her life. It was easy, all it would take is love and money, something they both had. They could have it all, all the pleasures that money can bring, they were popular on the social circuit but with planning they could develop an even larger social circle, this was something she could not manage on her own. If there was one thing she had learned over the years it was how to rise in social circles, she had needed a man to help her, now she had one and she was raring to make the most of all her experiences and knowledge. She wanted to be known all over America and not just in two or three states as the best hostess and be a regular top table guest at all the best of functions worth attending. This she had been planning and thinking about quietly over the last two years.

Her finances were beginning to cause her problems. Living a prominent life and mixing with high society cost lots of money to maintain and fund. She had seemed wealthy on paper but she had drained several oil wells full of money to fund the lifestyle and it would take more in the future. She needed Christopher on all fronts; as her partner, lover and she needed his money. Christopher did not have a clue.

He had sat down with Jennifer and told her everything she needed to know. He would never tell her everything, that would be fucking stupid. He had told her he wanted to make his home permanently in America with her, adding hesitantly, if she would have him. He had money, but was it enough to fund a lifetime in America. He was 50 years old now and was busy working out how much he would need, with investments, to have a good life until he was 80 years old. She had laughed at that figure, but he said in all seriousness, 80 years old was a good age to reach and his father had not reached that age. She asked him if he had enough money and seeing the worried look in her eyes, had airily told her he had tons enough to last them three lifetimes. She threw her arms around him and he could feel her body relax into him. He was determined that somehow he would get enough money to last three lifetimes. He was to work on that project to the detriment of Davies-Clarke for the next year.

Christopher liked to watch Jennifer walk amongst the rose garden he had supervised. She walked with a sway that was so sensual it made him feel good. He liked it when she wore one of those skirts that clung to her hips but was full enough and soft enough for the hem to gently sway from side to side in rhythm to the roll of her hips as she moved slowly but deliberately amongst -the flowers. She would often catch him "looking that look" as she called it and it gave her much pleasure and she would exaggerate the walk for his pleasure. He concluded watching Jennifer was like watching a racehorse with its beautifully elegant gait and long slim legs, and then there was the beautiful mane of luscious blonde hair tumbling down a long slim neck, whilst Alice was like a rag and bone man's horse, stubby, fat and no class. Christopher would have smiled at that analogy but thought it was actually rather cruel and made himself retract such an unkind thought about Alice. Still, Jennifer was a class act and he did love her very much.

Over the year he had looked fruitlessly into all legitimate ventures that would bring him in enough money to fund Jennifer and his lifestyle. The carefree days spent idling in the garden like a country squire were about to end abruptly. Christopher would need such memories to keep him going during the dark days ahead.

PART 2

CHAPTER TWENTY SIX

The idyllic life with Jennifer had been very easy to come by. He had the house, the garden which he loved. He had earned the respect and standing in a higher social group; he dined with well known stars for Christ sake! It was the life he had always wanted. Jennifer had freely and happily made available everything she had to him and had never asked for any reward except his love. It was on his 54th birthday that something changed and he knew it was now payback time.

She was worried; she had lots on her mind. She had looked at him with tears in her eyes and asked him what she should do. He knew he had no option, indeed, he would never have considered looking for an alternative. She told him she was going to lose the house, the servants, the money, everything. Of course he would help her, he had comforted her, promised her, and reassured her so she could go away and think no more about it. As he said, dealing with Solicitors was men's work and he would sort out everything. She, in return promised undying love, loyalty and anything he wanted from her. He was too burdened by the heavy weight of what he had promised to appreciate the loving, sensual words whispered in his ears.

That evening he had sat with one of many cigarettes and a large whisky or three considering what he had foolishly promised and trying to get to grips with how he could afford to take on this fight. He sat in the study, and tried to sink into the leather sofa, but the sofa was having none of it. Made from sturdy timbers and strong leather dimpled violently throughout it made him sit upright and tall. This was a mans chair and he knew that now, at the age of 54 years, he had to be a man and do the right thing. After an ashtray full of cigarettes smoked to the filter tip and after finishing the bottle of whisky, he had worked out a plan. Tomorrow he would phone Chuck, he shuddered at the thought but with a deep breath decided that as the clock chimed 3 a.m., enough was enough and went to join Jennifer in bed.

As he walked up the stairs he was amazed at how sober he felt, although he was to tell Jennifer in the morning how strange it had been that the stair treads kept moving as he walked up the stairs and how he had nearly tripped up. He cautiously picked his way up the stairs but why that made him start to giggle he didn't know. He climbed carefully into bed choking back the giggles so as not to wake a beautiful, peaceful Jennifer sleeping without a care in the world. He had intended to kiss her on the cheek but as soon as he lay back in bed the alcohol pushed his head into a downward spiralling fall which sped him to a hell he had never envisaged. His snoring confirmed the sleep of the damned.

He woke breathless the next morning from a night of constant nightmares, each individual nightmare would finish, with his heart pounding, and a fear that did not have time to recede before plunging him into a new evil, heart stopping situation from which there was no escape. He pushed the bedclothes off himself to try and rid the memory of the nightmares which were now a blurred memory of being smothered and strangled and drowned in a cesspit of stink. He got up and opened the window and breathed in deeply the fresh air and gazed at the lawns leading down to the lake which he loved. He felt better, but he needed to get rid of the headache and the taste of shit in his mouth. A coffee and an aspirin was what he needed and a fool proof plan.

At breakfast Jennifer noted the unkempt look and the distracted smile and silently, gently hugged him, words would have been an intrusion. Their closeness was such over the years that the merest gesture, a covert look was all that was needed to ease and understand what each wanted and thought. That idyllic calm and understated love was something he took for granted but he knew he could not live without her. The heady power of such strength and unity was something others had noticed. Their friends and associates saw them as a very strong couple who worked well together.

The comfortable and expensive lifestyle that both their money had brought them had never been taken for granted by Christopher, but he had got used to the lifestyle and the respect it had brought. He had "made it". He was better than his brother, he was better than his father. He wished they could see him now. His brother spent his day ploughing fields and he, Christopher Cross, was living a lifestyle that paid for someone else to shift the dirt. It was a bitter sweet triumph that could not be shared with anyone in England. He spent many evenings toasting their bad fortune with a glass of whisky.

Truth be told, Christopher's lifestyle took its toll on his working life. Many years ago he was considered one of the top salesmen for Davies-Clarke Plc – Luxury and Customised Vehicles for the Discerning. His customers had stayed with him and still bought from him and because of his new associations he had fielded more customers to Davies-Clarke without actually working very hard. There had been low rumblings of discontent from London but as he had brought some prestigious customers through Jennifer, they kept quiet and watched.

Christopher was a huge expense on Davies-Clarke Plc, his air fares and expenses which included his suits, petrol, meals at the best restaurants were all paid for by Davies-Clarke. Of course he pitched this years ago with James and put together costs. Christopher was a Salesman Supreme; he sold James the complete package. To sell in America, to beat the Americans at their own game would take style. An English Salesman had a believable authority of honesty that was not recognised in an American Salesman. He went on to say that with no class system in America except money, his Englishness appealed to the seriously rich snobs.

Christopher had studied the market place and knew that American companies could offer exactly what he offered in top quality cars and customising in any way the client wanted. His hold of the corporate American

Market would amount to the prestige of buying from Davies-Clarke and the after care service provided. Which, as he told James, is why he needed to be seen in the very best restaurants, in the best hotels and he needed the best suits to promote the exclusivity of Davies-Clarke. The showroom they opened in Atlanta and the internet site were put in place. He kept his promise that whatever the expenses amounted to, he would outsell and outmatch any other salesman with his yearly profits. The expenses were peanuts in comparison to the sales he made. Christopher had become the top salesman and generated a client list that kept Davies-Clarke buoyant even during the years of recession in England.

Christopher ran the company in America and it had been noted that he had personally slowed down during the past years. It had been hoped that Christopher would make the company bigger in America and the expansion would go into more States. He had a large team of salesmen and service engineers geared to accommodate the more discerning of clients to ensure their every need was catered for. The clientele was prestigious and big enough to satisfy Davies-Clarke at the moment. Christopher and sometimes James were vital in bringing their English quality to the sales. Christopher was well aware and very satisfied that he was irreplaceable in the Company.

James was getting old now and didn't make the journey too often. Still trying to be at the front of the company, James was running out of energy and there had been a few health issues over the years. No one can work at the pace James had for years without a few problems. The ulcers were dealt with but the heart problems were a nuisance and he had a pacemaker installed and was told to rest more.

Davies-Clarke had always been a successful Company in Christopher's working life, but now it was world renowned and had the royal insignia on its headed paper and internet site. Davies-Clarke supplied all the royal cars. This actually cost them dearly in profit. The Queen's household were canny negotiators and got an exceptional deal from Davies-Clarke.

To be able to use the Royal Insignia as part of the Company was a momentous moment in James's life. No one knew, but he had cried in private that this was a triumph of pride and joy that felt hollow without his beloved wife and his father, the Captain to share it with. The Captain would have blustered and complained that his son was far too above his lowly station. That "we Norfolk folk" as he liked to call himself, were used to having royalty in Norfolk and he would have scoffed at the press interest and scoffed at the champagne party James held to celebrate. Through his tears he laughed at the thought "oh dear God! He missed his father so much". Neil was there but they were quite distant. Neil was doing well and he was proud of him but the gap between them had got bigger and deeper and conversation was stilted and brief.

The Royal Insignia meant more business for Christopher. The American public loved the Royal Family and the prestige of buying from the Queen's suppliers was essential in the one upmanship game played by the seriously rich. Nevertheless, James had hoped the business in America would grow even bigger. Christopher was around enough to keep it ticking over at a good rate, it was a highly successful money earning venture with prestigious clients but the edge had gone from Christopher. He now wanted an easier life.

The meeting with her Lawyers last month had been an eye opener and a catalyst. She attended these meetings regularly, it was her business, not his, but this time she asked him to come along with her. She was worried, he knew that, but she wouldn't say why.

The Lawyer was a short, tight mouthed man who had seen better days. Christopher noted Hershel, as he introduced himself, had mopped his brow in a distracted and disturbed fashion that worried Christopher. Here was a man under considerable stress. Hershel had ignored Christopher. All his conversation was with Jennifer. He had obviously had a long association with Jennifer and felt able to admonish her with comments of "you knew this was going to happen" and "it comes as no surprise". What he proceeded to outline shocked the hell out of Christopher.

Jennifer had spent and cashed in a vast amount of money over the past few years. As the Lawyer kept saying, "selling your assets caused this. What did you think was going to make you money to maintain your lifestyle once your assets had been sold". Hershel was flushed and he had continually pushed up his large thick glasses that were forever slipping down his nose and threatening to fall off. Christopher had watched strangely detached, waiting for either the glasses to fall or the beads of sweat that were threatening to cause a puddle on the table to distract the tightly controlled Hershel. Hershel had told Jennifer, in a quietly controlled voice, that this was a red letter meeting. "Today", and he had thumped the table to enforce his words causing Jennifer to jump "was make or break day."

The meeting went on for three hours and Hershel stated that the house would have to be sold and Jennifer's lifestyle would have to change drastically if she wanted to maintain a respectable lifestyle.

Christopher had stepped in when the house was mentioned, this was non negotiable. The house was everything to Christopher and of course to Jennifer. Jennifer had got very animated when her lifestyle and house was mentioned, she could not and would not lose everything she had worked so hard to achieve. Almost crying, Jennifer retorted that she would rather die than lose her beautiful house and her position in the world of Charity. It was a rather emotional and theatrical statement which set Hershel back a little, making him hesitate, and look to Christopher for help. Jennifer needed him and Christopher knew it was time to be a man and step in.

Christopher and Hershel talked money. It would take $3,000,000 to get back on track with investments to maintain a lifestyle and keep the house serviced. It would take an additional $1,000,000 per year to account for the additional expenses accrued in servicing the charitable events and lifestyle they had developed. Christopher promised Hershel that the $3,000,000 would be no problem and he said that would be organised through a bank draft within a few months. He said that he needed to sort out his investments to make this possible. Hershel, for the first time, took a great interest in Christopher and offered his services in looking after his investments. Christopher thought Hershel was an expensive idiot and wouldn't touch him with a barge pole, but he smiled and thanked Hershel and said he would think about it.

"Of course," Christopher had smiled at Jennifer and Hershel and added, "I would expect to be the owner of the house, on paper only naturally, and would expect papers to be drawn up and signed to that effect when I hand over the bank draft for $3,000,000." Hershel's brow knitted in concern and he looked at Jennifer for her reaction. Jennifer was going to say something but Christopher added quickly, "That as Jennifer was to be my wife in the near future, the house in my name is of no consequence. I will ensure that the $1,000,000 additional monies is met each year." He saw Jennifer flush with pleasure at this impromptu proposal and she took Christopher's hand as her acknowledgement and agreement.

Hershel was going to worry about the paperwork later. The fact $3,000,000 was going to be invested and as a bonus for him, he saw this as an excellent opportunity for making money together with whatever Christopher was worth. He was going to look into Christopher's financial history when they had left. In the meantime a date in 3 months was diarised for their next meeting when the promised $3,000,000 would be available.

Christopher felt a weight so large and dark descend on his shoulders that he could hardly breathe. What had he agreed to? The words tripped off his tongue so easily and a $1,000,000 per year additional, what was he thinking! He needed to get out and think.

He drove Jennifer back to the house. He noted she was strangely quiet but the shock of nearly losing everything was a lot to cope with he surmised. Jennifer, who obviously knew the arrangements with Alice, broke the silence and asked when he was going to get the divorce finalised. "Yea Gods!" he thought, he had offered marriage without thinking, and he was still married to Alice and had no intention of divorcing her. He would lose the house and god knows what else. Alice would take him for everything she could lay her hands on. What had he done? The pressure was building and he needed to get the fuck out of the car and away from everyone to think. All he could muster as an answer was "soon."

With more good grace than he felt, he dropped Jennifer at the house and said he needed some time alone to work out what investments he needed to organise. Jennifer could see the look on Christopher's face and nodded mutely and left him blowing him a kiss as she turned and tripped lightly up the steps to the house. She could read him and knew when he needed time alone this had always worked well. Jennifer knew he had promised a lot, she felt good knowing all would be well, but Christopher would have to be handled carefully. She knew how to be compliant.

Marriage was quite a shock, she never expected

marriage with the Alice woman still around, but now he had suggested it, she smiled and wondered what he was going to do. Alice was his problem not hers and she contentedly helped herself to a glass of cold white wine to celebrate the good news. She went to the window and surveyed the lawns down to the lake and took a deep breath and exhaled with a contentment she hadn't felt for a long time. All was in place and well with the world. She loved her home and gardens more than anyone understood.

He drove for miles and eventually stopped at a roadside bar and got a drink from the man behind the bar. Christopher nodded to him and the skinny moustached man who would never know 50 years again whipped a glass off the shelf and put it in front of Christopher. Christopher was beyond worrying that the glass may be as clean as the stained off white apron the man was wearing. He poured the bourbon as directed. The bar man knew better than to say anything to this man who appeared to have the weight of the world on his shoulders.

Christopher gave a quick cursory look around him. The bar was a dump, along with Barman Les, as he called himself, the place had seen better days but at least it was empty. English pubs were solid buildings full of eccentric mementos. This was a small, plastic, holiday home type building with a huge car park outside. The music on the jukebox disturbed the air but made no difference to Christopher's concentration, he had to think, and think fast and clearly. He took a swig of the bourbon and it nearly gave him indigestion, but after a few swigs he got over that. He drew deeply on his cigarette. He had to think. Okay, he knew he wasn't broke, he had accrued a tidy sum from the drugs he carried into England. He earned very good money in America and his bonuses were such that if necessary he could lay his hands in total on $3,000,000 tied up in various off shore investments. But he had a family home in England and children and a wife to support. Jennifer had always been an expensive asset. All the additional entertaining and the events they attended which he couldn't offset to Davies-Clarke had cost him dearly but it was affordable up to now. He had to find $3,000,000 in 3 months, an impossibly awful amount to find. He could sell everything he owned in investments but he would still be $1,000,000 short for the year's running costs and he just couldn't be broke, Alice needed money. There again, he got to own the house and grounds and had Jennifer's undying gratitude for keeping her lifestyle. He would have to find the money.

The rash promise to marry Jennifer would have to wait. He would think of something, he wasn't going to divorce Alice. Jennifer couldn't have everything but he wanted the house and grounds very much. He could afford the $3,000,000 but it needed replacing and he needed another $1,000,000 for the running costs for the year. He wanted it all and there had to be a plan to get it.

He drank more whisky than he should and smoked a pack of cigarettes before leaving the bar. The bartender kept his distance but carefully watched this man wrestle with problems he could only guess at. He warily approached when Christopher gestured with his glass for a top up and then stepped back down the bar to clean glasses and watch Christopher under hooded eyes. He had learned over the years that a man troubled is like a volcano that can erupt without warning. He was careful not to disturb his mood by any sudden moves or unprovoked remarks, and was relieved and somewhat surprised when as Christopher left after paying the tab, he left him a big tip and distractingly thanked the bartender for everything. English manners never left Christopher, even in times of stress. He had a bit of a plan in mind. He was anxious to drive back to the house and make that phone call.

His meeting with Chuck had been arranged for a few days now. The telephone conversation had been strange. Christopher and Chuck had got an understanding over the years. They did their business and left. Chuck was not big on manners or etiquette. He had over the years hinted none too subtly to Christopher that there was more money to be made if he was up for it. Christopher had never been "up for it". He thought it dangerous enough to do what he did in being a courier for drugs between Amanda and Chuck and Chuck was not the sort of man he would want to do business with, he was a lowlife and a necessary evil that Christopher did not want to get further involved with.

Christopher had a few whiskies to steel himself for the call and the third cigarette seemed to help. Chuck had listened to the sorry tale of money being needed and doing anything that wasn't too dangerous to get it. If Christopher had seen the smirk on Chucks face he might have considered walking away but that wasn't going to happen.

They met in a dingy bar on the far side of town. Atlanta had a few out of the way places that no one would visit if they had a choice. This was another little tin pot shack just off the road with a car park big enough for 3 football pitches. Christopher was amazed at such a waste of land.

Christopher entered the bar and saw Chuck sitting in the far corner. The subdued lighting made the bar look dirtier. The slot machines on the far corner flashed lights of gawdy reds and greens across the tables. This was the most depressing bar Christopher had ever been in. He ordered a whisky from the bar tender and took his drink to the table and sat next to Chuck.

Chuck, sprawled inelegantly in the corner, was going to make Christopher work for his help. He idly watched through hooded eyes as Christopher walked slowly over to the table and sat down opposite him. He thought what a prick this limey was, so stuck up in his starched shirt and wearing a tie for god's sake, in this heat? It made him want to puke to look at him. Christopher wanted to get out of this place as quickly as possible and as far away from the look and stench of Chuck, didn't beat about the bush, he stated that he needed $4,000,000 quickly and what could he do to earn that. The macho stance crumpled as Christopher leant forward and whispered urgently to Chuck that he was open to anything. He was desperate for the money and needed it within 3 months. Christopher felt the sweat that had beaded up violently on his face begin to trickle down his cheek. He didn't want to wipe it away and let Chuck see just how desperate and scared he was.

Chuck smirked, he liked this, to have the limey, stuck up your ass, bastard, almost begging him for help was very satisfying. He had ideas, Chuck had many years to formulate ideas and he had a good one on the back burner. He whispered back to Christopher that for that sort of money the risk was big but possible. It would take two trips, that's all, and $4,000,000 was doable. Even one trip could do it but the size of the stash needed something special to carry it.

Christopher didn't want to know anything but, of course, he needed to know something. Where was the money to come from? Chuck became quite expansive and waved his hand in the air with a menace that scared Christopher Chuck whispered, "We is gonna steal from Peter to pay Paul, you heard of that limey?"

Christopher nodded and wanted to ask more but hesitated. He leaned forward again and asked: "what am I to do, what is my part in it?" Chuck was enjoying seeing Christopher so uncomfortable. He detested the creep who always looked too special to spit. He waited a few seconds more than was comfortable and said:

"You is gonna do what you always do and no more. Take to Amanda as usual."

"Is she in it too?" Christopher asked

"Yea, we can't do it without her, but she will be fine. Not your problem." Chuck was still economical with words. Christopher said that if he could get the Lear Jet then perhaps it could be done in one trip. Christopher's hands shook as he lit another cigarette, and he thanked Chuck for arranging this. Chuck smiled, he was going to enjoy this.

Christopher left knowing he must wait for a phone call. His part was the same as usual but he would be carrying far more drugs than usual. He would arrange to use the Lear Jet that James made available if and when necessary. Christopher would have to plan his reasons for using it and when he had he could bring a huge amount of drugs into the country unnoticed. The Lear Jet was never searched and the VIP lounge meant he got through easily. He spent the evening along with his cigarettes and whisky thinking out who he would take to England from America as his cover story.

He had a perfect cover. He would take Senator Murphy who worked with Jenny on the Aids Foundation to England and show him Davies-Clarke Cars and introduce him again to James. Of course James knew him well but this would be a special visit to promote the company. Senator Murphy and his wife were in the diary to come to dinner at the house next month which was just perfect. Christopher went to bed feeling very self satisfied. Not difficult, his role the same as usual. All was going to be well. The whisky left him with a glowing feeling of success and smugness that would cost him dearly in the near future.

CHAPTER TWENTY SEVEN

Pamela

Pamela from the office spoke to Christopher regularly. His call to find out when the Lear Jet would be available within the next 3 months filled her with excitement. He was coming home.

If Christopher had realised what this sort of devotion meant, he might have watched his words more carefully. Pamela studied everything about him and he would have been surprised how much she had gleaned from information he said, from telephone calls and how she spent the time putting everything together. The anonymity Christopher thought he had would have made the smug smile disappear. Although bravery never quite rested with Christopher he had become quite cocky over the years. The successful trips, the money had all come easily to him. The smug smile would have disappeared if he had realised just how much Pamela knew about him and what information she could give.

Neil was her favourite, a wonderful man with such exquisite old English manners. She knew he was an important business man in Norfolk and a JP as well so she always felt honoured at his attention whenever he phoned the office. He always asked after her health and made small pleasantries which made Pamela blush. Pamela felt a bond with Neil, she felt they both loved Christopher in their own way. She told him everything he needed to know on Christopher's whereabouts and contact numbers, but because of their special relationship with Christopher she always added in more. Pamela felt good to be able to share her knowledge, and to gossip with Neil. Neil listened and expressed surprise at Pamela's excellent understanding of events and always praised her reasoning powers. Neil had also built a picture of Christopher's life which he protected. If Christopher had known what Neil had rightly guessed, he would have been mortified. His secret life was discussed on a weekly basis.

Pamela knew his marriage was convenient by the way he was respectful but not personal to Alice. Her conversations with Alice only confirmed the fact that Christopher was far too classy for her. She was a snobby, silly woman who didn't deserve such a fine man. Pamela felt superior to Alice.

She knew the Jenny woman in America was his lover, well that was easy enough to gauge. He stayed there, he spoke in a hushed loving way and went quiet when Pamela came in the room. In idle moments thinking about Christopher, she begrudgingly conceded that Jenny filled a purpose in Christopher's life. Perhaps, with Christopher being so manly, this Jenny was just a necessary bit on the side for him. She didn't like Jenny; she didn't know why, just a woman's instinct she concluded.

The other woman, Amanda, she thought there was more to her than a mistress whilst he was in London because he jumped when she told him to. There had been many occasions that after her call he had rushed out of the office saying he would be back later, or take messages. That woman had some sort of power over him. She was desperate to find out why.

All his secrets were safe with Pamela, she took pride in the fact that she would always protect him and cover for him. Studying him and what he was doing was better than reading a book. She found everything so very fascinating. She saw the bag he used to carry the drugs when on commercial airlines. It wasn't hard to realise it had a use that only he knew about. He had his briefcase for his paperwork, he had his suitcase for his clothes and she had seen what goes in that... but he always took this bag empty, and she didn't know why.

She had never known him come straight from the airport to the office with all his bags. Christopher kept, as much as he could, this part of his life away from the office. But, on one occasion only, he returned, reluctantly to the office for a meeting with James. If James called, Christopher was there. He arrived at the office with his suitcase and briefcase but he only asked Pamela to put the usually empty bag in her cupboard and lock it away until he asked for it. He trusted her implicitly, he knew she would do anything for him. That one act changed Pamela's view of Christopher for ever.

She looked inside. Of course she did, as she told herself, no self respecting PA would do anything less. It was part of her job to oversee and look after her boss.

She didn't know exactly what the packages contained but she knew they contained drugs. She had seen enough programmes on the television to understand that. But why had Christopher got such things and she realised the bag had been used on all his flights to America. He left the office with it empty and, yes, of course, she was catching on very quickly. He came back from America with a full bag. It explained a lot. She knew how much he earned and he earned a lot. But the standard of living he had was way above his earnings. This was such a learning curve for her. He only came back because James had called a last minute meeting and ordered him to come straight from the airport to the office, in fact James said he was timing him. Christopher had no option and no time but to go straight to the office. God! She was shaking with the knowledge of what Christopher was getting up to. It was illegal and he, he was such a gentleman. She went and got a cup of tea to steady her nerves, or was it excitement, and sat down to think it through.

Her mind was racing and soaring and she could see everything. Of course, Amanda must be his contact in England and Jenny was his contact in America, it made sense. All those whispered calls. But why would he do such a thing. He was a gentleman. Then it came to her. She realised how silly and stupid she had been. He was, and she couldn't think of the correct word, but he must be like a James Bond person. Oh the thought of it made her hug herself and she quivered with the thought that she was his Miss Moneypenny. She suppressed a giggle because she always thought of him as her James Bond and it was so right and so true. She chose to believe he was on a mission for England, Christopher couldn't possibly be anything other than her shining knight. She hinted as such to Neil who, with gentle goading, made her tell him more than she intended to. Pamela tingled with excitement. It was wonderful to share her detective skills with someone as eminent as Neil, it made her feel important.

Pamela had got used to Neil ringing her weekly to find out how she was and how their friend, Christopher was. She took much pride in his amazement at how much she knew about Christopher and who he was talking to. She liked to dredge up every little bit of information she had just to bask in this wonderful and important man's gratitude. They would talk constantly about Christopher and she found it a source of great pleasure to have someone she could trust to share her love of Christopher with.

Christopher was special, she knew that, but now, he was something utterly magnificent. He was just so delicious. She would pause and lick her lips as she thought of him savouring real and imagined scenarios of being with him. They shared a secret that was naughty and dangerous and involved saving the world. She would never say anything to him but perhaps he had hinted over the years and she had just not seen it. She knew he trusted her and relied on her, he had told her how important she was to his work in keeping the office running smoothly for him and for keeping him informed of all the in house gossip and politics so he could steer clear and keep himself safe. When he was away he had no one to watch his back as he called it: to let him know if someone was muscling in on any of his clients. Pamela watched and made sure that never happened and if there was any sign she let Christopher know immediately. She was even more important than she realised and this made her gasp with a pleasure she hadn't felt for a long time.

Christopher had been away for 2 months and the thought of seeing him made her heart race. Everyone in the office knew when Christopher was returning. Pamela informed everyone in a tone which should have made them race to get the welcome home banners out, but of course, Pamela was the only one to be thrilled at the thought. When Christopher was coming home, Pamela changed from being quiet and studious around the office to animated and bright and happy, it was a source of amusement for everyone. She had her leg pulled so often she wondered how it was still attached, but she didn't mind. She would say, when necessary, that she was a good example of an excellent PA to Mr Cross and they could all learn much from her. The tea room clique of girls bitched often and Pamela would have been hurt to know how much she was mocked and laughed at. She never thought deeply about it, but she was quite alone and there was no one she could call a friend or confide to in the office.

Pamela worked according to Christopher's time scale. If he was around then she worked until he left and because of the time difference in America she would work late to talk to him.

Pamela's husband had got fed up with Christopher

years ago and wished he would piss off to America and stay there. Pamela had stopped talking about Christopher in his presence and he was grateful for that, she didn't say much to him these days and that suited him fine. She earned good money, and he conceded she must be good at what she does but when that Christopher Cross beckoned she got home late and his dinner was left to be microwaved. It infuriated him she cooked dinner in the early morning and left it plated to be reheated in the evening. He hated to smell chops and vegetables cooking at 6 a.m. it was disgusting. He wished she would work somewhere else but the money was handy. He was let go by his last employer. He never explained the reasons why to Pamela, and now he could only find odd driving jobs around town. He worked steadily and brought in some money but Pamela was the main wage earner these days and that bugged him badly. Pamela's success caused a brooding resentment that they both avoided discussing. She walked around him on tip toe to avoid any confrontation. He had learned to control his temper and didn't lay a finger on her anymore, not since the last incident when he went too far and Pamela called the Police. She had been very frightened and she thought she was going to die. His hands were round her throat and he only let go because she kicked him hard on the ankle. He got a verbal warning from the Police because Pamela said it was her fault and she had pushed his patience too far. He had hit her on occasions but she deserved it, the mouthy cow, but he never hit her where it would show. They had a nice little place in Ilford, nothing grand but money had been spent on it over the years and they were comfortable there. Neither wanted to lose their home so they lived in their own negotiated space and it worked well as long as no one rocked the boat and kept conversation to neutral and necessary areas. He had the pub to go to and she had her job.

Pamela's negotiation skills were awesome and although the Lear Jet was due to be serviced during the month of August, she spent the day rearranging the Lear's schedule, cajoling and smooth talking the pyramid of people involved in the use and repair of the Lear. She got her way and Christopher could have the use of the Lear. She rang him and said the Lear Jet was available for when he wanted it. She flushed at his words of how much of a treasure she was and how he just couldn't do without her. She would feast on those words and expand them and find more meaning in them. Pamela was to be instrumental in the downfall of Christopher.

Senator Murphy and his wife Sally were invited to dinner, it had been in the diary for months. Jenny, as usual organised a splendid meal of steak and young succulent carrots and baby potatoes tossed in butter, it was the Senator's favourite meal. They drank Californian wine in honour of the Senator who had an investment in some of the vine yards. After a very pleasant meal filled with laughter and some gratuitous rubbing of the Senator's ego, Christopher invited him out for a cigar by the lake.

The butler put a decanter of the finest Scottish Malt

on a small table in readiness by the river and 2 chairs. Christopher and the Senator, sated and feeling relaxed stood on the terrace and viewed the scenery. Christopher took a deep breath and enjoyed the air and the view. The two men didn't need words, just being there felt enough at that moment. The lake reflected the full moon in its ripples and they both smiled at the tranquillity of a warm, early summer evening. They walked down from the terrace to the lake with a Havana Cigar kept for special occasions. The Senator came to a gentle halt by the lake and sucked gently on his cigar, savouring the size and hardness against his lips. The smoothness of the cigar smoke filling his mouth and trickling down his throat. He waited for a flavourful moment and exhaled slowly. He rolled his tongue lazily around his mouth, tasting the ripeness and completeness of the experience. He closed his eyes for a moment to ensure nothing interfered with the pleasure. Christopher kept quiet and watched.

After 5 minutes, the Senator turned to Christopher and smiled. He thanked Christopher for a wonderful evening. He said that his life had been difficult and busy with Bills going through the Senate and always having to watch his back. He said he was ready for a break he needed a holiday. Christopher took this up immediately. He asked the Senator if he would like to come to London on Corporate Business for the weekend. The Senator looked at him dubiously and asked why on earth he would want to do that!

Christopher told him a story called Amanda and her friends. He painted the picture of complete pampering and every need catered for from bathing with the girls to massages. He told him about girls that were young and nubile but experienced and eager. He told him about a bed that could hold 6 girls comfortably, of satin sheets and lace, of wanton pleasures and quiet pleasures, of sensual and spanking pleasures. The Senator asked quietly of whips and leather and Christopher assured him there were plenty. Christopher promised it would be discreet and so wonderful he would not want to leave. The Senator was interested, very interested and Christopher could see his interest.

The Senator's interest in prostitutes was well known by everyone but his wife and the general public. The newspapers had never mentioned it. Christopher thought they were saving it for a rainy day. He knew that Amanda and the girls would be of interest to him.

Now he had the Senator's interest, Christopher filled in the other details. He told him he had organised the Lear Jet to be available in two months time. The visit could be official because Davies-Clarke was much respected in America and would involve the Embassy in London. He suggested he brought his wife with him. The Senator looked sharply at Christopher and before he could say anything, Christopher added that a full itinerary would be set for her to visit various charities in London whilst the Senator was busy meeting the girls. The Senator asked why he was arranging this for him, what was Christopher going to get out of it. Christopher smiled and said that quite simply it would be an honour for Davies-Clarke to have him in England at that time. He said that the Senator was highly respected in England

and he would arrange for a champagne reception with James, the Managing Director at Davies-Clarke which the press would be invited to. It was to be a big promotion for Davies-Clarke with the new Bugatti being shown. As this was the most expensive car in the world it seemed appropriate that an American Senator should be there to represent the excellent relationship Davies-Clarke has in America and to honour our valued American clients. The Senator liked that.

The Senator thought the two months notice was quite tricky, and that he would have other things in his diary. Christopher said he understood but reminded the Senator that the girls would be disappointed and the reception was a once in a blue moon event that would allow the Senator to be in London. After much thought, the Senator said he would get his secretary to move his appointments and it was agreed that he would travel to England for the reception and stay at the American Embassy. Christopher would organise everything.

The women laughed and thought it wonderful and very carefree to make such a bold decision. The Senator and his wife usually had their calendar full for the year ahead and to say that in two months they were going to London was just so unusual but such fun too. A shopping trip in London was good for both the women and they left the men to discuss what they would do and what shows they wanted to see. They all got out their diaries to consider which weekend in August would be the best and what they could rearrange. Christopher left them with the excuse he had to ring London and went into his study. He sat down in the safety and quiet of the room and exhaled loudly. He noticed his hands were shaking and he tried to control his urgent breath. He had pulled it off, a nervous laugh escaped his tight lipped grin, the Senator had agreed. He tapped the arm of his chair with a tight fist to reinforce the message. Tomorrow he would get Pamela to sort out the details for him. It was going according to plan and he was scared rigid.

James was put out. Why, he asked Christopher had the damn fool of a Senator got to come now! Christopher explained that in his busy itinerary, this was the only time the Senator could come. Christopher felt the beads of sweat breaking out as he spoke to James on the phone. Yea Gods! This can't break down at this stage, he thought. He could feel panic setting in and he had to hold it back and keep calm.

"James, this is good for us. The American market will love us. The Bugatti as the most expensive car in the world is the launching pad to advertise ourselves more. Trust me, I know the American market and it is still wide open to us." He hoped that sounded professional enough. He hastily added, "Her Majesty is in favour of companies bringing trade into this country and you will be doing your bit for her too." Christopher thought it a stab in the dark, but James was now so pro royalist it seemed a winner. James agreed reluctantly but said he didn't like the rush, but he saw the virtue of the idea and would go along with it. He thought the timescales for getting the Bugatti into the showroom on time might be a bit tricky but would pull a few strings. The damn Bugatti could wait as far as Christopher was concerned, it was the Lear Jet he wanted, but the whole package would be a good smoke screen.

Next was Pamela, she should have been easy but the damn girl was asking questions. Why will you have so much baggage? Where will you want it taken and why so many cars to carry you all from the airport? She was driving an already uptight and only just in control man up the bloody wall. He curtly told her what to do and said he would ring later to check it was all done. His voice rose through the conversation ending in a crescendo of "just get on with it!" as he finished the call and he slammed the phone down. Pamela was very upset but she did what he asked.

He had a whisky and a cigarette and sat still for a moment. He had to pull himself together. Jennifer had given him that look at him over breakfast as if he was going mad and she had kept very quiet. The servants noticed the atmosphere and that wasn't good. Everyone would notice something was wrong and the whole idea of this was to be normal. A trip on a Lear Jet to London is pretty normal. This made him laugh out loud. What on earth did he sound like. He had got pretty big for his boots over the past decade. He decided to walk around the estate, get some fresh air and lighten up.

He rang Pamela back and told her how sorry he was for being abrupt and that she was marvellous and he had every confidence she would organise this for him in her usual perfect way. Pamela purred and of course got on with the job for her Christopher. As he left the house he grabbed Jennifer around the waist and kissed her. He told her she was beautiful and he was sorry for being grumpy which put her mind at rest.

The walk did him good and he returned to the house

ready for the final part of the charade. He rang Amanda and told her what was required for the Senator and asked where the additional suitcases were to be delivered. Amanda told him not to worry himself. The Senator would have his mind blown along with everything else and the suitcases would be fine at her place as usual. She could always make him feel relaxed. She told him he was the best and he was going to be a very rich man when this stash reached her. Nothing was going to go wrong, the Lear made it easy and it would be the same as usual except there would be a few more suitcases. He felt good, it was all working out well. The Gods were on his side and he was going to be rich and own the house and land here. He decided this was the big one but he would never do it again, it felt too risky. He would replace his off shore money with his usual smaller deliveries. He had a lifestyle to maintain. He reasoned that he would work harder to improve sales in America and build up his legitimate money in sales.

His daughters had been a huge leak in his money but they were married now so were their respective husband's problem. The weddings had cost him a few trips between America and Amanda. He had to admit, they had been bloody good events and Alice had pulled out all the stops and produced weddings that were in all the local papers. The girls had married well and she now spent a lot of time visiting the girls in their homes. They didn't move too far away, one in Norwich and the other had married a farmer and had a huge house and farm near Potter Heigham. He saw the girls when he was back in Norfolk but the relationship was strained, they were closer to their mother than to him. With no grandchildren to keep them bonded, the girls had a wonderful life that didn't include him. He often thought how pleased the Captain would have been to have the girls staying in Norfolk. The Captain wouldn't have been so pleased to know what he had been doing over the years but he blanked that from his mind. His life was in America and he was about to own a fabulous house and estate which would ensure his rightful place here.

Having got the visit sewn up and ready to go, he now had to arrange for the off shore money to be sent to Jennifer's solicitors. The money would arrive, he was assured well within the time frame specified and Jennifer's solicitors would be informed that the monies had been deposited in Jennifer's account the day after they returned from England. Hershel assured Christopher that once all the formalities had been addressed, the meeting was arranged for 1 p.m. the same day so that Jennifer could sign over the house and grounds to Christopher.

Hershel stated quite clearly that he wanted the money, all $3,000,000 in Jennifer's account before the signing took place. Christopher felt a bit edgy about that and tried to argue the point to no avail. Jennifer's solicitor was adamant and would not step down; the money must be in Jennifer's account before the signing took place. Christopher wanted to punch the slimy toad in his sanctimonious face for pushing him into this corner. He had no where to go if he wanted this to happen. He was so close to getting what he wanted and he desperately wanted to own the house and grounds. It was an opportunity he couldn't let go.

Thinking back, it was madness and greed that had taken him over and blinded him to reason. After taking a far too short moment to think he grabbed the words of that slimy toad and chose to believe the money would be in Jennifer's account for no more than 2 hours before the papers were signed. He convinced himself that it was a breeze, what could possibly happen in 2 hours to make a difference he told himself. He laughed at his disquiet and agreed to the arrangement. Of course, he realised, that Hershel might be a slimy toad but Jennifer was wonderful and generous and didn't possess a dishonest bone in her trusting body. With the decision made, he slumped back and quietly and smugly rejoiced. Life was good, and it was going to get better. He was definitely a man of means. A drink and a cigarette calmed his nerves and he felt in control.

With everything on his mind he didn't notice what Jennifer was doing and he didn't ask her. In retrospect he should have watched her.

The day came for the trip to London. Christopher met with Chuck the night before and 6 large suitcases were filled with bags. It was the most he had ever seen and it made him very nervous. Chuck nearly smiled and told Christopher that everything would go according to plan except the drop off point. To hear this the night before the trip freaked Christopher out. He went white with terror. He had always taken the bag to Amanda and left it with her and that was the end of his part. He just sat back and waited for the money to be put into his off shore account. Now Chuck was telling him he had to do something else and he had 6 fucking suitcases to do something else with. He turned to leave saying he wanted none of it, it was too dangerous. Chuck grabbed his arm and attempted a bit of charm which freaked Christopher out even more. Everything felt different, everything felt very wrong and very frightening. He panicked and just wanted to leave and pretend it had never happened. He didn't need this.

Chuck quietly reminded him that oh yes, he did need this, and in fact without it he would have nothing. Chuck knew what a desperate man Christopher was to have come to him and almost begged and pleaded for a good job to earn him the money he needed. The charm instantly stopped and Chuck grabbed Christopher's arm tighter and pulled him so close that their noses were almost touching. Menacingly, he advised Christopher in a controlled urgent whisper to stop fucking about and get on with what he had to do. He hinted in venomous terms that the payback would be something he wouldn't like at all if he didn't do this. He asked through spittle and breath that made Christopher wrench, did he think the money involved in this was peanuts. This took top men to set up and they wouldn't take any shit from anyone.

Christopher took a few moments of wrestling with his fear and calmed down, he had no choice. Chuck gave him a key and an address in Muswell Hill. He said it was a big Victorian house and he was to drop the suitcases himself and put them in the drawing room at the back of the house. He was to lock the door and walk away, the rest would be done as usual and he would just wait for his money to be put into his off shore account.

Christopher asked how he was to get the suitcases off the Lear and to Muswell Hill. Chuck, couldn't hide his disgust, and told him to fucking sort it out. He was earning enough to make it worth his while. Chuck was losing patience and wanted to leave. He hated this jumped up bastard of an Englishman and had enough of his whining. "Get those cases into Muswell Hill tomorrow night that is all you have to do for God sake! Those cases need to go somewhere now ready for the morning."

The cases were put in his car and he drove back to the house but the nagging feeling was why was he allowed to travel alone with so much stuff. It felt wrong. Anyone could mug him for them. He had never been given stuff the night before, always on the day as he was about to go to the airport. It all felt wrong and he just didn't know what to do about it. He would be glad when tomorrow came and he could get rid of the cases. Again, he promised himself he would never handle such a big load again. In fact, he would think hard about ever doing a smaller job again. He had been lucky and perhaps his luck could be running out. He put the car in the garage and locked it. The cases should be safe there. He made his way to his study and poured a stiff double and drank it in one go. Feeling a bit better he sat down to think about how he would get to Muswell Hill as soon as possible to off load the suitcases. He went to bed worse for drink with a headache and feeling sick. He hoped tomorrow would come and go quickly so he could feel better.

It was Thursday morning American time and Christopher rang Pamela at the office. He asked her to come to the airport to help with his guests. His ETA was 1.45 a.m. Friday morning at Gatwick. In answering her question, he said that he had things to take somewhere and would meet them at the Embassy later but he would like her to accompany them to the Embassy. He asked her to arrange for 3 cars, one for the Senator and his wife, one for Jennifer to take her to the hotel and one for himself. Yes, he told her, he would drive himself, no chauffeur needed.

He had a piece of toast and 4 cups of coffee for breakfast. He was feeling sick and his head threatened to explode. He took some paracetamol and hoped all would be ok later.

Because he had things to arrange on the Lear Jet, he told Jennifer he would go ahead of her and meet her on the jet at 12 noon. At 10 a.m. he left for the hour trip to the airport. He opened the boot first and checked the 4 suitcases were there plus the 2 cases on the back seat of the car. He arranged that one of the staff would collect the car from the airport later. So far he had thought of everything. The 6 suitcases took up a lot of room and weighed a ton. The journey to the airport was stressful but at least he was moving in the right direction and was on the way to getting rid of the stuff. He rubbed his neck with his handkerchief; it itched with sweat and heat.

The Lear was waiting fuelled up and ready to go. Christopher drove the truck up to the Jet and unloaded the suitcases with the help of a mechanic. The Americans were always so helpful and Christopher not wanting any help but aware that any fuss made would bring it to the attention of bystanders, agreed to the help. Tony was the name of the mechanic and he asked why each case was so heavy. Christopher, blasé now, in a state of controlled panic, waved his hand in a dismissive way and said that it contained important bits of kit for customised cars. He explained that they were incredibly valuable and easily broken so was best transported in this way. The mechanic accepted the explanation and carried on pulling and pushing the cases into the hold. It only took 10 minutes to stash them well back in the hold but it felt like hours to Christopher. He was ready for a drink and walked into the aircraft looking for the whisky. The airport customs drew up alongside the Lear as Christopher took his first sip. It nearly choked him. He put the drink down, steadied his hands and adjusted his smile and walked out to greet them.

They had details of the flight they told him, they had details of the passengers they confirmed but what were they taking to England? He explained it was a courtesy visit to England for the Senator and his wife to cement international trade between the two countries. Christopher thought he might have gone over the top with such words but it seemed to impress them. They suggested they would like to look over the Lear, as a matter of standard procedure and asked if that was alright. The piercing look they gave Christopher ensured he gave an open response of, "be my guest" and with a smile, he swept his arm in the direction of the steps into the Lear and invited them to follow him. He was seriously on the edge of collapsing but held his panic and hoped the sweated brow that had beaded up wouldn't run down his face and sting his eyes. How could he stall them, stop them, but not make them suspicious? He really didn't know what to do. He walked ahead of them with his eyes darting this way and that, trying to think what to do to stop them. As he reached the top step into the Lear he heard a car stop and a booming "Hello Christopher, can you give us a hand with the luggage?" It was the Senator.

Christopher asked courteously if the customs men would just wait a moment. He walked up to the Senator and in a very tired whisper stated, "These men are just such a nuisance Senator, I want to get on and make you and Mrs Murphy comfortable. I don't understand why they are picking on us today, especially with someone as important as you on board." Senator Murphy just wanted to get going, he was looking forward to his trip to England. To enjoy such promised carnal pleasure away from the prying eyes of the American press was something special. He had been working very hard lately and this was to be his R&R and no one was going to mess that up. With a wave of his hand he called over to the two customs men.

"Thank you for being so efficient but not necessary, you can go on your way now. We will be leaving in a few moments and Mrs Murphy needs time to settle down."

The customs men tried to protest that it was their job but Senator Murphy was having none of it. They stated their boss would have something to say about this and Senator Murphy asked who their boss was. They replied that Kevin Peterman was their boss. In a gregarious wave of his hand, Senator Murphy said "Kev is a dear friend of mine, he won't mind, off you go now gentlemen, and let us get on our way."

As the men drove away, Christopher said that it had been great luck Senator Murphy knew Kevin Peterman so well. The Senator looked at Christopher quizzically.

"Nah, never met the man in my life, but it got rid of those men didn't it." Christopher chortled and realised the trip might not be as bad as he had envisaged. It was 8 hours flying time to London and England was 4 hours ahead. Arriving at Heathrow at 12 midnight English time was perfect.

The journey was good, Jennifer arrived within minutes of the customs men leaving and all baggage was put in the hold, leaving the 6 suitcases hidden at the back. A few whiskies, some amusing conversations had the occupants laughing and all were feeling good and looking forward to tomorrow in London.

Jennifer sat with Christopher for a while holding his hand and stroking his back. He felt very comforted by her and pulled her gently towards him to keep her close. She was an amazing woman. He felt very lucky to have her love. He could do this, he kept telling himself. He had done it often enough before, it was just this did seem different and more involved and more dangerous. But he was earning a tremendous payback for this trip so of course it is going to be different. He didn't know what he was carrying but for 6 suitcases to pay him alone $3,000,000 it must be pretty special. He chose not to think about it any more, he never wanted to know details.

After a few hours they all quietened down and slept for the remaining hours of the flight. Christopher could not sleep. He paced up and down for a while until he settled with a coffee. He knew he couldn't drink anymore if he was driving at the other end. The last thing he needed was to be stopped by the police for drink driving. He kept fingering the keys in his pocket to the house in Muswell Hill. He had looked up on the map whereabouts it was and he would have no difficulty in finding it. Besides the car had Satnav and it would sort the journey out for him. The journey was long and tiring and worrying for Christopher. He was pleased to hear the captain over the intercom tell everyone to put their seatbelts on for landing. At last he was in England and the last leg of the journey could happen. In a few hours he would be rid of the suitcases and on his way to being cash rich and a land owner in Atlanta. For the first time in the journey, he smiled and felt quite good.

They were all tired when they alighted from the Lear. Pamela was there as requested, and he thanked her warmly which made her blush. Christopher had forgotten just how late it would be for Pamela and he was grateful she turned up looking very bright and cheerful. She checked Christopher first to see if he was o.k. and on his instructions took control of the suitcases for Senator Murphy and his wife and showed them into their awaiting limousine. Tired as they were, they thanked the captain for the flight and the stewardess for her help. When their cases were put in the limousine they sped off to the Embassy for a night's sleep. No going through customs for them, this was dealt with by the car as an official saw them into their limousine. A brief word with Christopher and Jennifer and looking at their passports and they were allowed to leave. No heart stopping difficulties here Christopher thought. Jennifer got into her limousine and Christopher told her he would be at the hotel in about 2 hours and not to stay awake for him. She gave a tired smile and blew him a kiss.

Christopher had his car and proceeded to unload the 6 suitcases into the estate car organised by Pamela. It took him 20 minutes to get them out of the hold and into the car. He was feeling tired but the thought of getting rid of them in an hour or so put a spring in his step and he moved athletically between the plane and the car. He got into the Volvo Estate which was plenty big enough for the suitcases. A normal looking car and hopefully normal enough not to interest any police cars on route. He put the post code in the Satnav and started his journey. The woman's voice telling him every move he should make. He was careful not to go over the speed limit. So close to the end he didn't want to be stopped for speeding.

Muswell Hill was empty at this time of night. It was gone 1 a.m. when he arrived. He sat for a few moments looking at the house which loomed out of the darkness. There was no sign of life inside and Christopher, reluctant to move for the moment, wasted time having a cigarette and admiring the beautiful Victorian House with those wonderful pillars holding up the porch and the square bay heavy in its magnificence and solidness of the era. Looking up at the 3 floors he reckoned it must have 7 bedrooms. At a different moment, he would have ventured that Muswell Hill was somewhere he would have liked to live. As it was, this was not the moment to contemplate any warm and idle thoughts, he was on the last leg of the fraught journey and he felt apprehensive and unsettled. He didn't want to get out of the car because if anyone wanted to jump him, this would be the place to do it. The road was still and the streetlights did not pierce the darkness. After a few moments he stubbed out his cigarette and took a deep breath and found the keys in his pocket. He walked to the front door realising the tree in the front garden shielded him from any onlookers which gave him an itchy spooky feeling. He fumbled with the key and opened the door. The lights were working but the house was empty and hollow. He deftly carried the first case into the back room and moving quickly he had, within 10 minutes, put all the suitcases in the room and double locked the front door as instructed and hastily got back into his car. He took out a cigarette, lit it and drew heavily. He gunned the engine and drove off. God! He felt wonderful. It was all over. He had done his bit and now could go away and sleep easy.

He rang Amanda from his mobile in the car to say everything was in place and ready for collection. He sped back to London and to the hotel and Jennifer. He felt good and safe and knew that within a short time the money would be in his off shore account. Jennifer was asleep when he arrived but she had left him a bottle of his favourite whisky and a glass. She was so thoughtful and if he hadn't been so tired he would have ravished her there and then. After downing 2 glasses and finishing a cigarette, he wearily got into bed. He lay down thinking how wonderful life was. He put his arm around Jennifer and tried to cuddle her, he wanted to feel safe in her arms. Disturbed and slightly aroused she caressed his arm. Feeling so tired and comfortable, she muttered good night and turned over and fell asleep. He smiled, tomorrow they would celebrate and he would make love to her and make her remember how much she needed and desired him. He would have his stake money back in his off shore account of $3,000,000, he had Jennifer and he had the wonderful house and grounds in Atlanta. He had everything he ever wanted and it was just so easy. He fell asleep with a grin as wide as the grand canyon.

He woke gently and lazily, too relaxed to flex his muscles in a stretch, instead he sighed and turned over to feel for Jenny. The space was empty and his hands just felt the ruffled cotton sheet. He thought she must have gone for breakfast. Absentmindedly, he looked at his watch and it said it was 5 p.m. Stunned and unbelieving he reached for the phone and called reception. The Receptionist said yes, it was 5 p.m. He made her repeat her throw away comment that it was a lovely Sunday afternoon. She held the phone away from her ear as the caller ranted and blustered and shouted that it was impossible that it was Sunday. Receptionists are trained to deal with difficult customers but she thought him very rude indeed to slam the phone down when all she had done was answer his questions and offer him room service.

Christopher grabbed his cigarettes and tried to make sense of it all. Where was Jenny? Christ! What about the Senator, who was due to meet Amanda and have a promised full on sexual fantasy like he had never experienced before. He would be mightily pissed off if that didn't happen. He looked for the whisky bottle, he needed a drink, but it wasn't in the room. Did he imagine it all? No, that was not possible. He was in London as he should be and the last thing he remembered when he got back to the hotel was having a couple of whiskies and a cigarette. Where was Jenny? Was he going mad? He sat for an hour collecting his thoughts. He felt sluggish and confused. He ordered black coffee from room service and when it arrived Christopher drank deeply to clear his head and his thoughts.

The call to Amanda confused him. The girls said that Amanda had gone away for the weekend. When he protested that the Senator was due to see her and indeed, Christopher had booked this months ago, the girls reassured him that they had seen the Senator on Friday as agreed and he had a wonderful time with them. They giggled, and added that the 6 hours of pleasure was the best he had ever had and they hoped he had recovered. Amazed at such a question, they confirmed it was of course Sunday, and they fell short of asking him what on earth he was on. They sensed he was edgy and knew to keep their mouths shut. Christopher still couldn't believe he had slept through nearly two days. How could it be Sunday and why hadn't Jenny woken him?

He checked the wardrobes and Jenny's clothes had

gone, in a panic he opened all the drawers and found them empty, in a confused daze he looked in the bathroom, all her moisturisers, make-up and all the bits that made up her essential toiletries were gone. It made no sense and he thought he must be having a nightmare and he would wake up soon. His heart was racing, and his head had started to throb deeply on the left side of his temple. As he rubbed the spot above his left eye, he could feel the headache beginning to march across his forehead and in passing giving him a good kicking behind his eyes. He thought he was going to be sick. He didn't know what was wrong with him. He just wasn't thinking straight. He rang Jenny on her mobile but it went straight to answer phone. Where was everyone? Nothing made any sense.

At 6 p.m. he realised the Senator, his wife and Jenny would be on the Jet back to Atlanta and he was supposed to be with them. He still wasn't functioning at full pelt. All his thoughts were filled with why? But he still felt unable to think what he should do or where he could go for answers. At 7 p.m. after numerous calls to Jenny and messages left on her answer phone, he rang Alice.

He was surprised how calming and normal it felt to hear Alice's soft Norfolk voice talking ten to the dozen about things that didn't interest him and about people he didn't know. After quite some time of relaying all the latest gossip and doings in Winterton, she stopped to ask if he was o.k.? She wasn't used to him ringing and just listening in this way. More, his calls were usually focussed and to the point, albeit always polite and deferential. He told her he had been busy and although in London, he wasn't sure if he would have time to come home or not. This was quite usual for her to hear and she said that if he changed his mind, just to let her know so his room could be freshened for him. At that moment he realised how scared he felt and that to be in Winterton being fussed over by Alice, sounded safe and he wished he had settled for a safe and easy life, but those thoughts would have to wait for the moment. He said he would ring her if he had time to come home.

As the call finished, Alice thought he sounded different; the goodbye was hesitant and almost as an afterthought, just before he put the phone down, he told her to take care and he would see her soon. This was not the Christopher she was used to speaking with. They had an almost business like relationship which had suited them both. She had her home, girls and charity work, he had his career which also gave her much standing in the community. Christopher was viewed as an exceptionally successful business man in Norfolk and Alice as his wife was asked to attend many functions in his absence.

The unexpected warmth in Christopher's voice, and his words made her wonder, and in that wonder she discovered she liked the thought of them maybe getting closer again. They were both getting older and life would calm down as the years passed. She wondered if it would be possible for them both to maybe enjoy their village and events together. She put those thoughts to one side whilst she got on with sorting out her diary of engagements for the following busy week. Christopher had no idea what Alice was doing these days and how, in his absence, she was making quite a name for herself in the county.

Christopher headed for the hotel bar. He felt disorientated and scared. He couldn't think straight and couldn't work out what was happening. A stiff drink in normal surroundings would help him think and decide what he would do next. The two men in the reception area were working hard to look part of the furniture as they watched Christopher down his whisky. They would take their chance when he moved out of the public area of the hotel. He would either have to take a piss or leave the hotel sometime soon they wagered and they could afford to wait.

CHAPTER TWENTY EIGHT

Home Sweet Home

Amanda was sitting by her pool just outside her villa in the village of Karsiyaka near Kyrenia in Northern Cyprus. Her secret bolt hole. The fear was subsiding. Her body felt calm but her hands still had a tremor that threatened to spill the champagne in her glass. Krug Rose' was her preferred Champagne and at just under £100 per bottle she thought a lock on her wine cellar was a good idea. What she had done was the most daring, stupid, brilliant and deadliest scam. She had taken on the Colombians and beaten them. It was momentously awesome. No one in their right minds would do what she had done. She trembled at her audacity. Now, when it was all over and she had time to reflect, she knew she had done the right thing. It had worked.

Nearly four months ago she decided it was time to go. It wasn't just the Police that troubled her, they were just a frustrating annoyance. She had some influential top Police in her pocket together with the odd judge. No, the Police were not the major problem. Her contact in America was pushing her to shift more drugs more regularly but that was being handled. It was the CIA's sudden interest that bothered her enormously. She saw the CIA as a ruthless organisation she knew very little about and they had started to ask questions. The writing was on the wall. There were too many people too interested in what she was doing. All in all, she was tired of fighting, tired of watching her back and tired of pretending.

Here in Karsiayka she felt real and that is what she wanted. It was Saturday night. She had slept well Friday night, exhausted by the fear and daring of what she had done and had woken and found herself in paradise. She surveyed the quiet beauty with the sea ahead of her and the mountains behind her. The fragrant oleander bushes were in bloom with lots of deep pink flowers. As dusk approached she could smell the gorgeous white flowers of the caper bush, with their swirl of purple stamens a gentle breeze would carry the scent and fill the evening air. She visibly relaxed and thought that she had done the right thing to make this place her escape and her home. The estate contained orange and lemon trees and of course the wonderfully old and gnarled olive trees that bloomed and brought forth fruit at a very old age. She remembered when the villa was being built that an olive tree fairly close to the pool was going to be dug up. She was told in no uncertain terms that it was a criminal act to kill an olive tree because it took many, many years for them to fruit. She had laughed and thought that for all she had done over the years it would seem like divine intervention if she was placed in gaol for killing a tree. Of course the tree was moved and lovingly replanted by her gardeners. Yes, she breathed in the cool, fragrant evening air and thought it felt like paradise. This moment, this place, this feeling of relaxed pleasure, she would remember forever. She raised her glass to the sky in welcome to her new life.

Amanda was getting older and had become quite tired of it all. She wanted a semblance of safeness and respectability. She had run an impressive empire and since Peter had died, she had the advantage of running successfully and single-handedly the whole caboodle. Jennifer was no problem; she knew nothing about the business. Peter had been the brains in that relationship and when he died Amanda took everything over. She successfully ran the business and it got bigger and better. But it had taken its toll and at 50 years old, the fun and excitement had gone out of it. She had accumulated plenty of money but in order to fully retire, she needed something big to give her enough money to get Jennifer off her back for good and that bit more money to ensure she would be a rich woman for the rest of her life.

The drug run had been a little side line at the beginning but with Christopher working the America –England run so well, it had proved to be a big earner. There were Police, the drug barons, the special branch and lately the CIA who had started to take a bit more interest in her business. Enough was enough and Amanda decided it was time to get out. She knew her success was due in part to her ability to know when something was right and when it was starting to go wrong. The Colombians wanted her to move larger quantities through her courier, Christopher. Many of their previous couriers had been caught and runs were closed but Christopher had the luck and potential to continue to make them lots of money. Whilst the drugs had been a small and profitable business it was easy to manage but Amanda was beginning to feel threatened by demands to move more drugs more often. Christopher still had panic attacks when pick ups and deliveries happened more often than he liked and she had to work hard to get him to do it. Again, she saw warning signs to get out.

Amanda was a clever, ruthless girl, Peter had always said so. The plan was worked out overnight with the aid of a few glasses of champagne. Amanda called Jennifer the next day. Jennifer argued that she had never been "silly" with money, that her accounts were in good order but Amanda, with patience she found difficult to control explained again that she had to make Christopher feel she was broke and needed £3,000,000 to get back into control. Jennifer didn't want to do it. She wasn't used to being that devious. Besides, she loved Christopher and didn't want to do this. Her accountant was also Amanda's accountant and he was in on it too after being promised £500,000 for doing what he did best, screwing anyone that helped his clients stay viable. He didn't know the bigger picture but the £500,000 blocked out any need to explain to him. Poor Hershel she thought. He was about to lose her custom. As part of her plan to disappear, she had moved all her money overnight to a secure bank in Switzerland. They would charge her a vast amount of money to keep her investments safe and away from prying eyes. She surprised herself that she would walk out on her business so easily. Money was no good if you were in prison, or dead. She had earned enough to be very comfortable and this last big run gave her more than enough to invest and keep her in Krug champagne happily for the rest of her life. The business had been left to her girls who had worked hard for her. It was the least she could do and cannily, she knew that if she fell on hard times she could always turn to them. But that was not going to happen. Shrewd investments over the years had made her a wealthy woman and she would now want for nothing.

There was no extradition from Northern Cyprus. It was part of Turkey. She had loved the place for years and had visited secretly on a regular basis. It had a beautiful port for her Sunseeker yacht to moor in. Amanda was never going to "rough" it. She had a crew on board who at an hour's notice would be ready to sail anywhere she wanted. The luxury yacht had been her biggest indulgence and she loved it. The villa was her next indulgence and after finding the best builder in Northern Cyprus she purchased 3 dolman of land near the foot of the five finger mountains. Her villa looked out over the shimmering Mediterranean sea and from her balcony at the back of the house she looked up at the mountains.

Northern Cyprus could rival other Mediterranean countries with their 5 star hotels and casinos, she knew she would never be without company and fun if she wanted it. It was a good place to live and she felt safe here. It was the last place anyone would think to find her, and she had covered her tracks well. Her yacht was crewed by young, gorgeous Turkish men. There were no women and that suited her fine. She may have retired but she still had a healthy sex drive and knew the young crew could satisfy any needs she may have. Now was the time for her to be the recipient of much pleasure, not the giver.

Her very needy and strong sex drive was what got her into the business in the first place. She also remembered it was what got her thrown out of her upper class family. At the thought of them she raised her glass again in salute and defiantly shouted "Fuck you all". It didn't make her feel good, she felt rather sad actually.

She was going to enjoy her drink, and turning to look at the impossibly beautiful mountains she had to say that, quite frankly, she felt good. There was no guilt. Jennifer would be ok, she had promised to look after her. She smiled at how angry Jennifer was at the thought of Christopher buying her house. She had to laugh. The idiot had never realised how much Jennifer loved her home and grounds. He had never thought that something so beautiful and grand takes love, time and money to achieve such greatness. He never asked that the house was the love of her and Peter's life. He deserved her scorn, but she played her part well and she seemed to have lost her love for Christopher which was very helpful. Amanda had thought there would be lots of problems with Jennifer feeling guilty and still caring for Christopher, but he, bless him, ruined that in one fell swoop when he insisted he had the deeds to the house and grounds.

She didn't feel any guilt at Christopher being the "patsy" in all of this. He had been paid very well over the years and she had put up with so much whinging from him. He would never have made so much money in his lifetime, he should be grateful to her. Chuck had summed him up after one meeting. He was a stuck up prick. But well, she thought, that was that. He was a closed book and she would never think of him again.

The money had been paid on the Friday morning. A huge amount of money. The Cocaine had been exceptionally good quality and when mixed would earn street money way in excess of treble the amount paid out. The buyers were very happy indeed. Amanda paid Chuck £2,000,000 and he was disappearing out of the country but each never told the other where they were going. Jennifer got to keep the $3,000,000 from Christopher which would set her up for life. Hershel would invest it well for her and Amanda's promise of looking after Jenny was now fulfilled. Amanda earned $4,000,000 which together with her investments made her a very wealthy woman indeed. It had to be one of the biggest stashes to have ever got into Britain without being discovered.

She knew the Colombians wouldn't rest. No one duped them and got away with it. It was the biggest gamble of her life. Was it worth it? She had thought hard that night and decided it was damn well worth it. The Colombians would never find her. She had agreed with them to move this exceptionally large amount of the purest Cocaine. It was worth more than she negotiated with the South London crew. They couldn't believe their luck. She smiled at the thought. This was the largest shipment to come into the country for a very long time. She knew the South London crew well. They had had dealings over the years and they understood each other. For this exceptionally good price she wanted money transferred that night. A test of the quality of the drug proved it was a bargain. The going rate for pure cocaine was between £35,000 per kilo to £45,000 per kilo. They had 6 cases carrying 30 kilos in each. It was good shit and she sold for under £45,000 per kilo.

She told the Colombians that Christopher would be landing in England at 10 a.m. on Friday morning. She knew they would be waiting at the airport to see the cases unloaded and they would follow the car to the pick up point. They would leave nothing to chance with such a huge amount of Cocaine. She aimed to be out of the country by 6 a.m. Friday morning and the money would be in her suitcase. She flew to the continent, changing planes, and stopping off in Switzerland and depositing the money. She had paid Chuck by bank credit Thursday night so he could get away. Hershel had been paid his money. She could afford the £2,500,000 from her account. The £6,000,000 together with her other assets made her feel very safe and secure. She arrived in Kasyiaka late Friday evening. All her ties had been cut with England, her money was safe. She had an account in Northern Cyprus for her instant spend account. She had changed her name to Angela Coombes. A good fake passport was easy to get and all necessary papers were of the highest quality. She had covered herself. She shook at the thought of what she had done to the Colombians and what they were capable of. Everyone had been paid off. Her money was being looked after and no one could ever access Swiss accounts. The two bodyguards she employed at the moment made her feel safe, they were ex SAS and she reckoned she would only need them for 3 months. By then, if no one had come looking, she would be safe. She poured another glass of champagne and the trembling stopped. With a deep breath she realised she had everything covered and her future looked good.

If only her father could see her now. The smile left her face briefly at the thought. Well, she had succeeded. Ok, she realised, she came from a very rich background, she had the schooling, the horses, and the society parties. To have that all taken away and be thrown unceremoniously out of the family and never spoken of again at an early age of 20 years was very traumatic.

She had always loved sex. She had enjoyed many sexual partners since the age of 14 years and at 18 years old she decided to make it pay. She had the good fortune to meet Peter and he recognised her talent and that was the start of the films and the high class brothel. Actually, she hated the word brothel and always thought of it as a gentleman's club. More discreet and classy.

It was a tiresome story, but one of her clients knew her father and of course all hell was let loose when her father found out what she was doing. Actually, she supposed that as he was a Judge and a very religious man with many acquaintances in the higher church, it was inevitable she would be disowned. Although, she smiled at the thought, some of her clients were Judges and she had known the odd Bishop in a biblical way.

Funnily enough, it was only now that she missed her family. Her mother and father were in their 80s but still very much alive. Until now she hadn't cared about them, but at this moment, well, it would have been nice to see them. With no family ties and no children, Amanda had a plan to sail the seas and enjoy her life to the full. Her lovers would now be her choice and she would enjoy selecting them.

CHAPTER TWENTY NINE

On the plane Jenny was relieved to be away from England and on her way home, she needed time to think. It had all been a frightening whirlwind. She had paid Amanda back in full and no more favours would have to be given. Although, she conceded, it hadn't been all bad. When Amanda had suggested all those years ago that she could be very nice to this English man, Amanda would never have envisaged how close they would become. Jenny grew to love Christopher, and would happily stay with him for ever. He wasn't, of course, her one true love, there could only be one. Her one true love, her abiding passion, the one she got up in the morning for was her house and grounds. she didn't love him as much as she loved her home and grounds and lifestyle. She couldn't believe how he thought he could just take her house from her. It was the love of her life and the love of her deceased husband. She had promised him that the house and grounds would continue, be maintained and guided into something wondrous. It had become their child. Who would give their child away? Not her, she would fight for what was hers.

The money that had funded the house and grounds was her deceased husbands business. He was in business with Amanda. Prostitution and porno films were his area. He had funded Amanda and bought Zillion Films to produce the popular and sought after fantasy films bought on the internet. When he died, Jenny turned to Amanda for help in keeping everything going. Jenny wanted nothing to do with the business, she just wanted the money due to fund her life and home. Jenny owed Amanda big time. When police investigated the film company Amanda was noted as the owner. When the trail led to the house in London, again Amanda took full ownership of the house and stated it was a private club. Never once did Amanda involve Jenny, and all the publicity and notoriety was focussed on Amanda. Jenny still had thousands paid into her bank account every month. Jenny would never be poor. The account had $20,000,000 in it which was invested well and allowed her to live like a queen and adopt many worthy and charitable projects. Her profile was clean and untraceable, thanks to Amanda. Jenny always wondered if her husband and Amanda were more than working partners, but it wasn't good to dwell on such things. She owed Amanda, and she paid her back in full when asked for help.

Amanda had worked hard over the years, and now she wanted to retire, live the good life with plenty of money behind her. She had spoken candidly to Jenny about it and it was decided that she would retire with a big bang and have enough money to live on and Jenny would help.

Jenny was not a schemer. She followed. She wasn't

happy about duping Christopher. She told Amanda she loved him and it would be treacherous to deceive him in this way. Amanda, soothingly said that she wasn't doing anything terrible. In fact, it was going to earn Christopher and herself a lot of money. She said that Christopher being an upstanding English man would not do this off his own back, in fact he was a gentleman and would do it for Jenny. Jenny still argued but Amanda got tough and said Jenny owed her and this would pay everything off. This was the last time she had to do anything and the money would keep her in charity parties for a lifetime.

Reluctantly Jenny played her part and she was surprised at her acting skills. Hershel nearly made her laugh with his tough stance but Christopher had bought into it and she stayed in character. When Christopher said he wanted the deeds to the house and grounds her shock at such an opportunist move took her breath away. She could never forgive him for doing such a thing. It felt like a huge betrayal. She realised he had never understood her feelings for the house, he hadn't bothered to understand her at all. So she played her part, she spiked his whisky and she packed and left him on Saturday and went to stay at the American Embassy with the Senator and his wife. She would use some of Christopher's £3,000,000 to build the most fabulous orangery in America. Already she was excited about looking at designs. When she got back home she would start her new project immediately. Her love for Christopher had strangely dissipated and was replaced by indifference.

CHAPTER THIRTY

Lamb to the Slaughter

Pamela was in the office on Sunday morning. She knew it was silly but with Christopher in the country she wanted to make sure that everything was in order. With the Senator and his wife being here as well as the reception that had been organised for Saturday evening, Pamela had clearing up to do and paperwork to finish. It had been a shame Christopher missed the reception on Saturday evening. Apparently he had to go home to sort out something or other. Pamela thought Christopher's wife was really awful to ruin an important reception in this way. In fact, the Senator, she noted, looked a little under the weather and tired when he arrived quite late on Saturday night. She presumed it was still the jet lag. The reception was a great success and she prided herself on getting it just right and everyone had a good time. She wished Christopher had been there.

No one ever came in on a Sunday and the usually noisy office always felt strangely spooky to Pamela when it was so quiet. When the phone rang it made her jump and she nearly dropped a sheaf of important papers. Of course, she thought excitedly, it must be

Christopher, no one else would ring her at work on a Sunday. She rushed for the phone and answered breathlessly "hello", in a most unprofessional manner. She was disappointed to hear a strange voice. It was not Christopher.

The voice introduced himself as "a friend of Christopher." Pamela listened suspiciously. She asked what she could do for him and he responded in a most soothing and appealing way that he was most concerned for Christopher's safety. Pamela stiffened her back and the word "why" she asked was full of anxiety. The friend heard the concern and asked who she was. She explained her important role in Christopher's working life. The friend extolled her virtues as relayed to him by Christopher himself. She recognised herself in his words saying the beauty of her spirit, the handsomeness of her loyalty and the attractiveness of her wit and intelligence. She liked this man very much. He wasn't English, he had a foreign accent she couldn't place and thought that might account for the unusual use of words he had said to describe her.

He asked tentatively if she knew where Christopher was. She said she didn't. After a little questioning and flirting and suggesting of an important meeting, the friend said abruptly it was urgent that he speak to Christopher now and he needed to know where he was on the Friday morning when his plane had landed. All pretence of softness had gone and it was obvious that the friend had lost patience. Pamela was taken aback by such plain speaking after the warm and sweet words. She remonstrated that she couldn't possibly divulge such details of her boss's itinerary. The friend mentioned that possibly Christopher had made a delivery for him and because of Pamela's wonderful relationship with Christopher it was hoped she would know what had happened.

It was strange but suddenly all seemed clear to Pamela. She licked her lips and thought how to phrase such a question. "Are you the man Christopher deals with on his trips to America?" The man replied quickly and urgently, "yes, yes, that's me. Pamela, you truly are what Christopher says about you. His one true right hand person." Pamela liked that very much. She was keen to impress him further. "I know where Christopher keeps the bag, you know what I mean don't you, Mr, erm..." The friend responded quickly, "just call me Alfie" It didn't sound very foreign to Pamela but she continued. "Well Alfie, I have the bag here." She hesitated and asked, "Is that what you are looking for? I know it is very important to Christopher." Alfie responded quickly again. "Yes. Indeed. Do you know if it has a book with names and numbers in it?" Pamela, was excited now and said she would go and look. This man seemed to know all about her and her working relationship with Christopher and how important she was to him. She wanted to impress him more. There was a book in the bag but it didn't contain much. There were a few scribbles which she didn't recognise.

Pamela, continued talking to Alfie and asking what she could do to help him. Alfie asked if she knew where Christopher had gone on early Friday morning from the airport. Pamela, eager to please, thought hard. Although she didn't know where he had gone the Satnav had been set and she would check it. She had it in the garage at the office. Alfie said he would love to ring back in 10 minutes after she had looked. His parting words were what a deep, deep treasure she was to Christopher. Her heart was pounding. She loved the way he said treasure in such a meaningful way, it made her face blush. Pamela rushed to the garage to look for the Satnav. She knew she was helping Christopher in his secret work for the government. It was just so exciting.

Her ego was laying all her own traps. If only she knew what fate had in store for her, she may well have pleaded ignorance of Christopher's affairs and sought the safety of her home and anonymity.

She rang Alfie back with the Satnav details. He spoke so gently and soothingly to her she felt very important and special. Wanting to impress him further she coyly suggested that she was Christopher's right hand person and she knew everything about his secret work. Alfie was obviously very impressed by this and asked if she had the merchandise. Well Pamela didn't know what he meant but instead of admitting this, she again, coyly suggested that perhaps she might know something about this. He asked if she knew where the merchandise was now. She hinted she could find out. She licked her lips and smiled. This was such delicious fun.

They flirted and teased and Alfie cajoled and as the laughter died away Alfie said a tad too sharply for Pamela that she must bring the bag, book and information on where the merchandise was to him. He said he would ring in the morning with directions. The persuasiveness had been replaced with a cold, curt tone that scared Pamela. She protested that she couldn't do that, it was Christopher's belongings and the merchandise was no longer in it. He said she had to do what he said and she would bring the bag and tell him where the merchandise was.

The protests would have gone on for much longer if Alfie hadn't stated that Christopher would be dead by lunchtime if she didn't bring everything to him in the morning. He stopped any further questions from Pamela by saying he would call at 8.30 a.m. in the morning and he expected her to answer and be ready to take his instructions. He added chillingly that if she told anyone about this phone call, Christopher would be killed. With that he put the phone down. Pamela sat motionless in shock for a full 2 minutes.

"What had she done?" She kept asking herself. "What should she do?" The torment of it all was too much. She rang Neil, she trusted him to tell her what to do. Neil was on his way out for the evening to some Rotary event. He listened carefully and told Pamela in no uncertain terms to be there for the telephone call in the morning and then ring him and he would help her. All his questions on who they were, and who the caller had been was to no avail. Pamela knew nothing. Neil knew about the bag and the book and they contained nothing new.

Neil had recently started tracking Christopher. All his intimate conversations with Pamela had been helpful and something she let slip one day about the bag being full and in her cupboard had put in place the final piece of the jigsaw. Neil would always protect Christopher if he could, but he started to make enquiries through his Contact at Scotland Yard, DI Freddie Carrington. Why it had all taken such a giant turn at this stage he didn't know. The enquiries being made had not brought to light any contacts. But what he did know was Christopher was in trouble and needed his help. He got on the phone immediately to his contacts at Scotland Yard. Freddie Carrington was a friend and he asked for his help. Still protecting Christopher, Neil omitted to say anything about Christopher being killed. He wondered if Pamela was exaggerating. Christopher was not the sort to get into that type of trouble, surely not he thought. In the meantime, he asked Freddie to just check if there were any known intelligence on drug couriers in town. Why they wanted Christopher's courier bag he speculated must be because Christopher hadn't delivered this time. Neil was not a detective and had no idea what was going on, but he was sure Christopher was ok. This was not a film, bad stuff just doesn't happen to ordinary people. The morning would sort this out. Pamela was prone to flights of fancy. He had listened to enough of her conversations over the years to know that was true.

After a restless night Pamela sat by the phone in the office. She didn't go home. What could she tell her husband, he would never understand. She slept on the couch in the office. After a restless night she gave up any further attempts of sleep and got up at 5.30 a.m. There was coffee and milk in the office kitchen and some dry biscuits. She realised she had not eaten the night before.

She washed and was sitting ready for the phone call by 7.30 a.m. At 8.30 a.m. on the dot the phone rang.

She picked up the phone immediately and waited. She was told to bring everything to Liverpool Street Station. She was to wait by the Central Line entrance and she would be picked up there and taken to Christopher. What really scared her rigid was the words that she told no one, she must be at the station by 9 a.m. or Christopher would be killed. The voice told her that she was being watched and any deviation from her instructions would mean Christopher would be shot through the head without a second thought.

Pamela nearly fainted in panic. Her Christopher shot. It could be her fault. It just didn't make any sense, was she dreaming? These things don't happen to women like her. She so wanted to ring Neil. But there was no way she would ring Neil. In fact she wished she hadn't spoken to him last night, she might have caused harm to her Christopher. To be at Liverpool Street Station at 9 a.m. meant she had to leave 10 minutes ago. She grabbed the bag, her things and rushed out of the office. She ignored the telephone ringing. She knew it would be Neil and he would only get Christopher shot if she told him what was happening. She was on a mission to save her beloved Christopher and nothing would stop her.

She got on the Central line which would take her to Liverpool Street Station. It was a busy Monday morning rush hour and there were lots of trains. With a bit of luck she should be there with 5 minutes to spare. She got on the train and edged down the train past passengers.

Passengers streamed onto the train pushing her towards the middle of the aisle and left her holding the central pole for balance. She was being crushed by the crowds of people going to work and they hemmed her in on both sides. The air from the open top window helped her cool a little. She was agitated and those sitting in front of her noted her moist eyes and the chewing of her lip. Every now and then she would let go of the pole and pat the bag on her other arm for reassurance.

The train stopped abruptly in the dark tunnel. Only Pamela looked agitated and concerned. When the driver stated over the tannoy system that there was a delay due to a fault in the train at the next station. Pamela broke down in floods of tears. The passengers seated in front of her looked away uncomfortably. It just was not British to cry in public over such a normal event. Trains frequently broke down on this line. It was all very embarrassing. Within a few minutes the tannoy stated that the train would now be moving and apologised for the short delay. Pamela willed the train to move fast and she willed the time to move slower. She had to be at Liverpool Street Station by 9 a.m. and it was now 8.50 a.m. and she had to run to the entrance of the Central Line station at Liverpool Street. Her heart was racing, her mind was all over the place. All she could think of was her Christopher and if he was alright.

At 1 minute past 9 a.m. she got off the train at Liverpool Street Station. Blindly panicking, she had to push her way out of the train, everyone was moving so slow. She felt the whole country was conspiring against her to make her late and she could feel a deep headache stirring behind her eyes. The queue for the escalator shuffled slower than she had ever seen it. She pushed her way forward and ignored the angry commotion she left behind her. She ran up the escalators pushing arms out of her way and the tidal wave of anger followed her up to the exit point. She didn't care, she just wanted to get out and stand at the front of the Central Line entrance in Liverpool Street Station. She got there breathless and sweaty and 5 minutes late. She looked around for signs of someone but could see no one who looked interested in her. The mantra of "Oh God, Oh God, Oh God" kept going through her head. With time to think she felt scared and alone. She didn't know what to do for the best and hoped it would all be alright and the man would appear. Pamela knew she must stay where she was outside the Central Line entrance. She needed to go to the toilet but was too frightened to leave the entrance in case the man appeared and she was gone.

Scared, dejected and emotional she slumped in a corner feeling flat and deeply depressed. She had let Christopher down and she didn't know what to do now. The tears rolled down her cheeks in large droplets dripping off her nose and chin.

Alfie, as he called himself was in the upper level of Liverpool Street Station and looked down on her and watched her distress. He had to be sure she had not been followed there. He knew she would be late. 30 minutes to Liverpool Street was cutting it fine but the panic he caused her would concentrate her mind on getting here and leave her no time to think. He smiled, only 5 minutes late, she must have run all the way. He would enjoy playing with her. After 20 minutes if he felt certain she was not followed, he would go down and get her. The stupid bitch was crying and drawing attention to herself. He wondered if she would be a screamer too. He liked it when they screamed.

He had plenty of time. The others would not be back until the afternoon. They knew Christopher had been set up and they were after the others involved in this. They had some names and some leads but they had to move fast. Alfie was given Christopher to do with as he pleased and to get any additional information from him. Christopher, if nothing else, would be made an example of. Alfie enjoyed his work.

Neil was on the phone to Freddie Carrington. "We've lost her, she went without telling me what was said to her." Neil, through lack of sleep and frustration punched the wall in front of him, he gritted his teeth in anger, his knuckles bled, but he didn't feel the pain. He had been so stupid. He should have gone straight to London last night and stayed close to Pamela to make sure she didn't go anywhere without him. Freddie was having none of the self analysis pity. "What is her mobile number?" he asked Neil. Neil, with heavy sarcasm said "Well now, why didn't I think of that... I could call her. NOT! I tried that she is out of signal." This was so unlike Neil, usually dependable, business like and certainly not this panic stricken idiot on the other end of the line. Freddie was now getting impatient but he was trying hard to stay friendly. Again he asked Neil for Pamela's mobile telephone number. Neil sullenly gave it to him and waited for a sensible answer to his question of "What the hell do you think you can do with that?"

Freddie had left the phone hanging and Neil could hear him in the background passing Pamela's number to someone. After a few seconds he was back. Freddie explained to Neil, in tones sounding far more patient and relaxed than he felt, that people could be tracked by their mobile numbers and it was certainly worth a try because for the moment there was nothing else to go on.

It was 9 a.m. and Neil decided to do what he should have done last night. He told Freddie he was on his mobile and he was catching the 9.30 a.m. fast train to London. He would meet him at Liverpool Street Station and perhaps by then they would know where the hell Pamela was, and perhaps they might have found Christopher. He was to miss Pamela by just over an hour. He stood on the concourse of Liverpool Street Station at 11 a.m. looking in the direction of where Pamela had sat crying not knowing that she had ever been there.

Pamela looked up as a shadow engulfed her. "Hi, I am Alfie," he said with a winning smile and gentle tones. He extended his hand to help her up. She smiled, hesitantly at first, not knowing what to make of this man. His chiselled face and black hair gave him a sharp look that put her on edge but the smile with perfect white teeth looked genuine and warm and she pushed her wariness to one side. She recognised the accent from the phone call and knew it was him. She rushed her words to apologise for being late, stating the train had stopped and she had run up the escalator. He interrupted her gently and told her not to worry, nothing bad was going to happen. The tears that threatened to appear again subsided and she smiled at him.

He helped her to her feet. She could feel he had a strong grip but he was gentle and caring. His fingers caressed her hand and made her feel safe. She wasn't scared anymore. He led her along the concourse of the station, turning into another entrance to the Central Line. They went down the stairs and through the ticket barrier. She noted he had tickets for both of them. Instead of waiting for a train he led her along the platform and through an arch to the labyrinth of tunnels that took commuters to and from the underground system that travelled through Liverpool Street Station and crossed most of London and the suburbs. Pamela stayed silent. Alfie whispered kindly reassuring words that they would soon be there and all would be well.

The passages twisted and turned and they went down stairs and across. They moved purposefully along with the flow of people. It felt like they were walking for ages. Alfie halted suddenly, looked both ways, and moved quickly into what looked like a shallow cul de sac of a tunnel. A few steps ahead was a door. Alfie quickly and violently shouldered open the door beside them. It looked like one of those doors that never opened and was one of many you would pass on the way to a train.

Once inside, he closed the door quickly. From the modern and bright tunnels with the busy rush of commuters overtaking and brushing past, Pamela realised they were in a place that was all still and quiet and there were no people here. She looked around and the tunnel before them seemed to be locked in a time warp of old London. The ceiling was low and curved, the tiled walls dark with age and the dim lighting made Pamela breathe deeply and her breath jerked and stalled with trepidation at each intake. The atmosphere had changed and become airless and oppressive and heavy with a brooding shadow of fearful expectation. Pamela's step faltered and she was immersed in a feeling of deep foreboding.

Sensing her unrest, Alfie's grip got tighter and he pushed her to move quickly. She didn't want to go on, she didn't want to be here and she started to protest and pulled away from his grip. He would have none of that. He pulled her roughly close to him and moved her faster than she wanted to move. His tight grip on her upper arm ensured she could not escape his hold. He whispered words of encouragement, saying that Christopher needed her, that they were nearly there. He promised she could sit down with Christopher and rest very soon. Unable to think and unable to comprehend what was happening, Pamela was pulled along in a muted fog of panic.

There was another door and this opened easily and led to a small room. In the middle of the room was someone tied to a chair and gagged. She saw but couldn't register. That couldn't be Christopher could it? The man looked dishevelled and there were cuts on his face and a swelling around the eye that made it difficult to recognise who he was. Christopher saw her and from a slumped pose his back became as rigid and erect as was possible with the ropes. His eyes widened with horror as he looked from Alfie to Pamela. He tried to shout a warning but it came as a muffled blur from his gag. Pamela sensing the horror and feeling Alfie grip her more tightly she wanted to get away now and hide. She wanted to wake up in her bed and remember this as a nightmare.

There was rope that appeared from nowhere, there was a chair that she was made to sat on. He tied her tightly and sat her opposite Christopher but not close enough to touch. Pamela couldn't take her eyes off Christopher. She mouthed the word "Why?" Christopher's brow screwed up and he tried to say something but it came out as a muffled long murmur. He shouted at Alfie, trying to get him to take off the gag, he wanted to plead with him, to let Pamela go. Alfie was enjoying Christopher's response. It was satisfying to know he didn't like this at all.

He took the bag that Pamela had dropped. Christopher watched intently as he pulled out the book with all the scribbled comments in it. They were indecipherable and looked of no consequence. He tossed it to one side. He barely took his eyes from Christopher, ensuring the deadly meaning of his intent did not escape him. The bag was empty but he made a performance of examining it closely and then threw it carelessly across the room. He stared at Christopher, ensuring he had his full attention. His gaze was intense and he whispered menacingly, "This is all for you Christopher. All you have to do is just watch." His Cheshire cat like grin was the most frightening thing Christopher had seen so far.

Pamela had watched silently, afraid to make a noise

hoping he would not notice her and would forget she was there. Her panic had made her unrealistic and she wished for everything that was never going to be possible. People would miss her and send someone who would come and rescue her. Even more unrealistically, that Christopher would break free from his bonds and knock their captor out. They would escape and be free to go back to how everything should be. But that wasn't going to happen, deep down she knew that. She couldn't shake off the fear that something bad was going to happen. It was the dreadful thought that made her whimper in fear, that he might hurt her and there was nothing she could do to stop him.

Freddie was waiting with news. Pamela's signal which could not be found suddenly appeared at 9.05 a.m. on the computer console as in the vicinity of Liverpool Street Station. He exclaimed that the coincidence was unbelievable and fortunate. It disappeared again at 9.40 a.m. before they could find her. The satellite could pick up approximate areas of where the mobile was, but still could not pin point the exact spot. London was a big place and all around Liverpool Street Station were buildings and cellars which would take an army of men days to search. Freddie had arrived with 5 police officers to help him. Neil felt the frustration well up inside him: he walked away to calm down. It was impossible, how on earth would they find Pamela and Christopher.

Freddie continued to talk. "We have to think clearly about this. If the signal disappeared it either means she got on an underground train where the signal is lost or she was taken somewhere close by that is underground and that is also why the signal was lost." Neil turned around and came back, Freddie was making good sense. Neil added, "if the signal was seen for half an hour it supposes that she did not get on a train. It supposes that she was here to meet someone and they took her somewhere." Freddie picked up the idea and added "Yes, who ever picked her up would not take her on a train; too public. More likely took her somewhere close by."

Freddie sprung into action. He asked where the Station Master Office was and walked purposefully to second it for his use. This was now a case that needed immediate and dedicated work. Time was of an essence. He didn't want to alarm Neil just yet, but his instinct told him this was not going to end well. He barked his orders on the phone and to those around him. He sent an Officer to the CCTV room in the station and asked for all CCTV to be made available. He prayed they had digital CCTV, if not, he knew there would be problems in getting hold of the tapes quickly to view. Officers were despatched around the station asking questions. It had been rush hour and no one who worked on the station had taken any notice of commuters travelling. They drew a blank.

Meanwhile, Freddie had found the Station Master's Office and unceremoniously thrown him out. He told him to wait outside in case he was needed. The phone in his office was put to use immediately. More officers were needed to help and he shouted down the phone that he needed them now!

With everything nearly in place, Freddie grabbed Neil, sat him down and in tones far from friendly told him to start from the beginning and give him every fucking detail now! So far, Neil had given the impression that there was a potential problem coming on board and if monitored it could be halted before it got going. That was obviously at best a naïve notion, or at worst a fucking deception of the first order. Trafficking of drugs in a small way was of little interest to Freddie, but in kicking a can of worms you never know what nasty little insect is going to climb out. Freddie had thought it might have thrown up intelligence information that could be useful at some stage. But this turned out to be much more than a can of worms, it was a big fucking anaconda and he didn't like being taken for a ride.

Neil dredged up every bit of information that Pamela had told him. He apologised for not mentioning that Christopher might be killed. Freddie, amazed at the stupidity of a man he thought had more brains, held back his anger as Neil went on to tell him about the bag and the book which he had looked at once whilst visiting his father. He had gone into Christopher's office at Pamela's invitation and looked at the bag. It seemed to contain some form of cover and a book with scribbles he couldn't make out. Freddie by now spitting nails of anger shouted "Didn't you think man that this was important stuff to tell me? Your friend is threatened with being killed and you thought it not important? Gees, save me from the righteous!" Neil started to say that Pamela exaggerates, that it couldn't be true, but the words fell short of being spoken.

Neil was overcome with embarrassment and unbelievable remorse. Of course Freddie was right, what the hell had he been thinking of. This was not a film, this was true life and his friend was in danger and he had allowed Pamela to be taken. He should have come clean earlier with Freddie and he should have travelled to London last night. He would never forgive himself if anything happened to the two of them. He was a Magistrate but he only dealt with lesser crimes. He wasn't worldly like Freddie. He would beat himself up for years on his stupidity and naïvety that might cause the death of two people.

Freddie was not the sort of man you messed with. London was his patch. A slightly antiquated idea in this modern day and age but he never bought into the PC world of niceness. He had seen too much in his considerable career to go down that candy-assed way of thinking. Tall, lean, and wearing a moustache that was out of fashion and a suit that would have looked good in the thirties: Freddie was a smart man who didn't give a shit about fashion but liked to be turned out well. He demanded respect and got it in bucket loads. His men, and he called his women DCs his men too, loved him with a loyalty not seem by many in the force.

He had met Neil at some Met function in London. He was never keen on such events but was told by his superiors to "network". Stupid saying he thought. Networking didn't catch thieves and villains. He met Neil during the polite talking at the dinner table and strangely they seemed to get on. It was an unusual friendship that no-one would have put money on as succeeding but it did. They had the same values and levels of integrity which made their conversations interesting. They had been long distant friends for a few years now. They met occasionally for a drink when Neil was in town.

Neil was a good man and a good friend but work was work and this was turning nasty. Freddie knew something big had happened. If this Christopher had been couriering drugs for a few years and everything had run smoothly, you don't get kidnaps, and potential killers raising their ugly heads unless it was something worth their while or something had gone wrong. Villains want an easy life too. They don't want to make waves unless they have to. His gut instinct was this was nasty, very nasty indeed and he didn't want his town messed up with gunmen going off half cocked.

The one female officer in the group had spent time with a girl who worked in the kiosk close to the Central Line Underground entrance. Her name was Tracy and she told the officer that there had been a woman slumped for a while in a corner of the station crying. She fitted the description of a middle aged woman, dark hair and wearing a beige coat. She had what looked like one of those flight bags you carry on board a plane. Tracy said the woman was cuddling it like it was a teddy bear. All in all, it was too much of a coincidence that this person sounded like Pamela.

Tracy had gone on to say that she felt so sorry for the woman, but she couldn't leave her kiosk. She said her boss would have fired her if she had done that. She added that after a little while a very kind man did go over to her and help her up and seemed to make her feel better and she had left with him smiling. The girl thought it was dead romantic; two strangers meeting on a station and thought it would make a good film. On being asked, she said she didn't know which way they were walking because she had customers who needed to be served and when she looked up again, the man and the woman had gone.

This piece of news excited Neil. They had to be close by. Again, Freddie reminded him that they lost the mobile signal at 9.40 a.m. so they couldn't have gone far and they had to be in a cellar somewhere, but where? Freddie got on the phone again and asked someone at New Scotland Yard to find out which buildings had cellars around Liverpool Street Station. He estimated cellars had to be within 10 minutes walk of the station. They waited. They were told it would all take at least half an hour. The officer finding out about the CCTV should be back soon. It was a waiting game and Neil had run out of patience at the same time as he had run out of hope. It all sounded impossible. How would they find anyone in this maze of trains, platforms and exits.

Fired up and jittery, Neil needed to calm down. He hadn't had a drink for hours and to fill in the time, he bought Freddie and himself a coffee. Freddie spoke in quiet tones to officers coming and going with information. No one had any idea of where to look first. The CCTV would track the direction they had gone. This was one of the biggest stations in London with enough cameras, to make the BBC jealous. God! He thought, how could 30 minutes feel like 30 hours?

He would have been physically sick if he had known what was going on whilst he sipped his coffee.

He seemed to have finished talking to Christopher and Pamela saw him turn and come towards her. She pulled and struggled to get out of the ropes, she didn't want him near her, she didn't know what he was going to do. He smiled and made shushing noises, he stroked her hair and petted her like a dog. She calmed a little and waited. He took off his mac and placed it carefully away from them both in a clear corner.

Gently, he undid the ropes and uttered, "Careful of your arms my dear. That's better, now you can stretch a bit and feel more comfortable." Pamela didn't dare look into his face, she averted her eyes, not knowing what to do. He helped her out of the chair and looked into her face, pushing her hair away from her eyes. "You have beautiful eyes my dear," he purred. "Now I want you to take off your coat." She hadn't buttoned her coat, so it lay across her open and ready to take off. She didn't want to take it off and pulled her coat across her to stop such a thing. He gently chastised her and pulled the coat open and eased it from her shoulders. She let him, knowing she couldn't do anything else. Her low moan of anguish excited Alfie.

Getting her to take off all her clothes was not very easy, she refused and cried and pushed him away. It was ok for a few minutes to see her resisting, he liked a bit of fight but enough was enough. He slapped her face hard. He didn't punch her, he wanted her to feel told off but not damaged. More, like chastising an hysterical child. He lovingly touched her face where the glowing red mark appeared and whispered soothing words. "My poor darling, I had to do it, you were getting hysterical and I don't want you to suffer." He kissed her cheek and promised all would be well. He helped her take every item of clothing off. Pamela whimpered and tried to stop crying. She so wanted to go to the toilet. She stood in front of him naked now and saying she needed to go to the toilet. He laughed... it was a joyful, engaging laugh. "You poor darling, if you want to pee go into the corner over there." He pointed to a dark recess. She moved, trying to cover as much of her private parts as she could. She had never been naked in front of her husband, let alone like this. Her hair was dishevelled, her face wracked with tears and trepidation, her body shook with fear. Her degradation was nearly complete.

The message came that the CCTV was ready to be viewed. Freddie got up and Neil jumped up and followed him. The CCTV room was very modern and thank goodness it had digital. It was also like a glass box and all commuters rushing past could see them in the room. Freddie didn't want to draw attention to his men, as he said; you never know who is watching. He was in plain clothes and so was Neil. He told the rest of his men to go look around the station but listen to their radios, he would call them if he needed them. There was a bank of monitors to view the different cameras. "Yeah Gods!" Neil thought. He asked how on earth all the various cameras could be viewed in a short time, it would take hours. The CCTV operator got his instructions from Freddie. He asked to see anything from 8.30 a.m. to 10 a.m. He asked for the camera outside the Central Line Station to be shown first. The operator assigned to them shuffled around and acted like he had never moved fast in his life and it was driving Neil mad.

Freddie kept busy, he was on the phone again. Earlier, he had sent for one of the top DI's from the Drug Squad and told him to get his arse over to Liverpool Street Station CCTV room. Valuable minutes had passed and as they waited for the CCTV to work Freddie sent out another call with dire warnings of having his bollocks for breakfast if the DI wasn't here in 5 minutes. DI Thorpe walked in as the phone was put down. Everyone he needed was here now and he was conscious that they were running out of time. Freddie shouted at the CCTV operator to get a bloody move on.

DI Thorpe, or Kev to those who knew him was an enthusiastic DI who had risen through the ranks on a fast track scheme for University graduates. Not overly tall at just 5'6", he made up for lack of height with a bounding, youthfulness that filled the room. What he didn't know about drugs and the big boys who dealt in them, was not worth knowing. "Ok old man, why have you summoned me to this place. I was in the middle of something important." Freddie gave him a withering look "And what computer game was that may I ask, sonny boy!" This banter went on for a few minutes until everyone's attention was drawn to the screen showing a woman standing by the entrance to the Central Line Station. "My God, it's Pamela," Neil exclaimed.

Nothing seemed to be happening and the film was fast forwarded. They watched as she slumped down into a corner by the station. A man came up to Pamela and bent down to help her. They slowed the picture down and freeze framed it as the man appeared to be looking directly at the CCTV camera. "Fuck! What's he doing in England?" DI Thorpe exclaimed as he pushed the other two out of the way to get a better look at the screen. On being asked who he was, DI Thorpe answered in hallowed terms "It's Alfie Como! And if he has got your friend, they are in big fucking trouble."

Neil asked who that was and DI Thorpe gave a potted history. "He is part of the Colombian mob. Where ever he is they are close by. They use him to get information and he is known to us as The Animal. He is the mob's torturer and he loves his work. His *Uomo Picollo*, Little Man in English, is infamous and scares the hell out of anyone who sees it." Neil laughed. It might have been the incredible tension that was in the room and the reference to such a phallic term "Little Man", but he roared with laughter and was utterly shocked that he could laugh at such a moment. DI Kev Thorpe gave him a withering look. "You have no idea what I am talking about have you?" He turned to Freddie and asked if he had heard of it. Freddie nodded and got on the phone to the station and asked for some armed undercover police, he added, "Don't send the SO19 bastards, they would scare the shit out of anyone on the station: trampling over everything in their size 12 boots! We need subtle." He told them to report to the Station Master's Office and he would ring them and tell them what he wanted. He added they had 10 minutes to get their arses in place and make sure they were not late. The grim look on Freddie's face together with DI Thorpe's enthusiastic, "Hell we are in for some action today," panicked Neil in a way he had never experienced before. With handkerchief in hand mopping a leaking face, he asked quietly what now?

The CCTV operator was told to get a move on and make sure where ever the couple were going he got the right camera on them. The digital CCTV recordings made using the system much easier to manipulate. With all eyes on the CCTV operator, he nervously fumbled his way across the key board. It was tortuously slow but they were getting there. It looked, at first, as if Pamela and Alfie were going to get on a train but with each new camera shot of the couple, they could see the pair going off into another tunnel. In anticipation of where the pair were walking, the operator showed the next camera they should come onto. They were not on the next camera. They had lost them. Freddie asked how that was possible, he asked where the fuck were the cameras when they needed them. They went back to the previous camera which showed the last place they were seen and as they watched, they saw them turn left into what looked like a recess. Freddie was shouting now at the operator who said that there was no camera in that area.

The Station Manager who had been in the background watching, was unceremoniously dragged by each arm to the monitor and told to look. Both Freddie and Kev, hyped up and ready to punch his lights out if there was a wrong answer given, shouted at the Station Manager "What is this place, where is it and how do we get there?" He knew his station and exactly where this was. No cameras were needed there because it led to a disused passageway for access to parts of the tunnel track. Freddie was on the phone to the armed police to meet him on the concourse by the Central Line entrance in 30 seconds, he added dryly, "Try and be as inconspicuous as you can, and don't scare the real people out there." 4 men running at full pelt with hands on their chest to hold something still was not as inconspicuous as was hoped for but time was of an essence. Kev had been on the phone to his people to tell them the Columbians were in town and to scour all haunts and get what information they could. He rang again to update them on his tracking of Alfie and it was now a searching procedure.

She was in the corner for far too long. Alfie called her and told her to come to him now. She was cowering there and whimpered when he came over. He was impatient to get a move on. The playing had to finish he wanted some real fun. Everything was for Christopher to see. "I am showcasing this just for you," Alfie told him. He wanted recognition for his ingenuity, for his creativity but above all, he wanted to see real terror. The show was about to begin.

She didn't want to move. If she stayed huddled in the corner he might go away. The panic she felt was like nothing she had experienced before. She was giddy with fear and she wanted to scream but she couldn't. He came over and dragged her to the centre of the room and stood a short distance in front of Christopher.

Christopher was shouting and pleading and shaking to get out of the ropes. But that translated to Alfie and Pamela as muffled urgent noises. His face had gone red from the exertion and his eyes held a terror that matched the terror in Pamela's eyes. He watched as Alfie stood Pamela in front of him and put his left arm across her to hold her body and arms tight. Both Alfie and Pamela faced Christopher. She had made an effort to cover herself with her hands but to no avail. Her fear was plain to see. Now held tightly, she stood erect and still, nothing moved except her eyes which darted this way and that in terror but never rested on Christopher.

Alfie whispered in Pamela's ear that she was quite a sweet little thing. His right hand caressed her left nipple. She hardly dare breathe, in case he hurt her. His hand trailed down towards her belly and rubbed the little hairy mound above her vagina. Her breathing had nearly stopped and she was gripped with a fear that knew no boundaries.

Christopher couldn't bear to watch. All the time Alfie was looking into Christopher's eyes and smirking. He licked Pamela's ear and nibbled her lobe. An anguished moan from deep down in her soul forced its way into her throat. "Please don't," she pleaded. He stopped and looked at Christopher and said. "Are you ready for the show?" It was like the world had stopped and that they were the only people alive. All of Christopher's senses tuned into the monster before him. Alfie deftly parted Pamela's legs with his right leg and he violently and swiftly jerked them apart. He whispered shushing noises to calm Pamela's anguished cry and with his eyes on Christopher, told Pamela to say hello to his Uomo Picollo.

Christopher saw a glint of metal but he didn't know

what he saw, he just knew it was bad. Pamela was rigid, not a movement in her body, just her eyes staring and darting this way and that. Her mouth moved quietly as she pleading with him to let her go. It was unbearable to watch and he didn't know what to do. "No, no, not Pamela," he cried, "she is an innocent in this." Alfie watched Christopher and could see the utter horror and frustration in his eyes. He knew exactly what Christopher was trying to say, the pitch was near screaming point. This made him smile.

Christopher watched, now silenced by the sheer horror of what was to come. He couldn't take his eyes off Alfie or Pamela. He willed everything to be alright, that she would be let free but he knew this wasn't true. Her rigid body tensed even more as he felt for the lips covering her opening and he parted them gently. He kissed her on the back of her neck and told her all would be well and she would be free soon.

Christopher held his breath as he watched, he could see the metal object attached to his finger gently laying across her pubic hair. He felt sick, he could guess what was to happen but he prayed so hard he was wrong. Again, his adrenalin kicked in and he shouted and pleaded, and begged for Alfie to stop. He shook violently on the chair to break the ropes to escape and help Pamela. He cried for him to leave her alone that he would tell him anything he wanted to know but leave Pamela alone. Of course, it made no sense to anyone listening. It was just a frantic muffled noise behind the gag. But Alfie understood and he appreciated the show of begging.

Christopher, now so exhausted by his frustrated

efforts, watched fearfully and with a dread no one should ever experience. There was a stillness and a calm. Pamela was hardly daring to breathe. Her face looked like a death mask; hideous and frightening. Alfie continued smiling at Christopher. It seemed like a shocking pageant that was held in a frozen tableau, nothing moved for what seemed an age. As his brain tried to make sense of what he was seeing, there was a flash of movement, a thrusting and a grunt from Alfie.

The suddenness of the movement, the shocking sound of Pamela screaming with her legs flaying and her body writhing in an unspeakable blistering, penetrating, torment of pain caused Christopher to nearly pass out. She screamed and cried, "Oh God, oh God" in a deep and guttural way that sounded terrifying. The fiend was still thrusting his right arm into her and as she writhed, her back arched unnaturally and her mouth opened wider as she screamed in a pitch he thought not possible. It was unbearable, he had to watch, he had to be with her in some way, oh the pain, he could see was more intense as she wriggled and writhed to get away from him. The knife dug deeper inside her and cut and stabbed and chopped what was her womanhood. Christopher heard her call for her mum, for God and anyone who would help her. She screamed and pleaded for him to stop. Her screaming begging to stop felt like a hand grabbing his heart and ripping it out of his body. The blood had started to pour from her and his hand was covered in blood. After what felt like hours to Christopher, the fiend stopped. Pamela was quiet and looked almost dead and he just let her drop to the floor in a bloody heap. It was all too much for Christopher, he felt he had gone mad and he just wanted to get away, to die and be at peace. How would this end? He was hysterical with an explosion of hatred and fear and an anger he had never experienced before.

Alfie was quite exhausted. He was breathing deeply and fast. It had been good so far and the look on Christopher's face was worth it. He showed Christopher his little friend. As he told Christopher, it was his little man, Uomo Picollo. He took out a handkerchief and lovingly cleaned the knife. "This was specially made for me, see how it sits on my finger," he held it up and showed Christopher how the leather finger stool was a perfect fit and on the end was a securely positioned knife which was only 2" long and tapered to a sturdy point. Alfie showed Christopher close up how sharp the edge was, stating it was sharper than a Stanley knife. With a pride that only the fiend could have, he bragged, "I can gouge out eyes with this, and I can kill someone easily and quickly." He waved the little man in front of Christopher. "In fact," he said quite airily, "I will show you". He picked up Pamela by her hair. She was like a rag doll and he needed both hands to keep her upright. Christopher watched as the bastard then kissed her passionately on the lips and after a moment, in a brazened flash, he cut her throat from ear to ear. As he tossed her to one side, Alfie told Christopher in a matter of fact tone, "I have had better than her."

Christopher watched her fall. For a few seconds she appeared to be gasping but that stopped and there was silence. She lay on the floor, eyes wide open and looking accusingly at Christopher. He was smothered with grief and guilt. It was all his fault, he had got her killed. She didn't deserve this. He wanted to die with her, he didn't deserve to live. But the steely part of him wanted to live long enough to see this bastard die slowly and painfully. All he had left was his anger, he let it get stronger and fiercer. He wanted it to blot out what he had seen. He was focussed on this murderous bastard and wanted to see him in hell!

They were all on the move following the Station Master. Neil hoped they were in time. This Alfie had a head start on them of at least 3 hours. "Please God, they are alright" he prayed.

Neil looked around to find the group had suddenly got bigger. 2 DCs from DI Thorpe's team had come along to help, the police on the station joined them and together with the armed police, about 15 of them strode purposefully down staircases and along corridors with Freddie and DI Thorpe directly behind the station manager who was leading the way. Neil trailed behind playing catch up with the professionals ahead. His head was spinning and he was fighting with himself. One part of him wanted to be at the front telling everyone to hurry, that time was passing and anything could be happening. The other part of him wanted to stay at the back, away from what sounded like an inevitable fatal find.

It wasn't time for Neil to reflect, it wasn't time to consider options. It was time to "do" and "be" the person he should be. He had always owed Christopher. He owed him his protection during his school years which were tortuous until Christopher stepped in. He owed him for his support when he started his business. He owed him for his continued friendship. This was payback time and what was he doing? He was straggling at the back. Neil picked up the pace and ran forward, he was now beside Freddie and was determined to stay there and be there for both Christopher and Pamela.

Alfie, sidled up to Christopher and stroked his head. "See what you have done." He whispered. "What happened to your little treasure was your fault." He poked Christopher in the chest. "Our little treasurer told me you had taken something to an address in Muswell Hill." He walked around Christopher, wanting the pause to allow Christopher to realise what he had done. "If you had told me about the drive to Muswell Hill, she might be alive now." He loved the way Christopher got so animated, he pushed and pulled and rocked and tried to get free and in doing so, nearly pushed the chair over. "You want to get at me do you?" he teased. Christopher would have strangled him if he could get hold of him. He had used up all his energy and was now overcome with a tiredness and hopelessness that drained any hope he could have had. He knew that nothing could be done for Pamela and he would not be freed. He gave up. He looked coldly into Alfie's eyes and willed him to kill him. He thought he should just get it over with. Alfie was having none of this.

Alfie lit a cigarette, he was bored and wanted to get

away from this dark damp place. He told Christopher that the bitch Amanda's place was where he would go soon to meet with his boss. He wanted Christopher to know that he was nothing to them. Contemptuously he added that Christopher was just the patsy in all this. They knew he didn't have the brains to organise such a shipment. He was wiling away the time just ensuring all the information Christopher had was known and could be put together. Menacingly he said that everyone involved would be dealt with. There were only 4 people big enough in the country to take such a huge consignment. Two of them would only use their own kind so they were ruled out and the other two were based in London and Manchester. They have been visited. Alfie thought Christopher would be riveted to know this. He said his work was nearly done except, and he smiled and paused a moment as he looked into Christopher's eyes, "Except for you telling me absolutely everything. I know where your wife lives and you have 2 beautiful daughters I hear. I would enjoy meeting them." Christopher knew exactly what he meant and nearly fainted at the thought.

The gag was roughly taken off and Christopher lost no time in telling Alfie everything from meeting Chuck, the flight, how many suitcases, where he went with them in Muswell Hill. He told Alfie everything he could think of. Out of breath and pleading he asked, "Please don't touch my wife and daughters. They know absolutely nothing. It is all to do with me and Amanda." Alfie's face was inches from Christopher's and he asked through gritted teeth, "Where is the bitch Amanda?"

Christopher didn't know. He hadn't a clue, he wished he knew and if he did he would have told him. In a panic, he told Alfie everything he knew about Amanda. Actually, it boiled down to not much at all. She never confided in him and he realised he had never taken the trouble to ask her about herself. What a pathetic low life he was.

Christopher had plumbed the depths of despair and seen his life as a hedonistic waste. How selfish and egotist can one person be? He asked himself. He had caused the death of a poor innocent woman and his family could be tortured and killed all because of his love of money. He deserved nothing, he was scum.

Alfie put on his mac, he needed to cover the blood stains and got ready to leave. His parting gift to Christopher would be the knowledge that before he returned to Colombia he would visit his wife and show her his Uomo Picollo. He whispered in hallowed terms "I will take my time and ensure a long and lingering death for your wife." With pride he added, "I can make it quite exquisitely long and the pain will be unimaginable. Will she scream that high pitched terror scream that pain inflicts, and will she call your name do you think?" He smiled and asked Christopher "Can you imagine her tied down and naked. I will spread-eagle her legs and tie her ankles so she can't move at all. Just imagine how easy she will be to play with. The screams I can make go on for hours. I could gut and rip out her intestines and lay them out for her to view." He laughed as Christopher screamed and begged.

He got up to leave. "Before I go, I have one present

for you." He took out Uomo Picollo. Christopher hoped he would kill him. He didn't want to live. Alfie cut Christopher across the chest. It wasn't very deep but it was bleeding. He also cut him across the arms, just enough to bleed profusely but wouldn't kill him. Christopher could feel the heat of the cut, but he was past physical pain, it was his mental torment that filled his body. Alfie watched as the blood dripped to the floor. "My present for you is the rats." Alfie smirked as Christopher realised what he was saying. "They will come when I have gone," Alfie confirmed. He looked at Pamela on the floor and said, "Your treasure will attract them and they will see you too. This place is full of rats, they could eat you alive and I am sorry not to stay and see that." He laughed again, "But you will have time to reflect on what I am going to do with your wife before they eat you alive."

The smile left Alfie's face, and with a deep breath to calm himself he told Christopher that he and the others had made a fool of the Colombians when they tried to scam them. The haul was so big everyone knew about it. This was the biggest scam ever pulled and for the honour of the Colombians his death, and all the others involved would be known to everyone. So his death had to be particularly spectacular and the death of his family spectacular too. It would serve as a warning to everyone not to mess with the Colombians. With that Alfie turned and left the scene of carnage.

Christopher could hear Alfie's footsteps echoing along the tunnel as he left. Soon there was silence and Christopher heard the first rustling sound and the squeak of rats. There seemed to be hundreds of them and at first he felt something at his feet and he lashed out with his foot. The little light was still on and it looked as if Pamela was boiling with rats; they covered her body. He could still see her looking at him accusingly and he couldn't bear it. Her head shook as they tore at her cut throat and still she stared at him. His eyes were locked into hers and he could almost hear her begging for her life again. The torment was broken when he felt the rats at his feet jump up on his leg. He looked down and screamed. He shook himself and wriggled, but he was still tied so tightly. At first they jumped off when he moved but they seemed to be getting braver and jumped back on his legs. They hadn't as yet moved up to his chest but one was near his arm. He could feel them. The terror of what they would do engulfed him and he shook with fear. Pamela's eyes still staring directly at him, the images of what would happen to Alice and his girls and the terror of the rats filled every crevasse of his mind. The madness had started.

The station master stopped. All behind came to a disorganised halt. Freddie looked and frowned at all the officers behind him. "What the bloody hell are you lot all doing here?" he asked. He picked the 4 armed officers, himself and DI Thorpe to go forward. Neil raised his hand hesitantly to argue that he too must go, only to be rudely pushed back and told to stay exactly where he was. The station officer pointed at the only way through the alcove. He was pushed to one side and all 6 moved forward cautiously towards the door.

Neil watched as the door was gently and quietly pushed to see if there was movement in opening it. The door opened suddenly and swiftly inwards. All stared in stunned surprise. For a few seconds no one moved. Alfie glaring at all the police ahead of him and at the 4 guns pointed in his direction and in a blink of an eye he turned to run. The melee that ensued with shouts of "Get him," was watched by Neil. It seemed such a small space for so many men to bundle into. Alfie was put to the floor and handcuffed in seconds. Neil's adrenalin rose to dizzy heights and no one noticed when he slightly staggered against the wall and held his chest as he breathed deeply. He was not used to all this excitement.

Freddie shouted to his men to, "Hold him here" as he beckoned to DI Thorpe and the armed police to follow him down the tunnel. They moved quietly but decisively, listening to hear if any more Colombians were here. The emergency lighting was depressingly dim with just enough light see where they were going. The tunnel wound its way this way and that for what was a good few minutes. A door to the right side of the tunnel was opened and a flashlight showed nothing was inside, it was just a disused storage area and they moved on. At the next door they heard a noise and cautiously listened for clues on how many people were in there.

On a count of three, they burst open the door and after a quick look for any Colombians, they looked in shock at Christopher looking more dead than alive on a chair and a woman obviously dead on the floor. The last of the rats scurried away but not before the full horror of what was happening was seen by all. Freddie shouted for one officer to go and get paramedics. He looked at Pamela and shuddered. He found her coat and covered her with it to give her some dignity in death, she deserved that.

It was about then that the screaming started. Christopher raised his head as he was being untied and was told that he was safe. It sounded as if he was trying to speak, the noise was soft and came out as a low moan which rose into a high pitched scream that didn't stop. He wouldn't let anyone touch him. He scurried into a corner and sat on the floor and every time some one tried to speak to him, to gently help him he screamed and shook.

"God help us," Freddie whispered. He turned to one officer and said, "Go get Neil, he knows him and he might help us find out what is going on." The officer didn't move quick enough for Freddie and was told "fucking move now you bastard, we have no time to lose."

Neil arrived minutes later having been unceremoniously dragged faster than Neil was used to moving. The sight before him caused him to stop in his tracks and throw up. Pamela was not fully covered and Neil saw her face and recognised her. He could see the slashed throat, the eyes were open. He had never seen a dead body in such a state, her hair was dishevelled, her face looked wracked, and he saw the blood. More blood than he had ever seen, it seemed everywhere. The gaping gash around her neck had bits coming out of it as if, and he threw up at the thought, that something had eaten it.

"Yeah Gods, protect us from the normal people," was the wail given up by Freddie. He had no time for all of this messing around. He pulled Neil over to where Christopher was. Neil wiped his mouth on his sleeve and peered into the corner. He saw Christopher, at least he thought it was Christopher. This mound of humanity huddled shaking and cowering in the corner couldn't be Christopher could it? Freddie prodded Neil and nodding his head in Christopher's direction mouthing "go on" for Neil to say something.

Neil, shaken to the core by the sight of Christopher cowering in the corner, edged forward. "Christopher old chap, it's Neil," he whispered hesitantly. He offered his hand out, "Come on old chap, lets get you out of here," he added gently I bet you could do with a stiff drink. Christopher looked up and Neil could see a glint of recognition in his eye. Neil thought he saw a glimmer of a smile but it disappeared quickly and was replaced by a fearful look. "Neil, is Alice safe?" he asked urgently.

"Gosh yes, nothing is going to happen to Alice, I promise," Neil responded, not sure what he said was true but it was what Christopher needed to hear at that moment.

With a bit of coaxing, he got Christopher to move out of the shadows. Freddie was getting impatient. He wanted to know whatever Christopher knew. They had Alfie but where were the rest of the Colombians? The Paramedics arrived and helped Christopher into a wheelchair. They said he was in shock, dehydrated and exhausted. A drip was set up by his wheelchair and he was made comfortable. Neil left with Christopher and

Freddie barked orders to everyone to keep the place clean for the SOCCO to check over. After many photos were taken, Pamela was put on a stretcher and taken out. As they left the scene, a policeman was put on guard at the entrance to the tunnel to stop anyone going in and further contaminating the scene.

Freddie and DI Thorpe had a brief conversation and parted. Freddie was off with Christopher and DI Thorpe would join him soon at the hospital. In the meantime Alfie had been taken to the local nick and would be interviewed. It was paramount to find out what Christopher knew about the Colombians and where they might be. No one thought Alfie would say anything, but of course, they would ask. At least they had that murdering bastard in custody. DI Thorpe wanted to be in the custody suite to ensure Alfie was read his rights and securely locked up until he was ready to interview him. It was quite an achievement to have the infamous Alfie in custody and DI Thorpe wanted to bathe in that particular bit of glory and covert the limelight before someone else grabbed it. There were going to be drinks in the pub tonight he told everyone.

Neil waited outside the curtained examination room. Christopher was quiet now. Freddie murmured quietly to Neil that it was imperative that they talk to Christopher to find out what he knows. There were Colombians in his town and they were dangerous. Neil was trying to come to terms with it all. Pamela was dead. How could Pamela, an innocent, naïve woman in all of this be dead? By all accounts, she had been tortured and as Freddie explained what he thought had happened, Neil curled up and hugged himself. The awfulness of it was too much to bear.

The curtains opened after an hour of doctors and nurses going in and out of the area. Christopher, they were told had been put on a drip to rehydrate him. The knife cuts had been glued together and they had given him a high dose of diazepam to calm him down. The doctor on call whispered that he was teetering on a breakdown and they must be careful how they talk to him. A Psychiatric Consultant had seen him and would be organising treatment for him in the morning.

Christopher was asleep. He hadn't slept for 24 hours and the diazepam had relaxed him enough to send him off into a deep sleep. Freddie cursed, he wanted Christopher awake to talk to him. Today had felt like a botched up mess and he wanted this all dealt with quickly without anyone else being hurt. His bosses wanted to know what was happening and he needed something to tell them.

While they waited for Christopher to wake up, Freddie got on the phone to DI Thorpe and asked what was going on. The initial interview of Alfie was a no comment interview just as they predicted. The SOCCO had taken samples from Alfie's clothes, fingernails and his Uomo Picollo which had been put in a plastic holding tube to keep it safely until it was needed for court evidence. Police officers in the station got wind of this and many had made their way to the Custody Suite to take a look at Alfie through the spy hole in the cell door and to look at Uomo Picollo. No one had seen this before; it had just been part of the urban legend of Alfie.

Freddie left Neil for an hour to chase up leads. They had a good idea of what part of town the Colombians had visited but there was no sign of them now. On his return, Freddie was in time to see a nurse wake Christopher by taking his pulse and temperature. They had to keep him awake and find out what he knew. Still groggy, Christopher tried to make sense of the questions being asked. The diazepam had kicked in and he felt great. It wasn't until Freddie talked about Alfie that the horror came flooding back. To the dismay of the nurse, Freddie would not let Christopher go back to sleep, or let him try to ignore his questions. Between Freddie and Neil, they wringed all the information from him. He started at the beginning and told them about the suitcases full of drugs on the Lear jet. Neil held his breath and realised his father, the company and the Senator had been used badly. Christopher broke down when he told them about Pamela and what Alfie had done to her. They asked again and again, did he know where the Colombians were now? He couldn't remember. They pushed and pushed for every bit of information Alfie had given him. Christopher was becoming very agitated and a little hysterical. The nurse was about to tell Freddie and Neil to go, she had had enough of their bullying. Just as Freddie was about to give up as hopeless any further help from him, Christopher remembered Alfie mentioned something about the bitch Amanda's place and that he was going to meet them there. Freddie didn't wait to find out who he was meeting, it had to be the Colombians.

Freddie took the address and rang base and told them to send for the SO19 bastards. He knew he would need them now. Neil realised that "bastards" was a term of endearment as far as the SO19s were concerned. Freddie loved them. They were big, armed, professional and no nonsense. In an emergency you couldn't ask for a better squad to get the job done, and besides, he added, they scared the shit out of anyone they were pursuing. His work with Christopher was done for the time being and Freddie left to go to Mayfair to get the Colombians.

Neil rang Alice to tell her where he was. He asked tentatively if all was ok and she laughed and said of course everything was ok. For the next ten minutes she told him what she had been doing, and how Mrs so and so had said this and the man from the old rectory had done such and such. It was all gossip and it made him smile. Life in Alice's world was a warm and gossipy place which Neil found very comforting.

They had become quite close over the years at first through Christopher, and then when they went into business together. Neil was successful and as a Justice of the Peace had his own contacts but he never quite knew how to use them to his advantage. Alice had no qualms in getting to know the right people and then on how to use them to further her work. The combination of his business acumen and her networking proved very successful. He always called her "my dear" and she loved the gentleness of Neil. They worked well together and had expanded businesses around Wroxham over the years. Neil found Alice had grown into a very accomplished business woman and her contacts in the

County were legendary. If you needed any help, advice, networking done, Alice was your woman. She was always working, either for her family, her voluntary work or her businesses. He admired her greatly.

Neil stayed at Christopher's bedside. He wondered what on earth was he going to do to sort this mess out. There was Alice and what was he going to tell her? She had to be protected from the sordidness of Christopher's life and the affair with Jenny. How was he going to explain Pamela's death? Of course Alice knew Pamela and spoke to her often in the office. It was one way that Alice could keep in touch with Christopher and what he was doing. Alice so deserved better. Neil, for a second, felt a bubbling fury over what Christopher had dragged his family into. His father's company should be told what their Lear Jet had been used for, or could he talk to the police and keep the company out of it. He tried not to think of it, but there was Pamela's husband to be contacted and what could he say to him? The police would obviously contact Pamela's husband and give him the dreadful news.

The burden of it all felt too much for Neil to cope with. He looked across at Christopher, he was alive and that was a miracle. The lights had been dimmed in the hospital room as night fell. Tomorrow he would deal with everything for now he needed to rest. Exhaustion and all the emotion of the day had taken its toll and Neil nodded off in the chair beside a drug induced sleeping Christopher.

EPILOGUE

The September sunshine warmed him. Everything felt so peaceful and calm. The breeze was playful and light and it barely ruffled the leaves of the sturdy oak tree on the village green. It was a good day to sit and watch.

He nodded and slightly raised his cane in acknowledgement when someone on a bicycle passing by shouted cheerily "Good afternoon Colonel". He was used to being addressed in such a fashion. He looked like an old man sitting comfortably in the late sunshine. His back was bent and his thin arms poked awkwardly out of the short sleeved shirt. His face was the face of someone who had been through the wars and the locals respected him for it. No one knew exactly what he had done in the war, but everyone knew it was something clandestine and brave. Alice had hinted and given suggestions but she told everyone it was more than her life was worth to tell more.

He looked tired and some would think he was in his 70s but in reality he was the right side of 60. The sunken eyes had seen more than most and the lines deeply etched dropped from his cheek bones, curving either side of his mouth and down to meet his chin. It gave a hang dog expression that showed a deep sadness. He often sat and just looked at the beauty of Winterton. Nature, he surmised was perfect and right, it was people who were imperfect and so very wrong. A tree that had stood for generations, grew bigger and stronger and formed part of the landscape. It deserved respect.

He looked around him. Everyone had somewhere to go and somewhere to be. Alice was with Neil talking about the farm. His daughters were looking after his grandsons and keeping home for their husbands. He could do whatever he liked to do.

Neil had done so much for him. The trial was big and went on for months. He was never identified and was part of a Police resettlement programme due to the exclusive information about the Colombians. He never understood what Neil did to get him off so lightly. He was sentenced to 3 years for his part in the drug run. It was acknowledged that he had helped put the Colombians away and he was medically disabled by the events. He did, in fact, spend the 3 years in a mental institution. He remembered the madness.

Again Neil, oh blessed Neil, told Alice that Christopher was working on a special assignment for the Police. He spun her a story of his contacts in America being vital in this assignment. He said that Christopher was a hero and although he could not be contacted, he would try and write. Alice was used to Christopher not being at home very much and wallowed in the glory of such an assignment. Neil visited Christopher and on good days got him to write a short note for Alice.

When he got home Alice noticed how worn and

quiet he was. The medication was a permanent thing and he had 10 tablets to take each day. He needed nursing and reacclimatising to the world of Winterton. He became Alice's project and she bustled and organised him and got the local woman's guild to visit him and keep him cheerful. Alice enjoyed looking after Christopher, it made her feel good. She would sit at the meal table and tell him about everything she had done during the day and he would listen. She chose his clothes and had them laid out in the morning for him. He smiled when she smiled at him and he nodded when she spoke. He was so compliant and pleasant. It felt very comfortable and she liked it. He wasn't any trouble, she just had to make sure he took his tablets.

Neil never visited him again. It was explained to Christopher that he had paid him back and now they were quits. What Christopher had done to his own family and to Neil's family business, was unforgiveable. He added that for the 3 years Christopher was away Neil had covered for him and now enough was enough, he wanted his life back. Neil added that they would, of course, meet at various functions and that was fine, but the friendship had been used up. Christopher understood. The tablets kept him on an even keel and not much emotion got through to him.

Alice used to take him to the farm that Neil had set up for disadvantaged children. Alice had helped over the years to grow this project. It was a success and well known in the County. Many inner city children had stayed in the hostel attached and school day visits were standard as well. It was a hive of activity. She thought it might be good for Christopher to be around youngsters. At first it seemed to do him a lot of good. The children's laughter and the obvious pleasure they got out of being around the animals seemed to boost him and he became more animated for a while. He couldn't go there anymore now. It was the rats you see. Christopher saw one running through the barn. Rats were fairly common place but when Christopher started screaming, she didn't know what to do. He went into a corner and huddled and was crying like a baby. It scared the children near him and they had to be led away quickly. She was shocked and after seeing Christopher's local doctor, it was decided that Christopher's trauma as the doctor put it, needed to be managed carefully.

Most days now he didn't stray too far from the house. The village people kept an eye out for him. The short walk to the village was a pleasure for him and sitting there looking at the village green Oak tree was the highlight of his day. He would then walk on to the Fisherman's Rest Public house close by for a few whiskies before dinner. He had his own chair that was always put near the fire in the winter to warm him. The locals enjoyed having him there and he said very little but they knew he was thinking. Whenever someone asked what he did years ago, Christopher would tap his nose with his index finger and shake his head. They all laughed when he did that and thought him a most modest and brave man.

He had his study at home where he would drink the evening away. The nights were long and he did his best to stay awake. He always hoped the drink would make him comatose and he would just sleep. But as soon as he closed his eyes he saw her. It was the eyes, always the eyes that haunted him. They were accusing and cursing and that tormented and horrified him. She was still looking at him, she would never stop until he was dead. She would always be with him and silently make him pay for his treachery.

He had been saving his tablets up and one day soon, he would take them all and together with a few glasses of the finest malt whisky he could buy, he would lay down to sleep and never again wake up in a cold sweat and terrified.